'What are we going to do, Harry?'

He put her from hi⋯⋯⋯⋯⋯⋯⋯⋯ou
so. Forgive me darling⋯

Frightened her? Sh⋯⋯⋯⋯⋯⋯⋯⋯ ⋯ch
a thing. Her whole b⋯⋯⋯⋯⋯⋯⋯ he
didn't realize it. She ⋯⋯⋯⋯⋯⋯ ⋯ing
with frustration. A Russian ⋯⋯⋯ she
told herself angrily. Why were Englishmen so slow? Such
perfect gentlemen? Yet no Russian had ever moved her
like this English sailor.

ZENA MEYLER

Shadows on the Ice

PARRAGON

A Grafton Paperback Original 1987

This edition published 1993 by
Diamond Books
77-85 Fulham Palace Road
Hammersmith, London, W6 8JB

Printed and bound in Great Britain by
BPCC Hazells Ltd
Member of BPCC Ltd

For my sons
Richard and Clive
Hamerstey

. . . Who order'd that their longing's fire
Should be, as soon as kindled, cool'd?
Who renders vain their deep desire? –
A God, a God their severance ruled!
And bade betwixt their shores to be
The unplumb'd, salt, estranging sea.

Matthew Arnold: *To Marguerite*

Part One
1881

1

The Merchant's Daughters

1

Nicolai Mironovitch Urosov, the timber merchant, was immensely proud of his three daughters. When he entertained some of his fellow merchants in his great house on the Moika Canal in St Petersburg, he could never resist leading them across the room to a picture hanging on the wall between two windows. The walls were covered in handpainted Chinese paper, the curtains were a rich red satin: the late Madame Urosova had possessed a refined taste unknown in her husband. It was she who had insisted on retaining the original wallpaper when they had bought out an impoverished nobleman several years earlier. Urosov had hankered after something a bit more modern (a popular word just then) but he had loved his wife and was glad to let her have her way. After her early death, he lost interest in his home. For him it now served only one purpose: it housed his treasures and by this he meant his daughters.

The lovely watercolour was chastely framed in plain gold and the three little heads seemed to float out of it, each pressed against the other in a confiding manner: Marie, Laura and Anastasia.

The little merchant would rock on the balls of his feet as he pointed gleefully at the picture with his cigar. 'My daughters, gentlemen! My true treasures on earth!'

His guests, politely concealing their amazement that these beautiful children had sprung from the loins of their ugly little host, would murmur quite truthfully that the children were indeed adorable – little beauties without flaw!

The medium of watercolour suited the delicate looks of the three children. The artist had painted only their heads and three pairs of trusting eyes looked out on the world. Marie, the eldest, had very dark hair and a long fringe just skirting a pair of remarkable greenish-blue eyes with very dark pupils. Her full lips had firm corners and there was an air of immense seriousness about this twelve-year-old child. The second sister's head was pressed against hers: Laura had dark hair too, but smoothly drawn back under a ribbon leaving her round white forehead exposed. A pale flush moulded high cheekbones and her eyes, tilted upwards at the corners, held a green glint. Little Anastasia had pale apricot hair curling in tendrils about a face that was still roundly babyish.

Four years divided the two elder girls but Anastasia had come late in Madame Mironova's life: it was seven years after Laura that she was born. At Anastasia's birth, her mother had died from puerperal fever and only Marie could remember her at all clearly.

Poor Urosov! people had said at the time. Surely he had wanted this last child to be a son to inherit his many businesses and immense fortune? Perhaps he would marry again – not that he would find it easy to find a young woman to breed from with his face and at his age despite all his money!

But Urosov had shown no desire to marry again in order to sire a son. Instead he had brought home his spinster sister Kitty to run the house and bring up his children. Kitty he knew to be a fool; a religious maniac with a huge collection of jewelled icons which she brought

10

with her and strewed about his house. She also harboured
absurd superstitions and went several times a year to
fashionable seances at the homes of like-minded friends.
'The spirits say – ' began most of Kitty's conversations as
she predicted disasters that never happened. Even worse,
she couldn't manage the servants. But he endured her
shortcomings because she lent respectability to his household. One only had to look at Kitty to know that she
would never countenance shady behaviour of any kind.
The children's upbringing was safe with Aunt Kitty in
charge.

So they grew up docilely and correctly with English
nannies and French governesses and the excellent manners instilled by these good women. But by the time she
was eighteen, Marie had begun to pester her father.
'Can't we get rid of Aunt Kitty?' became a daily litany.

Urosov was shocked. 'Do you want your mother to
turn in her grave? Who would lend countenance to my
daughters as they entered society?'

'Society!' Marie shrugged her pretty shoulders. 'Oh,
Father, you know that's all nonsense! We can never be in
proper society and you can't call taking tea with the wives
of the professors at the university going into society! Nor
attending the doctor's wife's At Home on Wednesdays!
That's not society. We're just too bourgeois for real
society so don't let's pretend. Besides, Aunt Kitty is a
rotten duenna,' Marie added wickedly. 'She was so busy
talking with Father Basil at Madame Mendorva's At
Home that she let me spend the whole afternoon with
Ivan Mendorv. Don't worry. I think him a great bore.
Besides, he has horrid spots.'

Urosov was horrified. He had suspected for some time
that Kitty was getting worse at guarding his treasures. He
would have to speak to her. What a fool the woman was!

Marie was watching his face, closely. 'Do let me

manage the house and servants, Father! Let Aunt Kitty go back to her own home and take her wretched icons with her – '

'Silence!' Urosov thundered. 'Have you no respect, girl? Your aunt stays – no, not another word. She will just have to be stricter with you.' Urosov was adamant and Marie had to flounce sulkily out of the room without achieving her aim of getting rid of Aunt Kitty. After she had gone, Urosov sat at his desk and smiled under his whiskers. The saucy little puss! he told himself fondly. He had great plans for this eldest girl who filled the place of the son he had never had. For years now – since she was fifteen – she had been coming with him to his timberyard that had its own dock on the Neva. She was the only one of his children to show an interest in what was their very lifeblood. She was developing a sharp business brain and she could handle those timberyard ruffians as if they were lions and she their tamer. She was a beautiful girl and her tall slender figure – a fully developed woman now – wearing furs in winter and plain costumes without bustles in the summer would move about the yard checking the numbers on the huge piles of planks being seasoned, beckoning the foreman out of his noisy shed to have a word with her. This shed that housed the huge circular saws both fascinated and terrified her. She liked to watch the powerful saws biting through the giant trees as easily as if they were made of candlegrease. But the noise! Even with her fingers in her ears it made her dizzy. The men who worked there became deaf in a very few years while some others lost fingers, arms and sometimes their lives. Perhaps that is what fascinated her most of all: the danger. When those round saws whirled so fast they became a white blur she was drawn against her will to stand and watch.

One man, grey bearded and pallid, seemed to spend his

life underground with the two boilers built in Lancashire, England and imported by Urosov thirty years earlier, before he began to make his fortune. He had lived on nothing in those days, ploughing his slender profits into the timberyard and it had paid off – by God! how it had paid off! he reminded himself gleefully from time to time. The boilers were the first of a new kind and two Englishmen had come to install them. At five o'clock each morning, with a prolonged hiss, the heavy fifteen-foot flywheels would begin to turn their belts. Down in the tunnel, the shafting began to drive the saws. The two circular saws would begin to scream like demons and the three four-cutter planes would begin to hum a descant from the other side of the open shed. Steam and sawdust would choke the air, a deadly mixture that found its way into the lungs of the workmen causing a terrible irritation.

To Marie it was simply the breath of life. She knew with confidence that she could run this place if anything happened to her father. She knew (because he had told her so often) that it might be up to her some day to provide a livelihood for herself and her sisters. She knew every one of the men by name and knew also that they respected her; she had noticed that their language became very careful when she was near. There were people in her class and upwards who feared the workers, the Dark People as they were called, but she wasn't one of them.

Aunt Kitty moaned that Marie was being ruined for young ladyhood. Pretty though she was she would never find a husband if she spent half her days down at the timberyard. What man would want a wife who could only talk about the price of timber, where the best oak could be found at the right price and how quickly and cheaply ash could be grown?

It was meant as sarcasm but Urosov only laughed. He knew that this first-born daughter fitted completely into

13

that corner of his heart that might have been occupied by a son. She would inherit his empire; Marie Nicolaievna Urosova was his heir and one day would be one of the richest women in St Petersburg. Finding a husband for her would present no problem.

He showed far less interest in his other girls. Laura was fourteen now and had been at the Imperial Ballet School in Theatre Street since she was six. Like all the boys and girls living there she seldom saw her home any more. Entering the Ballet School at the end of babyhood was almost the same as becoming a novice in a nunnery. From that moment of selection, the child renounced its family and instead became a member of a family of one hundred and fifty children at whose head was the Tsar Alexander III whose money paid for the school.

Seven-year-old Anastasia lived hidden from the world and guarded by her governess. There were few who knew a third daughter existed until shown the watercolour in the salon. She had no talents but promised to be another beauty like her sisters and Urosov was confident that he could marry her off well, even into the nobility when the size of her dowry became known. Urosov was a cynic and his mouth under the grey whiskers would pucker with suppressed laughter at this thought. He had learned early in life that money could be the entrée to much that was desirable and no questions asked.

2

That spring the thaw was late. The dock that belonged to the Urosov Timberyard on the River Neva was still empty. The tall masts of boats from several countries would usually be crowding the sky above the basin; now there were none. From October St Petersburg had been icebound and cut off by sea. The network of canals that criss-crossed the city were still covered with ice that was hard enough to be driven on; tramlines were laid across the Neva from the right bank to the left where the workers lived and where the red-brick buildings of the university were visible through the icy fog that still hung about. The streets were covered with hard-packed dirty snow and bonfires still burned on street corners to thaw the fresh piles of ice. People asked each other: would spring never come?

Day after day, Marie drove with her father in the sleigh to pay their daily visit to the timberyard. Urosov's business interests stretched further afield now, but, like the good businessman he was, he kept his hands on the reins of all his commercial interests and no manager or foreman had complete autonomy. He trusted no one.

'Look, Father!' Marie clutched his arm one day in late April. 'At last! Look, the ice is breaking!'

A distinct report emphasized her words. Yes, the ice was breaking at last, the first signal of spring.

Urosov called to their driver to stop, then he and his daughter stared in fascination as the ice on the Neva began to move slowly and reluctantly, breaking into a raft here and there, and clinging stubbornly near the banks. They had seen the same phenomenon many times and it never ceased to move them. *Spring was coming*. Only those who had spent the dark winter in St Petersburg could understand their joy.

Marie looked up and there – sailing like a bubble through the thin screen of clouds – was the sun. Her lovely face flushed as if already touched by its rays.

'The boats will be putting in by the end of the month,' Urosov said with satisfaction as he settled back under his fur rug. A rich chuckle rumbled through him as he

15

thought of the piles of seasoned timber waiting in the drying sheds.

'Yes,' Marie agreed and turned her head away.

Captain Harry Croxley would be returning.

With the colour still beating in her cheeks and her huge eyes shining like candles, her face softened under the grey chinchilla bonnet. Only to think of Harry made her heart beat fast. He attracted her as no other man had done in her eighteen years.

Her father, she saw as she gave him a nervous glance, didn't notice her excitement. He had no idea of what was going on – thank heaven! Squeezing her hands together inside her chinchilla muff, she tried to appear composed but her longing thoughts were dwelling on the English sailor, Harry Croxley, the captain of a big timber boat owned by one of their regular customers, Howarth and Hawksley of Hull. He was twenty-eight, a fair-haired giant of a man with an imperial beard and bright blue eyes always full of fun. His Yorkshire accent made his English difficult to her ears but they knew each other so well now that it no longer mattered what they said.

They had fallen in love the first time he had invited her aboard the *Sylvie-Rose* of Hull. How cosy it had been in his cabin, just the two of them while Father thought she was going over the way-bills with his clerk! The captain's steward made tea in a big brown pot and brought in a pile of moist buttered toast to be eaten with the heather honey the captain always brought with him. She had never tasted toast before and the tea had not been like their Russian tea brewed in a samovar and golden brown in colour. This was queer-tasting stuff, very black and with tinned milk added to it! She had drunk it valiantly, her heart jerking every time her eyes met his.

When she got up to leave he had taken her hand and kissed it. 'Th'art a gradely lass,' he had told her, his eyes

16

twinkling because she couldn't understand a word. He kissed her hand again. 'That means you're a girl after my own heart,' he said in her ear. 'I'll be back in a month. Will you take tea with me again?'

Under her petticoats her legs were trembling and weak. But she promised to return. Later, back in her home, she examined the strange feelings she was experiencing. Really, it was very odd. Could it be that this was – well – love? Could she really be falling in love with Harry Croxley, a foreigner from a strange country? She went hot and cold at the thought. She was being silly and miss-ish just because the man had kissed her. All the same, Harry Croxley remained in her mind.

Now spring had come at last and every day she eagerly examined the masts of the boats jostling with each other in the timberyard harbour, longing to find the dark-green pennant with the entwined double aitch of Howarth and Hawksley flapping in the breeze. Three weeks later, the *Sylvie-Rose* was there at last and while the seasoned timber was being loaded, Captain Croxley was to spend most of his time courting Marie Nicolaievna Urosova in secret.

The second day after his arrival she was helped aboard the timber vessel and escorted to the captain's cabin by Johnson, the bow-legged steward, who wore a crisp white jacket and a big knowing grin of welcome. 'Lovely weather we're having, miss,' he remarked as he led her aft.

With dry lips, she attempted to respond but her heart was pounding like a drum and had taken all her breath.

Crikey! The old man wasn't half going it with this lovely little Rooshan gal, Johnson told himself gleefully. The girl following him with her graceful swaying walk seemed a creature of light and shadow in her white dress and shady hat wreathed with green leaves. The brim was lined in pleated green silk to match her parasol and it cast interesting shadows over her pale skin. There was a very faint flush running under her cheekbones and her full red lips were parted in a painful anticipation she could not conceal. Her whole body was alight with it and aching for her lover's touch.

'Miss Urosova, sir,' Johnson announced.

She stumbled over the threshold and fell into Croxley's outstretched arms. 'Get out!' he growled over her head and the disappointed steward departed reluctantly. 'Darling,' he said in a shaky voice and began to draw the long pins out of her concealing hat. Casting it aside, he buried his face in her hair, holding her close so that each was astounded by the sound of the other's heart. 'It's seemed like a year since October!'

'Harry!' she gasped again and again.

Hungry for each other, they collapsed into a deep chair. He kissed her so fiercely that soon they were both trembling with frustrated desire. He could feel her soft body through the muslin dress as she pressed ever closer.

'What are we going to do, Harry?'

He put her from him with an effort. 'God! I want you so. Forgive me, darling, have I frightened you? It's been so long.'

Frightened her? She was amazed he should think such a thing. Her whole body was crying out for him and he didn't realize it. She lay back in the chair, almost crying with frustration. A Russian wouldn't have held back, she told herself angrily. Why were Englishmen so slow? Such perfect gentlemen? Yet no Russian had ever moved her like this English sailor.

'We must get married,' she announced, coolly matter-of-fact now.

He looked intently into her glowing eyes. 'You mean it? You would marry me and leave your father and sisters

18

and live in England? It's a very different country to this one. You love me enough for that?'

'You know I do,' she murmured, sliding into his arms again. She glowed with love for him and he had to struggle to keep his head; to put her from him again. She was so young! He took a deep breath. 'Then I shall go and see your father tomorrow.'

She nodded. 'Twelve o'clock. Don't be late, my love.'

3

'What does he want to see me about?' Urosov poured himself a glass of wine, his noon *apéritif*. 'Why couldn't he see me at the yard?'

Marie murmured something about 'very special business' and retreated quickly to her bedroom before he remarked on the hot colour in her cheeks. From behind the lace curtain that overlooked the road, she saw her lover emerge from a *droshky*. Her heart trembled with terror. What if – but no, he couldn't, her father wouldn't be so cruel! In a quarter of an hour she would know her fate. Father couldn't turn him away! Harry was such a fine man.

She took a tiny lawn handkerchief from her sleeve and patted her moist face with it. She began to pace her room restlessly, looking for comfort at the many small treasures she had amassed during her life. She would be nineteen in two weeks and that was a good age for marriage. She was no longer a child, she told herself fiercely. Father must realize that.

She sank onto a small velvet buttoned-back chair and tried to be calm, her eyes on the little gold clock ticking on her desk.

After fifteen minutes she could bear it no longer. Why hadn't she been summoned downstairs? She opened her door and leaned over the banisters to peer down the well into the hall. Far down below a door opened. A manservant with measured tread was going across the marble-floored hall to open the first door. The keeper of the outer door, an old man who sat huddled in a canopied chair in the outer hall, wouldn't open the great outer door until the guest had been ushered through to him. Harry was leaving. She hadn't been summoned to her father's study . . .

A little cry of anger and despair escaped her and she flew back into her room to press her face against the window pane. Yes, there was her sea captain crossing the road, striding away from the great house on the Moika Canal with angry steps; she could tell he was angry by the set of his shoulders and the thrust of his head. Tears began to trickle down her face. She tasted their salt on her tongue as she licked them childishly away. Father hadn't given his consent, then . . .

Never a girl to evade direct action, Marie ran helter-skelter down the long staircase and with only a brief tap at the door burst into the study. 'Father, how could you? You've sent Harry away! It's not fair – '

The merchant had been standing at the window and he swung round to face his angry daughter with a face as angry as her own. 'What is this, Marie? How have you contrived to meet this fellow behind my back?' He leaned on his desk and thrust his red face into hers.

Recoiling a little, she still managed to stand her ground. 'Not really behind your back, Father. We met over business in the timberyard. I love him and I intend to marry him.'

'Intend to marry him?' Urosov repeated, bringing his fist down with a crash on the green leather top of the

20

desk. 'No! Never! Your place is here in Petersburg. You will marry a man of my choice who will help you when you inherit the business!' He paused for breath as anger had made him choke. That Marie, his jewel, should have been nearly filched from under his nose by this English sailor! But everyone knew the English were a perfidious race. Cunning devil. After the Urosov fortune, of course. His legs now weak, Urosov sat down suddenly. He could find no words to express his grief and rage. The idea of Marie leaving him to go to live thousands of miles away frightened him very much. What would he do without her? What was left in life, then? He had been building up the business for *her*; there was no point in anything without her at his side.

Marie was trembling violently but forcing herself to remain dry-eyed. She gripped the back of a chair and steadied her voice. 'It's no use trying to stop me, Father. I won't marry anyone else. I can't! I only want Harry and you're not going to stop us marrying, so there!'

They glared at each other, all love between them suddenly dissolved.

'We'll see about that, miss! Now be off with you. I'm not going to discuss it further. But from now on remember one thing: you're forbidden the timberyard. I see now that you're not to be trusted.'

Forbidden the timberyard? She stared in horrified disbelief. He couldn't do that to her! He knew she had her own little carriage and could continue to go there on her own. Indeed, she would go this very day to talk things over with Harry and persuade him to take her away with him. They could be married in England.

She wheeled and left the room without another word. She felt very bitter towards the father who had hitherto given her everything she had asked for. How could he be

21

so cruel? But of course he was old and the old never understand the powerful force of love.

She reached her bedroom and began to open drawers and cupboards to find suitable garments, something that Harry would find irresistible like this demure grey muslin threaded with black velvet ribbons –

'Where are you going, Marie Nicolaievna?' Old nurse, her face long with suspicion, was standing in the doorway with her hands on her broad hips.

Marie tossed her head. 'Out,' she announced airily. 'Please order my carriage to be brought round, Nurse.'

'I will do no such thing. Does Katrina Mironovna accompany you? Or the governess?' Nurse never gave Miss Hardwick the dignity of a name. 'I thought not! You put those clothes right back in that cupboard or I go straight to your aunt. Understand me? You know very well you aren't allowed to go calling or shopping without a companion. Now don't you toss your head at me, Marie Nicolaievna! It's not a pleasant thing to do to old nurse who's only got your best interests at heart.'

Marie sank onto the bed in her chemise and drawers. She could have yelled with frustration.

Nurse nodded approvingly. 'That's a good girl,' she said fondly and hobbled away.

Marie was not renowned for patience in the family. But she was patient that day; patient and cunning. She knew that old nurse was fond of a nap every afternoon when her eagle eyes became very heavy-lidded. So Marie went down to luncheon with a sulky face, refusing to be drawn by puzzled enquiries, refusing to eat.

'Leave her alone! Leave her alone!' Urosov said impatiently. 'She's a silly child but she'll come round, you'll see.' He plunged a spoon into a bowl of thick soup and the aroma stung Marie's nostrils making her hungrier than ever.

22

Urosov raised his brows at Aunt Kitty who was looking stupidly from one to the other: what was wrong with everyone today?

Afterwards, the timber merchant shut himself in the study, Aunt Kitty went up to rest (although why she should need one when she did so little no one knew) and Miss Hardwick, martyred by one of her headaches, took Anastasia to the schoolroom and told her to keep quiet. A profound silence descended on the house.

Hastily and silently, Marie dressed herself in the grey muslin dress and tied the matching lingerie bonnet, a mass of lace, frills and ribbons, round her firm little chin. Smoothing on fresh white gloves she opened the door and listened. Not a sound. Like a ghost, she flitted down the stairs and out into the vestibule. As the old doorman came out of his doze, she passed him quickly and was through the heavy street door before he could get out of his chair. She had decided to take a cab: ordering her carriage would have made her conspicuous, she told herself as she walked swiftly down the broad sunlit road towards the main thoroughfare, Nevsky Prospekt.

The sun was hot even through her parasol and beads of sweat appeared on her upper lip as she hastened towards the cab rank. She disliked the idea of taking one of those dirty-looking cabs but there was no alternative.

It seemed to take an age to get there. Telling the driver to wait, she got down with difficulty, twisting her ankle on the rough road. Limping to the timberyard gate, she rang the bell imperiously.

The old doorkeeper, who wore a shabby fez winter and summer on his unkempt head, shuffled out of his cabin and stared at her through the iron gate. Slowly, he shook his head. 'It's no good, Marie Nicolaievna, the master has given orders that you're never to be let inside these gates again. Very sorry but I don't want to lose my job.'

23

Marie's full bosom heaved with fury and her dark eyes were suddenly full of sparks. Telling the cabby to drive her home, she flung herself back against the seat, her face stony. Father thought he'd won but she would soon show him how wrong he was! For now she knew what she must do.

4

Laura Nicolaievna Urosova was not pleased to have her practice interrupted just to see her eldest sister who had called on her at the Imperial Ballet School. Visitors were usually frowned on by the teachers but star pupils were often granted favours and Laura was a star pupil although still only nearly fifteen.

She came running down the stairs, a little frown on her face, to find Marie pacing the cool hall with its marble floor. From upstairs floated the sound of a piano, of a voice shrilling instructions and the steady thump of feet dancing. Laura was wearing her practice tutu and had wrapped herself in a black shawl for there was sweat on her body and all dancers dreaded the ache that came from chilled limbs because stiffness was sure to follow.

'Well, Marie, what is it? I'm practising for our performance before the Imperial Family next week.'

Marie nodded. She knew that the Tsar Alexander and his family came occasionally to see the most promising pupils perform in the perfect little miniature theatre upstairs. 'I'm sorry, darling. It was just that I needed to see you . . .' Her voice trailed away, but Laura, self-absorbed confident Laura, noticed nothing.

'To see me? Good God, I thought at least Aunt Kitty must have died!' and she gave an explosive little laugh for Aunt Kitty was not a favourite with her. 'And is that all?'

'Laura darling, if you hear – if I do something soon – go away from home, I hope you won't feel too badly. I mean I want you to understand why I'm doing it. I love someone very badly but Papa won't hear of it.' She spoke in rapid French and Laura replied in the same language. At home, Urosov insisted on Russian being spoken but here in the Ballet School only French was used. It was the language most suited to the romantic expression of love and Laura listened with sparkling eyes to the tale of her sister's romance – and right under the nose of Papa, Aunt Kitty and old nurse, too! 'Oh, Marie, how did you manage it?' she burst out enviously. 'Oh, you have been clever! How furious Aunt Kitty's going to be!' and she burst into hearty laughter that she had to muffle in her shawl.

'Ssh!' Marie begged. 'So you see why I must go away with him and marry in secret. You do understand?'

'Oh, yes,' Laura assured her, her eyes still dancing. 'I think it's wonderfully romantic. Marie, my sweet sister, I salute you,' and she flung her arms round her so that both were buried in the black shawl. 'And you will come home again?'

'Certainly,' Marie assured her. 'I shall travel with my husband on his boat and visit St Petersburg every summer. I'm sure Papa will forgive me very quickly. Harry might even settle here and help me run the timberyard when Papa gets old. Oh, Laura, you will like Harry, I know. He is big and strong and so droll! He is very like a Russian except in one way – ' She hesitated.

Laura's eyes were fixed on her face. 'What way?'

'He is too gentle with me and *so* respectful. Oh, I hope he's not like that when we get married!' Marie added anxiously.

"Course he won't be, silly.' Laura hugged her. 'I *must* go or I'll be in the most awful trouble. Write to me – tell me what happens, Marie. Oh, how I'd love to see Aunt Kitty's face!' She laughed gleefully as she hugged her sister for the last time. 'Oh, help, there's Mademoiselle Creuset looking for me! I simply must fly.' She ran up the stairs, a sturdy well-knit figure in darned black tights and a grubby tutu. At the top she turned and waved the shawl like a flag. 'Hurrah, Marie!' Then with the ballet dancer's penguin-like walk she strutted down the landing and out of sight, Mademoiselle Creuset pouring out wrathful words as she followed her.

Marie drove home comforted that Laura understood why she must leave home and go to Harry.

Anastasia was sitting at the top of the marble staircase when she entered the house. 'Marie, come here!' She crooked a finger excitedly.

Marie went up, untying her bonnet as she did so. 'What is it, Stana? I'm late for luncheon – '

Anastasia drew her into a curtained archway. Her small face was filled with importance. 'I've got a message for you. When I went shopping with Miss Hardwick this morning, a man put this in my hand – don't worry, Miss Hardwick didn't see him do it. We were in Elisev's and she was too busy choosing those marzipan sweetmeats she adores.'

'Was this man in a sailor's uniform?'

'Oh, no, he was just a *moujik*. I think he'd followed us from outside this house – I'm sure I saw him standing here. I thought he was a beggar.' She had put her hand under her frilly lawn petticoats to find the pocket on the leg of her drawers where a spare handkerchief was usually kept. Marie waited, biting her lip impatiently. She felt sure this was a message from Harry: he wouldn't accept his dismissal as final.

'There!' At last Anastasia withdrew a crumpled envelope in triumph. 'It was scratching me! Is it a *billet doux*?'

'Of course not, silly!' Marie lied lightly. 'Just a bill, I should think. How silly of the shop not to post it to me. Have you washed for lunch? Then hurry. You know how Papasha hates to be kept waiting.'

She went into her room, closed the door and leaned against it. She had recognized the writing at once: it was from Harry. With trembling hands she opened it and read that the *Sylvie-Rose* would be sailing for Hull on the tide at three o'clock that afternoon. *I must see you*, Harry wrote desperately.

You will, my love! You will!

With a little laugh of excited happiness, Marie tucked his note into her waistband, her mind working rapidly as she tidied her hair. On the way back from the Ballet School she had stopped the carriage and made some surprising purchases. The parcels, she had instructed, were to be taken up to her room during the luncheon hour.

With a light heart, she ran downstairs but she entered the dining room wearing an air of depression: lowered eyes, a tight mouth and a refusal to eat the *zakouski* being handed round. Normally, she loved these little dishes of highly-flavoured foods that began their meals and from which everyone was expected to choose at least five portions: smoked salmon, pickled cucumber, some black olives, and so on. Their varied smells tickled her nostrils but she shook her head firmly all the same.

Urosov looked gloomily at his eldest. Perish the girl! He wished Harry Croxley at the bottom of the sea. Missing her company sorely, he was only too ready to make it up with his daughter. But she kept her eyes averted and even refused the glass of white wine from Georgia that he offered as a favour. The silence between

27

them was obstinately solid. Aunt Kitty felt it and looked in mild confusion from one to the other, forced in the end to make conversation with Miss Hardwick whose papery skin and whiskers seemed to her so unfortunate.

After luncheon came a siesta for the whole household.

In her room, Marie wasn't resting. Writing her farewell note in a firm hand, she paused to look wistfully at the treasured possessions she must leave behind: the pretty clothes and hats, her little gold clock, the picture of her mother, many favourite books. But it wouldn't be for long, she told herself. Next summer she would be back and by that time Papasha would have forgiven her.

She changed rapidly, giggling under her breath at her changed appearance, and encountering difficulty with her abundant dark hair that must be tucked under the canvas peaked cap. Into a piece of cloth, she folded her dress, petticoats, a change of underclothes, a toothbrush and powder, a sponge, a piece of soap and her nightdress – the very pretty one of fine lawn and lace with threaded blue ribbons. It made a bulky parcel but she managed to tie the four ends into a knot and then it became a tidy bundle to carry over her shoulder.

Opening the door of the now cold stove in the corner of the room she rubbed her hands over the interior and then here and there on her face. It changed her gloriously and now she looked a grubby urchin and not Marie Nicolaievna any more.

She was ready. Creeping out, she looked over the banisters. There was no one about. The servants were in their own quarters until three-thirty which was calling time for St Petersburg ladies, who came to have tea and stilted conversation with Aunt Kitty. Marie looked towards the closed schoolroom door, making the sign of the cross. 'Farewell, little sister! God be with you.' Then

28

she was flitting noiselessly down the stairs and opening the heavy front door.

Out in the street she strolled along, noiselessly whistling, her bundle over her shoulder and one hand in her pocket. She was enjoying her new role as a cabin boy and couldn't resist stealing glances at herself in the shop windows as she went down Nevsky Prospekt to the trams. No one looked twice at her: the disguise must be good.

It was two-thirty by the time she reached the gates of the Urosov Timberyard. Usually she never went anywhere by tram and had made the foolish mistake of taking one going in the wrong direction. It had wasted precious time and in her new guise of simple English cabin boy, she had been forced to ask directions in halting Russo-English – oh, yes, it had wasted precious time! But she was here at last and she gave the bell an imperious pull more fitted to the owner's daughter than to a cabin boy.

Old Lev hobbled out of his cubbyhole and stared suspiciously with his one good eye.

Marie's pulses raced. Would he recognize her? She pulled her face into a vacant stare and saw with glee that Lev didn't know her at all.

'Well, lad, what d'yer want?' he asked gruffly in Russian.

Marie said haltingly, with many gestures: 'Me, from *Sylvie-Rose* of Hull. Me Captain's boy.'

Lev digested the few words he had picked up from the English sailors. 'Where's yer card, then? Card, boy, *card*.'

Too late, Marie remembered the seaman's card that always had to be carried by the sailors. Picked up dead drunk, they could always be forcibly returned to the right boat. She pretended to search her pockets and then said tearfully: 'Oh, sir, me lose card! No card!'

Old Lev cuffed her neatly on the side of her head,

nearly sending her sprawling. 'Sodding little bastard!' he scolded. 'You'll cost me my job, just see if yer don't! Go on then – get along with yer afore I kick yer!' and he gestured with his boot.

Marie, her head reeling from the blow, went as fast as her legs could carry her, one hand holding on to the canvas cap that had nearly fallen into the dust under Lev's hand. She had a pain in her side and was breathless by the time she reached the place where the *Sylvie-Rose* was berthed. Seamen were making fast the huge pile of timber on her deck, lashing ropes round it and covering it with tarpaulins. Only one spared a glance in her direction as she clambered aboard and he merely said to himself: 'Looks like the Ol' Man's got a new boy. Anything would be an improvement on that last little varmint.' Then he went on lashing timber.

She was aboard. Leaning against a bulkhead she tried to draw a steady breath. They would be setting sail in twenty minutes and she would be with Harry for ever! The idea made her quite faint with emotion and the St Petersburg skyline of towers and minarets seemed to swim in front of her eyes. When would she see that beloved outline again? The golden spires were shining under the sun and the majestic buildings on the quayside seemed suddenly the finest in the world. How could she leave her home, the only city she knew, for an unknown country and a man she barely knew? For a moment – but it was only a moment – she nearly changed her mind and got off the boat. There was little Stana and Papasha – oh, poor Papasha! How angry he would be at first! But he'd forgive her. He always forgave her in the end because he loved her so much: she had basked confidently in that love for almost nineteen years and it had never failed her.

Her courage began to blossom again. She *loved* Harry

30

and it was simply silly to try to part them. Nothing should ever do that.

She made the sign of the cross against the skyline. 'Goodbye, Papashi,' she whispered. 'I'll be back soon. Goodbye, little sisters, Marie won't forget you.'

Choking under her breath, longing now for the comfort of Harry's arms round her, she took up her bundle again and went down the hatchway to the captain's cabin. She knocked timidly and waited. A voice growled, 'Come in!' and, taking a deep breath, she stepped over the threshold and closed the door.

His cap on the back of his head, Harry sat at his desk checking the way-bill. He had his back to the door. 'Well, what is it?' Not receiving an answer he swung round and glared at the cabin boy who stood so dumbly by the door. 'What the hell is it, boy? You're not in trouble again, are you?'

For answer the figure in the shadows removed his canvas cap and a wealth of rich black hair tumbled out. 'Harry,' said Marie falteringly.

'For God's sake!' He leapt up, his face scarlet. 'Marie, Marie, what prank is this? We're just about to sail – oh, Marie, my darling girl, I've got you in my arms again!' He was crushing her to him, kissing her fiercely and she went limp.

'I'm coming with . . . you . . .' she managed to gasp.

He stiffened and thrust her from him to stare into her grubby face. '*What*?'

'I've run away from home. I'm going to marry you, Harry. I don't care what Father says or does!'

'Are you mad? You'll be ruined.'

'Yes, I know and then we'll have to be married!' She laughed exultantly and perched on his desk, smiling into his harassed face. Then she glanced down at the clock. 'In five minutes or so you will be sailing and I shall be

31

with you for ever and ever! Oh, Harry darling, say you are glad!'

He kissed her with rueful tenderness, his heart exultant but his conscience uneasy. He had been bitterly hurt by Urosov's sneering rejection of his suit. *How dare you consider yourself a suitable person for my daughter? You are only interested in her fortune.* But stealing Marie from this man had been no part of his intentions. 'Oh, Marie!' he sighed, burying his face in her hair. 'My sweet Marie, you've burned your boats with a vengeance now!'

'Burned my boats! No, no!' Marie protested, puzzled. 'I should not dream of doing so, Harry.'

He looked at her disguise and broke into unwilling laughter. He found her irresistible and she knew it, the rogue. 'Your father will never forgive you – never.'

For a moment, her heart failed her as she thought of Papasha, always her friend – until now. 'But we shall have each other,' she said with a wavering smile.

He hugged her once more than snatched up his cap. 'Wait here while we cast off. We must catch the tide. I'll see about a cabin for you after we've sailed and I'll telegraph Hull to get us a special licence.'

5

As she watched the St Petersburg skyline drifting past the porthole, no inkling of the long unforgiving years touched her. The merchant didn't acknowledge her existence after this. Marie Nicolaievna Urosova could be considered dead from now on. All her clothes and possessions were packed up and despatched after her to Hull, care of the shippers Howarth and Hawksley. Urosov wrote personally to Abel Howarth and warned that any boat putting in to his dock with Captain Croxley aboard would be turned away.

And so he turned his ambitions in other directions. The timberyard was run down, its turnover shrinking. He could no longer endure going there for Marie's shade was everywhere and the men continued to ask about her long after she had gone.

With Laura swallowed up by the Imperial Ballet School, Urosov considered he now had only one child. For her, his ambitions became high.

Part Two
1894

2
The Prince's Son

1

It was on the first day of November that Tsar Alexander III died in his palace at Livadia in the Crimea. He was only forty-nine, a huge bear of a man who fulfilled his role to the letter and was adored by his people. Alexander *was* Russia, and everything that was best in it.

Ten days later, the coffin arrived in St Petersburg. In front of a silent multitude and to the sound of muffled drums, the cortège moved off at walking pace from the station.

In the last carriage, alone except for a lady-in-waiting, rode the new Tsar's betrothed, the shy Princess Alix of Hesse who was Queen Victoria's favourite granddaughter. The people, craning forward eagerly, could just see her as she stepped into the carriage and the blinds were pulled down. They reported that she had red-gold hair just discernible under the black veil of mourning; grey eyes that held reserve and a clear-cut profile which a strong little chin dominated.

Watching the coffin moving off on its gun carriage, the people whispered to each other: 'She comes to us behind a coffin . . .' They shuddered and crossed themselves.

Standing among the crowd behind the barriers in the railway station was a tall seventeen-year-old boy who had been waiting there for some hours. His train had been held up by the imminent arrival of the funeral train and of course it had been late. However he couldn't have felt the cold for he was warmly dressed in a long fur-lined coat with a big collar, a Cossack hat of black fox and high soft leather boots. He was a handsome boy with intense blue eyes that missed nothing, cheeks reddened by the frost, a high-bridged nose and a firm humorous mouth. The face was as yet unfinished and young but it held promise of being intelligent as well as good-looking.

It was snowing now and he brushed the flakes from his lashés, his eyes intent on the Imperial Family driving away from the station. His mother, Princess Rakova, was somewhere in the long line of carriages for she was in-waiting on the bereaved Empress Marie.

Prince Alexander Rakov hunched his shoulders impatiently and turned away as the last carriage moved into the screen of snow. Pushing his way through the crowds, he made his way back to the waiting train that would take him to their family estate south of the city. He plunged a hand into one of his pockets to make sure he still had the ticket to Tatarskino and smiled with relief when at last he found it. He had never made the journey alone before but always accompanied by Monsieur Boulet, their Swiss tutor, who had had to remain at home this time with Alex's young brother. It was glorious to be free, a man of the world, Alex told himself happily as he found his seat in an empty compartment. He had begged his mother's permission to go there on his own for a couple of weeks while she was away at Court. The city was going to be insupportable during the next few months with the court in mourning and all fun of any sort cancelled and frowned on. At Tatarskino he could shoot foxes with Ivan Fillipov, the schoolmaster's son who was exactly his age. So Alex smiled with happy anticipation of the days ahead as he leaned his head back against the lace antimacassar and willed the train to get steam up and depart for his beloved Tatarskino.

The train started with a jerk but soon gathered speed and the outskirts of St Petersburg were quickly left behind. Snow spattered against the windows, slid down the glass and began to gather thickly round the edges as with a shriek the train began to roar and rattle across the flat marshy plain to Tatarskino.

As Alex gazed at his reflection in the glass his thoughts were far away. He had always taken his parents for granted; they were *there*, in charge of his life. He was even a little afraid of his father: Prince Peter was an immensely tall man with a narrow face that perpetually wore an expression of boredom and disdain. Between him and his elder son was a strange gulf that puzzled the boy. Alex held his father in awe, he admired him and wondered what he could do to please him; but there was no warmth. Lately, as he grew up and became more aware of the strange adult world in Petersburg, he had begun to be troubled. Something was wrong between his parents; they didn't share anything any longer, from a bedroom to conversation. The princess had to pretend she knew where her husband was when he was absent from home but Alex had a shrewd idea that she knew of Madame Sophie Clèmont about whom she could say nothing.

How had he first heard of this 'bundle of French charm'? Those were the words used by one groom to another in the stableyard behind the Rakov palace. 'We've been to see our cosy bundle of French charm,' the man had chuckled as he entered the tack room. Too late, his colleague had given him a warning signal: *the young master's over there*!

Alex had jerked his head and seen the warning and the man's look of dismay. He had known then what he had only suspected before, but pride made him pretend he hadn't heard. He had asked them to look at his horse's fetlock, discussed it with them and then gone back indoors. His father had just arrived home and was demanding tea in his study. Three days he'd been away this time.

A week later, he had gone again.

Alex found himself watching, counting the days, wondering how his mother could remain so calm . . .

Then Ivan Fillipov, the schoolmaster's son at Tatarskino, had told him bluntly not to be a fool: all the aristocrats had mistresses, he had said scornfully. It was only part of their general rottenness!

They had fought over that, fought, laughed and made up. Alex ceased to worry about Madame Clèmont (it was Fillipov who told him her name) but he also cared less and less about his father's approval. In some ways, he deliberately sought to hold opposite views to Peter Rakov on every possible subject, but because they saw so little of each other it had ceased to matter to either of them. A sort of armed neutrality became the conduct expected by each of them.

'He's decadent,' the boy would say scornfully in the privacy of his bedroom.

'The boy's a fool to meddle in politics,' the prince would tell Henri as the valet tied his cravat. 'Depend on it, he'll find himself in trouble before long.'

Outside the train window lights began to appear in small bunches: they must be nearly there. A minute later, with a grinding crash of brakes the train slid to a halt. Tatarskino was a special stop and no one else got out besides himself, Alex noticed as he jumped down into the snow.

'Excellency, they have sent a troika for you!' The fat little stationmaster, almost square in his sheepskin coat,

40

was bustling up to him bowing and beaming. 'We are honoured! Only two hours ago we welcomed his excellency, Prince Rakov himself!'

The boy paused, blank dismay on his face. What awful luck! His father was here, too.

2

Alex woke next morning in his own room at Tatarskino and lay back contentedly as he savoured the feeling of being *home*. Only Tatarskino gave him that feeling.

Tatarskino in winter was so different to Tatarskino in summer that it could seem two places. From the shelter of the dark woods would come the howl of wolves yet all one saw of them was their paw marks in the snow. There were a lot of woods around Tatarskino, four thousand acres of them, and they were looked after by the forester who had to keep to an approved government plan for felling and planting: all private forests were under the central jurisdiction of the government forestry department. The woods were part of Russia's great riches: the hardwoods went for a hundred uses and were exported in great quantities; only the softwoods were sawn up to feed the stoves that kept the house warm all through the long winter.

A mill for grinding the corn stood on Rakov ground and to this would be brought the meagre yields of the villagers themselves who would have it ground up for their own use. The Rakov yield fetched a great deal of gold and it was this that was beginning to disturb Alex. The peasants toiled on Rakov land and could spare very little time for their own patch: how could they be expected to live on that poor weed-choked grain?

41

Apart from the farms let to tenants, Prince Rakov owned a home farm. Here everything was on a vast scale: there was stabling for forty heavy horses, for the riding horses and the brood mares. The estate depended heavily on horses to work the rich black valley soil. Hundreds of pigs were housed in the long low pighouse and their continual squealing could be heard at the big house itself. By contrast, the estate office where the factor worked was the meanest building of all, a mere log cabin in the shadow of the mill. Stout wooden sheds housed the vast herd of cattle all winter but in spring they were driven out daily by the herdsmen and brought back for milking at dawn and dusk, raising clouds of dust in the air as they stampeded back to the sheds. How wasteful it all was! Alex thought, staring out of the window moodily as he sat up in bed. No wonder their milk yield was low. His father had given the farming side of the Rakov inheritance no thought at all and yet it was an essential part of their lives, indeed of the lives of everyone in the valley. Nothing had been altered in a hundred years – perhaps longer.

He got out of bed, a tall lanky boy in a white nightshirt, and perched on the windowsill. The stove's warm air kept an even temperature but outside everything was frozen and still, the snow very white because it was the first fall. The house had been built on a knoll and the valley lay stretched out in a broad plain below it. It was watered by a wide river, smooth-flowing in summer but now already frozen hard as steel. Now the village could take its sledges straight across to the other side to visit relatives instead of travelling miles down to the bridge, so winter had its advantages.

The village lay only a short distance from the Rakov house and consisted of two or three rows of crude log cabins with thatched roofs that were full of vermin.

Hardly a winter passed without one or two of them being set on fire by the blazing stoves inside. A well with a see-saw pole stood in the middle of the huddle of houses; it never froze and here one met one's neighbour daily. There were no lavatories and in summer the smell was sometimes unbearable; swarms of flies infested the big house so that fly-screens had to be put in place. It was in summer that people died of dysentery and the Rakov children were forbidden the village.

Biting his finger, a habit of his when absorbed, Alex dreamed of main drainage and a pumping system such as he had seen depicted in a book from America. If only he could persuade his father! There must be the money to do it; it was just a question of getting his father interested. Surely he loved the place as much as he, Alex, did?

It had been too dark to see much last night and it was still dark grey outside now at eight o'clock. But the way the house and formal gardens looked was still vivid from the last time he had seen them. He had come down in time for the big fair held on St Sophie's Day in September. It had been a stifling day, golden and misty, and the fair had lasted from dawn till dusk. It was always an occasion of great excitement locally and Alex had gone round meeting the peasants, having a word with those he knew, rather enjoying his role as the inheritor of this valley. How lovely the house had looked, too! It was a huge place, square and built of locally made bricks painted white. Hidden at the back was the long servants' wing economically made of timber, but from the front the house had looked serene and dignified with the creeper turning red and orange and late roses climbing over the porch. He had looked up at it, feeling for the first time great pride in his inheritance and a strong sense of responsibility, too. And that was why he had come back now in November; he wanted to get to know the place on

43

his own. It was very annoying to find that his father had also decided to come down to the country.

It isn't as if he cares two kopecks for the place, the boy told himself resentfully. I suppose he needs more money as usual. What does he do with it all?

His father could spend money like water: he spent it on horses and cards and probably Madame Clèmont, too, and was known and admired for it in Petersburg. The princess, on the other hand, was rather feared and resented for being too straitlaced and far, far too economical. 'My dear, she actually *thinks* about money,' her acquaintances told each other with a laugh. It was put down to her Swedish ancestry.

He bathed quickly and decided to shave, too; his fair stubble was still pretty tentative and normally he shaved every other day. He had just lathered his face generously when Henri, his father's valet, bustled in and began to fuss over his small clothes. 'Your excellency takes no care of his possessions,' he scolded. '*Tiens*! Another button off.' He began to carry off a bundle of soiled garments when he stopped and shook his head at the young prince. 'Not like that, excellency! You will make your skin sore. Allow me.' He ran an expert finger over the razor and shook his head again. 'Your excellency is forgetting to use the strop. This is very blunt. I really think it's time we found you a body servant. I will speak to his excellency at the first opportunity. I really cannot be expected to do everything,' Henri added huffily in his strong Parisian accent. After twenty-three years with Prince Rakov he still refused to speak Russian. He was over fifty now and his thin dyed hair had to be spread carefully over his cranium. To Alex and Feo, Henri was the benevolent influence in their lives. Seeing little of either parent it was to Henri they turned for advice or praise; he was in fact a sort of father to them. He had

44

been part of the family before they were born and he knew every ramification of it. If he had been suddenly removed from their lives both boys would have felt orphaned.

Released at last from Henri's expert hands, Alex finished dressing in a very great hurry and took the stairs two at a time to the ground floor. He was very eager to see the little colt born in the summer to one of the brood mares. It had been sired by his own horse, Ajax. Ajax was a big powerful creature with the nature of a pampered pet dog. The prince said Alex had 'ruined him' but Alex (refraining from contradicting his father) knew better: Ajax understood his every mood and had a great heart and courage. His coat was like black satin and he had a sensitive mouth that had not been ruined by the stable lads for Alex only allowed Mikhail, the head groom, to ride the horse. Now it looked as if Thor, the little colt, was going to be exactly like him.

He opened the side door and an icy blast hit him full in the face. Pulling his fur hat down well over his ears he trudged across the frozen snow, every step cracking the thin surface, to an arch in a high wall. Behind this were the stables for the riding horses. The smell of horse manure, too strong before breakfast for some people, only made Alex smile with anticipation: the stable yard was his special domain and if he hadn't been born a prince he would have been a stable hand.

The yard was lit by lamps hung at intervals on the walls that nearly enclosed it: the fourth wall was a row of twenty stalls for the horses, each door with the name painted over it. Coming through the arch, Alex drew up sharply in utter surprise: the yard was full of people standing in a circle, the light from the lamps lighting their faces grotesquely. What were they watching? A bear baiting or a cock fight? Their faces were intent on something in the centre of their circle. As he stared a girl's anguished scream rent the clear cold air; a girl was crying for mercy as if she were caught in a trap.

He leapt forward, pushing to the front of the circle, bent on stopping whatever was making the woman cry out. He stopped and breathed hard, barely able to believe his eyes: a young peasant girl, clad only in a loose woollen garment, her hair falling over her ashen face, was receiving a beating from a wooden-faced servant whose arm went up and down rhythmically while she dashed from side to side of the circle trying to escape. Her mouth was stretched wide and screams poured out, her terrified eyes white in the lamplight. With spittle slavering from the corners of her mouth she looked demented. As she turned, Alex saw with horror that she was in an advanced state of pregnancy.

'My God! What's going on here? What are you doing?' he shouted, snatching the whip from the groom's hand.

'Alexander!' The sound of his father's voice cut into him like a sabre blow. He wheeled, his face set in astonishment. Prince Rakov was leaning against a stable door, calmly smoking one of his favourite Turkish cigarettes. 'Don't interfere. The girl has to be punished.'

'But, for God's sake, Father, don't you see? She's *enceinte*!'

'That is why she is being punished.'

Alex rushed across to him and put an imploring hand on his sleeve. 'I beg you to stop them! It's infamous! She could lose the child!'

The prince struck his son's hand away, his pale grey eyes blazing with rage. But his voice remained coldly calm. 'Don't interfere with my orders. I hope the girl *will* lose the child. Go indoors if you haven't the stomach for it. How will you ever be master here?' The jeering tone

46

was unmistakable. Turning, he pointed an imperious finger and the man began to beat the girl again.

She was lying on the ground now, drawing up her legs in the first pangs of labour. Beneath her, blood began to stain the snow.

'God, it's brutal!' Tears stood in the boy's eyes. 'You'll kill her and the child. I beg you, Father, stop it – in the name of God, stop it!'

'Unfortunately, God has nothing to do with it,' his father murmured with a twist of his thin lips. 'It was your brother Feodor.'

Alex felt the blood drain from his face. '*Feo*? But Feo's only fourteen!'

The prince shrugged and threw his cigarette away: it described a glowing arc against the still dark sky. 'Throw the hussy out,' he directed and his servants obeyed with wooden faces. The girl was one of them but in the valley of the Tatar the prince was all-powerful: from him they got their daily bread. Without a backward glance, the prince strolled away, his fur collar turned up to shield his face from the cold.

Alex turned to Mikhail, the head groom. 'Who is the girl?'

'Daria Kvitkova, your excellency. She worked in the stillroom,' the man muttered, his head down. Suddenly he lifted his eyes and Alex saw the naked hatred blazing in them. 'She is my sister's child.'

They were carrying her past him now. Someone had wrapped a horse blanket round her. Alex could see that despite her bruised and battered appearance she was very pretty. Suddenly, her eyes opened, huge with hatred. With what strength she had left she spat at him.

He recoiled, feeling the hatred like a blow between the eyes. Never before had anyone manifested such open malevolence but now he had seen it in the eyes of Daria

47

Kvitkova and her uncle, the head groom. At that moment he had the strange feeling that they were – all of them standing round watchfully – ready to kill him and his family. This was the moment when he realized how privilege had kept this feeling from him before; he had been cocooned from it but it was here, naked in the eyes of these people. They had been freed as serfs but had gained very little as citizens. They were still misused and starved, ground into the mire of the disease-infested village outside these princely walls.

Revulsion choked him. Wheeling, he ran across the snow, stumbling in his long coat and calling out loudly as he entered the house: 'Where's the prince? Where's my father?'

Ivan Ivanovitch Sablin, his father's major-domo, drew himself to his full height. 'His excellency is about to have breakfast,' he announced. 'I advise your excellency to hasten and follow his example.'

His father was already making short work of croissants and coffee in the breakfast room. In between eating and drinking he smoked one of his little cigarettes and a ring of scented smoke hung over his head. Now and again he fed tidbits to his favourite elkhound Perseus. His expression and tone were soft and doting as he spoke to the dog.

Stopping short in the doorway, Alex was aware once again of how much he disliked and distrusted this man who was his father. Once, he had been ashamed of these unfilial feelings but no longer. How could his father cuddle the dog and eat so unconcernedly when he had just witnessed a young woman heavy with child punished beyond her endurance? The man was a fiend and he hated him!

Sleek and comfortable as a cat, the prince drank his coffee, lazy smoke from his cigarette curling between his fingers. His moustache and hair smelled of a delicate pomade and he was wearing his pale biscuit uniform with long black boots. Handsome and self-assured he eyed his dishevelled son with disfavour. 'For God's sake, boy, look at yourself! Go and brush your hair; you look like a *moujik* just in from the fields.' He spoke in French but used the Russian word for peasant with good-humoured contempt. 'I'll ring for fresh coffee while you're gone.'

'Father, I must speak with you! Father, what we both witnessed just now was horrifying. Surely you agree?'

The prince's face froze. Then a look of contempt twisted his features. 'Alexander, you are my heir. Some day you will be master here and have to deal with a similar situation no doubt. Do you think there will be room for these *girlish* emotions?'

Inside Alex fear fluttered but he had to go on. 'I call my emotions common humanity. How do you know this won't kill the girl or the child? That girl, Daria Kvitkova, is being punished for Feo's offence against her. Is he to be punished also?'

A spasm of surprise had crossed the prince's face. Why, the cub was daring to challenge him! He languidly buttered a piece of croissant. 'Don't use that tone to me or I'll have to box your ears and that would be a bore. No, Feo will not be punished. The girl is just a part of his growing up. Have *you* had your first woman, my son? Don't leave it too long, or I shall begin to think you are not fully a man.' He smiled maliciously, enjoying the red flush suffusing his son's face.

The taunt sickened the boy. 'I shall never want to know a woman if it means this terrible punishment for her,' he managed to say without choking. Then he jerked round and rushed from the room, taking the stairs two at a time to his own set of rooms.

Henri was tidying up, fussy as an old maid over details.

49

'Your excellency has forgotten to bring enough shirts and where are your hair brushes? Really, your excellency, you're old enough – '

'Oh, don't fuss!' Alex shouted and sat down on a chair. He suddenly felt very young and in need of comfort. 'Oh, Henri, I'm sorry. I shouldn't speak so but I'm upset. There's this girl, you see,' and he began to pour out his story.

Henri listened enigmatically. He had known for years that his master had this cold sadistic side to him but he loved him and served the prince devotedly despite his weaknesses: he had such charm! No wonder women fell in love with him so easily, the valet thought as he stripped Alex's sweat-soaked silk shirt off and tried to explain his father's nature to the boy. But Alex had made up his mind and Henri got no response to his plea to be patient, to love his father blindly and to do all he asked.

'You don't understand,' the boy said impatiently and stepped into the bath that had been prepared for him. He caught sight of his naked self in the cheval-glass and stared sombrely at his reflection. Was he fully a man? he wondered wistfully. His father didn't believe he was. It was true that he had not yet known a woman and was simply attracted to a passing pretty face. True, last summer he had thought himself mad with love for chic Madame Chevnenka, their doctor's wife in St Petersburg. They had gone skating together and he had bought her hot chocolate and cream cakes afterwards. But of course, she had been quite old, at least twenty-six.

In the mirror he saw a tall, broad-shouldered youth who had not finished growing and filling out. His body still had a lingering summer's brownness and was well-knit and muscular. He was hard and healthy because he had spent part of the summer working in the fields with the men. His father, if he had known, would have thought him mad. In the winter, forced to stay in St Petersburg most of the time, he would go each morning to a gymnasium for a work-out or to box or fence. In the afternoons he skated. He hated parties and knew that he was reaching the age when he would be expected to attend balls and make conversation with people he hardly knew. He much preferred leaning against a wall, talking politics with his friends.

Yes, the face looking back at him already had strength: his eyes had a new awareness, his mouth a new firmness. Last year, he had been a boy, looking up to his father with a blind faith: the prince had seemed then to inhabit a different world, a mysterious exciting place where he wielded much power.

He began to soap himself all over, washing away the dried sweat. Perhaps he washed away something else at the same time for he knew now that never again would he be frightened of his father.

3

The Captain's Daughter

1

As soon as the school bell rang at four o'clock, thirty-six girls put down their pens with relief and began to babble like a flock of starlings.

'Girls! Girls!' their teachers implored, 'remember you are Hill House young ladies.'

Hill House School in the Yorkshire port of Whitby prided itself on turning the doubtful material sent them by hopeful parents into a semblance of young ladyhood who would grow up to marry local young men and in turn produce more fodder for Hill House. The two old sisters who ran this establishment that took fifteen boarders had been doing so for over twenty years: Miss Lesley taught the older girls and was the titular head; Miss Mabel Lesley taught nobody but was a first-class cook and housekeeper. The other teachers were brought in from outside and managed to push a little knowledge into unwilling heads. On the whole, parents were satisfied they were getting value for money, a great consideration in this part of the world where money was scarce.

'Now do remember to walk *quietly* through the town and stand aside to let people older than yourself pass you on pavements. *Never jostle.*'

A girl of twelve, her tam o'shanter slammed anyhow on the back of her dark curly head, her leather satchel bumping at her side, was running across the yard to freedom when she ran full-tilt into Miss Mabel Lesley. 'Katherine Croxley, you look a perfect disgrace to the school! Go and wash – your face is covered in ink smudges. What will people think if they see a Hill House girl in such a state walking through the town? What a dreadful advertisement for the school, Katherine!' Miss Mabel stretched her little eyes to an alarming width.

So the girl who was Katherine at school and Katya at home was at least ten minutes late when at last she was allowed to walk sedately out through the gates to her home high above the harbour.

'Gently, Katherine, gently,' Miss Mabel had urged but once out of sight of the school windows, Katya broke into a run, her long thin legs in their brown woollen stockings making short work of the ground between school and home.

It was her twelfth birthday and Mamma had promised that Annie would bake a special cake covered in marzipan and candles: eleven coloured ones round the edge and a big white one in the middle. Katya had asked eagerly if she could have a party but Mamma had been nervous as usual and had put it off. 'When your father's at home,' she had promised as she did each year. Katya had not yet had a party although she asked every year if she could invite her school friends. Even after all these years in Whitby, Mamma was still very shy and nervous with her neighbours, the child had noticed. Perhaps it was because they called her 'that Rooshan' and looked at her with open curiosity. They found her accented English as difficult to understand as she did their Yorkshire dialect. To the local people Russia was a strange heathen country where they worshipped a powerful Tsar who put thumb-screws on his enemies. One good lady was amazed to find that Mrs Croxley, born in St Petersburg, was actually a

Christian like herself; she even knew the Bible! But most people remained suspicious and gave her a wide berth, so the woman who had been Marie Nicolaievna Urosova became selfconscious and withdrawn and very, very lonely.

Katya had been born in Whitby and so was a Yorkshire girl in their eyes. But she knew about her Russian side; she felt it there under her heart, tugging mercilessly at her nerves and sinews.

'Tell me about Tante Laura and Tante Stana,' she would beg her mother sometimes, climbing on her knee to listen to tales of Tante Laura, the beautiful ballet dancer, and Tante Stana who was the prettiest of them and who lived with Katya's Russian grandfather in a huge house like a palace on the Moika Canal in St Petersburg.

Sometimes the tales brought a smile to her mother's lips, lips that had so seldom smiled since the death from diphtheria of four-year-old Matthew Croxley two years ago. It was after Matt died that her mother ceased to go out, Katya had noticed.

The girl noticed a good deal. She saw how different her mother was from the short sturdy-boned Yorkshire folk: Marie looked foreign, with eyes too dark and haunted and skin too white for her to be overlooked in the little streets of Whitby. Besides, those who came to the house saw in its dark-papered walls covered in icons, and the scents of sandalwood and camphor, a strangeness that made them uneasy. They didn't mean to be unkind but they kept their distance.

So as she ran home in the early November gloaming Katya's thoughts were all with her mother and the possibility of a birthday cake. In the centre of town near the brightly-lit shops a newsboy was carrying a poster to his news-stand at the bottom of the street. DEATH OF RUSSIAN TSAR it proclaimed.

Katya clapped her hand to her mouth: that was Mamma's Tsar! Oh, she would be sorry! Finding a half-penny she bought a newspaper and ran on, a stitch forming in her side as she climbed up to the broad terrace where her home stood. Fog was settling over the town and she could clearly hear the buoy outside the harbour sombrely ringing its bell. Just as if it knows Mamma's Tsar is dead, the little girl thought, opening the front door and crying 'Mamma! Mamma! Where are you, Mamma?'

Annie, the cook-general, looked out of the kitchen and scolded: 'Now, Miss Katya, less noise, if you please! Your ma's got one of her headaches and is lying down. I'll send your tea up in a minute but you just be a good girl and keep quiet.'

Katya's spirits sank. 'But it's my birthday! There's going to be a cake! Mamma promised me – '

'Now stop that. Think of your poor mother for a change,' scolded Annie, who was making bread and too busy to be bothered.

Katya felt tears spring to her eyes as she climbed the stairs. It was her birthday after all so why had Mamma got one of her headaches?

Marie spent most of the day in her bedroom when Harry Croxley was at sea. Not that he suspected how unhappy she was because when he came home she would be sparkling and happy, wearing her best dresses with her hair newly curled and with something delicious ordered for his dinner. She was standing now at the broad bay window. Darkness was enclosing the landscape outside but she could still discern the heaving grey sea through the salt-rimmed glass. Her huge eyes, wide and strained, stared unblinkingly at it as if too fascinated to turn away. She turned as Katya came in and embraced her tenderly. 'My darling child, I'm so worried about

55

your father.' She spoke in French in which Katya was as fluent as herself.

'Mamma, why?' Katya stood with her arms round her mother's waist feeling a great wave of tenderness sweep her. 'Papa is all right or we should have heard.'

'His ship is late – I'm sure it's late. I have today telegraphed Howarth and Hawksley and all they send me is *this*.' She held out a crumpled orange form.

Katya read it slowly, wondering how to comfort her mother's fears. The telegram was laconic like all the shipping line's telegrams in answer to Marie's frantic enquiries. There was no need for anxiety, they assured her: only twenty-four hours late. 'You see, Mamma? There's no need for anxiety. They're not worried themselves.'

'*They* are not worried – oh, no!' Marie retorted sarcastically. 'Why should they be? They can get plenty of sea captains but I have only one husband – my Harry! Without him, I would die,' she added in a low voice and turned back to stare at the sea with despairing eyes.

Katya sighed. She had inherited her father's calm commonsense and found her mother very difficult to understand. Her father used a Yorkshire expression to tease her mother sometimes: *Don't cry before you're bit*, he would say tersely. She went across and drew the heavy velvet curtains to shut out the sight of the sea, pushing her mother away from the window towards the brisk fire in the steel grate. 'Please don't fret so, Mamushka. Father would hate to see you unhappy when really there's no need. His boat has often been late. Come and sit down.'

Her mother stared at her in a puzzled way: never before had her Katya spoken so firmly, in such an adult manner. For a moment she was reminded of her sister Laura and then – like a thunderclap in her mind – she remembered it was the child's birthday: twelve years old

56

today! Crushing her daughter to her, Marie cried: 'Oh, my darling, I forgot your birthday! There's no birthday cake, I'm afraid. I've been so worried about Father that I have thought of nothing else – oh, my Katya, forgive me! Forgive me!'

Swallowing her disappointment, Katya hugged her mother back. 'It's all right, Mamma. I – I don't mind. Shall I make toast and we'll have tea here in front of the fire?'

Marie nodded, dabbing at her eyes. To her, anxiety was like an illness, bringing on palpitations and an aching head so that she had to spend most of the day lying on her bed and not eating. There was very little left of the gay and lively girl who had once lived in St Petersburg and been the apple of her father's eye. Her love for Harry Croxley had consumed her; she barely lived when he was at sea. Deprived of her own background, she was a lost unhappy woman who made no effort to make friends with anyone. Life came to her through the medium of her daughter. Katya knew everyone, even the fishermen down on the harbour, and brought home snippets of gossip for her mother's pleasure. But Marie could only be diverted for a short time. She hated the dampness and fog, the cruel look of the German Ocean outside her windows. For thirteen years she had tried to come to terms with the country in which she had chosen to spend her life; to like this ugly red-brick house that had belonged to Harry's parents, with its tiny staff of cook-general and little housemaid which was all they could afford. Here the carpets and furniture were the same as they had been for forty years because Harry said they were too good to be got rid of. So Marie had to be content with changing the wallpapers and hanging rich curtains, placing her collection of icons in corners and burning sweet-smelling incense in her bedroom. Frightened and lonely, she still

57

had the courage to conceal these feelings from her husband and he never guessed at her anguish when he went back to sea for weeks at a time and winter storms raged beyond the harbour bar. Hour after hour she sat in her room holding her gold icon and praying for Harry's safety. If anything happened to him what would become of them? They had saved nothing. And how could she go on living in this alien place among people who were strangers? She couldn't go back to St Petersburg – she wouldn't have even enough money to live in an apartment on the Islands! Papa would never help her: he had forgotten her.

The worry was telling on her health: her face was growing whiter and more pinched with the years.

If one day that cruel sea swallowed up Harry for good then she would be lost indeed. *I would kill myself*, she thought one night, and the idea brought relief as a way out of her dilemma.

However, Harry was not completely blind: he knew his Marie too well not to know that she suffered when he was at sea. His solution was always the same when he saw the familiar pinched expression clouding her face: he would take her to bed and make love to her so ardently that she would fall asleep at last convinced that she was a lucky and happy woman just because his arms were round her. Then he would go back to sea and the horror would begin all over again.

Carrying up the tea-tray herself, Katya pushed open the door and dumped it on the table. 'I've got a jar of Annie's bramble jelly – oh, Mamma!' She stopped to stare wide-eyed at her mother who was turning from the wardrobe with something in her arms: a beautiful little dress on a pink velvet hanger.

'For you, darling child. I wore it at your age.'

Katya wiped her fingers down the sides of her serge

skirt, her breath catching in her throat. Such a dress! A fairytale affair of white silk and narrow Valenciennes lace threaded with coral satin ribbon. Underneath peeped a taffeta petticoat that rustled and was edged with more lace. Katya had never seen anything like it in her life and her round eyes went to her mother's face. 'But – but where can I wear it? I don't get asked to any parties – but it is beautiful, Mamma!'

The smile on Marie's face faded. It was true; because they invited no one inside their door, they got asked nowhere themselves. So now mother and daughter looked at each other blankly.

Then Marie said gaily: 'We shall give a party! Yes, for Christmas. At home we were always very gay for Christmas and so it shall be here. You shall ask all your class – and their brothers! – and we'll hire a waiter and bake a special cake and you shall wear this dress as I did on such an occasion.'

Katya smiled and kissed her. 'It's a lovely idea, Mamma, and the dress is beautiful. After tea I'll try it on to show you.' She knew this would be the only occasion she would wear the dress: to an audience of one.

It was after they had made toast and drunk their tea that she remembered the evening paper she had brought home. Putting it in her mother's hands she pointed at the headline.

'My God, this is terrible!' Marie turned towards the lamp and tears began to pour down her cheeks. 'He was so big and strong and not at all old – ah, the poor Empress with her young family! Nicholas, the new Tsar, is just about to be married, too. Oh, my poor country!'

Katya bit her lip. Too late she realized that she should have hidden the newspaper for the news it contained had quite ruined the happy atmosphere. It would now occupy the rest of the evening for her mother. Without a word,

59

she slipped the dress back on its pink hanger and brought out her homework.

Marie went on sitting by the fire, staring into the little blue flames and thinking tearfully of her family and friends in St Petersburg. Stana had been younger than Katya when last she had seen her, she remembered wistfully. Not once had she heard from the little sister she had helped to bring up but of course she wouldn't be allowed to write. She would be twenty-three and surely married by now. And what of Laura? Past her prime as a ballerina, what course had her life taken?

Looking up from her Latin declensions, Katya saw fresh tears stealing down her mother's cheeks.

2

After Marie's elopement, Urosov had become a very strict parent. That fool Kitty, as he wrathfully described his sister, no longer had charge of his youngest child who was the prettiest of the three daughters. He dismissed Miss Hardwick and engaged a strict Scotswoman as governess. Every hour of the day had now to be accounted for to him. Anastasia was a sweet-natured not very intelligent child and she never rebelled against the life now imposed on her.

She was twenty when her father approved a very satisfactory marriage for her; satisfactory from his point of view that is. Count Sergei Barinsky was nearly twice her age and with the reputation of being a rake and a gambler. He would never have considered marrying the timber merchant's daughter (although he owned she was amazingly pretty) if he hadn't been in deep waters and unable to pay his gambling debts. He had met the girl through her sister Laura, now one of the principal dancers with the Imperial Ballet. It was the fashion for young noblemen to lay siege to the beauties of the Ballet, showering them with jewellery and flowers. Home on a long leave from the embassy in Tokyo where he was a junior secretary, Barinsky went with his elder brother to the ballet every night and was soon declaring that he was madly in love with Urosova.

His brother Sasha grinned. 'Too bad, old boy, but she's the Grand Duke Philip's property. Didn't you know?'

'How could I know, dolt? I've been confined in that fiendish Nippon empire for two years! Hell's teeth! Just my luck. Shall I try and cut him out?'

'Better not try! Philip can be an ugly customer and he's the Tsar's cousin to boot. Besides, the little dancer's in as snug a nest as she could wish for. They say her jewels are beginning to rival the Empress's – he's mad for her, you see.'

Laura had met the Grand Duke Philip through his second cousin, the Tsarevitch Nicholas. Both men had been on summer manoeuvres with the Horse Guards at Krasnoe Selo outside St Petersburg. Krasnoe Selo was another Salisbury Plain and its miles of flat fields and open plains were given over to the army for its war games every summer. The officers were housed in luxurious wooden bungalows, looked after by their servants, and so enjoyed a sense of 'roughing it' without much distress to themselves. As they were out in the saddle most of the day they were all fitter for their sojourn at Krasnoe Selo. Evenings were given up to gambling, bridge, dining in each other's bungalows and attending performances at the little theatre.

The best theatre companies were invited to perform in the wooden theatre and the Imperial Ballet was invited back time and again. It was after just such a visit that Mathilde Kschessinska became the mistress of the Tsarevitch Nicholas. Although then only seventeen, she was already a star of the ballet, dancing with brilliant naturalness; at first sight her tiny body and pretty face with its dark sparkling eyes had captivated Nicholas. Until his marriage four years later they were to be together. The little Pole hoped against hope that he would never need anyone else but her, that they could be together always. Nicholas, however, knew he must marry some day.

In the summer of 1892, when the lilac bushes at Krasnoe Selo were filling the air with their heady scent, the Imperial Ballet put on a performance of *The Sleeping Beauty* with both Kschessinska and Urosova in the cast. Dancing to Tchaikovsky's music, Kschessinska was at her brilliant best, but Urosova drew many eyes too. She was five years older than Kschessinska and her face held a quiet maturity and beauty that fascinated many of the men in her audience.

The Grand Duke Philip had had many mistresses in his thirty-four years but not until he set eyes on Urosova did he know what it was to feel like a young and ardent lover, nervously unsure of himself. The other women had been only too delighted to receive his *carte blanche* but Laura held herself aloof. She was to keep him at bay for months while his desire to possess her mounted to fever pitch and he could think of little else.

Unlike Kschessinska, Laura had not been out to Krasnoe Selo before and was charmed to find it a very civilized camp indeed with delightful little wooden bungalows where the officers entertained lavishly. Two of these bungalows were set aside, one for the male dancers and the other for the girls. They were resting and drinking tea here after their arrival when Kschessinska ran in looking radiant. 'Laura! Come and help me by taking the Grand

Duke off our hands! Nicky and I cannot be alone because this cousin of his will not leave us – oh, do come, Laura!' She took the tea glass out of Laura's hands and set it down. 'Please, Laura, fascinate him and keep him busy!'

Philip was several years older than Nicholas, taller and powerfully built with a forceful nose, splendid teeth and a small trim moustache as fair as his thick head of hair. He was immensely attractive and Laura felt herself drawn to him at once. As she was being presented to the delicate-looking Tsarevitch, Philip came forward to stare hard at her.

'Present me, Mademoiselle Kschessinska.'

'Willingly, sir,' and Kschessinska dipped in another graceful curtsey. 'Laura Nicolaievna Urosova, your highness, who will be dancing with me tonight. His highness the Grand Duke Philip Alexandrovitch.'

He and Laura measured each other with curious eyes. Then he smiled as he lifted her from her curtsey with one hand. 'Come, Laura Nicolaievna, we will take a stroll about the grounds and leave these two lovebirds to their own devices.'

There was a glamour about him as there was with all these royal princes. Their stroll ended at his bungalow. On the verandah a rattan table and chairs were set invitingly. 'Come, let me show you my temporary home,' he suggested, holding out his hands to help her up the steps.

A manservant brought out vodka and wine but Philip sent him back for champagne. Her heart gave a nervous thump as he drew his chair near and toasted her in champagne. 'To Urosova and her brilliant career! To success tonight.' He set down his glass and looked alertly at her. 'You are married?' he asked in abrupt French.

She flushed under the shade of her hat for suddenly she knew this man desired her; but first he wanted to make sure the way was clear. All she wanted was to be left alone to devote herself to her dancing. Her last love affair had ended two months ago. The man had been her partner in several ballets. He had left to go to the Moscow Ballet and she had – after a week of missing him acutely – been glad to be free once more. Now this fascinating man was making it very clear that he desired her – but she didn't want an involvement with him! Her career – oh, her career must come first from now on! There was so little time left in which to make her mark and already the talented little Kschessinska who was so much younger was making tremendous headway, as being the Tsarevitch's mistress seemed only to put a finer edge on her talent. Laura knew that becoming Philip's mistress now would blunt her own. He would want all of her and there would be nothing left over for dancing. So she flushed nervously and stammered that, no, she was not married, none of them were nor wished to be. 'The ballet is a hard taskmaster.'

For answer, he leaned over and stroked her bare forearm where the lace of her sleeve fell away. A *frisson* chilled her spine and her legs trembled. *Be strong*! she exhorted herself silently.

'You are lovely, Urosova, very lovely indeed.' He ran his fingers down to her wrist, then lifted her hand and held it against his lips longer than was usual for such a gesture. 'Already I am falling in love with you,' he said softly.

She gave him a beseeching look then rose, gently disengaging her hand. 'Sir, I must take my leave. We have a rehearsal very soon and I shall have to change.' She hesitated, lowering her eyes. 'I thank you, sir, for your kind hospitality but pray forget me. My life is ordained: I must devote myself to my dancing.'

For a moment he looked astonished: he was not used to

being rejected. Then he recovered himself. An admiring, laughing look came into his eyes. 'Beware, Urosova! You are never going to be safe from me!'

Her rejection of his *carte blanche* had only served to make him more ardent. When the company returned to St Petersburg, Philip took a permanent box at the Maryinsky Theatre. Now every night, by himself or in the company of his guests, he watched her dance. Now he began to bombard her with gifts of precious stones to be set to her instructions, strings of huge pearls, soft furs fashioned into graceful flowing garments, a pair of grey horses and a red sledge for them to pull . . .

She accepted everything, glowing with delight at the beautiful things he chose, and perfectly aware that the day was drawing near when she would yield to him. She would, she reminded herself, have to be made of stone to resist such a man – and such gifts.

She let him dangle after her for a year: everyone in Petersburg was talking about it, declaring that Urosova was frigid and Philip had better forget her, or that she was an unkind tease who enjoyed seeing the poor fellow miserable.

Laura realized that she must capitulate eventually but she was determined that it was to be on her terms, not his. He had discarded many women before her, now her aim was to see that their relationship endured. Neither of them were children, nor were they virgins. She needed a permanent home, status as the mistress of a royal duke.

Spring arrived after the usual long cold winter and as it turned into glorious summer the Guards were again on manoeuvres at Krasnoe Selo. Once again the Imperial Ballet were invited out to the barracks to perform on three nights.

On the last of these three nights there was a party in the little theatre after the last performance. The young officers were in high spirits and there was much laughter and teasing and the popping of champagne corks.

Laura was in the midst of a happy circle when Philip came forward and put a commanding hand on her arm. The other young men fell back, suddenly silent and deferential. 'Come,' he said.

She opened her mouth to refuse such a cavalier command but something hard in his eye made her change her mind. He drew her out, his manner gentle now, into the translucent night where the heavy smell of lilac seemed to envelop them and the white sky (which was what passed for night so far north in June) hung over them like a canopy. He steered her in the direction of his own bungalow: here on the verandah a table set with silver and crystal with lighted candles flickering awaited them. His manservant silently poured cooled champagne into tall wine glasses and handed round delicious *zakouski* to tempt their appetites.

In the dusk, a woman's light laughter rang out; there was the tinkle of glass and silver as midnight picnics took place under the sheltering lilac trees.

As they ate and drank almost in silence Laura knew that tonight she must surrender to her Grand Duke or get out of his life. He knew it too as he calmly refilled her glass; he could see the white oval of her face floating outside the circle of candlelight and an urgent desire to seize her there and then and carry her indoors was sternly repressed. Not yet. Not yet. 'To us,' he murmured, smiling. 'To the realization of a hope. Laura . . .' He took her long white hand and pressed it. 'I love you and want you. You have my word that I'll be good to you.'

'Yes,' she said with difficulty, the pounding of her feverish heart almost suffocating her.

'I'm seriously in love with you,' he persisted. 'I'm on

66

fire for you,' he suddenly added, slipping on to his knees and grasping her in his arms.

She caught her breath, desire shooting like a bolt of lightning through her responsive body: his nearness, the lilac's scent, the warm night all pleaded his cause for him and she felt every resolution she had held slipping away from her. 'Philip – ' She choked over his name and he laughed joyously, knowing that he was winning.

Burying his face in her neck, he whispered: 'I need you. You are the light of my life. Laura, sweet darling, *please* . . .'

She was a passionate woman and had missed her dancer-lover in the long spring nights although she knew it was not he she really missed but the closeness of a relationship.

Suddenly he scooped her up in his arms; and her champagne glass fell to the ground and was crushed beneath his feet. 'Laura?'

'Yes – yes!' Her breath was against his mouth.

With a whoop of triumph, a hunting cry, he bore her indoors and closed the door with his heel.

There were two lamps burning in the bedroom but turned low and the mosquito netting round the narrow bed had been looped back. Silk sheets and soft pillows awaited them, together with another bottle of champagne in an ice bucket.

Throwing her on the bed, he roughly began to tear off her clothes.

Laura was outraged: there was no need for this! She had intended giving herself willingly but he was bent on raping her! She uttered a stifled scream of fury as a rending sound gave evidence of the demise of her beautiful chiffon dress with its appliqué satin leaves strewn across the bodice and the wide skirt. 'Stop it! Stop it at once! This is uncivilized,' she protested, all desire for him now gone. How dare he use her like a common trollop? She was Urosova, a shining star of the Imperial Ballet, whose favours were sought by many but given to few. 'Oh!' He had hit her across the face because she struggled. She could feel his beautifully manicured nails tearing the skin on her breast and she shrieked with pain and rage. 'Beast! Brute! Let me go – let me go, I say!' Tomorrow she would be black and blue from this assault and no amount of greasepaint would conceal it from her audience. She would be humiliated! Anger giving her strength, she bit his hands; first one, then the other as, blind and deaf to her pleas, he struggled to tear her clothes off and force open her thighs. Again and again she bit him, tearing at his reddened face and the sandy hair that now fell over it. Strong from hours of practice at the barre she suddenly proved too much for him. He rolled off her.

'Why, you viper! You've drawn blood!'

'How dare you?' she hissed. 'How dare you lay your hands on me without permission? You've ruined my dress, you brute, and bruised my body for all the world to see. I hate you!' She fled to the door and fumbled for the handle, tears pouring down her face, great gulps heaving her body.

The blood had drained from his face. 'But what can you mean? That is how women like it, isn't it? The assault, the quick thrust and – *la voilà*!'

She panted, trying to draw fresh breaths. 'I don't know what women you've been consorting with but that certainly doesn't apply to me!' she gasped, the French guttural and deep in her throat.

He threw himself at her feet, gathering her firm and pliant body tightly in his arms. 'Forgive me – forgive me! Please forgive me, darling. I have never known anyone like you before. You see, the others liked to be tamed. They expected it. Oh, Laura, I need you! This is different.

68

I didn't understand.' The face he lifted to her was quite despairing. 'Show me,' he begged humbly. 'Show me how you would like to be loved.'

She stared at him, knowing that this was a Philip no one had ever seen before: a man deeply in love and unsure of himself, fearful that he had lost her. A little uncivilized still, like all the young royal princes who had always had everything they wanted in life granted at once. 'Get up,' she said in a gentle voice and in Russian now. 'Don't you see? Love doesn't mean the humiliation of one person by another. My feelings are as strong as yours and I love you, too, but I'll not be used by any man as his plaything, to be bruised and battered like – like a dog with a bone!'

For answer, he picked her up and carried her back to the bed. Throwing off his own clothes he lay down beside her. 'Show me,' he said in her ear. 'Show me how we can enjoy each other. There will never be any other woman in my life except you. This will last for ever.'

3

It was a good relationship. In those first months they were hungry and thirsty for one another every moment they were apart. Unlike the passion they had felt for others, this passion didn't burn itself up and become indifference. They knew that they could never marry: no member of the Imperial Family could marry a commoner. They would be banished from Russia if they did.

Kschessinska, who felt as passionately about the Tsarevitch as Laura did about Philip, refused to listen to her friends' repeated warnings that he would have to marry a suitable princess before long and produce an heir. Deeply in love, the Polish girl danced during those days as she had never danced before: she was like an incandescent moth fluttering round a dangerous flame. A month later, Nicholas went to England for the marriage of his cousin, the Duke of York, to Princess Mary of Teck.

'He wishes me to accompany him,' Philip revealed one night as he and Laura lay in bed. 'I'm afraid we shall be away about six weeks.'

It would be their first parting since they became lovers. Lying in his arms, she was sick with fear and jealousy. In London she knew there would be beautiful women only too ready to divert him and make him forget her. There might be many of royal blood who would make him a highly suitable wife – but she would never share him – never! Sitting up in bed she stared bleakly into his face on the pillow. 'Promise me if you fell in love with someone over there that you'd tell me at once? Promise me?' She slid down and pressed her warm, pliant body close to his. They spoke softly in Russian; to them both it was far more the language of love than French.

'Why disturb yourself about something that will not happen?' His lips were warm on her breasts. 'Ah, Laura, there never will be anyone else – never! If only we could marry . . . it would mean exile, of course. Could you bear to leave Russia and the Imperial Ballet and come with me to the South of France? It would be a pleasant life there.'

She drew in her breath: what a terrible choice! She who had never been out of Russia to leave it for good? Never to return? Russia was her bones, her flesh, her mind and heart. To leave it for some alien lotus land where their love would dwindle and die like a plant put into the wrong sort of soil – no, no! It was unthinkable! And yet her sister Marie had gone to her lover without a backward glance . . .

70

'You're shivering, my love.'

'I couldn't leave,' she whispered. 'Nor could you, Philip. Russia means too much to us both.'

They were silent, pressed close together in what had been the drowsy aftermath of lovemaking. He wished now he hadn't brought up the subject because she was shuddering inside; he could feel her. Tightening his arms about her he sought to reassure her by revealing that he was going to put her in a delightful villa at Tsarskoe Selo, the Tsar's village. 'It's not far from the palace gates. We shall be very comfortable there. It will be particularly useful when I'm on duty there. And there are trains to run you into Petersburg at any hour you wish.'

She was delighted. 'Oh, Philip, how good you are to me,' she murmured before they fell asleep.

Two months later, when the Tsarevitch Nicholas and his cousins and the rest of the wedding party returned from England, he wasted no time in telling Mathilde Kschessinska that their affair was over and that he intended marrying Princess Alix of Hesse. But the Grand Duke Philip had met no one who would replace his dancer who was waiting for him in their home at Tsarskoe Selo and their reunion was as passionate as ever.

4

Contentedly established in her villa, Laura now turned her attention to her beautiful young sister who was being guarded as strictly as a young nun in her father's house on the Moika Canal. With her connection with those at court and friendly with Philip's brother officers, Laura was in a splendid position to further her sister's interests.

Her father was now almost a recluse, going out only to

inspect his businesses but no longer mixing socially. He knew nothing of his second daughter's liaison with one of the Imperial Family and perhaps would have cared little if he had known. His only concern was to guard his youngest girl so that she couldn't run off behind his back as her eldest sister had done. He needed to know where she was every minute of every day; it was only because she was naïve and sweet-tempered that Anastasia didn't rebel.

Laura, on one of her rare visits home, summed up the situation at a glance. She determined to take Anastasia back to Tsarskoe Selo on a visit and had little difficulty in persuading her father to let the girl come.

'My dear Father, you can surely not have the slightest objection?' Peeling a grape, Laura quizzed him with her large green eyes. 'I live in the Emperor's own village; he and Marie Fedorovna are but a stone's throw away. I assure you I am very privileged to live there.'

'I suppose it is a reward for long service with the Imperial Ballet,' Urosov grunted. He took up the silver scissors and snipped another small bunch for her.

She did not correct him. 'I have a perfect dragon of a housekeeper who will take care of Stana when I'm not there. Let her come to me and I'll guarantee I'll find her a good husband in no time at all. The child is good and beautiful and no doubt has a large dowry? Then what are we waiting for?' Laura cried gaily. 'I shall take her back with me tomorrow. You would like her to marry into the nobility, wouldn't you, Papa?'

Urosov shrugged. 'I just don't want trouble of any kind. If she disgraces herself then I wash my hands of her, too.'

Laura looked at him with the first real pity she had ever felt for him. He looked ill and old with lacklustre eyes and deep lines carved into his face. 'Ah, Papa, if

72

you could but forgive Marie!' she said impulsively. 'Wouldn't you like her to come on a visit? She has a little girl called Katya now. You would like to see this grandchild surely? Let me write to Marie on your behalf and ask her to come home.'

'Never!' The word was snapped out. 'Never use your sister's name to me again, Laura Nicolaievna. *She is dead.*'

Laura sighed, throwing down her damask napkin. What obstinacy! He would die without seeing again the only one of them he had really loved. Pride was forcing him to close his heart to Marie and her little girl.

When Laura set her heart on something, she pursued the objective mercilessly. Anastasia and her trunks (but without Aunt Kitty or her governess) accompanied her worldly sister back to Tsarskoe Selo the very next day. That Urosov and his sister Kitty had no idea of the sort of household she was going to went without saying. How nice, they told each other, that Laura was taking an interest in her little sister at last!

Anastasia was so excited at escaping from the home that had become her prison and coming to live in Laura's delightful house opposite the palace gates, that at first it didn't register that the Grand Duke Philip was much in the house. It was only when she saw him one night closing the door of her sister's bedroom (with himself on the other side) that she understood. She was a well brought up girl from a sheltered environment and she was horrified. The Grand Duke wasn't just a friend – he was *more*! He was – he was Laura's lover!

She went back into her own room, closed the door and burst into tears. Papa would be so angry! Of course she would have to go home now; that went without saying – and oh! she had been enjoying herself so much, so much! Walking up and down her bedroom, twisting her small lawn handkerchief into knots, Anastasia fought with her conscience: fought and won. She decided not to say a word. Indeed, she would go on pretending she was just a naïve child. It was, she told herself as she blew her nose on her ruined handkerchief, much the best solution.

Whether Count Sergei Barinsky could be classed 'a good husband' was open to question. He had looks but no money, a job as Third Secretary at the Tokyo embassy but few prospects. Worse, he had a terrible reputation and a whiff of wickedness about him that made him irresistible to girls like Anastasia. He was twenty years her senior and knew that he must marry a rich wife soon or be disgraced. Debts of every kind had mounted astonishingly and it was only a question of time before he went under.

Laura met him through the Grand Duke who had played cards with him. Inviting him to dinner she inspected him coolly and calculatingly and came to the conclusion that dear little Anastasia could not hope to do better; not in a legal marriage that is. He was only a count but it was a title that the dear child would enhance. No doubt he'd finish sowing his wild oats and she would give him splendid children – yes, she couldn't expect better than that.

Anastasia fell in love on their first meeting. His olive skin and black hair and moustache took her youthful fancy at once. There was a piratical quality about his good looks that thrilled her even as it frightened her.

It took Barinsky longer to make up his mind. He was proud of his lineage and he would be marrying beneath him. All the Barinskys were proud, unpleasant people, his sister Nada especially so. She had herself married into one of the two hundred princely families of Russia: a rich, powerful, land-owning family. No one knew how

74

she had managed it for she was a plain girl and there was no money but Prince Guriev was rumoured to have had a debauched career and needed to marry quickly and produce an heir or be cut off with a kopeck by his incensed father.

For once Barinsky refused to listen to his sister. 'Yes, yes, I know she's from the people,' he said impatiently, 'but I can't allow that to be a consideration. I must have money and old Urosov has a great deal. Laura Nicolaievna tells me he's prepared to give her a great dowry. Besides . . .' a slow smile spread over his face, 'she is beautiful. Admit, dear sister, that my Anastasia is beautiful?'

'I admit only that you're a fool!' Nada Gurievna snarled.

Sergei lit one of his tiny yellow cigarettes, still smiling his cat-like secret smile. 'Well, of course, how can you understand? You're not a man. Besides if I don't return with a bride when my leave ends next month I shall be up to my neck in hot water. I'm getting too old for duels – one needs young hot blood for that – yet that hothead Skernevitsky will insist on it – '

'You've been having an *affaire* with Xenia Skernevitska?' Nada sat bolt upright, her eyes bulging with horror.

He laughed aloud at the sight of her face. 'My dear Nada, stop behaving like a provincial! Doesn't everyone have an *affaire* with Xenia at one time or another? She's a great overblown flower whom we men cannot resist. Little Skernevitsky nearly has a seizure every time he finds her in bed with someone other than himself – depend upon it, it will kill him off and then, alas, half the fun of pursuing her will be finished. And now unfortunately she has got over-serious about me and is demanding a divorce, believe it or not! I'm supposed to adore the prospect of going into exile with her: she's forty-five and is getting fat, poor dear. So I've got to find a bride quickly and take her back with me to Tokyo next month. Anastasia Nicolaievna Urosova fits the bill quite admirably and one would never guess she wasn't from a noble house. And old Urosov has agreed to pay all my debts, too. What do you think of that?'

5

Behind the quiet façade of the house on the Moika Canal, Anastasia was preparing her trousseau. Laura and she spent part of every day now at fittings and a spare room had been given over to receiving the new garments, including a fairytale wedding dress. She was young enough to be thrilled with having so many new clothes made by Madame Brissac, the most expensive dressmaker in St Petersburg who made the clothes of the Empress Marie.

The idea of taking the Trans-Siberian Express half across the world to unknown Japan was another thrill for the girl. Only one thing troubled her: she didn't know what to expect on her wedding night. She timidly approached Aunt Kitty who, to hide her own ignorance, threw up her hands in horror: 'What a question to ask, you naughty girl! Just do what your husband requires of you, that's all I can say.' Seeing the girl's troubled face, she relented. 'You'd better ask your sister. She's experienced enough, heaven knows,' and she hurried away to pray before her icon.

So Anastasia asked her sister and Laura in plain blunt language told her. Seeing the shock in Anastasia's big blue eyes she added quickly: 'Don't look so, Stana! You won't believe me now but in time you'll come to enjoy it.

Most people do. But if he asks you to tie him up and flog him with a whip, *don't do it*. You are entitled to refuse and if that's what he needs he can go elsewhere for it. Understand?'

Her head reeling from so much extraordinary information Anastasia nodded. She felt suddenly sick and panic-stricken at the thought that from tomorrow her body would never be her own again. She shed tears on this last night of her girlhood and slept little. In consequence it was a very pale bride in heavy satin and lace who stood beside her bridegroom while the crowns were held over their heads. Behind her she could feel the many hundreds of people who filled the Cathedral of Our Lady of Kazan; she was encircled by both families; she was trapped . . . Feeling faint, she closed her eyes and swayed. Then she felt Barinsky's hand on her wrist: he meant to give her support but to Anastasia his fingers closed round her like steel handcuffs. Two tears welled in her eyes and spilled over. Those who saw this emotion were touched but none guessed the terror in her heart.

After a reception in the Urosov home (a reception even Princess Nada Gurievna couldn't find fault with because Laura had seen to everything herself), the bridal couple left for the railway station under a shower of fresh rose leaves. In her turquoise velvet outfit with its short train and matching toque of velvet leaves, the new Countess Sergei Barinskaya looked carefree and happy and flushed with the several glasses of champagne she had consumed. A small party of Sergei's intimates escorted them to the station where the huge express was waiting to carry them across Russia to Vladivostok five days hence.

'Goodbye! Goodbye!' Laughing faces bobbed far down below them as the train began to move; hands waved and someone threw a handful of rose leaves. There was a last glimpse of these friendly faces then the steam came between them like a grey curtain and they were gone. Anastasia turned from the window and towards her new husband. He bent and kissed her gloved hand. 'All mine!' he whispered and a frightened shudder went down her spine.

They had been given the most luxurious suite on board (paid for with Urosov money) and his valet and her maid were in small cabins on either side.

Her head aching with nervous tension, Anastasia ate very little dinner. Night, the speedy all-enveloping night that fell without the overture of dusk in Russia, descended and the heavy velvet curtains were drawn across the windows. The rhythmic hum of the train's wheels and an occasional shriek of its whistle were the only sounds to be heard and she had to force herself to listen to her husband's conversation across the table.

Sergei talked easily of the life they were going to in Japan and pretended not to notice how her fork chased food round and round her plate without once conveying it to her mouth.

'I – I think I'd like to go to bed. I'm very tired,' she said as he attempted to refill her glass. 'No, thank you, I don't think it suits me. I've drunk enough already today.' Her eyes looked pleadingly at him. He bent his sleek head and kissed the tips of her fingers.

'Very well, my dear. I'll probably walk along the train to the bar. I need the exercise after that splendid meal.'

With the help of her maid, Zeneide, she undressed in the confined space of their sleeping quarters and then directed the woman to turn out all the lights. If Sergei found her asleep he would perhaps leave her alone this first night of their marriage. She was tired and over-excited and presently fell into an exhausted sleep shot through with queer images that made her twtich and turn

78

restlessly. She dreamed she was a child again and darling Masha, her eldest sister, was there. She hadn't run away to England, hadn't left her Stana alone in that great house with Papasha and Old Nurse and Aunt Kitty. She cried out 'Oh, Masha!' and woke with a start: it was still dark in the cabin but she knew he was there.

A light clicked on and she saw he was standing by the door wearing a Japanese short gown. Seeing her eyes were open and staring at him, he suddenly stripped the gown off and stood there naked, letting her startled eyes study him, smiling his secret smile.

She had never seen a naked man in her life and had only guessed what he would look like. Secretly she was horrified, thinking his body covered in black hair was like an ape's.

He had picked something up from the top bunk and now held it out to her: a pair of handcuffs such as a common thief would have to wear. 'Put these on me,' he directed, a dark flush beginning to change his pale face. 'Here's the key. Now take off your nightdress and beat me hard with this riding crop – as hard as you like! Make me cry out – Anastasia!'

For she had slipped down in her bed again and had pulled the sheet up to her chin. 'Go away!' she ordered, her voice shaking.

He grasped the sheet and wrenched it off her. 'You're my wife and you'll do as I say!'

She sat bolt upright suddenly. 'I don't have to do that! Laura told me. If that's what you need you can go elsewhere for it. Laura says that now I'm a titled lady I can even appeal to the Tsar himself – so there!'

He was staring at her in complete amazement. Then a curse was wrenched from him. 'Damn and blast your sister Laura!' He was furiously angry; he felt he had been cheated. He had thought he had married a complete innocent, a girl who would obey him blindly because she knew nothing. Instead the new Countess Anastasia Barinskaya, married to him for only a few hours, was sitting up in her bed spitting defiance at him. It was a sign of the age, he told himself sorrowfully: girls nowadays knew too much.

He was forced to put away the handcuffs and whip and seek his bunk in sulky silence, aware that her eyes watched his every movement as he pulled on his nightshirt and brushed his hair. He lay awake a long time and presently heard her gently breathing in sleep. He'd have to make it up with her tomorrow, of course; pretend he had been drunk. But it was damnable he should be flouted in this way and all Laura Nicolaievna's fault. Fortunately there was a little Japanese girl in Tokyo who would be happy to accommodate him. He would use Anastasia just to breed from; hopefully she would have several sons and grow fat and ugly. It would serve her right.

4

The Howarth and Hawksley Heir

1

The offices of Howarth and Hawksley, the German Ocean shipping line and timber importers, occupied a depressed-looking six-storey building near Hull's main harbour. From this area drifted the rich smells of fish, tar and tanning which mingled to permeate the offices of Howarth and Hawksley. How these smells managed to squeeze inside the building remained a mystery for the windows were always kept firmly closed in all weathers; some were even nailed up. Perhaps clients and visitors brought in the smells on their clothes, and left them to drift like ghosts when they departed. Whatever it was, the building reeked of the harbour and a stale smell of gas. Outside, the sun might shine and playful little sea breezes might whisk through the company flag fluttering from the roof; it might even be spring and the flower woman at the end of the road might be selling violets. No matter. Inside it was always bleak mid-winter.

Young Mr Robert Howarth, who had left school for good only two months ago, stood on the opposite pavement with his hands in his pockets and looked with some dismay at his inheritance. Golly! What a terrible tomb of a place! Just because *his* father had set up business in this very building sixty years ago the pater went on using it. The place was a slum, Robert decided airily. Should be pulled down.

He was a pleasant-looking youth with an open face and crisp hair threatening to curl. He wore a well-cut tweed coat and trousers with a gold watch-chain across the waistcoat, a brown corduroy cap and very well polished hand-made boots. He looked the prosperous son of a prosperous father and certainly not a junior clerk beginning his first day with the shippers and importers. He was Abel Howarth's only child and (secretly) the apple of his eye.

Hearing a clock strike nine, young Robert sighed. How sickening that he had to go to work for the first time on such a perfect September morning! The rugby club would be having its first practice of the season this afternoon and he wouldn't be there. He had forgotten how truly awful the family business house looked: peeling, its windows smeared with sea mist, seagull droppings all over the roof. It was no better than one of the run-down warehouses on the dockside. His father ought to gut the place, rebuild – yes, that was the answer! Sweep away this rotting edifice and let a beautiful neo-Gothic building rise in its place. After all, the pater could afford it. Business had never been so good and they seemed to be getting richer every year. Newly honoured by the Queen for his gifts to charity, his father ought to be thinking of expanding the business premises now. Robert narrowed his eyes and conjured up a magnificent turreted building in red brick and white stucco with a roof of blue Westmorland slate unsullied by seagulls and – by jove, yes! – a new house flag! The one flying from the roof was positively dingy.

Someone cleared their throat. Opening his eyes with some annoyance, Robert saw Amos Stuttle, his father's chief clerk and a pillar of the firm for more than thirty years, standing in the doorway across the street staring anxiously at him. He wore black sateen sleeve protectors and held a pen in one hand; the other tugged at his grey beard.

'All reet, lad?' he called.

'Yes, of course, Mr Stuttle.' Flushing with annoyance at being caught day-dreaming, Robert sauntered across the road. 'Good morning,' he added, raising his cap. 'What a lovely morning.'

Fancy manners, Stuttle told himself pityingly. That's what came of sending t'lad to private education down south. 'Morning,' he growled and led the way indoors. 'By thy manner of shutting th'eyes I thought thee were taken bad or summat. Here, where you going?' he added sharply.

Robert, one foot on the bare wooden stairs, paused and raised his eyebrows. 'Why, up to my father's office, of course. Isn't that where I'm to work?'

'It is not,' retorted Amos Stuttle with emphasis. 'Start t'lad at bottom were Sir Abel's instrooctions and bottom's reet here, lad.' He pointed a stubby thumb over his shoulder. 'This here's t'shipping office where we whip you into shape.'

'Lad looked fit to bust,' he told Mrs Stuttle with relish that evening. 'But I'll say this: he said nowt. He took off his fancy jacket and got reet down to it.' Spearing a hot potato he put it into his mouth and said indistinctly: 'He'll be *all reet*.' And by this Mr Stuttle meant that Robert would turn out a true son of his father's after a spell; that is after he, Amos, had had a hand in the lad's education he would become *upright, hardworking and thrifty*.

Those three words summed up Sir Abel's recipe for a successful life. His son thought he harped on them a little too often. He had begun to hate the words by the time he was twenty – especially *thrifty*. Starting at the bottom on

83

a guinea a week he asked for a rise at the end of the year.

His father's pained face and voice were used to hammer home a lesson. 'That guinea a week is more than most working men get to keep a family on, Robert. Do you really think it would be justified?'

'I should jolly well think so, Pater,' Robert retorted indignantly. 'I simply *slave* for that guinea and it goes simply nowhere, you know.'

'You're living free, my lad, while you're at home.' Sir Abel hooked his thumbs into his waistcoat and prepared to preach a little. 'Many a man has had to bring up his family on less. When my old father set out in life – '

Robert groaned.

'What's that supposed to mean?' his father demanded sharply.

'Nothing,' Robert said quickly with one of his disarming smiles, 'only how could I possibly keep a family on a guinea a week?'

Sir Abel immediately looked alert. 'Keep a family?' he repeated. 'What's this? Why haven't I been told? Does your mother know? Who is she? You're far too young. It's absurd.'

'For heaven's sake, Pater!' Robert began to shake with laughter. 'I'm not thinking of marriage – what? on a guinea a week? I think it's a disgraceful wage for a man with a family. They must be going hungry.'

'You're talking rubbish,' Sir Abel retorted in much the same spirit. 'This country has the cheapest food in the world and they're eating meat every day. You're spoilt, m'lad,' he added, shaking his head anxiously. It had been his dread from the beginning that he and Alice would spoil the boy with all that education and nice clothes and anything he wanted. A heavy sigh shook him as the mental picture of Robert rose before him, drunken and dirty, found lying in the gutter and being rescued by the Salvation Army having spent all the Howarth and Hawksley money by the time he was thirty . . .

Neither knew it about the other but both father and son possessed vivid imaginations.

'No, I'm not talking rubbish,' Robert argued stubbornly. 'It's time the firm branched out and started spending some money – '

Sir Abel recoiled. '*Spending money?*'

'Yes; a lot of money. Some thousands. Just look at these offices – '

'Nay, we're not starting up that old hare again surely?' Sir Abel leaned back in his chair and a terrible creak echoed through the room.

'You see? Even the chairs have got woodworm,' Robert was quick to point out. 'These offices are awful. They must frighten off potential customers. We could do double the business if we had a better building – I know what we should have!' He leaned forward. 'An office, a bright clean new office in the town centre. What d'you think of that idea, Pater?'

'What for?' Sir Abel asked. 'Have you any idea what it would cost? A pretty penny I can tell you – '

'Oh, I don't mean we should move these offices. I mean a place where people can go and buy their tickets and book a berth.' He saw that his father's attention had been caught.

'An office in the town, eh?' Sir Abel mused, rubbing his chin.

Three days later Robert saw the senior partner in a firm of local architects emerging from his father's room and he grinned to himself. In his own good time the pater would tell him about the new office; of course he would pretend it was his own idea, but no matter. It meant progress.

2

Lady Howarth gave a party that winter, a full-blown affair with hired waiters and wine cup to drink.

Dressing for it, Robert knew that it was for his sake his parents had shaken themselves out of their usual social stupor and were throwing open their doors to their neighbours. Tying his white tie, Robert groaned gently to himself. He would be expected to dance attendance on the local maidens, none of whom had ever attracted him. At the moment he was in love with one of the little waitresses at the chop house near the harbour where he went daily. She was half-Chinese and the most delicious morsel he had ever beheld. They were at the stage of smiles and timid snatches of conversation under the disapproving basilisk stare of the girl's father, but Robert's dreams always included her. The rest of the time he was too busy working or playing rugger in winter and tennis in the summer, to remember her much.

He inspected himself in the cheval-glass, tucked a snow-white handkerchief in his pocket and squaring his shoulders went down to do social battle.

Miss Trotter, the neighbourhood spinster who went to every party, was already at the piano, a smile fixed to her long face while Mr Huxley, the bank manager, turned over for her. Dotted stiffly about the over-furnished rooms were the local families: only those with daughters of marriageable age had been invited, Robert noticed with amusement. His feelings for his parents consisted of this amusement mixed with a deep and tolerant affection: poor dears, they were so innocent, he thought as he hurried to join his mother who was receiving in a very stately fashion.

'You're late, Robbie,' she chided him under her breath but her eyes beamed proudly on this only child: there wasn't one in the room to touch him, she told herself tremulously. The girl who got her Robbie would be a lucky lass, that went without saying.

And several tried that night, pushed on by their mothers who had spent the night before calculating the wealth of the Howarths. There was Miss Freda Jackson, the architect's daughter, whose girth could not be contained by the pink slipper satin dress she wore and who panted as she danced. There was tiny Miss Umpleby and tall Miss Metcalfe whose long neck reminded him of a poppy stalk. There was a girl who giggled self-consciously and a Miss Rawnsley whose front teeth fascinated him: they reminded him of a horse laughing. He went to bed with relief at one o'clock.

In their big double bed his parents went on talking: Sir Abel had indigestion from eating too much lobster and Lady Howarth had drunk too much coffee and was lively and unable to sleep.

'I thought he quite took to Hilda Rawnsley,' Lady Howarth said.

Sir Abel pummelled one of his pillows and turned restlessly. 'I hope not. She's got buck teeth.'

'Abel! She's a *nice* girl: sensible and steady. Her mother told me.'

Abel Howarth grunted disbelievingly. What fools women were about other women, he ruminated. There wasn't a cat's chance in hell that young Robert would look at the rum lot assembled downstairs this evening. Why, he himself was over fifty and he wouldn't have looked at that job lot. No man in his senses wanted a sensible and steady girl – not unless there was summat wrong wi' his works, Sir Abel told himself crudely. No; they'd have to look elsewhere for a bride for their son. Sir Abel smiled to himself: he was not without an idea or two that would surprise Alice when she found out – but not yet, not yet.

'Are we to get some sleep tonight or not?' he demanded. 'Put that lamp out, Alice, and cease your chattering. I've an office to go to tomorrow if this damn lobster will let me get some rest.'

'I told you not to eat it,' his wife reminded him tactlessly.

3

That January Alex Rakov began his compulsory military service and was therefore in time to join the manoeuvres in June at Krasnoe Selo. He was enjoying himself. The life suited him with its early bugle calls, hours spent on the back of Ajax, his wonderful horse, who had been brought up from Tatarskino, and then in the evenings going to see one of the theatre companies or the Imperial Ballet performing at the little wooden theatre.

He was young and strong, slept like a young animal and was up at dawn with a raging appetite for breakfast. He began to broaden out, to thicken and to look more like his mother's Swedish ancestors as his fair hair became lint-like and the light in his blue eyes became more intense. But much as he loved army life he knew it was not for him. This was just a lighthearted interval; he intended to enrol in law school at St Petersburg university when his two years were up. It was not so much that he was interested in law but in law school politics were the main interest and he was interested in politics. He had read a great deal and kept his eyes open and he was beginning to see, as many of the young did, that change must come in Russia or there would be a disaster. The rich got richer every year, the bourgeoisie who were the bureaucrats did very well and kept much power in their hands, but the poor were getting poorer and dying from hunger and disease in their thousands. On the head of the Tsar, because he was the Autocrat, would fall the savage wrath of these people one day. Alex intended to join a liberal party that might one day be in a position to prevent this; that might be able to persuade Nicholas II that a Duma must be inaugurated where decisions could be taken collectively and not solely by the Emperor. But as a soldier in the Tsar's army he was not supposed to take an interest in politics.

But there were already rumours flying round the dinner tables that the young Empress was influencing her husband against democratic government, was indeed insisting that he remain the only powerful voice in the land.

Alex didn't altogether believe these stories but he knew that although the Empress was a shy and retiring young woman, she was supposed to hold very strong views on certain matters. His mother, Princess Rakova, was now attached to the young Empress's household and sometimes brought back stories about the young couple who were still living in a suite at the Anitchkov Palace with the Dowager Empress Marie. Not a good thing because there was already disagreement between the two women over the young Tsar whom they shared so jealously: Alexandra believed he spent too many evenings with his mother when he should have been with her, while Marie, in her turn, was exasperated by the cold formality of her daughter-in-law.

He was thinking of this now as he showered and changed with the help of his servant into the blue and white mess dress. The Imperial Ballet had arrived to perform this evening and he was hoping to persuade one of the *corps de ballet* to honour him by accepting an invitation to dine. He had had his eye on this girl for some time and she hadn't seemed averse to his presents of flowers: tonight he would put it to the test and ask her to dine. He shared his bungalow with another officer but it would be a simple matter to persuade Bulganin to join another party. So Alex whistled under his breath as he pummelled his thick bright hair with a pair of gold-backed brushes and dismissed all thoughts of the Empress and politics from his mind as he practised what he would say to his little ballet dancer.

'His excellency the Grand Duke Philip,' suddenly announced his servant in a scared voice, and was swept aside by Philip's powerful body.

'Look here, Rakov, will you do me a favour? Laura Nicolaievna's sister has suddenly turned up without her husband and we need someone to partner her at dinner. Nine o'clock sharp. Oh, by the way, I think she's in some marital trouble so try and cheer the poor little thing, will you?' He had gone before Alex could protest that he was planning a dinner *à deux* himself tonight. He put his brushes down and went to cancel the meal: to be summoned by a grand duke was in the nature of a royal command and one couldn't refuse. But what a bore!

4

In the event, it wasn't a boring occasion at all. Urosova's sister, Countess Barinskaya, was a pretty, gentle creature. Her huge blue eyes dimmed often with tears as she spoke of her baby daughter left behind in Paris with her nurse.

'My husband is in the diplomatic service, you know, and we have moved about a great deal since we were married.' There was a plaintive edge to her voice as she told him this.

'And you don't like a nomad's life? I would ask nothing better myself than to see the world. Surely, Countess, you are very lucky!' and his eyes twinkled at her.

Her nose wrinkled with distaste. 'But Japan was horrid!'

'But not Paris, surely?'

'N-no. But I'm often lonely there.' Then, afraid of having given herself away, she added quickly: 'Perhaps lonely is the wrong word. I mean I feel homesick for Russia sometimes. Do you ever come to Paris, Prince Alex?'

'Occasionally. My parents have an apartment there and my mother likes to go in the autumn to order clothes.' But they were seldom there together and he looked with ill-concealed pity at this young Countess Barinskaya who was probably just finding out that her marriage was a failure and that she would have to spend the next forty years living out a lie. 'May I call on you next time I'm in Paris?' he asked impulsively.

Her face lit up like a child's. 'Oh, please do! To have a Russian friend call is such a very great treat.'

'I shall show you the Paris I love,' he told her masterfully. All thought of the girl in the *corps de ballet* had vanished: Anastasia Nicolaievna Barinskaya was an exceedingly pretty woman and just that much older than him to be interesting, he told himself.

'Oh, that would be delightful! And in return I'll show you my charming little girl; she's so pretty and bright and I miss her so much.' Suddenly, her lips trembled. 'I'm so homesick for her. I shall have to go back soon.'

He pressed her hand: no doubt she had run home to

91

her sister from that brute Barinsky whose reputation in St Petersburg was of the lowest. Why on earth had lovely Anastasia married him? 'I shall look forward to my next visit to Paris, Countess,' he assured her.

5

The coronation of the new Emperor and Empress of All the Russias took place in 1896 eighteen months after the death of the Tsar Alexander III. The young couple, deeply in love and with a six-months-old baby girl Olga, still lived in the Anitchkov Palace with the Dowager Empress Marie Fedorovna. They lived very simply like a middle-class couple despite being surrounded by a large staff and the rich trappings of their position. Their happiest times were when they had shut the world away and were alone behind firmly closed doors in the rooms Alix had furnished to be cosily Victorian and ordinary. This was the background she liked best, felt safest in. Their greatest joy was the hour reserved each evening for bathing their baby. They were twenty-three and twenty-seven, a good-looking young couple who seemed to have everything they could wish for in the world. Yet already there were shadows at their feet.

They played with their child every evening, Alix wearing a white flannel apron and Nicky leaning against a wall chain-smoking as usual. Alix scolded him for his nicotined fingers but he never made an effort to cut out the habit. Before an open fire with a guard, Alix bathed her baby in the special rubber bath on a stand they had had sent from England. For an hour or so they could be Mr and Mrs Romanov, cut off completely from the uneasy world of government officials waiting for interviews with their

Tsar. 'Let them wait,' Nicky would say with a shrug as his wife nodded vigorous agreement.

The nurses, who in the beginning had hovered to see that all was well, were always dismissed now for Alix had become very proficient at handling the vigorous slippery baby.

'Nicky, I don't think you should smoke in here. Just look how it's getting in her darling little eyes!'

'Very well,' Nicky said equably and threw his cigarette in the fire. They always spoke in English in private. Alix's Russian was coming on well but her French was halting: she had been brought up at Hesse with English, the language of her mother, as her second language. The Tsar leaned against a wall enjoying the pretty picture before the fire: his wife, her girlish face serious and flushed, her red-gold hair falling in tendrils round it, and his daughter so pink and strong, kicking and crowing in the bath. He sighed. How perfect it would be if he had no heavy responsibilities awaiting him outside that door! Witte with his sharp mind demanding instant decisions on a dozen questions; or the Minister of the Interior bringing him more evidence of sedition in the cities. This hour together was a blessed relief to them both, especially to the Tsar who was bored with having to meet his ministers and listen to petitions with a desk loaded with papers awaiting his signature: he always put off this work until the last minute. Perhaps he hadn't had a long enough youth; certainly he felt resentful of the curtailing of some daily activities he had always found pleasurable; playing tennis, dancing and going to the theatre. Becoming Tsar left little time for any of these pastimes.

'Look out, Sunny, she's got the soap!' He laughed with delight at his daughter's antics and suddenly his pale thin face looked young and carefree again. Reaching down, he lifted the crowing baby out of the tub and held her high above his head so that droplets of water ran off her body and sparkled on his beard. The baby seemed to know no fear and she reached determinedly for his fair hair, giving it a sharp tug.

'You rogue!' He kissed her and handed her back to her mother. 'Take her, beloved; I must go to Mamma.'

The Tsarina took her daughter and with her head bent over the child said: 'But you promised to read aloud to me, Nicky.'

Halfway to the door, he stopped uneasily. 'But Mamma expects me. She does so hate being alone – '

'Alone!' Alix's breast heaved and there was a dangerous light in her eyes. 'She doesn't know what being alone means! I am the one who is alone – yes, all day alone with strangers! People I barely know! Mamma is surrounded by people who know her well and care for her while I – ' She choked and the child, sensing the emotion in the air, jutted her lower lip and began to shake with sobs.

The Tsar hesitated, biting his lip. 'But, Sunny, Mamma is expecting me.'

'Then go!' She was now just an angry, jealous girl, not Empress of All the Russias.

He went on standing and staring unhappily at her. As she finished drying the baby he went across and, kneeling down, put his arms round his wife. He felt her physical response at once: never did this fail him. Her face flushed and she pressed against him. 'Oh, boysy-boysy dear, your girly dear loves you deeply!'

They murmured together and the baby began to coo contentedly. Presently, handing over the child to her nurse, they went back to their room together. Nicholas did not go to see his mother that evening despite an imperious note from Marie.

Lying in bed beside him that night, Alix told herself

she must begin to build a circle of loyal friends round her; friends who would serve her unquestioningly.

Dressing her for the Coronation in the Kremlin a week later, one of her ladies pricked a finger on the shoulder clasp of the Empress's coronation robe; a droplet of blood fell on the white satin dress, with its sparkling jewels sewn on the corsage and skirt. The concerned eyes of the Princess Rakova met the scared eyes of the culprit: *don't say a word*, one pair of eyes told the other. This was a bad omen and both women pretended it hadn't happened. Neither ever referred to it again, but both remembered the incident twenty years later. Curtseying, the ladies surrounding the Empress stood aside as the Emperor entered the room.

Nicholas, already dressed for the ceremony, took the Tsarina's crown from one of his attendants and practised placing it on his wife's head; he would have to do this at the coronation. Alix was taller than he and had to bend from the waist towards him. Her hairdresser, hovering anxiously, waited to fasten a diamond clasp into the mass of red-gold hair. After seeking her permission to adjust it, he pressed the clasp against her head and she cried out in pain. 'Oh, that hurts!'

Abashed and murmuring florid apologies, the man hastily removed the clasp and with fumbling hands tried once more, this time successfully. Everyone agreed that the Empress looked very lovely but she was still not wearing the Imperial jewels that by right ought to be hers; only a diamond necklace encircled her throat.

Suddenly, the big double doors were flung open and the Dowager Empress Marie, followed by the Imperial Family and all their attendants, swept into the room. Marie's tiny figure was glittering from head to foot with the crown jewels she should have handed over to her son's wife months ago.

'You're looking very nice, Alix,' she observed graciously, a strong hint of patronage in her voice. Like her sister, the Princess of Wales, she hated Germany and the Germans for what they had done to Denmark in the past and Alix, despite her English mother, was after all a German. It would be years before Marie accepted as her successor this young woman from Hesse on the Rhine.

Alix flushed with suppressed indignation as she beheld the Imperial jewels covering the breast of her mother-in-law. Catching her husband's troubled eyes and chiding herself for calling him weak in her heart of hearts, she forced herself to smile tranquilly at him. Poor Nicky. When would he summon up the nerve to ask Marie to return the jewels? The jewels in themselves meant little to the new Empress but the possession of them would have meant that she was truly Empress now. But with an effort she put them out of her mind and said, 'I would like to see my baby before we go.'

The nurse was summoned and she came in bearing the tiny Grand Duchess Olga Nicolaievna in her arms. The baby was wearing a pink ruffled dress with bows tied on her fat little shoulders. Her mop of dark curls had been brushed into a glossy crown of her own and as she saw her young mother she stretched out her arms and smiled delightfully.

'How lovely! What a splendid child!' the onlookers murmured admiringly.

'She is indeed a fine child,' agreed the Dowager Empress with gracious approval, 'and we must all pray that the next one is the Heir.'

There was dead silence. Then Nicholas came forward and took his wife's hand: it felt icy. 'Come, Sunny,' he said for her ear alone. 'We must go.'

Her fingers clasped his convulsively, seeming to draw strength from his thin warm hand. She took a deep breath as she prepared to face the long ceremony ahead of them. Only she knew how she dreaded the huge crowds that had flocked to the capital. But in a few hours it would be over and she would be safely home again, the door firmly closed against the world. Until then she must gird herself to face the stuffy Ouspensky Cathedral nearby where the ceremony was to take place.

Much as she dreaded the ordeal (and she could feel the trembling inside already) she knew she must somehow find the strength to go through with it for she had prayed long and feverishly never to let Nicky down. 'I am ready,' she said.

6

It was in the spring that Abel Howarth began to look mysterious. His small puckish face would break into unfinished smiles, his small eyes would disappear in a sunburst of wrinkles and even his beard looked waggish.

At dinner one night, Robert noticed these visible signs of a secret and stopped in mid-sentence to stare at his father. 'Now what did I say to make you want to laugh, Pater?'

Sir Abel hurriedly changed his gleeful expression. 'Nowt,' he said innocently. 'Nothing at all, m'boy – good soup this, Alice,' he added as a red-herring.

But Alice Howarth had noticed something strange about her husband, too; an inclination to cut off a half-begun sentence; a nervous airiness and a lack of concentration on the matter in hand. 'Abe, you're not going to start acting silly at your age, are you? It's not that new girl typewriter you've taken on, is it? Girls in offices! I don't hold with it.'

'Alice!' Sir Abel dropped his spoon. 'Good God, woman, what'll you say next? And in front of t'lad, too! I'll have you know I've never looked at another woman since the day I married you!'

'And better not, too. But I know you too well, Abe, not to know that you've something up your sleeve. It's all over your face.'

'Is it?' Sir Abel was offended. He had thought he had covered his tracks very successfully, but Alice always could ferret things out. 'Very well, I'll tell you.' Then he stopped for his wife had pressed the new electric bell for the next course and he was not prepared to divulge his secret in front of the parlour maid. By the time the fish had arrived he had had second thoughts.

'Out with it, Pater.'

'No; I'll tell you tomorrow.' No amount of cajoling would move him now. 'Tomorrow,' he reiterated and with that they subsided.

The next day was Sunday. They went to church, they ate roast beef with Yorkshire pudding and then prepared to disperse: Alice to her room for a nap; Robert for a walk with the dog Rags.

'I've ordered the carriage for two-thirty sharp,' Sir Abel said suddenly. He consulted his watch. 'You've two minutes to get your hat on, Alice.'

Mother and son wheeled round. 'I'm going for my rest, Abel! I don't want a carriage ride in this weather,' Alice Howarth protested.

'Didn't I tell you yesterday I had a surprise for you? Well, you'd better come along, then.'

At two-thirty the carriage came up St Osyth's Road and stopped outside the door. John Coachman looked disgruntled for he too had planned a Sunday afternoon nap and the master seldom if ever went out again after church on Sunday. Somewhat reluctantly the family got

98

in. Despite Robert's plea for him, the family dog Rags was excluded from the expedition.

'It's not the day for a drive,' Alice pointed out. She drew her broadtail coat about her and exchanged an eloquent look with her son: *your father*!

'What's wrong with the day?' Sir Abel was beginning to be irritable with his recalcitrant relations. 'It's a grand day. Just a little drop of rain now and again,' he added defensively as a shower of hail clattered against the carriage windows. 'A grand day,' he repeated.

His wife sighed, remembering the bright fire in her bedroom and the daybed drawn up invitingly before it. But the success of their marriage owed much to her capacity to admit defeat gracefully and let Abel have his own way, so she snuggled into the corner of the carriage and wondered what Abel was up to now.

Robert was looking about him. 'Now why should we be taking the Beverley road halfway to nowhere on a wet Sunday afternoon?'

'It's a grand day for a drive,' his father repeated obstinately.

They bowled along in silence. Outside the carriage window the scene changed as they left behind the outer fringes of the city and began to drive through real country. Flat land lay spread out on either side of the road. It was March and a north-east wind blew in from the sea over the empty landscape. Yesterday there had been a real smell of spring but today it was winter again. Gulls had settled on the ploughed brown furrows and rose in a screaming mass as the horses clattered past.

Looking out of his side of the carriage Robert suddenly exclaimed: 'Hello! John's turning off the road!' He glanced at his father. 'I do believe, Pater, you're considering setting up as a country gentleman! Isn't this the beginning of Wentworth Park?'

Alice sat up with a jerk. 'Abel Howarth, you haven't? You know I can't bear the country!'

For answer, he pulled out of the capacious inner pocket of his coat a bill of sale and handed it to her.

Robert leaned over his mother's shoulder and read aloud:

'Particulars of the Wentworth Park Estate situate 8 miles from Hull. It consists of a mansion, a finely timbered Park in the centre of a noble domain of nearly 3,000 acres. Divided into excellent agricultural holdings with superior homesteads, an extensive Lake and a Decoy with its beautifully secluded Waters.

'Nearly the whole of the village of Wentworth comprising another 2,000 acres is for sale as a whole with the estate.

'Further particulars from Humphreys & Co, Hull. For sale by auction at the Mart on Wednesday, May 12th 1896. As an entirety in one lot.'

The carriage suddenly took a right-angled turn. They dropped the bill of sale and stared out of the window. They were passing through a fine pair of iron gates held open by a woman in a man's cap and a shawl who curtsied as they bowled through.

'My sainted aunt!' Robert choked with excitement. 'Pater, you're not joking. This *is* Wentworth Park!'

'Abel, are we buying this place?'

'Maybe,' Sir Abel conceded cautiously, avoiding his wife's horrified eyes.

As they got down from the carriage and looked at the vast house, he added, 'It's all right, Alice. The old marquess has been dead this twelve month. There's a caretaker will show us over.'

Lady Howarth had found her voice again. 'Abel, you're mad! It's much too big! Why, it's like a palace! What do we want with a place like this? Anyway, we can't afford it.'

100

'Now you mind your housekeeping business, Alice, and leave the big business to me. How d'you know what we can afford, m'girl? It's time we went up in the world for t'lad's sake,' he added in her ear. 'Thirty-three St Osyth's Road is no great shakes, you know.'

She thought of her comfortable villa with its deep Turkey carpets and glowing warmth, the fine new patent boiler that gave them as much hot water as they needed, the curtains she was just going to have made for the spare room, and she could have cried. Why did Abel have this itch to uproot them and replant them, plain Hull people, in this huge mausoleum of a place? She knew what it was: he was ambitious for their son.

He had taken a plan out of his pocket and was pointing out the rooms: she heard in a dazed fashion of the drawing room, the library, the small library, the salon, the billiard room, the dining room, the entrance hall, the morning room, the owner's room, the little sitting room – 'Why, it's as big as the White Swan Hotel at Harrogate!' she expostulated. 'We'll never need all that to live in! Think of the staff we'll need. Abel, you've bitten off more'n you intended here, lad. Let's go home.'

'Now, Allie, hold your horses,' Sir Abel said soothingly but she had flounced away, her face red with indignation. Why, he was getting senile! she told herself.

But senility had nothing to do with it. Sir Abel's dreams for his son included a wife of charm and social standing and several well-behaved good-looking grandchildren to follow. That Robert had no eyes for the neighbourhood's young ladies had become obvious. What alarmed him was Amos Stuttle's story about some half-Chinese wench down on the waterside. *Half-Chinese!* The idea had nearly given him a stroke. He had wasted no time in finding a property of suitable grandeur and although he hadn't told them this, contracts had been exchanged. The auction to be held in May had been cancelled.

'Pater, this is a place and a half and no mistake!' Robert's eyes were shining as he followed the caretaker from room to room. Good old pater! He'd come up to scratch at last, he told himself gleefully. Yes, he'd beaten his friend Bundry into a cocked hat! Bundry with whom he had shared a study at school, had asked him to stay last summer and he had thought their house in the country a magnificent place. What price Bundry, now! Why, Bundry Hall would look a small place set down next to Wentworth Park. 'You've seen the place before, Dadda?' he asked as they crossed a broad landing.

Sir Abel swallowed, unable to believe his ears. The lad hadn't called him *Dadda* since he was a little chap in knickerbockers! It had been worth the vast sum he had given for Wentworth just to hear the boy call him Dadda in an intimate voice. 'Last month. Knew at once it was right for us,' he replied gruffly.

Alice Howarth's lips tightened. He'd not said a word to *her* – not one word!

'I daresay we'll be moving in before the summer. We shall have to get a lot more staff.'

'Are you off your head?' Alice Howarth hissed in his ear.

Robert left them to their wrangling. Running downstairs, he let himself out by a side door into the garden. The rain had stopped but it was bitterly cold and he turned up the collar of his overcoat before plunging down the steps of a broad terrace and across a lawn to the park railings. Here he turned and faced the property. Someday it would be his and he would be Sir Robert Howarth. He would live here with his wife and children. The children would play cricket on this very lawn. He would like several sons and at least one daughter (for he must have

102

a daughter to cherish and spoil). He could see her wheeling her doll's pram along the terrace and going for walks with her governess along these well-kept paths. Yes, he could see this mythical family quite clearly but not their mother. The girl who would be their mother remained a misty creature. He thought of little Susie Wei and regretfully discarded her. Ah, well. There was plenty of time; he was only twenty.

Turning, he leaned on the fence, staring at the clumps of oaks and elms dotting the park. He felt very happy.

Part Three
1899

5

The Shadows Lengthen

1

The head *vendeuse* of Monsieur Geralde's dressmaking establishment on the rue St Honoré had herself escorted the Countess Barinskaya down to the main door: word had been sent up to the fitting room that Lady Mary Cairns' carriage was awaiting her.

Anastasia had begged her friend to pick her up from the dressmaker's at three o'clock: she had so much to tell her, she wrote in a fairly feverish note, and badly (scored under three times) needed her advice.

Mary Cairns was not averse to giving advice whether she was asked for it or not because she thought herself admirably placed to do so. Everyone said she was so full of commonsense. *Ask Mary* had become the axiom in her circle. She certainly looked the part of a serious-minded young woman with responsibilities. She had produced five children before she was thirty and her husband, Mr Alfred Cairns, was a rising young Liberal MP with ambitions and a great deal of money. They owned a house in Paris to which they repaired twice a year, in spring and autumn. She knew no one from the Russian Embassy until she met the Barinskys through a French friend. Anastasia knew at once that she could talk freely with this English friend for that very reason: she knew no one at the Embassy and none of Anastasia's revelations would ever get back to Sergei's ears. Once she had confided her troubles to a young Russian whose husband was a colleague of Sergei's; she had sworn secrecy but of course had told her husband almost at once with the result that Sergei knew about it within forty-eight hours. He had been furiously angry and had shaken her until her teeth rattled in her head; then (his favourite trick) he had forced her into a corner and directed heavy blows with his fists within an inch of her face. If she had struggled or moved, he could have broken her nose or her teeth so she stayed perfectly still until his fury abated. Unfortunately, it became his favourite form of torture for her after that.

So now she chose her *confidantes* with great care. Mary, who was neither Russian nor an embassy official's wife, had therefore become her best friend.

Monsieur Geralde having bowed like a mechanical toy to each lady in turn, the green clarence moved off. Only very grand people used a clarence in Paris and people on the pavements looked with interest at the two women as they bowled smartly along.

'My dear, you must have been spending a fortune in there! Monsieur himself to see you into the carriage!'

Anastasia's eyes shone like a child's with excitement. 'Oh, I have! I've chosen three beautiful outfits and they are finishing them now I've had my second fitting. The street outfit is to be delivered tonight and I can wear it to the de Puisseys' tomorrow.' She gave an excited laugh for clothes had the effect on her that a magnum of champagne had on others. She was intoxicated by them and could hardly wait to show them off.

It was a glorious spring afternoon and Paris, putting forth new leaves and new clothes, looked its best. It was so warm that Mary, who was always tight-laced, perspired gently under her frilled parasol and her broad cheeks reddened to an unbecoming lobster shade. Anastasia continued to look cool and beautiful in her favourite biscuit shade braided in black with heavy black lace trimming the bodice and matching hat.

'I've so much to tell you, Mary dear!'

'Well, we've plenty of time.' Leaning forward, Lady Mary poked at the coachman with the tip of her parasol while she said in loud clear English: 'Drive round for twenty minutes.' Although she had been coming to France twice a year since she was married, her French remained abominable. By raising her voice and pronouncing each word clearly, she was quite certain her servants understood well enough. 'I suppose it's Sergei again? Really, Stana, I don't understand why you aren't firm with him! Men need a good deal of firmness. Look at Alfred. I was firm from the very beginning and he has *never* strayed.'

Anastasia considered Alfred Cairns: who would look at the little man with his bulbous nose and short legs? True, he had fathered several healthy children but it was his only attainment in life. Sergei, now, was beautiful. Remembering this, his wife gave a sigh. When she looked at him she never could resist him for long and he knew it, the wretch. There was a lot to be said for having a plain, good husband, someone who wouldn't allow himself to be attracted by every pretty ankle! She began to pour into Mary's ear all Sergei's iniquities: his disloyalty and extravagance, his downright cruelty. She had, she announced defiantly, reached the limit of her endurance. 'I'll not stand it any longer! This time it's the little seamstress who comes to the house, so Corinne informs me and she's seldom wrong. How could he sink so low?'

'Oh, I don't know. It's a compliment to you really that he only does it with people of the lower orders.'

'The Duchesse de la Touraine is not of the lower orders.'

'No, I forgot her. That's over, isn't it?'

Anastasia nodded. 'Louis de la Touraine put his foot down.'

'And quite right, too. That's what you must do, Stana. *Be firm*.'

'But Sergei doesn't care how firm I am!' Anastasia wailed.

'Besides, men are like this,' Mary went on, ignoring the interruption. 'I'm sure Russians are as bad as most English gentlemen in this respect.'

Anastasia pouted. It was all very well for Mary to sit there, calm as a statue, lecturing her on how to keep Sergei tied to her apron strings. Mary's life was totally different with that little Alfred who wouldn't say boo to a goose. She herself was only twenty-five and had been married five years. Her little girl was now four and she had determined not to have any more children. Sergei didn't know it but she had sought the best medical advice on how she could prevent herself becoming *enceinte* again. She would no longer put up with Sergei's flamboyant behaviour. He was incorrigible and a brute! She felt herself go hot under her clothes when she thought of all he did to her body – and she was supposed to accept it all meekly! Well, she wouldn't. Not any longer. 'If only we could divorce. But the Tsar would banish us, you know.'

Mary raised her brows. 'The Tsar would interfere in your lives? Surely you exaggerate, Stana.'

'I assure you I do not. The nobility are not allowed to divorce in our country – not that the peasants would dream of doing so. It would not be tolerated, especially as Sergei is in the diplomatic service and therefore representing his country. I assure you the Tsar is equally hard on his own relations. No divorce, no morganatic marriages, no scandals, or they are sent out of Russia. Is it not so in England?'

110

'Certainly not.' Mary drew herself up. 'The idea of Queen Victoria banishing anyone is simply ludicrous! Of course divorce is very much frowned on and one is banned from Court functions and the Royal Enclosure at Ascot but as for being sent away to live in another country, why, it's undreamed of! I must say – and I do not mean to offend you, Stana – Russia sounds quite mediaeval.'

Anastasia nodded sadly. Living in Paris this past year had shown her only too clearly how mediaeval her country still was. Here, she breathed the air of freedom and was beginning to resent her husband's brutal treatment of her.

'In England the children are usually taken from the mother when there is a divorce,' Mary added, remembering a recent court case that had been splashed all over the English newspapers. 'I suppose it's so in Russia, too? Men always succeed in getting what they want, I'm afraid. The law is on their side not ours. Women have no jurisdiction over their children in England.'

Her companion turned an ashen face towards her. 'No! You mean I should lose my Tanya? I would die!' To have her darling baby taken from her! Her blue eyes filled with terror and tears.

'There, don't get upset, my dear! You aren't going to involve yourself in a divorce; you won't be so silly. Much better to pretend to know nothing. Just go on with your life and make the best of it. Order yourself a lot more new clothes – oh, you already have, haven't you? Splendid! How are you off for hats and underlinen? Then what about scent? Henri,' she poked the coachman's back again, 'drive to the rue de Rivoli. I'm sure you have accounts at all the best shops so we shall spend a very pleasant hour or two.'

Even while agreeing, Anastasia shivered inwardly.

111

Then she bolstered herself up by reminding herself that it would be her own money she was spending – although by the way Sergei kept his hands on it one wouldn't think so, she told herself resentfully. She remembered that little seamstress coming to the house as meek as a mouse and stealing her husband's affections – no, that wasn't strictly true. Sergei's affections had not been directed towards her for a long time, if ever. He came to her bed occasionally and she endured his attentions because he would hit her if she didn't, but there was no love between them.

Her mouth drooping woefully, she sighed. 'I wish I could go back to St Petersburg.'

Lady Mary looked at her pityingly: how could anyone long to go back to Russia? It sounded too frightful. And how strange not to fall in love with Paris as everyone else did. But knowing that the Russians were a touchy lot she held her tongue and said nothing.

2

The parcels began to arrive that evening.

A trickle at first and then an avalanche as equipages with well-known names painted on their sides trotted smartly into the street and stopped outside their house in the Bois de Boulogne.

Corinne, her rather sour lady's maid, brought the first consignment into the boudoir where Anastasia, clad in a pretty wrapper, was writing letters at her little desk. With glee she began to undo the gold string and pink ribbons; every shop, it seemed, had tried to outdo its rival in the beauty of its wrappings. A sea of tissue paper floated across the floor as Anastasia plunged her hands into the exciting boxes. Exquisite silk and lawn underwear (one could never have enough lingerie, she reminded herself sagely), a gold-mesh purse to carry her handkerchief in the evenings, gossamer silk stockings, a dressing jacket trimmed with swansdown that tickled her nose, a pink peignoir with ribbon ruffles, large cut-glass bottles of scent and even some curled ostrich feathers to trim a hat, spilled out of the boxes. Monsieur Geralde's creations in their restrained white boxes trimmed and fastened with emerald ribbon she put on one side for Corinne to unpack and hang up.

When Sergei suddenly appeared in the room she raised a flushed excited face. 'Just look at these exquisite gloves – one could only find them in Paris!'

'In God's name!' He looked at the boxes spilling beautiful things over the chairs, the floor, everywhere, and his face darkened. He had had a frustrating morning at the embassy over an important paper carelessly lost. He had been the last to sign for it but of course it wasn't his fault. It was the clerk's and the little worm had tried to wriggle out of it by pretending ignorance, but he hadn't let him get away with it – by God, no!

Picking up the swansdown-trimmed jacket he rolled it into a ball and hurled it roughly across the room where it unfolded and drooped over a lamp. 'Who has sent you these things? You'd better tell me at once before I shake it out of you.'

The light died in her face. 'No one has sent them. They're not presents, Sergei. I bought them myself this afternoon.' She retrieved the crumpled dressing jacket, smoothing the swansdown with a loving finger. 'I went shopping in the rue de Rivoli – oh!' His fingers digging cruelly into her shoulder, he swung her round to face him. 'Let me go!'

'You bought them yourself? Who gave you the money?'

113

'Well, not you, of course! I put them down on account everywhere. You can pay for them with Papa's money. You're hurting me – oh!' She gasped again as he hit her across the face with the back of his hand. Quite cool and unmoved, he hit her again and again until blood began to run from her nose and spotted her blue wrapper. Her hair fell out of its pins and across her frightened face which was now scarlet from the blows he was dealing her.

Stopping suddenly, he grasped her by the arms and shook her. 'You've been using my money, you bitch!'

'Yes, why shouldn't I? Papa sends you money – I never see it. You have my dowry – ' Her breath came to an end as he hit her in the stomach, across the back as she turned, anywhere he could reach.

'I'll teach you to spend money that doesn't belong to you! These things go back at once. Understand?'

Losing her balance, she fell against the side of a chest and the corner struck her in the centre of her forehead. She lay stunned but conscious, feeling his boot kicking her in the kidneys and the spine. *He wants to kill me*, she thought dully. Then she fainted.

When she came to he was gone and Corinne was trying to raise her and drag her to the daybed.

'Oh, *excellence*, this is terrible!' she was crying. Suddenly she ran to the door calling for the valet, 'Louis! Louis! Here, help me raise Madame la Contesse – gently, you fool! This is your master's work and not the first time. He needs locking up – yes, I shall say what I like and you're not going to stop me!'

Their French voices irritated and brought her out of her faint. 'Stop it,' she mumbled. 'Send him away, Corinne, I don't need him.'

'There, madame, we have you. Lie back and rest. He's gone. That Louis! Cut from the same cloth, those two. I have some arnica here but first I must bathe you. *Mon*

114

dieu! The brute!' Corinne muttered as, pulling down the wrapper from her mistress's body she saw the extent of the damage inflicted by Barinsky.

Anastasia ran her tongue round her teeth: yes, they were all still there and unbroken but how she ached! Every bone in her body was protesting; she burned with pain. Tears ran out of her eyes and smartingly into the broken skin of her face.

'*Excellence*, you should not put up with this,' Corinne said, bending over her. 'It is not the first time and it's not right. He will *kill* you!'

Anastasia turned her head away. No, it was not the first time and it shamed her to think that Corinne knew this, had heard her cries and seen the bruises. *I wish he had killed me*, she thought miserably.

3

For a week, in perfect weather, she had had to cancel all her engagements and stay in the house to allow the bruises to fade. She saw hardly anything of her husband who came and went like a stranger. She realized all too well that he had no feeling left for her if he ever had had any. For herself, she knew she couldn't love him. He was greedy, brutal and spoiled and as he grew older the number of his seductions grew. The thought of having to stay with him for the rest of her life made her cry a great deal in secret.

Her little girl was brought to see her twice a day and as the child climbed on to her lap and touched her sore face with her soft little hand, she hugged her convulsively. How terrible it would be to have her child taken from her! Tanya was four, a silent child whose eyes seemed to miss nothing. How like Sergei she is, Anastasia thought sadly.

After a week indoors the bruises began to fade, so wearing a shady hat and a veil she was able to go driving in the Bois and even paid a visit to the races with friends. It was on her return from a morning drive that she was informed that Prince Alexander Rakov had called and was waiting for her in the small salon.

It was more than four years since they had met but she remembered how kind and sympathetic he had been. Forgetting her bruises she threw back her veil and went to greet him with outstretched hands. How he had changed! And how handsome he had become! All signs of the boy had disappeared and in his place stood a very tall, broad-shouldered man in a grey jacket and trousers of impeccable cut. His cravat was of dark green silk and he held a straw boater with a green ribbon. His crisp fair hair had darkened and he now possessed an interesting sabre cut across one cheekbone almost to the ear: that it had not long been inflicted was apparent from its pinkness but it didn't detract at all from his good looks. She was delighted to see him again and told him so.

'But you have been defending some fair lady's honour, my friend!' She looked teasingly at the scar. 'How truly romantic!'

He was still able to flush darkly although he laughed lightly enough and said that he and a fellow officer had had a slight disagreement a year ago.

'A year! It must have been a deep cut. You are no longer in the army? Your service is over?'

'I'm at St Petersburg university studying law and living at home. My mother and Feo and I are here for a month so I hoped I would find you still in Paris, Countess.' He avoided looking at her face with the unmistakable marks of blows on it. That brute Barinsky of course: how he

116

would like to call him out! It was time someone gave the wretch a thrashing. 'I hope you will do me the honour of taking *le five o'clock* with me this afternoon at the Ritz? It is becoming very popular, this English habit, all the rage as they say.'

Her eyes sparkled. She loved going to the Ritz for a tête-à-tête over English tea and *pâtisseries*. 'Thank you, I would like that.'

He bowed. 'Then I will call for you at four-thirty.'

It was when she went up to her room after luncheon that Sergei followed her, shutting the door behind him. She retreated to the window, quaking inwardly.

His lips curled. 'Don't worry; I shan't come near you. I simply wished to inform you in private that I've been ordered to Washington. It's my new posting and I sail next month. You can follow with the child when I've found a suitable house.'

Her heart had leapt hopefully at the news but his last sentence dissolved the hope almost at once: she was expected to accompany him to this outlandish place. 'Washington? Is it in England?'

'Your education at the hands of your Miss Hardwick leaves a lot to be desired, my dear. It's the capital of the United States of America.'

America. That was thousands of miles away. Panic constricted her throat. She would be alone with him there with all her friends left behind in Europe. 'I don't want to go!' she burst out. 'I'd like to go home to Papa. He won't make me go with you when I tell him how you behave to me.'

'Please yourself. The child will come with me, of course.'

She opened her mouth to protest then closed it. For a minute there was silence while he waited. 'Very well, I

117

will follow you later.' Inwardly she said: *But I shan't go, of course.*

'Don't plan to stay behind permanently, will you?' He could obviously read her thoughts. 'I should simply get leave and come over for Tanya.'

4

Taking her to tea at the Ritz Hotel, Alex noticed that the little countess was very quiet. It was only after they had drunk a cup of China tea apiece and she had chosen a pastry oozing cherries and cream that she suddenly opened up and poured out all her worries to him: they were going to Washington and she didn't want to go! But if she didn't, then Sergei would take her child from her . . .

She was several years older than he was, but Alex suddenly felt the older of the two. 'If he is a bad husband to you you should go home to your father and tell him so – yes, take your little girl with you.' He added softly: 'Go now before the bruises fade, Anastasia Nicolaievna. Have you money? I can lend you some. Believe me, you mustn't allow him to do such things to you. Your father will tell you so, I'm sure.'

Her face lit up: he might have been murmuring words of love to her by the expression in his eyes. 'Oh, how you relieve my mind! I am so grateful. Yes, I have enough money for the tickets home. Papa will be kind to me, I know.' Her joy at the thought of getting away from Sergei seemed to him quite pitiful. She cheered up considerably and ate another pastry with the enthusiasm of a child. They talked of other things and at six-thirty he dropped her at her house.

118

'Tomorrow, Countess? Shall we go on the river tomorrow?'

She gave him her hand. 'It would be delightful.'

'Then I will call for you at three.' He kissed her gloved hand and watched her until the servant closed the door behind her. She was adorable, he thought fondly, and he was quite ready to have an *affaire* with her. A pity if she went back to St Petersburg next week because Paris was perfect for an *affaire* with a pretty woman. He got back into the cab and mused about Anastasia Nicolaievna Barinskaya: was he falling in love with her?

He was never to know. When he called next day a servant told him she had left for St Petersburg at midnight: her father was very ill and not expected to live. Yes, Count Barinsky had gone with her.

119

6

The Dark House

1

Katya was sixteen when they left Whitby for good and found a new home inland. Holyoke was a small market town twenty miles inland across the moors and with a better rail connection for Captain Croxley. That they moved at last was due to a conversation she had with her father.

They had gone for a tramp over the hill to Ruswarp. The captain was on leave and for the first time he found himself more concerned about his daughter than his wife. He began to watch her covertly, uneasily aware that the girl was unlike her contemporaries: she was too quiet, too serious for her age. When he came to think of it she had always worn that rather anxious air and had been too ready to defer to her mother's whims and fancies. Was her mother the burden that weighed her down?

He was a man who believed in a blunt question. They were hardly at the top of the hill before he had got his answer.

'You see, she's a very different person when you're away, Father,' Katya explained, linking her arm in his as they descended the hill on the other side. The view spread out to encompass the blue-green moors and they were no longer in sight or sound of the sea. 'She's so unhappy then, so frightened of the sea. One night last

120

month when the maroons went off to launch the lifeboat she thought it must be your boat and she was in a terrible state all night.' The girl shuddered, remembering that night. 'Oh, Father' she said, impulsively turning to him, 'can't you leave the sea?'

'Leave the sea!' Captain Croxley stopped dead. 'And how would we live with me not able to save a penny piece? No, no, my girl, I can't do that. I want to see you go to college and make us proud of you. I'm sorry your mother's troubled but I would have thought that she'd learnt by now that my new boat *Hull Lady* is a good modern one. I'm Howarth's senior captain now, you know, so they're giving me the first off the line. Six keels have been laid down – think of that! Trade's booming again at last. Leave the sea! Good God, girl, what an idea!'

They walked on in silence, Katya thinking of her mother's agony of anxiety all the time her father was at sea, on those nights when the storm beat against their windows, when the wind nearly took the roof off, when the mewing of the gulls sounded like lost sailors crying for help. She sighed, stealing a glance at the ruddy-faced vigorous man striding along, always a little ahead of her. He was a stolid, unimaginative, hard-working Yorkshireman not given to nervous fancies himself and therefore totally unable to understand them in others. Yet he and her mother adored each other: what could it be that bound them together when they were so different?

Inexperienced herself she couldn't recognize the strong physical attraction between her parents. It was the difference between them that made her marvel.

An idea struck her. 'Father, what would you say to moving inland? Away from the sea?'

He considered this, his hands behind his back, a little frown between his light blue eyes. 'But you're doing so well at Miss Lesley's, puss. We shouldn't move just yet. You've a good brain, love. That last report was the best yet. Miss Lesley wants you to go over to Scarborough once a week to the boys' high school for coaching in Latin – Latin! Fancy that, now. It's from your mother you get it. Masha was like a son to her father and she was to have been his heir and taken over the running of the business from him. Aye, it was me changed all that for her, poor lass,' and he looked guiltily at his daughter.

She laughed, tugging at his arm. 'Oh, Father! You know Mother adores you and doesn't regret it at all. What was an old timberyard to a girl when she could have you?'

He grinned. 'You're a flatterer, my girl. D'you think she's been happy in England? No, she's never settled and that's the plain fact of it. She loves me but it's not been enough, I fear.'

She knew the story of that runaway marriage. It had always seemed so romantic; the young Russian girl dressing up as a cabin boy and running off with the handsome sea captain. How furious Grandfather Urosov must have been! He had never communicated with her since and it was this, Katya suspected, that was the cause of her mother's depression. She longed to see him again, to visit St Petersburg and talk to her sisters. Tante Laura scrawled a letter once a year on Mother's name day and Tante Anastasia had sent her a present from Paris once, but the lack of regular communication was beginning to tell on the exile. She sighed and returned to the matter in hand. 'Next summer I shall be leaving school for good so it won't matter if we leave Whitby then. We could be looking for a house now in some of the little towns on the moors. Oh, Father, tell her we're leaving, *please*!'

He agreed but with reluctance. He had been born and brought up in that house and anywhere far from the sea and the north-east wind would be stifling to live in. But he knew that the time had come to give way to the needs of his wife and child. 'Very well, puss,' he said gloomily.

Marie was overjoyed at the idea. Only she knew how many nights she lay sleepless with the icon in her hands, praying, praying. Away from the sea, it would be easier to forget its terrible power, perhaps even find peace of mind. She was only thirty-seven but knew she looked older and she was uneasily aware that her health was deteriorating. She had a strange lump in her breast and some pain . . . but of course it was nothing really and was bound to clear up when they moved and she was happier.

So they spent several fine Saturdays that spring taking a train from one small town to the other. Sometimes they brought a picnic: if it rained they ate it in the train on the way home; but if it was a fine day they would find a dry stone wall on the outskirts of the town and eat it there. Colour appeared in Marie's cheeks and she really seemed to be taking a new interest in life at last.

They came to Holyoke quite by chance when the engine of their train broke down and they had an hour to wait. They strolled about the little grey stone town that was just ten miles from Whitby and nestling in a depression on the moors. A clear, murmuring beck tumbled down the main street and was crossed by a stone bridge. Holyoke was bigger than a village and yet hardly a town. A cattle market was held once a week, a shop-keeper informed them as they bought his little beefsteak pies to eat in the train.

'Let's come and look at it again next Saturday,' Marie suggested as they got back into their train. 'I like this place.' It had not occurred to her that her daughter found the place remote and depressing, filled with old people and so quiet that the blows of the blacksmith's hammer from his shop were as loud as the maroon going off at Whitby. To Marie, the place seemed like a blessed refuge out of sight and sound of that horrible German Ocean.

So they came on the following Saturday and almost immediately found Updown House was vacant and to be rented quite cheaply to a good tenant. It was a severe-looking upright grey stone house with a high slate roof with two dormer windows in it. It had two bay windows and a large brick porch that had been stuck on as an afterthought. An imposing entrance gate between stone pillars brought one within a few yards to the house: there was just sufficient space to turn a carriage in front. The house's name was picked out in stone pebbles on one of the pillars and they learned that it had belonged to an Anglo-Indian gentleman who had recently died.

There was a half-light inside the house that seemed to delight Marie although Katya found it chilling: no winter sun could find its way past the trees that surrounded it. But Marie felt safe in this dark cocoon and planned to cover the windows with calico blinds and Nottingham lace. It reminded her in some ways, she said dreamily, of her old home on the Moika Canal. The bright light off the sea at Whitby had made her feel, she added, as if they were living in a goldfish bowl. This would be much nicer!

And Katya, anxious to see her mother happy again, readily agreed. But in her heart of hearts she found the prospect of making their home there quite daunting.

That summer she left school having passed her London Senior exams with distinction, the only girl in the school who had been capable of taking them. That she did so was due solely to the efforts of a schoolmaster at Scarborough to whom she went for coaching twice a week.

Miss Lesley was overjoyed: how well it would look in the new prospectus! *Girls prepared for London Senior exam.* She tried to keep Katya as a low-paid pupil teacher but Captain Croxley decreed that his bright girl must be allowed to spread her wings: nothing less than teachers' training college at Harrogate for her. She would lodge in a students' hostel and come home for an occasional weekend. He was determined that the girl should have some youth and the chance to be carefree before it was too late.

'Mamushka, are you sure you'll be all right without me?' Katya was as anxious as if she were the parent and Marie her child.

But Marie smiled with new confidence. 'Darling, I have good Annie for company and this delightful house to prepare for Father's homecoming next month. I shall be busy all day and I won't be able to hear that horrible roar from the sea.' She really did seem happier although she was very slim and pale. Her once abundant dark hair was getting thin and flecked with grey and although she spoke cheerfully her eyes were huge in her small face. However, when the day came for Katya to leave for Harrogate she waved her off quite happily. Katya's last glimpse of her mother through the steam of the train was of her wide smile beneath her grey hat. How distinguished she looked, how different to the others on the platform! the girl thought proudly as she drew her head in and pulled the window up by its leather strap.

Marie turned away as the train disappeared round the bend, her smile fading. She had made the Russian traditional sign of the cross over a departing traveller but to herself she had prayed: *let me see her again – just once more.*

3

It was a big step for Katya to go away from home on her own and she was full of excitement. Her father had been frank with her. 'I can just afford the two-year course, puss. After that, you'll have to find a job and keep yourself.'

'Oh, I shall be able to easily, Father!' Katya assured him. It was now the goal she had set herself: to be independent by twenty. How proud he would be of her then!

Harrogate seemed awesomely big with its splendid shops and brilliantly lighted streets overflowing with the carriages of the country folk. The new teachers' college was on the outskirts of the town but a horse-drawn bus clip-clopped with regularity down the road to take the students into the town to the coffee houses or to press their noses against the shop windows that were filled so enticingly with rich goods.

It was while she was in her first month there that Britain was suddenly plunged into war in South Africa. The Boers, those 'pigheaded farmers' handed in their

126

ultimatum to Sir Alfred Milner and mobilization was ordered.

Life was full and she began to enjoy herself; tentatively at first because it was such an unusual feeling to be happy and carefree, to feel young again. She made friends quickly with the other students, both men and girls, and to her astonishment found herself sought-after. The men lived in a hostel a mile away from the main block and the only chance of meeting them was at lectures. Sometimes, on Sundays, they could come to tea downstairs under the watchful eye of a chaperon but this was not a popular pastime. Walking on the Stray, that beautiful stretch of common in the middle of the town, was a good deal pleasanter and so long as the girls were never on their own with the men, it wasn't frowned on by authority.

For Katya it was a new experience to be surrounded by friends, people who smiled back at her at lectures, girls who asked her advice, men who invited her for walks. She was amazed. The pinched look faded from her face and she regained the pretty looks that had always been there under the strange look of anxiety that her face had worn for so long.

She took up hockey with enthusiasm and, longing to be selected for the team, played every afternoon. Up against girls who had played hockey at school (Hill House had disapproved of games), she had no chance of that just yet but was encouraged to believe she might achieve it next year. It was such fun! That was what was so amazing, the amount of pure enjoyment in her new life.

There was a great jubilation in the air: England was going to lick those Boers in a few weeks, by jingo, just see if they didn't. A column of Yorkshire Yeomanry, resplendent in their scarlet uniforms, swung through the streets to the railway station and Katya stood on tiptoe to wave her handkerchief. 'We're soldiers of the Queen, me lads!' roared out the crowd. How smart they looked, she thought admiringly.

Alas, it was those same scarlet uniforms that were to prove the undoing of these soldiers of the Queen just two short months later. By Christmas, the horrifying lesson learned that scarlet against the olive veld made too good a target for the Boers, the fresh battalions sent out would be clad in their new and ugly khaki uniforms.

But now in October all was patriotic excitement and pride and Katya and her friends bought maps which they hung on the walls of their rooms and stuck with coloured pins.

There was only two months of it. Early in December she received a telegram from Annie: *Your mother very ill. Come at once.*

4

Getting permission from her tutor, Katya took the first available train home. She sat in a stuffy third-class compartment with a lot of coughing people and wondered what ailed her mother. Annie must be exaggerating! Only last month, she had spent a weekend at Holyoke and her mother had seemed much as usual. Perhaps a little thinner. Or had she, Katya, forgotten how thin and white Marie normally was? Perhaps she had a bad cold and it had gone to her chest. There was no use speculating; she would be home in an hour and would know what it was. Nevertheless, anxiety gnawed at her as she waited impatiently at Malton for the branch-line train to Holyoke.

Mother very ill. What could it be? She hadn't – oh,

128

pray God, she hadn't done something to herself in one of her moments of despair?

As this thought occurred to her, Katya realized how long this dread had lived with her. After her husband's leaves ended (and Harry Croxley would have rejoined his boat two weeks ago) Marie was at her lowest ebb, weeping in her room, totally without appetite or indeed any interest in daily life. Being on her own with only the old servant for the first time might well have proved too much for her.

I oughtn't to have left her, Katya told herself guiltily.

She walked up from the station, carrying her small valise with a change of clothing. Miss Porter, her tutor, had given her two nights' leave only, but if Marie were really ill, then she would give her an extension. But the end of term exams were so near that Katya hoped she wouldn't be away too long. The ticket home had taken most of her slender pocket money or she could have taken the station fly up to Updown House. It was raining, a typical day for early December with the fallen leaves sodden and black on the road making walking a slippery business. The beck was bubbling and full as it ran under the village bridge; much rain must have fallen in the last few days. The misty rain clung to her lashes and tendrils of damp hair hugged her cheeks as she made her way up the hill in the early darkness of afternoon.

At last she saw the twin stone posts with Updown House picked out in pebbles and the nerves tightened in her stomach as she saw the thin bars of light escaping round the edges of the curtain in her mother's room. She stopped, shifted the valise to her other hand and took two deep breaths.

There was a smart gig waiting before the front door, the horse tied to one of the porch posts. She guessed it was the doctor's and as she cautiously opened the front

129

door she smelled the antiseptic smell doctors seemed to carry round with them. The lamps were lit and as she stared upwards she saw shadows flicker over the wall as Annie, in a clean white apron, led the doctor down the stairs.

'Oh, Miss Katya, it's you!' The old servant wiped her eyes with a corner of the apron. 'She's mortal bad, my dearie.'

Katya held her lips steady even as her heart lurched. She looked at the thin-featured man with white whiskers who was the village doctor. 'I'm her daughter. Please tell me what's the matter with my mother.'

He was shrugging into a waterproof cape. 'How-de-do, Miss Croxley. Your mother's very ill. She has left things too late, I fear. There's a growth in the breast that is attacking her spine now. Must have had it a deuce of a time, poor woman. There's only one answer to a growth and that's the knife. It's too big for that now and there is nothing else I can do. I'm sorry. I've given her an injection and I'll be in to give her another tomorrow. I've left some tablets for her in case the pain gets very bad. She'll sleep a good deal now.' He patted Katya's shoulder. 'Be strong for her sake. Your father has been sent for. She'll only last a day or two more.'

Katya heard the door close behind him. Feeling sick and dazed, she sank on to the oak settle. Beside her, Annie wept freely. 'Oh, Miss Katya, we can only pray it's not long. The pain she's in!'

Katya nodded. Very slowly, as if her hands were weighted, she took the pins out of her hat and hung it, soaking wet, on the stand. Then tucking wet tendrils of hair behind her ears she went upstairs. Outside her mother's room she took a deep, nervous breath and the smell of illness rushed out at her and up her nostrils. She retched, cold sweat breaking out on her face. Her mother's room had always smelt sweet and fresh with heliotrope and cologne. Now it smelled of her rotting flesh, of death and the grave. She wiped her forehead with the back of her hand and went in.

What was left of Marie Nicolaievna lay propped in the bed. Starched white linen framed her diminished face. Her eyes were closed and a deep shadow lay on her face cast by the shaded lamps. Katya knelt by the bed and held the emaciated hands to her lips. The change wrought in the face she knew so well stunned her. The light and life had gone out of it and she already looked dead.

'Mamushka, it's Katya.' The whisper seemed to reach the still figure for the fingers twitched faintly. Then the heavy lids opened a little and Marie's voiceless mouth formed her name.

'Yes, Father's coming home! Mamushka, d'you hear me?'

Again there was a slight pressure on the fingers. *I'm still here*, Marie seemed to be saying.

Leaning forward to kiss her, Katya touched her mother's breasts under their lawn robe. She recoiled in horror: they were as hard and cold as stone. How long had Marie known of the creeping horror in her breast that had now seized her spine? Tears rolled down Katya's face; her mother had successfully concealed her terrible illness from everyone until now when it was too late to save her.

5

As Alex Rakov ran up the steps of his home on the Catherine Canal, the door opened before him and the old doorman wearing the Rakov livery with a colourful bandolier bowed him in. He spent most of the day in a canopied leather chair just inside the door. No one arrived or left without Timotei to open and shut the door. The Rakov children had believed he lived in his chair and had no other home for he was never absent; to them he was like a great friendly dog with his grey beard and whiskers coming out of his kennel to greet them. As they grew up, old Timotei grew older and more decrepit but he still bowed them in and out of their home.

'Your excellency smells the change in the air?' he asked now in his gravelly voice.

Alex grinned. 'Why, Timotei, don't tell me spring's begun! We haven't had Christmas yet!'

'No, no, excellency, not spring but much snow. The real winter is here. Ah, there will be much want, I fear, when the cold begins.' And his old eyes watered at the thought of the hunger among the Dark People. 'Every winter I fear it, excellency. The cholera has begun, you see, and it's difficult to stop. I have a little granddaughter.'

Two footmen were sent by the butler to stop the doorman buttonholing his excellency. 'He's getting senile,' the man muttered as the footman held open the door to admit Prince Alex and the butler went forward to bow and relieve the young man of his burden of books, elk-skin coat and fur cap, fur-lined heavy boots and a long woollen jerkin that were necessary to withstand the cold of the tram journey to and from the university buildings on the Islands. The butler disapproved of the prince's insistence on behaving like all the other students at law school: no good would come of it, depend on it.

As Alex ran up the marble staircase in his soft leather boots to change for dinner, he found Henri, his father's valet, waiting to pounce.

'Your excellency dines in tonight?'

'Yes. Is the princess back from the Anitchkov Palace?'

'She arrived at luncheon, excellency. I understand she does not return there for three weeks which is good; she appears to be tired. I believe she is wishful to see you.'

'I'll bath first.'

Henri continued to hover.

'Well, what is it?' Sometimes Alex's impatient tone sounded very like his father's.

'I'm worried, your excellency. The prince has not been home for four nights. He never stays away so long without me to accompany him to see to his linen. Your excellency has no idea where he might be?'

'None at all,' Alex said with a shrug and continued down the long broad landing to his suite of rooms. But when he'd shut the door behind him his expression changed, became charged with speculation and grim anger. How dare his father behave like this? It was an insult to his mother and the servants were no doubt all gossiping about it. Where in God's name was he? The suspicion that something might have happened – that indeed his father might not be coming back at all was beginning to weigh heavily on him.

The relationship between father and son had deteriorated further these last few years. After his two years' compulsory service Alex had opted to go to law school at St Petersburg university. The decision had infuriated Prince Rakov: all the eldest sons in the Rakov family made the army their career, he had pointed out angrily.

133

Alex had obstinately refused to listen: army life in the long term didn't interest him in the least and the idea of staying in the regiment, idling his time away until his father died, had been repugnant to him. He had enjoyed his two years' service and made new friends but the life as lived by a young officer had seemed too wasteful of life's opportunities. Besides, his real interest was in politics and this was outside a serving officer's province. Since he was seventeen, he had been burning to do something for his country, to help steer Russia from the disaster most liberal-minded people predicted now loomed ahead. Two terms in law school had opened his eyes completely for here were most of the revolutionaries of the future. He had attended enough secret meetings held in basements (with lamps and candles the only light) to know for certain that this wasn't just a student idea. Real revolutionaries came out of hiding to talk treasonably of getting rid of the Tsar and ravenously eat the cheese and rye bread provided; hollow-cheeked men who had been to Siberia or who were likely to be sent there and in whose eyes burned the light of fanaticism as they spoke in low hoarse voices of their plans for a new Russia.

Last night he had been at such a meeting. The man who was addressing them had been sent to Siberia for distributing the revolutionary paper *Liberation*, printed in Germany and written by those Russians who had been exiled for their political activities. As this man Kornilov talked, the cellar became still and tense. Glancing about him, Alex saw the fervour on the faces gathered under the candlelight. The speaker was making Alex uneasy; he was haranguing his audience on the need to kill and bomb. 'To cleanse with the bomb' as he put it. Alex was a radical in outlook but now he realized he was no revolutionary. All he wanted was an end to autocracy on

134

the part of the Emperor and the beginning of parliamentary government: the *Duma* that liberals had been urging for some time. He had no desire to kill his Emperor or even replace him with a president. He simply wanted the people to have a hand in government, for Russia to become a democracy. Was it an impossible dream and did all these people sitting in this cellar want more drastic change? The speaker seemed to think so.

As he listened, he became more uneasy and indignant. Glancing casually to his left he caught the eye of a young man of about his own age. Funny: he hadn't noticed him at these meetings before and he knew most people there. From the man's expression it was obvious he was thinking much the same as Alex and now he shrugged expressively in his direction as if to say, 'Really, what next!' At the end of the meeting, he strolled up and said in a confidential tone: 'We have too many hotheads in the movement. Do you know who they all are?'

'No, I don't,' Alex said bluntly. Even if he had known the so-called 'hotheads' he would not have divulged their names to a total stranger. 'We haven't met before, have we?'

The other held his hand out in an open fashion. 'I'm Valerian Andreyevitch Netchaev.'

'Alexander Petrovitch Drusov.' Alex shook the proffered hand.

'Drusov?' Netchaev raised his brows knowingly.

Alex looked at him with a new alertness. Was this someone who knew him by his real name? Drusov was the name of his mother's family which he used at the university without his title. 'Yes, Drusov,' he repeated firmly and turned away. The man was altogether too friendly. Alex knew that spies from the Tsar's secret police, the dreaded *Okhrana* were all over Petersburg, disguised and unexpected. *Beware your best friend* was the cynical joke of the moment. He saw that Netchaev was now talking smilingly to other people. Alex noticed that there was a lighter patch of skin on his upper lip as if he had recently shaved off a moustache. Netchaev had very fair hair but the roots were dark. In the lamplight it looked very obvious – or was it a trick of the light? All his suspicious instincts were aroused by this man's over-friendly approach to his fellow rebels. Getting up, Alex slipped away.

6

The man, Netchaev, was aware that his quarry had gone: he had seen him slip into the shadows out of the corner of his eye, those eyes that had been highly trained in such work. Presently he left himself. His next call was to a house on the Mohovaya, the headquarters of the *Okhrana*. It was late but lights still burned from every window for here no one ever slept. Here dwelled the thousand eyes and ears belonging to the Tsar and deemed necessary for the confounding of his enemies.

Sending his name up, he was admitted to see General Boris Igorovitch Davidov, a thickset man with an eye-patch who sat behind a large desk.

'Ah, Netchaev, what news?'

Netchaev sat down without being asked and helped himself to a cigarette from a silver box within reach. He knew the worth of the information he was bringing Davidov. Lighting his cigarette, he puffed out a cloud of smoke. 'He's there.'

The general looked down at the papers in front of him. Confound the man! He was behaving as if the place belonged to him! He'd given himself away too much and

Netchaev had guessed the rest; he was no fool. 'That was all I wanted to know,' he said stiffly. 'Now, your next assignment – '

'I spoke to him. Don't you want to hear?'

Davidov controlled himself with an effort but under the desk his hands formed into fists. 'Well?'

'Calls himself Drusov.'

Davidov nodded. 'I see.' That had been *her* name before she married. What on earth was she about to allow the boy to get into the company of revolutionaries?

'Seems a nice chap,' Netchaev observed casually. 'His face reminds me of someone. I can't think – yes, general, I know! He's like *you*.'

The general rose. 'Thank you. I'll let you know if I follow this up. You've been helpful, Valerian Andreyevitch, and I'm pleased.'

After the man had been shown out, General Davidov sat for a long time doing nothing, staring ahead. But his mind was busy. So, Prince Alexander Rakov called himself by his mother's name at the university: plain Alexander Petrovitch Drusov. *His* son. Not Peter Rakov's heir but his, Davidov's son! Born of a wild affair when he was a young officer and Countess Natalia Drusova was the prettiest girl in St Petersburg and engaged to marry Rakov; an arranged marriage, of course. She had been rebelliously against it and for a time they had contemplated eloping but he had thought about his career in time. They had quarrelled bitterly then and she had married Rakov: the child had been born 'prematurely' but he had known all along it was his, only he had been too afraid and weak and young to acknowledge it even to himself. Perhaps that was what had changed him into the man he was now: known for his hardness and cruelty to those enemies of the Tsar whom he crushed daily under his foot. He gave a short, harsh laugh. God! How odd

137

life was! He couldn't see the young fool, his own flesh and blood, clapped into the Fortress of St Peter and St Paul! God knew he'd sent a good many people there – fools who thought that by subversion they could overthrow the Autocracy.

I'll have to do something, the general thought, stabbing the blotting pad with his sharp paperknife. I must warn him off somehow before he gets picked up by someone else in the secret police. I can't protect him then.

He got up and strolled to the uncurtained window. He didn't see the lights winking all over the city but a boy's face shown him in a photograph some days ago. It was that of himself when young. Netchaev had guessed at it; how many others would see and recognize the uncanny likeness?

7

Having bathed and changed without Henri's help, Alex took his white tie in one hand and went across to his mother's rooms: this would be as good an excuse as any in order to see her, he thought.

He opened the door of her sitting room and looked round it. Eliseveta, the *dame de chambre*, was tidying the room and hustling the two poodles from their sleep by the china stove. Seeing Alex she said in her cross old voice: 'Her excellency is not available,' and continued to shoo the poodles from the room.

Alex ignored her and went across the room to another door that was half open. 'Mamma? It is I, Alex.'

The princess was seated at her dressing table having a jewelled comb fixed in her hair by her maid. She smiled at her son through the glass and said impatiently to her maid, 'Enough. It will do very well like this. Please leave us.' Then she swung round holding out her hands.

He bent and kissed them.

'Alex, dear boy. How are things at class? You are enjoying it still?'

'Very much, Mamma. The lectures are dreadfully boring so I never go, I'm afraid. But it's not necessary. One can get most things out of books.' He held up his white tie. 'Mamma, will you tie this for me, please? I don't seem to have got the hang of it and have ruined at least six in the attempt.'

'With pleasure, of course, but where is Henri? He should be available to you when he has finished attending the prince.'

Alex squinted down at his mother's face just below his chin. 'I forgot. As you've been at Court you may not know that Father is away.'

She stepped back. 'Away? And without Henri?'

'Well, he sometimes does that,' Alex said, embarrassed. 'The thing is, Henri is becoming worried. He says it's unlike Father to stay away so long without him to see to his linen.'

The princess had quickly recovered herself. She completed a perfect bow, patted it and went to sit in a pink velvet chair, motioning him to sit near. 'I daresay he's at Tatarskino for a fox shoot.'

'No, he isn't. The factor called yesterday with the rents but I couldn't tell him where he might find Father.'

'Then I daresay he is staying with friends.' She smiled composedly into his face. 'And he probably has a change of linen there.'

'But where, Mamma?'

She was silent for a moment or two. Then looking up she smiled at him. 'You are quite old enough to know the

139

truth, I think. Your father has a mistress whom he keeps in an apartment in the Vassilyhov district.'

He stared. She seemed totally undisturbed by the information she was giving him. 'You don't mind?'

'No longer. The prince and I live separate lives now. Once I did mind; but that was long ago.'

He thought of himself and Anastasia Barinskaya. That was what she had said when he first heard of her unhappy marriage: *we live separate lives*. But his parents were quite old! Surely they ought to have overcome their differences by now? He felt deeply resentful that his father should continue to behave like a young buck and probably bring disgrace on them all. He got up. 'Thank you for telling me, Mamma.' Smiling at her, he added: 'We shall meet at dinner shortly. Have we guests tonight?'

'The Gusevs and, I believe, your Aunt Nada without your uncle. He has the gout.'

He nodded and shut the door. In his rooms Henri was still hovering, pretending to brush Alex's discarded clothes but keeping one eye on the door. His expression said clearly: Well, what have you to tell me?

'I shouldn't worry about the prince,' Alex said carelessly but secretly moved by the worry on the man's face. 'The princess assures me he will be back in a day or two.'

Henri's face cleared. 'Oh, if her excellency *knows* where his excellency is then I am quite satisfied. There are so many of these dreadful revolutionaries about nowadays that members of the nobility are no longer safe.' Smiling again, he took up an armful of linen and went away.

7

Company Orphan

1

All that day and the next, Katya sat by her mother's bed.
The doctor came and went, saying little. There were no
friends to call on them bringing comfort because they
knew no one in Holyoke. The one thought that kept
Katya going, forced her to rise each morning, forced her
to brush her hair, to eat and drink and to sit helplessly
waiting hour after hour by Marie's bedside was the
thought that soon her father would be here. *Hull Lady*
was modern and equipped with wireless telegraph so by
now he would know the terrible news, the mate would
have taken over and he'd be on his way home from
Hamburg overland to Rotterdam and then Hull. She
prayed he would be in time.

But Marie died on the second night, about two o'clock.
Katya was dozing in a chair by the fire. A coal slipped
and startled her to wakefulness. Stooping, she pushed it
back and added a couple more pieces to the dull-burning
fire. Then she straightened and went across to the bed.
She knew at once what had happened for the figure in
the bed was no longer her mother but a waxen effigy.

She stood a long time looking at her. Never again
would she hear the deep, accented voice telling her stories
of her youth in St Petersburg; never again would she see
those sombre eyes light up as her father walked into the

room. Some instinct made her go to the window and open it: it was raining gently, hissing on the fallen leaves below. Thank God her mother had died far from the sea she dreaded so much! But it was going to be terrible breaking the news to her father when he arrived.

Later that day she telegraphed Howarth and Hawksley again. This time there was no reply. This must mean that they had no news or were still waiting to hear from her father, she told herself.

She watched the doctor sign the death certificate. 'How long have we before we must bury her?'

'A week. I'll get the undertaker to come and see you, Miss Croxley.'

She closed the door behind him and went to the kitchen to comfort Annie. All that day she watched the road for the station fly. Only the undertaker came. That night she slept deeply, worn out by the past few days and nights when she had kept vigil by Marie's bed. She felt too stunned to cry and slept as if drugged. Waking at seven, she felt herself fall into a bottomless pit as she remembered. If only her father would come!

She trudged to the shops for provisions in the morning. 'The captain likes his vittles,' Annie reminded her as she planned steak and kidney pudding for dinner. 'Death or no death, we're all better for a warm meal inside us.'

Coming back half an hour later she prayed she would find her father waiting for her. How she longed for his arms about her! She could cry then, relax.

But there was no one but Annie. No message. Nothing.

She tried to eat the steak pie but it stuck in her throat. She sipped some water, and, leaving the table, sat huddled over the fire. How long she sat she didn't know but suddenly she became aware of wheels on the gravelled drive, and there was the station fly turning in at the gate. He'd come! He'd come!

142

She flew into the hall and wrenched open the front door, running out in the rain in her thin slippers and with nothing over her shoulders. 'Father! Oh, Father, I – ' The words died on her lips. A stranger, a young man, was telling the cabby to wait. He had a fresh plain face, blunt-featured and strong, and he uncovered crisp curly brown hair as he removed his bowler hat.

'Miss Croxley? I'm Robert Howarth from the Hull shipping line. May I come inside?'

She nodded, her throat dry with instinctive apprehension.

2

'You'll have to go and break it to t'young lass,' Sir Abel had decreed. 'How old is she, Amos? You know all these details. You were his friend, weren't you?'

'Aye, I was. The best captain we had.' Stuttle pulled his beard as he thought. 'T'lass will be nobbit sixteen or seventeen. The only child, too.'

'Well, Robert'll go – '

'I can't do it, Father!' Robert cried in alarm. Then he looked at his father's grey face and was ashamed. The terrible accident to *Hull Lady* had been a ghastly shock to them all but most of all to his father. He had put everything into this new boat: the best captain, the best crew, every modern device available. And the whole lot had perished when they were run down in thick fog – a thousand to one chance.

'Best go tomorrow morning, lad,' his father said heavily. 'The poor bairn might hear the news in some other way and I wouldn't like that to happen with the mother just dead.' He heaved a sigh. 'Of all the bloody luck,' he muttered. '*Hull Lady* – the best boat in the German Ocean – going down like a bloody stone – '

And so Robert, dreading the task before him, set off at first light for Holyoke in a cold train that halted at every village it passed. He came prepared to meet a tear-stained schoolgirl with her hair in pigtails, talking in broad Yorkshire like her father. The appearance of Miss Katherine Croxley rendered him speechless for a minute or two. The slim, pale young woman was beautiful. She had eyes like a hunted doe's and full pink lips. Her abundant hair was inclined to curl and fell in untidy tendrils round her face as she stood in the rain staring dazedly at him.

Oh, God, what can I say to soften the blow? the young man asked himself helplessly as he gazed into her agonized face. 'Come inside. It's raining,' he said in a low voice and put a hand on her arm. He could feel the apprehensive shivers racking her body but she controlled herself and walked ahead of him into a cold little room that a dreary fire was doing nothing to warm.

Her hands tightly clasped in front of her, she whispered: 'Tell me quickly, please. Has something happened to Father?'

He told her quickly, taking her icy hands in his own strong warm grasp as he did so. For a moment, he thought she was going to faint; she swayed and his hands slid quickly up to grasp her arms. A greenness underlay the natural pallor of her face but taking one or two quick breaths she composed herself. Tears glistened but didn't fall.

'So he never knew . . . Thank God, he didn't know about my mother!'

'No. When we tried to contact *Hull Lady* by wireless telegraph we couldn't make contact. She had already sunk. It was a collision in fog, you see, and in the dark. There were no survivors.'

144

She turned swiftly away and put her hands to her face. She stood very still and he could hear the harsh breath in her throat as she realized the full horror of what had happened at sea and in blackness. 'Oh . . . Father . . .' she muttered to herself, thinking of that vigorous ruddy-faced man defeated by the sea at last. As if her legs could no longer support her, she sank down and buried her face in a red velvet button-backed chair. Perhaps it had been his chair, Robert thought, as he watched in helpless pity. 'Father, I needed you so much!' she cried and beat the chair with her fists. Suddenly the tears came and overwhelmed her in a great gust of weeping.

Robert continued to watch helplessly. If only his father or Amos Stuttle were here! He was too young to comfort her, too shy to put an arm round her as an older man could have done. He felt angry and bitter at a Providence that allowed good men like Croxley and Matt Humble, the mate, and all the other good fellows who made up the crew of *Hull Lady* to go to the bottom of the German Ocean. They were so near home, too! She was right to be angry, to beat those cushions.

She fumbled for a handkerchief in her waistband, mopped her eyes and looked up at him. 'I don't know what to do,' she said helplessly.

He raised her and helped her to a chair. 'Leave everything to me. I shall stay at the inn near the station and see to everything for you. Don't worry about money, please, my father is seeing to all that.'

She liked his deep, steady voice and his kind plain face. Exhausted with grief, she was thankful to leave everything to him.

3

The day they buried Marie it was dark and bitterly cold, the sky heavy with snow. Sleet cut their faces as they stood on the hillside and the vicar intoned the burial service hurriedly in his light thin voice. Katya could feel nothing as she stood with Robert's arm supporting her and Annie weeping noisily on the other side. She couldn't help contrasting this bleak service here in the country Marie had never come to love with the richness and colour of the Russian Orthodox Church in which she had been brought up in St Petersburg. Did she know? If she did, would she care?

The vicar paused and looked at Katya and Robert bent and put a lump of frozen soil in her gloved hand. She let it fall gently on the coffin. 'Goodbye.' Her lips were stiff.

It was over. Robert led her back to the hired carriage that had brought the four of them up this hillside. He could still find no words of comfort but as they waited for Annie and the little clergyman to rejoin them, he held her hand tightly in his.

She was glad he didn't try to make conversation. She was drained of words as if the waters of life had run out of her. Going up to her room, she closed the door and flung herself face down on the bed. No tears came, only a fierce anger. Why? Why *both*? Why had she been abandoned by them both and left to face life alone?

Her thoughts were quite without logic; primitive despair held her in its grip. Had it really been worthwhile for her mother to give up so much for love? Remembering the passionate love shared by her parents, she knew that Marie had found it all worthwhile. And they had gone together so neither would ever know the pain of losing the other . . .

She sat up, comforted by this thought: Marie Nicolaievna Urosova was at peace at last.

An hour later, coming downstairs outwardly composed, she found Annie making up the fire in the living room. The remains of tea were on the table.

'Yes, he's gone. Told me not to fetch you. He's a nice lad, that one. I don't know what we'd have done without him. You're looking starved, Miss Katya. Come and sit by this fire, lovey, and I'll fetch you something nice.'

Katya held out her hands to the blaze aware of a sinking in her stomach. He'd gone. Her support for the past four days. Now she would have to turn to and face reality again. This very day. As soon as she had had tea. There were letters to be written and her precarious finances to be gone into. She couldn't tell Annie yet but she would have to let the house go in the New Year. And of course there was no possibility of returning to college at Harrogate. She would have to find a job.

Annie pulled at her sleeve. 'He said to give you this. It's your papa's pay cheque but they've made it out to you, he said.'

She opened the envelope and found the Howarth and Hawksley cheque for thirty pounds. There was also a short message on a piece of paper. *I shall be back.*

4

The week that followed was one of the most difficult of her life. She had become seventeen a month ago and was a woman and no longer a child, she reminded herself. She must stand on her own feet now and not be so easily

147

daunted. But it was terribly difficult with so much to decide and no one to advise her. It was snowing outside and a bitter wind whirled the snow into deep drifts. She sat at her mother's desk in the bay window trying to go through papers, but her feet were like lumps of ice and her brain refused to work. Annie had told her that morning that coal stocks were low and they'd soon be without any as horses couldn't get up the hill. So she had gone into the garden and sawn up a fallen branch into neat pieces that Annie was now drying out on the stove. But even when horses could get up the hill again, would she be able to afford coal?

There was no will for Marie had had nothing to leave except two gold icons, a little gold watch and chain and an old-fashioned pearl brooch. Robert Howarth had promised to let her have all details of her father's affairs when they were settled. There was a little money in the bank and the funeral to be paid for, but there were no other bills. Robert explained in his letter that she would have to take out letters of administration and he would show her how to set about it.

Drawing a sheet of paper towards her, she wrote to her tutor explaining why she would not be returning to the training college. She sighed to herself as she licked the envelope: at Harrogate she had felt young and carefree for the first time in her life. But that there was very little money and an unknown future was now certain. Her father, always openhanded and generous, had saved nothing. He had enjoyed life and had never contemplated an early death. Well, poor Annie would have to find another place and she herself would have to find a job of some sort. She took up her pen again and wrote to her grandfather in St Petersburg to tell him of Marie's death. She was never to receive a reply for Nicolai Mironovitch Urosov had died.

As Katya finished her letters, the door burst open and Annie entered, flapping her apron in agitation.

'Eh, Miss Katya, the butcher's just been with the silverside and he says there's terrible news!'

Katya's heart gave a nervous jump: what more terrible news could there be?

'We've lost to them Boers! They're calling it Black Week in't paper. See here – eh, the old Queen'll feel this, I'll tell you.'

She took the proffered newspaper, wet with the snow, and stared at the black type with a frown of dismay. Far from winning the war in a couple of weeks as had been confidently predicted, British troops had lost three battles in a row. The names Magersfontein, Stormberg and Tigela River leapt off the page. Here, thousands of British soldiers had been resoundingly beaten by bands of farmers calling themselves *commandos* who fought in a totally unorthodox way and who were deadly shots. The proud Highland Division had been cut to pieces and there was universal mourning in Scotland.

Remembering some of the young soldiers in the Yeomanry who had mustered in Harrogate in October, Katya looked at Annie in dismay. Defeat and disillusionment were facing the nation it seemed.

5

'No, Pater, I couldn't do it,' Robert said decidedly. 'If you think a girl like that would accept charity from me you're wrong – '

'From the firm, lad, from the firm!'

'She won't see it like that. I'm too near her age to offer it her. Send someone else.'

'He's right, Abel,' Lady Howarth interposed, looking up from her embroidery. 'Any girl of pride would be affronted to receive financial aid through someone of her own age. It's not at all suitable. Get that Mr Moyes of yours to send a letter on behalf of the company and that'll give her time to think it over.'

'An excellent idea of yours, Alice,' said the fourth member of the party sitting in the drawing room after dinner. Sir Abel's sister was also doing a little genteel embroidery. She was known by everyone as Auntie Polly and had spent every Christmas with them since old Abraham Howarth, her father and Abel's, had died.

Now her brother turned irritably on her (a week into her bi-annual visit Sir Abel's liverishness became pronounced). 'Who asked you to put your two pennorth in, Auntie Polly? This is nowt to do wi' you – *nowt*.'

Auntie Polly drew in her chin repressively and little lines tucked up her mouth. If Father was alive he'd not let Abel talk to me like that, she told herself tearfully. Most nights she retired to bed in tears after 'words' or imagined slights.

Lady Howarth shook her head at her husband and bent over her frame again. Her mind was working fast. She had caught the look on her son's face as they discussed the orphaned Katherine Croxley; he had looked tender and self-conscious suddenly. *He's fallen in love with that girl – now, that would be the answer*! Yes, she told herself as she made rapid plans, Robert should marry the girl, and give her and Abel some longed-for grandchildren.

She revealed this brilliant idea to her husband as he struggled into his flannel nightshirt that night.

He turned on her, his sparse hair on end. 'Marry that half-Russian girl? Good God, woman, have you taken leave of your senses? The girl's a nobody. Oh, aye, pretty

150

enough and no doubt he's taken with her but that's not the daughter-in-law I want – not by a long chalk!'

'Oh? So you've decided who our Robert's to marry, have you?'

'Certainly I have. We've got a place and money and the title. One of Crochester's girls would do well to have him.'

Alice Howarth burst out laughing. 'Why, Abel, you old snob! Those girls of Lord Crochester's wouldn't look at the boy – not unless they were fat, forty and desperate, which they aren't. You're flying too high, m'dear, they'll never marry into *trade*.'

Sir Abel hated being laughed at even in the privacy of their bedroom. 'Well, I won't have him marrying that girl of Croxley's. I liked Croxley, he was the best. But the girl – she's an unknown quantity.' He continued to mutter huffily under his breath as he kicked off his slippers and climbed into the high four-poster bed.

'Nonsense! I'm all for a bit of fresh blood in the family,' his wife retorted.

'Don't be a fool, woman!'

'You're the fool,' Alice said firmly. 'I thought you had a steadier head, Abel Howarth! Have you forgotten I was only the cobbler's daughter when you got sweet on me? That my old dad liked a drop too much? That my sister Winnie got into trouble before she was seventeen? You've been a good husband, Abe, and you've never said a wrong word to me about my family although you did have to keep the lot of them for years. You married me despite *your* old dad, and he never forgave me for it, but if you think Lord Crochester would even begin to consider us a suitable family for one of his girls to marry into then you're doddering.' She slapped cold cream on her face and rubbed it in as if applying polish to old furniture.

151

Sir Abel groaned and lay back on his pillows. 'All this comes about just because our Rob suggested making the girl a company orphan! You know she's too old for that – we only look after them to sixteen – but no, he would have his way and now we're going to pay for a college education for the girl until she's nineteen. I dunno. We're setting a precedent and it's going to cost us a fortune, just you see if it doesn't.' He ruminated in silence for a few moments broken only by the vigorous sound of his wife's nightly toilet. Then he heaved a sigh. 'But the lass'll starve if we don't see to her – someone's got to do summat, Allie.'

By his slipshod speech, Alice knew he was deeply concerned for the unknown Croxley girl. Climbing into bed, she kissed the bald patch in the centre of his scalp. 'You're doing the right thing, my dear, like I knew you would. But don't let our Rob be the one to tell her: my guess is that she won't feel like accepting it from him.'

Mollified, Sir Abel grunted: Yes, he thought he was doing the right thing, too. He had been very fond of his senior captain, Harry Croxley.

6

'A company orphan?' Katya repeated. 'What does that mean exactly?'

Mr Moyes, a precise little man who looked like a worried mouse, proceeded to explain. Howarth and Hawksley, being good employers, considered it their duty to care for the fatherless children of dead employees until they were sixteen. In her case, they were making an exception and were willing to pay for her education until she was nineteen.

'You mean, I can go back to college?' Her eyes lit up. 'But that's a wonderful piece of news, Mr Moyes! I'm very grateful to the company. How many company orphans have you got?'

'Forty-one since the loss of the *Hull Lady*.' The little man sighed as he took off his glasses and polished them. 'A bad business that. Our best captain and crew and a brand new boat. Your father was a fine man, Miss Croxley, and everyone liked him. We shall miss him sorely.'

Her eyes filled with tears and she bent her head. 'Thank you,' she said in a muffled voice.

He decided to be brisk. 'This house is rented? Then you must let it go and sell the furniture. We usually arrange hospitality for our orphans in the holidays. Friends of the company take them in.'

'Oh.' She tried to hide her dismay at the idea of spending the next two years being a cuckoo in other people's nests.

'You may not like the idea at present, my dear young lady,' Mr Moyes said kindly, 'but we shall endeavour to send you to – er – suitable people.'

She attempted to smile. 'Yes. It's very kind. And it is only for two years, I know.' But she felt afraid. She was no longer in charge of herself. She was company property and would be sent where the company decided was best for her.

Mr Moyes, who had a daughter of his own, patted her shoulder as he rose to go. 'Don't worry, my dear. It's going to be all right.'

As she shook his hand, Katya said impulsively: 'I feel I owe a great deal of this to Mr Robert Howarth. Please thank him most sincerely for me, Mr Moyes.'

'Certainly, my dear young lady, if you wish. But why not write to him yourself? He would appreciate it, I think,' and he gave her a surprisingly roguish smile.

'Well, I will.' Katya smiled. 'I'll do it at once.'

153

8

Head of the Family

1

Rattling across the frozen Neva in the overcrowded tram, Alex clung to a strap and wondered if his father would have returned home yet. He had been gone almost a week and there were only two weeks to Christmas. He had been to the last classes of the term and for five weeks could enjoy all the skating and tobogganing down the snowhills he could fit in. They might even go to Tatarskino for a week's shooting, he thought as he jumped off the slowing tram and crossed the road.

It was very dark and a fog hung about the quays so that the street lamps looked like balloons floating into the distance. He turned up the collar of his coat and hurried along Nevsky Prospekt with its brilliantly lighted shops to turn down into Catherine Canal where he lived.

Timotei, the old doorman, was strangely unresponsive as they exchanged greetings and the butler took his coat and outdoor boots with a low bow. 'Her excellency wishes to see you at once,' he said, summoning a footman to take the garments.

Alex looked up sharply. Something had happened. It was heavy in the air like a smell. He went across the echoing hall and up the marble staircase to the small yellow salon that was always in use in winter when they were *en famille*.

She was standing facing the door, her hands clasped in front of her. 'Oh, Alex, I'm so glad you've come! Didn't they give you my message? I sent word at four o'clock that I wanted you back home.'

He kissed her. 'I'm sorry, Mother, it will have been my own fault. I skipped a lecture and went out to a coffee shop with a group of friends.'

'Talking politics, no doubt,' she couldn't resist saying. Then she bit her lip. 'I have bad news, my dear. Your father.'

He felt a shock in the pit of his stomach. 'Is he – has he been found?'

'He's dead. He was found this morning in Madame Clèmont's apartment. She too was dead. They had been dead some time, I'm afraid.'

'Oh, Mother!' He took her icy hands in his, knowing full well what this would have done to her pride. Now the whole world would know that the prince had led a double life. The Princess Rakova was known for her stiffly unbending moral attitude which was a reflection of her royal mistress's. 'Mother, you mustn't mind,' he muttered. 'We must just show the world a united front.'

'You're right, Alex, but it won't be easy.'

'How did they die? Did he – '

'No, thank God. Madame Clèmont had a small revolver in her hand. She had shot him in the back of the neck and then shot herself in the mouth.'

He felt sweat break out on his face. 'My God, how awful! But why?'

She shrugged, turning away. 'Perhaps he was tired of her . . . who knows? There could have been someone else – someone new, I mean.' There was no bitterness in her voice. Peter Rakov's love life was an old story to her. Already she was recovering the composure that seldom left her for long.

He rang a bell. 'You must have some brandy, Mother, then we will discuss the whole thing.'

'Yes, I'm a little worried, you know. *They* are sensitive to every rumour and I don't want to lose my place at Court.'

He knew that she referred to the Imperial Family; it wasn't long since she had gone into waiting on the young Empress as one of her older ladies-in-waiting after serving the Empress Marie for years. The young family with children arriving every year were now her life and it would break her heart to be dismissed. What a selfish fellow his father had been! Why hadn't he thought of his family before embarking on this disastrous affair with the hysterical French woman? 'People forget these things very quickly,' he reassured her. '*They* will realize you know nothing about it.'

She accepted a small glass of brandy and sipped it thoughtfully. 'Feo,' she said suddenly. 'We must send for your brother Feo.'

'I'll ask his commanding officer to send him home at once. Leave all that to me, Mother.'

She looked up quickly, realizing that imperceptibly he had stepped into the shoes of the head of the household. 'And the police want you to identify the body, Alex. Perhaps you had better go at once.'

He drained his glass. 'No, we must dine first. I'll go and bath now and order the carriage for nine-thirty. A message must be sent at once to Tatarskino: our house flag must be flown at half-mast.'

She nodded, pleased that he was proving himself fit to follow his father as the most prominent landowner in their province. There were certain things to be done and instinctively he was doing them. Before dinner, he summoned the senior servants to the library and told

156

them their master was dead and he hoped they would go on serving him as well as they had done the late prince.

But before that he had turned to her and said frankly: 'I hope you will continue to make your home here with me and Feo, Mother. I have no thought of marriage yet.'

'And when you do, I will make my home elsewhere,' she assured him with a wry smile. 'You see, I remember vividly playing second fiddle to Grandmother Rakova in this house! I see it daily at Court: there is resentment between the two Empresses. Human nature is the same whether you are placed high or low, Alex!'

He agreed. 'Now I must go and see Henri.'

He found the valet standing by his late master's bed. He was still as a statue, his face ravaged. Only his eyes moved as Alex came in and tears began to roll down his grey cheeks as his new master put a hand on his arm and said gently: 'Henri?'

The man's voice was broken as he mumbled: 'Nearly thirty years I served him. He was just a boy of seventeen home from the Corps de Pages – so handsome – so wilful. He was always the same – ' Tears choked him.

'Come, Henri, old friend, don't cry. He is at peace now. You served him well and loyally all those years. No one knew him so well, I think. If he cared for anyone it was for you.'

The valet wiped his eyes. 'Your excellency is right. I was almost a father to him.'

'Better than a father,' Alex said with a slight smile. 'What father would have waited up for him night after night for years? I don't believe you ever went to bed before him, did you, Henri?'

'Never once, sir. I used to scold him, you know, and he allowed me to do so because he knew I cared for him with all my heart.'

'Will you stay and look after me?'

157

Henri stared at him. 'Your excellency means that? I have always thought you would need a younger man, one of your own generation.'

'Not I. You've looked after me from time to time in the past and I think we shall get on. You always say my clothes are a disgrace – well, now I'm head of the family you must help me change my ways!'

The man bowed his head. 'While I have the health and strength, your excellency, I shall look after you as I did your dear father.'

So, Alex thought as he went to his rooms, I have lost my freedom for good. I am Prince Rakov now and all these people, here and at Tatarskino, are my responsibility in the years ahead.

For a moment, the thought oppressed him. Then he straightened, opened the door of his room and went in.

2

The black hearse bearing the remains of Prince Peter Rakov made its way very slowly over Palace Bridge from Vassili Island. The four black horses wore black plumes that swayed and tossed with the motion and with the bitter snow-laden wind sweeping across the Neva. Behind the hearse in a carriage with its blinds down rode his two sons, Prince Alexander and Prince Feodor. They were bringing the body home to lie in state before the long rail journey for burial in Tatarskino. The ballroom of the family home on the Catherine Canal had been prepared for the five days' lying-in-state which would begin that evening and three priests were already waiting to receive the coffin.

Old men shovelling snow into great heaps to be melted

by bonfires paused and leaned on their shovels to watch the cortège pass. As they stared, they crossed themselves. One said: 'Is that the prince whose sweetheart shot him? Poor devil. You can't trust a woman, that's what I always say.'

Smartly-dressed people in Nevsky Prospekt turned their heads away hurriedly. So Peter Rakov had got his deserts at last, they thought with self-satisfied malice.

'I must say, Father seems to have been an absolute fool to trust that creature,' young Feo was saying loftily to his brother as they passed down Nevsky Prospekt. 'A mere tart from Paris – what was he about?'

'The same as you with Daria Kvitkova, I suppose,' Alex said, his expression hardening as he glanced at the soft and handsome features of his younger brother, the young officer of Hussars.

The boy's face reddened. 'What the hell do you know about that?'

'Only that she was beaten and forced into premature labour for letting you lie in her arms! All right, it's over and done with and you were only a child yourself. But do think of the consequences, Feo, before you ruin another girl's life.'

Feo fell into sulky silence. He and Alex seldom met and when they did, they could not agree. Smarting under the rebuke he had just received he muttered: 'You prig!'

Alex pretended not to hear. The carriage stopped: they had brought Peter Rakov home for the last time. They got down, stiff with cold, and slowly followed the coffin into the house. Old Timotei, tears running into his beard, made the sign of the cross as they passed him. In the brilliantly lighted hall stood Natalia Rakova dressed in black with a long black veil over her head and face. The priests came forward, one in front, two others following him. The family fell in behind them and processed slowly

159

into the ballroom which had been hung with black crêpe and filled with tall white lilies and flickering candles. The footmen closed the tall double doors and the brief service began.

Standing close by his mother's side, Alex glanced briefly at her. But not a muscle moved in her impassive face, not the glimmer of a tear dimmed her eyes. It was too late for her to feel love and regret for the husband who had never really been hers.

3

The scandal of Prince Rakov's murder at the hands of his mistress and the subsequent enquiry had rocked St Petersburg society for the past week.

Anastasia Nicolaievna Barinskaya was on her first visit home from the United States of America. Everything was sadly changed now that her father was dead. He had been the one stable influence in her life and it had been a frightful blow that he had died before she could – at last – unburden herself on the subject of her marriage. It had been young Rakov who had urged her to seek asylum with her father, but poor Papasha hadn't even known her when at last she reached his side. It had proved impossible to tell Laura because Sergei had been too watchful.

Somehow it had leaked out in St Petersburg society that the Barinsky marriage was in trouble but no one was surprised: what could be expected of such an unequal marriage? Only a timber merchant's daughter – besides, Sergei was known everywhere for his womanizing. It served the little countess right: she should never have aimed so high. These people ought to learn to keep to their own class . . .

Now that her father was dead and the old home sold, Anastasia had nowhere to go but to Laura in the Grand Duke's house in Tsarskoe Selo. She didn't like it but beggars could not be choosers, she told herself bitterly. The money her father had left her had gone straight into Sergei Barinsky's pocket as was his right.

The two sisters were preparing to go to the lying-in-state of Prince Rakov. Neither woman had known the prince well, but Laura had met the princess when she was at the Alexander Palace at Tsarskoe Selo and Anastasia considered herself a close friend of the son.

'We nearly had an *affaire* in Paris,' she confessed, tilting her velvet tricorne a little further over one eye.

'My God, weren't you taking a risk?' Laura swung round on her dressing stool where she was passing *papier poudre* over her rouged cheeks.

'It came to nothing. Sergei couldn't have proved a thing.' There was a defiant look on Stana's face as she faced her sister. 'But it might have been worth it, Laura! The daily unhappiness I endure! The endless empty nights! I'm not old but I'm forced to lead the life of a widow through no fault of my own!'

'No? He's always known you've never loved him, my dear.'

'Love? Sergei doesn't know the meaning of the word! Oh, Laura, what am I to do? Must I go back to Washington? Can't I make the break with Sergei? Heaven knows I have enough evidence of his adultery with several women!'

'But you know it wouldn't work,' Laura said forcefully, alarmed to see that her sister was in earnest. 'What could be proved? Only that he had slept with other women but most men do and if their wives are wise they pretend not to know it. After all, the status of being Sergei's wife should surely count for a great deal. You would dislike being a divorcée very much, my child.' She looked rather hopelessly at her sister who seemed to have a genius for running into trouble. 'You see, divorce places you in a terribly difficult position and Sergei might well be dismissed the service. Then where would you both be? Father left us both much less money than we expected and you and Sergei have only the settlement to fall back on.. You'd have years to face on your own and after all you're only twenty-five.'

Anastasia had gone to stand by one of the windows overlooking the road. Just down there were the gates to the beautiful little Alexander Palace where the Imperial Family had gone into almost permanent residence in this, the Tsar's own village. 'Yes, only twenty-five!' she repeated bitterly, 'and I've no happiness to look back on. Why did you encourage the marriage? He's years older than I am and he's getting fat and I hate him!'

This was a real crisis. Laura unpinned her hat, put it carefully down and went across to her sister. Taking her cold hands in hers, she shook them. 'Now, Stana, pull yourself together! Why must you be so impulsive? You're just like Marie was. You'll ruin your life if you aren't careful. Please be sensible and go back to Washington and behave as if you haven't a care in the world. Enjoy yourself. Take a lover – Sergei will turn a blind eye, you'll see. In fact, he'll begin to respect you when he sees you standing on your own feet. Besides, he's getting old – '

'You mean he'll die soon?'

Laura closed her eyes in despair. Really, there were some things better left unsaid: didn't Stana understand that? She jammed her hat on, stabbed it with a long hat pin and picked up her furs. 'The carriage has been waiting quite ten minutes to take us to the station so do come along.'

162

Anastasia wiped her eyes and blew her nose, shrugging into her long sable coat. What was the use? Someone like Laura with a satisfactory lover had no idea of the frustration of being locked in a loveless marriage. Of course she would have to return to Washington as she had feared from the beginning, sailing from a French port because Russia was icebound. A searing wave of homesickness swept her at the thought.

'Anastasia! Do come along.'

'Yes, I'm coming.' She wiped the expression of despair from her face as she had learned to do and replaced it with the social expression with which she faced the world. It was still on her face when she shook hands with Princess Rakov and turned to greet her elder son. He thought that the little countess was looking simply splendid and his eyes told her so.

4

Spring was early in England that year. Katya, who was in the college hockey team, found the exercise and the clear air of Harrogate suited her very well: she had never looked better than she did one day in March as she ran off the field after a match and saw a familiar thickset figure in an ulster and a tweed hat standing on the edge of the field looking at her. Catching her eye, he raised his hat. He was waiting for her when she emerged after changing.

'Miss Croxley, I've come to take you out to tea.'

She shook hands. 'That's very kind, Mr Howarth, but I'm afraid it's not allowed.'

'Oh, but it is! I've seen your Miss Richards and

obtained permission. A Miss Sarah-Jane Hollis is to accompany us.'

And there was Sarah-Jane smiling like a plump pussycat at the prospect of tea in the White Swan. Another surprise awaited them: Mr Howarth was the proud possessor of a motor! The girls gasped and tried to look nonchalant as he handed them into his yellow and black machine: neither had ever ridden in a motor before. He gave them chiffon scarves to tie round their hats and under their chins and they were away. The two girls clung to each other as they plunged down a hill into the town, but both were aware that they were being looked at enviously by other members of the college and assumed haughty expressions as they careered past.

'Did you see the envious look Paula Hodges and Lily Baker gave us?' Sarah-Jane muttered.

The engine made so much noise that Katya couldn't make out what she had said.

'Hold on to your hats, girls!' yelled Robert. 'I'm going to let her rip!'

Fifteen miles an hour! Both shut their eyes in delicious agony as the motor tore down the straight road as Robert showed off.

Tea at the White Swan, eaten in front of a large log fire, was everything two hungry girls could wish for.

'College food is terrible,' Katya told him, eating a Sally Lunn dripping with butter. 'We use up all our money buying food to eat in our rooms.'

'My father's a farmer,' Sarah-Jane explained. 'Mother sends me a hamper every fortnight.'

Katya stared at her: so that was why Sarah-Jane Hollis had a round smooth face and an even rounder figure by the end of term! She caught Robert Howarth's eye and knew that he was thinking the same thing. Giggles seized them which they valiantly suppressed although Robert

164

choked over his tea. It forged a link between them and all Katya's shyness left her. She began to chatter quite naturally, telling him about college life and the hockey team's successes.

'What are your plans for Easter?' he asked as they stopped outside the women's hall of residence and Sarah-Jane had gone inside. 'My mother and I would very much like you to come to us for a week.' He was amazed at the relief and delight that crossed her face.

'Oh, I'd love that! I was going to spend the whole vacation with the Miss Lesleys – that's at my old school in Whitby.'

'Then my mother will write to you.' He was aware of delight himself at the prospect of a week in the company of this pretty and intelligent girl. He suspected he had fallen in love with her for now he could see her as the mother of that large family with which he intended to fill up Wentworth Park. Why hadn't he realized it before? This girl was the shadowy figure, the missing mother of those mythical children. He took her hand and held it tightly in his. 'I have enjoyed my afternoon.'

'So have I, Mr Howarth.'

They exchanged smiles, reluctant to part. It was only after he had gone in a cloud of smoke and dust that doubts began to assail her. Wentworth Park would be full of servants. There'd be a butler. Late dinner. People wearing lovely clothes. The light faded from her face. How could she possibly go to stay with a meagre wardrobe like hers? She had one day dress and a coat and skirt. For evening she had made herself a dark blue dress with long sleeves and a white muslin collar. Everyone said it was a great success but it looked home-made. She would resemble a tweeny on her day out! A little moan escaped her. It was no use: she would have to refuse the invitation when it came.

Robert brought it himself the following week and she told him firmly that she was very sorry but she would have to go to the Miss Lesleys after all. They had been expecting her and she couldn't disappoint them. In her neat clear writing she wrote back to Lady Howarth refusing the invitation.

Alice Howarth saw the disappointment on her son's face. 'I'm sorry, dear,' she said gently. 'It looks as if Miss Croxley doesn't want to become involved with us. Maybe she feels her position as a dependant of the company – whatever it is, we must respect her feelings.' She longed to give him his heart's desire but this was one thing money couldn't buy.

'I don't think it's that, Mother – honestly I don't. I'll ask her next time – '

'No, Robert, leave the girl alone. She would have come to us if she really wanted to. Let's ask some young people from Hull. Freda Jackson and her brother and the Metcalfe girl.'

Robert said dully: 'All right, Mother. Anyone you'd like.' But there was not one girl to touch Katya Croxley. He had seen her sad and gay and each mood had touched him. He loved her. Surely she would love him in return some day?

5

The Princess Rakova, dressed in half-mourning for her late husband, came out onto the balcony where her royal mistress was sitting and smiled involuntarily at the pretty sight she discovered. The Empress, heavy with her third child, sat in the early May sunshine, her red-gold hair uncovered and her feet up on the *chaise longue*. Nearby,

166

watched over by their nurses, the two little Grand Duchesses played on the rug spread out for them: Olga aged four and Tatiana just walking at two years.

The princess curtsied and came forward. 'I've brought up some of your post, Your Imperial Majesty. There is a letter from the nursing institute that Your Majesty must see.'

'Thank you, Natalia. Put it on the table.' Alix spoke languidly and the older woman looked closely at her. Alix's pretty white hands were suddenly folded protectively over her stomach. Looking up, she caught the look and laughed. 'Yes! I do believe it is starting – no! no! not yet,' she added in the same low voice as Natalia Rakova moved towards the bell. 'It will be a long time yet and it is so lovely out here.' Her glance went down into the formally laid-out garden of the Alexander Palace. 'The Emperor has a great deal on his mind,' she added. They both watched the figures in the garden: the towering figure of the Tsar's uncle, Grand Duke Nicholas, and the slight boyish figure of the Tsar himself pacing between the flower beds deep in talk. 'I'm afraid we have bad news of the Emperor's brother.'

'The Grand Duke George, Your Majesty?'

'Yes, poor George. He is at Livadia now but even that dry climate is no longer helping him. I fear he is playing a losing game.'

The princess nodded, feeling a faint amusement at the English simile used so unconsciously: *playing a losing game*. Alas, poor George had never done anything so healthy as playing a game. Burning the candle recklessly at both ends he was at the age of twenty-seven dying of a rabid tuberculosis and not all the doctors in Russia could save him now. When he died, Michael, his much younger brother, spoiled and totally unsuitable to sit on the throne, would be the Tsar's heir. Unless –

167

'This time it *must* be a boy!'

Princess Rakova turned her head quickly at the desperate tone. 'Why, of course it will be, Your Majesty! By this time tomorrow we shall all be listening to a salute of 300 rounds for the Heir!'

The rather cold grey-blue eyes warmed suddenly with hope. 'Oh, you do think so? I have been carrying this baby very low for the whole time and they do say that means a boy.' She picked up a small icon from the table at her elbow and held it fast. 'It has got to be,' she said between her teeth as a real labour pain suddenly gripped her. Sweat broke out on her forehead.

Natalia Rakova spoke sharply in Russian to the nurses who, looking up startled, hurried to collect the two children and take them indoors. Then she pressed the electric bell. 'Your Majesty, I've taken the liberty of summoning your doctors – no, lie back, relax. I found that helped in my day.'

Alix ungritted her teeth. 'Yes, and you had two sons. How I envy you! How proud you must have been. It's so unfair my sister-in-law Xenia has three boys and we – who desperately need an heir – have not one! You do think – ' Her voice faded as another pain struck. 'You do think that this time it will be a boy?'

'Yes, Your Majesty, I do.' Gently, Princess Rakova wiped the sweat off the pink skin that was inclined to freckle.

'So do I,' Alix sighed.

But next day 101 rounds from the guns sounded out all over the city telling its citizens that the Tsar and Tsarina had a third daughter.

Part Four
1904

9

The Estranging Sea

1

Perhaps Katya felt she owed the Miss Lesleys something just because Hill House had been her home each vacation. So, fully qualified as a teacher at last, she had agreed to come back to teach 'for a time'. That time had stretched to two years now and 'Miss Katherine Croxley, highly qualified, will teach the older girls' had become a proud part of the Hill House School prospectus. Because she was conscientious, doing her work well and gaining successes for her girls, the number of pupils increased each year. Now, soon, she promised herself, she would look round for a job in a state high school where the salary would be twice that paid by the Lesleys. She had fully repaid her debt to them.

As she trudged up the hill to the school one Sunday evening in November she was thinking hard. She had been out to tea – a good satisfying Yorkshire high tea – with friends of her father's in their large house overlooking the harbour and Mr Horrocks himself had taken her to task.

'Now, look here, Kate, I've got to speak my mind. Mother thinks same as I do, don't you, Mother?' He prodded his plump wife.

'Yes, yes, Kate, I think the same as Father.'

Katya smiled: did placid Mrs Horrocks ever think anything that wasn't an echo of her husband's thoughts?

'We reckon you're wasting your time up at yon place. It's dying on its feet and if it weren't for you it would have been dead long ago. Time the old ladies retired anyway. How old is Miss Lesley, Mother? Sixty if she's a day. Any day now they'll decide to close and you'll be forced to take the first job that's offered you. Now I've been a friend of your poor father's nigh on forty year – boys we were, getting up to mischief round the harbour – and I'd be failing in friendship to him, m'girl, if I didn't tell you straight: you've got to give them notice.'

Katya put her knife and fork down. 'I know you're right, Mr Horrocks, but even if I gave them notice tonight I would have to stay all next term. It's in my contract. A term's notice or I lose a term's salary. I can't afford to do that. You see, I've not been able to save anything more than a few pounds in the Friendly Society.'

'That'll take you to next Easter,' her host grunted. 'Well, do it. Give 'em notice as soon as you can and then apply for a job in a big school somewhere.'

'It's a pity you didn't marry that nice young man,' his wife interposed tactlessly. 'Plenty of money, too. You'd have been safe for life, Kate.'

How they had learned that Robert had proposed and been rejected, Katya didn't know. Perhaps because his attentions had ceased so abruptly last year when she told him that she couldn't marry him: she was not in love with him, she had said gently, not in love with anyone yet. Now, a faint flush staining her white skin, she said: 'Robert Howarth and I were only friends, Mrs Horrocks. The company paid for my training after Father died. They were very kind.'

She thought about Robert as she hurried through the damp fog up the dark tunnel of road, the street lamps swimming past like nebulae. From the harbour came the clang-clang of the swinging bell on the buoy anchored out

172

in the bay over a sunken wreck. As a child, it had made her shudder and cry, it had sounded so like a desperate call for help out there in the roaring darkness of the sea. Now, she hardly noticed it as she hurried along, coughing a little from the fog, damp tendrils of dark hair escaping from under her hat.

How funny life was, she thought. She had never dreamed that she would come back to Whitby to work. It was more than two years now and Mr Horrocks was right: it was time she moved on, broadened her outlook and saw something of life. Should she have married Robert? He had been a tower of strength to her; he had taught her to laugh and take life lightly; he had been a good friend. When one day he had turned and folded her in his arms she had been foolishly surprised: she ought to have guessed that his feelings for her were deep and serious.

'Katya, please say you'll marry me! I can't imagine life without you.' He had crushed her to him, burying his face in her hair, muttering 'Katya . . . Katya . . .'

She had struggled free, staring into his face with frightened eyes. 'Marry? You can't marry me! I'm no one. Your parents – '

'Would want me to be happy. There's never been anyone but you in my life. It will finish me if you don't marry me.' He held her pinioned in front of him, his eager, pleading eyes drinking her in thirstily. He knew her face so well: her eyes so wide, such a very deep blue, the skin pale and flushing easily, her abundant dark hair framing her oval face. Half her charm lay in the fact that she didn't consider herself beautiful or unusual in any way. She knew she looked different to most of the other girls and would laugh ruefully at her 'Russianness'. This pretty, passionate creature was trying so hard to make herself into a prim school teacher and he wouldn't have

173

it! He wouldn't allow it to happen! He wanted her to share his life and have his children, to stop struggling to make ends meet, to have pretty clothes and to laugh and sing and bring him happiness. All this he poured out as she stood with averted head waiting for him to stop.

Looking up, she met his eyes squarely: 'Robert, dear, Robert! My best friend. I had no idea. You see, I thought it was possible to have a close friendship with a man and you have been that: the closest friend and confidant I have. But I'm not in love with you. I know I *could* be very much in love with someone some day. To marry you now at twenty-one and then perhaps to meet the man I really wanted a few years later – ' She saw him wince and her eyes filled with tears; she knew she was hurting him and she had never had to do that before. 'It's no good, my dear,' she said in a low voice.

He took it well, simply because in his heart he believed he could still win her. But it was after this that she changed towards him, becoming cautious, losing her hitherto unselfconscious friendliness towards him. So they began to see less of each other until now, a year later, he had ceased to come over to Whitby to see her. She hoped and believed he had found someone else to be the future Lady Howarth. But – oh! – how she missed him! It was tragic that the only deep friendship of her life had had to be with a man who inevitably wanted it to be more.

Now she had a new admirer in Doctor Ernest Hanson whom she sat next to at the Choral Society evenings and she was beginning to fear that he was becoming serious. Mr Horrocks is right, she thought, I'm going to have to leave Whitby but for a different reason to the one he put forward. I just couldn't bear to be Mrs Hanson and not allowed to have a free thought – at least one not approved by Ernest! – in my head.

She turned sharply left and saw the tall shape of Hill

174

House looming ahead. The road was quite empty on this miserable evening and every curtain was drawn in the shadowy houses on either side. Hill House was a tall red-brick house with black-edged windows and it stood behind a hedge of variegated holly that was as thick and high as a wall. 'Good evening, miss.' A neat elderly maid opened the door to her. 'This fog, Gets right to your throat, dunnit?'

Looking round the dim cold hall, Katya asked if Miss Lesley was in.

'Yes, miss. Up in the study as usual. Miss Mabel's gone to church.'

Katya nodded. Taking up a corner of her skirt with one hand, she grasped the banister rail and went swiftly and quietly up to the first landing. The study door was ajar, a fan of dim lamplight spilling from it. Miss Lesley always kept this door open so that she might hear the comings and goings in the house. She would probably be at work on her accounts (her usual Sunday evening task) and by this time she would be convinced that ruin stared her in the face. By Monday morning she would be putting new economies in force.

Hoping her employer would be too absorbed in figures to notice her arrival, Katya stole like a ghost past the study door and up a second and narrower flight of stairs to another landing where the lamp was a size smaller and the air several degrees colder. Here the fifteen boarders slept in two long rooms and here, too, was her own little bedroom which was her home for several months of the year. It wasn't much of a room. The wallpaper was faded, its one window looked out on to the roofs and backyards of boarding houses and the plain deal furniture had lost its varnish.

She began to take the pins out of her hat. No one had been in with a can of hot water for her nor had the curtains been drawn and the room was cold. She lit the small lamp that was all she was allowed and took off her jacket, brushing it carefully before hanging it behind a curtain in the corner that served as a wardrobe. Above this was a shelf and here she kept her hats. The room was not as good as the servants' rooms in her old home; it was certainly much shabbier and colder.

She nodded laughingly at her reflection in the spotted mirror. She believed she only had to say the word to become Mrs Ernest Hanson . . . what a choice lay before her! To be at the beck and call of Miss Lesley or the wife of an overbearing bore who believed a woman's place was firmly in the kitchen and nursery.

Doctor Hanson was the local doctor, a short, square young man with decided views about women. Women were, 'in his opinion' (and how fond he was of that phrase!), only slightly superior children whose quirks and fancies could be attributed to hysteria. Women needed 'firm handling' and this was how he attempted to manage Katya, brushing aside her opinions as 'mere foolishness'. He was only physically in love with her she knew, for their minds were poles apart, and although she had told him frankly that she could never marry him, he put this down to maidenly modestly: he would soon wear her down!

She turned away and poured some icy water into the basin. She washed herself vigorously with violet soap and emerged with pink glowing cheeks and nose. As she straightened her muslin ruffles she saw her natural paleness return and remembered wryly that Ernest had once called her his 'pale lily-girl'. Drat the man! Why did she keep thinking of him all the time? She felt automatically for the little pearl brooch at her throat, consulted her watch and smoothed her hair once more. With these deft strokes, she had made herself once more the image of a sedate schoolmarm.

Turning the lamp down, she opened the door and went downstairs. At the study door she paused and took a small gulp of breath before knocking gently.

'Yes, who is it?' Miss Lesley was sitting at the roll-top desk that had belonged to her father. She was, as Katya had guessed, doing the accounts. She was a large, majestic woman with a quantity of snow-white hair piled into a cottage-loaf style and studded with strong black hairpins. She wore a grey alpaca dress with a froth of snowy lace showing round the collar, black jet earrings and brooch and a mauve shawl round her ample shoulders. Miss Lesley considered mourning colours 'suitable' for one of her age and she regretted that her sister, Miss Mabel, didn't share her views. Mabel had a taste for magenta, olive and mustard that Miss Lesley deplored.

She removed her gold-rimmed pince-nez and regarded Katya short-sightedly. 'Oh, it's you, Katherine. Did you have a nice time at Mrs Horrocks's?'

'Yes, thank you.'

The conversation seemed to dry up as it always did after Miss Lesley had made the same inquiry each time. She shuffled the papers on her desk. 'Dear me, how the price of everything does go up! We shall have to start making a few economies before long – loath though I always am to take this step. Now, I don't think the girls need to wash in hot water *every* morning. When I was a girl we did very well with cold – it made us hardy. Very healthy and bracing it was.'

'Perhaps this isn't the time of year to start, do you think, Miss Lesley? Wouldn't it be better to start in the summer – '

'Nonsense! I shall be ruined by the summer. It will brace the girls first thing in the morning. Excellent for

177

the liver and therefore the complexion. Some of the girls are very spotty, poor little things.'

Katya refrained from mentioning the thick slices of suet pudding that were served several times a week for she saw that Miss Lesley had quite convinced herself that she was actually benefiting her pupils with her proposed economy. She groaned to herself. If Maggie brought her cold water in the mornings she would resign without delay.

'Now if I were you, dear, I should go to bed. Don't forget you're on early duty tomorrow. Don't keep your lamp burning late, Katherine: remember your pretty eyes.'

Katya concealed a smile: the old skinflint, she thought, she'll be measuring the oil in teaspoons soon. 'Yes, Miss Lesley. Good night.' Katya shut the door with exaggerated care, although she longed to bang it. As she walked through the hall, she could hear the voices of the boarders getting noisy under Mademoiselle's feeble restraint. She shrugged. She wasn't in charge until tomorrow. They could create mayhem for all she cared.

She knelt before the grate in her room and carefully created a small fire. The teachers had to pay for every scuttleful of coal used in their rooms so she had learned to be careful. Soon a small blaze was causing shadows to leap and dance on the walls and Katya sat for a while on the hearth rug hugging her knees and letting the warmth play on her body. Then she adjusted the lamp and pushed the one basket chair close to the fire. She put a small iron saucepan containing water and a tablespoonful of ground coffee on to the coals; soon a fragrant smell of good coffee filled the room as the water boiled up. Setting it aside to settle she slipped out of her clothes and unpinned her hair, letting it fall over her white shoulders. She regarded her reflection in the speckled mirror with some interest: was she pretty? Her body was white and well-shaped, her breasts firm, her waist only nineteen inches. She revolved slowly, examining herself with a little uncertain frown. A wry smile touched her lips: this warm shapely body was a secret between the mirror and herself. Only a lover would ever see it. If she married Ernest – she shuddered; a *frisson* of repulsion at the thought of his stubby fingers touching her flesh. She knew then, at that precise moment of truth, that she could never marry him. She could never become mistress of the tall house across the square, pay calls in a neat victoria, bear his children.

Quickly, she donned a scarlet wrapper, and lighting a cigarette put it in an amber holder. The coffee was ready, fragrant and hot. She sighed, stretching her bare feet to the now blazing fire. All the minor irritations of the past week began to seep away; now she could see how petty they were. Why did she let Hill House get on her nerves? She ought to have more control over her feelings. She blew an inexpert smoke ring: she was getting better at it! How annoyed Miss Lesley would be if she knew one of her teachers smoked! She considered it fast and altogether shocking.

Looking into the red coals she wondered about her future. If she didn't accept Ernest (and she was now quite decided on that point) what was to become of her? She would be condemned to this sort of existence for ever; there were few bachelors who were suitable in Whitby. And did she want to go on teaching all her life? It would seem that marriage offered her the only escape . . . If only girls possessed the same freedom as men to carve out careers for themselves! Even though the Prime Minister, Mr Balfour, professed sympathy for women's suffrage, he had done nothing constructive to bring it about. It was all soothing talk, Katya thought angrily, designed to keep them quiet. In reality, they were as

179

helpless in directing their lives as in her mother's youth. She was condemned like so many of her sex to remain an underpaid teacher or nurse, the only two professions open to girls like herself if they were not to remain prisoners of their relatives' selfishness at home. 'It's maddening!' she said aloud and threw her cigarette into the fire. Stooping, she parted the coals and the fire flared weakly for the last time. Throwing off her wrapper she leapt into bed to find that Maggie (bless the old thing!) had put a hot brick wrapped in flannel in the middle of the bed. Hugging it to her, she wasted no more time in brooding but fell asleep at once.

2

She woke to Maggie's knock on the door and another cold dark Monday morning. She hated these early duty mornings and as she rolled out of bed, she was dismally aware of being in the grip of black depression. Ugh! How she hated this place and what a fool she was to stay!

Outside her door she found the usual copper can of hot water awaiting her. Miss Lesley's threatened economies had evidently not been put into force yet. I shall leave – yes, this time I *shall* leave if she sends me cold water. Katya promised herself as she shivered in the icy air of the bedroom. 'Katya, you're a spineless creature. I dislike you more each day,' she said aloud to her reflection as she struggled into her corset and corset cover, lace-edged drawers and flannel petticoat. Her black woollen stockings had a hole in them but she thrust her legs into them with a defiant gesture. Let Miss Lesley notice if she liked!

Soon she emerged as a schoolmistress: neat and quiet

mannered with smooth hair and calm expression. Miss Croxley in person. Carrying a lamp and a handbell, she went into the two dormitories shaking the bell ruthlessly. She was followed by Amy, the between-maid, loaded with four cans of hot water, two to each hand.

'Can you manage, Amy?' she asked with some concern for she could hear the girl's laboured breathing. By the light from the lamp she saw the naked panic springing into the girl's eyes. Katya knew she would never admit that the cans were too heavy, that she lived in fear of losing her job, for she was the eldest of a large family living in a hovel down on the harbour. In bed last, up first in the morning to light the boiler, Amy wore a hunted air of fatigue. 'I'm – all right, miss,' she gasped fiercely, dumping the first of the cans.

Katya rang the bell loudly. 'Come now, girls!' she called and went across to lift the calico blinds.

Reluctantly obeying the rousing bell, the girls struggled out of bed to stand on the icy linoleum that covered the floor while they pulled off flannel nightgowns and pulled on wool chemises, yawning as they laced up boots and quarrelled sleepily over possession of the one mirror in each room. Then downstairs they trooped to the classrooms to work for half an hour (on empty stomachs) learning the collect for the day and revising their prep of the night before.

This was the time Katya disliked more than any other: the sheer discomfort of the draughty old house with the winter wind off the sea pouring through badly-fitting doors and windows; the half-asleep grudging pupils stuffed unwillingly at desks while outside the dawn had barely broken up the night sky. Besides, the sound of her own rumbling stomach exasperated her.

Then, at seven forty-five another bell rang and this was the signal for morning prayers led by Miss Lesley. As usual, Miss Mabel hurried in late from the kitchen, buttoning her cuffs and pretending not to be the establishment's cook-housekeeper but merely a partner in the school. Her guilty eyes tried to avoid her sister's accusing ones as she buried her long pink nose in a hymn book.

After prayers, breakfast came at last. Bowls of thin porridge, thick doorsteps of bread (with plenty of farm butter and treacle to spread), and jugs of hot cocoa that was watery but satisfyingly hot. This was the boarders' first meal since six o'clock the previous day. The poor girls were famished and ate with ravenous haste despite Miss Lesley's reproofs. She herself was toying delicately with a lightly-poached egg and fragrant coffee.

Katya eyed that repast with yearning. She always refused porridge and somehow the slabs of bread stuck in her throat. Out of the corner of an eye she saw Mademoiselle Dupont pushing aside, with a look of horror, the bowl of porridge. Miss Lesley saw it too but remained blandly blind to a gesture that was made every morning.

At eight-thirty the girls were sent out into the bare narrow garden at the back of the house. They were expected to run round it in an effort to keep warm. This morning, sleet was falling.

Katya shuddered as she saw them out and then hurried away for a blessed half-hour in front of the schoolroom stove. She would be certain to get it to herself as Thérèse Dupont preferred the fug in her bedroom where she would have stoked up a good fire which she kept going all day. Katya suspected that she spent most of her salary on coal for her bedroom fire. Miss Aylward, the third member of the staff (and a great crony of Miss Lesley's), lived in the town and didn't come to the school until nine o'clock.

Whipping out a copy of *An African Farm* from her

desk, she prepared to bury herself in it. Ernest Hanson, she knew, thought the book gave her bad ideas. Ideas about female liberty and even of sexual equality that quite alarmed the good doctor. For nearly half an hour she was lost to all sight and sound of Hill House and its petty miseries. When the children trooped in again at nine, it entailed a great mental effort to bring her mind back to Monday morning's time-table.

If only women had another purpose in life besides being wives and mothers! Katya thought as she got up and began to write on the blackboard. Her wide reading from the really admirable library old Doctor Lesley had garnered and left to his daughter, had opened her eyes to the possibilities of a full life for girls like herself that hitherto she had only dreamed about.

Writing the first lines of a Wordsworth sonnet with a chalk that squeaked, her thoughts were angry and frustrated. There were so many things she longed to do and was prevented from doing simply by being a woman. Suddenly, she wiped the board clean and turned to the class. 'This morning,' she said firmly, 'we are not going to study the sonnets of Wordsworth after all. I am going to talk to you about being women. Some of you will be leaving next summer. Do you know what you're going to do with your lives?'

They gaped at her. They were not the most intelligent of the town's children but their parents hoped (by paying the fees) that they were buying a little culture, and keeping them out of mischief until they put their hair up.

'Marry, I suppose,' said Sylvia Mary Hodges with a giggle. She fiddled with the black moiré bow on the back of her head. 'What else is there to do, Miss Croxley?'

Katya took a long breath, looking round the circle of upturned faces. 'I'll tell you,' she said crisply.

Ten minutes later, Miss Lesley chanced to walk down

183

the passage and past the door of Katya's classroom. She paused as usual to listen. It was not difficult to hear every word spoken beyond the door that had a frosted glass pane let into it. Katherine's voice was raised quite passionately, she considered. What could she be talking about?

'Do you want to be underdogs all your lives? For that's what you are. *Females*, otherwise second-class citizens. Do you really want to be tied to a man without knowing anything of the world? To bear children year after year whether *you* want to or not? To be virtual slaves? To have no laws to protect you because you are women? To have no legal right to your own children? Well, I believe there is more to life for women than that. We've brains, haven't we? Brains as good as men's but with very little chance of using them. We could earn our own living – yes, even you, Sylvia Mary, if you sit up and pay a bit more attention – we could not only be teachers and nurses but scientists, doctors – even MPs! The time can't be far away when we get our freedom – '

'Good heavens!' Miss Lesley felt gooseflesh creeping up her neck. 'She's gone mad!' Opening the door she said in a shaking voice: 'Miss Croxley, one moment, if you please.'

Katya, the flush of enthusiasm still on her cheeks, came reluctantly. It was just like Miss Lesley to interrupt at a crucial point: the girls had just begun to sit up and listen. Leaving the door ajar behind her, she said, 'Yes, Miss Lesley?' It was difficult to conceal her impatience.

Miss Lesley smoothed the lace frills at her throat. Her voice shook with anger. 'What in the name of heaven are you teaching those girls, Katherine?'

Katya reflected. 'A new philosophy, Miss Lesley. I'm trying to open their eyes a little.'

'Oh, no doubt you've done that! Dangerous stuff,

184

Katherine. It won't do, you know.' She looked suspiciously at her junior teacher. 'Katherine, are you a follower of that woman's?'

Katya's smooth young brow wrinkled in puzzlement. 'What woman, Miss Lesley?'

'Why, that – that suffragist creature – Pankhurst, isn't that her name?'

Katya smiled. 'Oh, I see. Yes, I suppose I am in a way. But I've really been teaching the girls what I've learned from Olive Schreiner – oh, Miss Lesley, she's wonderful! She's put into words what I've been feeling for a long time.'

'Good heavens,' Miss Lesley murmured faintly. This was even worse – the teachings of a Boer woman and the war only over a couple of years! They would lose every pupil in the place if this got out. 'Katherine, you mustn't do it – you mustn't, really. The parents won't like it. I shall lose all my pupils. The school would have to close!'

Katya opened her eyes very wide. 'But, Miss Lesley, surely it's our duty to educate these girls? Isn't that what education is? Enlightenment? We could never progress otherwise. Oh, Miss Lesley, please don't stop me talking to the girls! I must blow some air into their minds.'

'Not in my school.' Miss Lesley's mouth shut like a trap as her eyes bored into Katya's. 'Do you understand? Don't let me have to mention it to you again, Katherine, or I may have to terminate our association.'

Otherwise give me the sack. Katya stared mutinously after her headmistress's well-cushioned figure as it sailed grandly down the corridor. Miss Lesley always walked as if acknowledging applause from an unseen audience.

With a sigh she turned back into the classroom. The old wore blinkers, she told herself bleakly. Why couldn't they acknowledge that the female revolution was only just round the corner? Couldn't they see further than

185

their noses? Sadly, she looked round at her pupils. They were so young, so foolish and she wasn't even to be allowed to enlighten them about the world and what was happening in it, a matter of paramount importance to them.

'Open your Wordsworth,' she said dispiritedly. 'We've only ten minutes before the bell so be quick, please.'

Dinner was at twelve-thirty, the main meal of the day. It was substantial and tasteless: huge cauldrons of stew with penny-sized blobs of golden grease floating on its surface and spotted dick to follow.

Immediately after this repast, the girls put on their coats and hats, tied on thick scarves and struggled forth in a long crocodile for the daily walk with Katya at one end and Miss Aylward at the other. The wind was bitter, whipping the sea into wild horses and blowing spray high into the air so that they could taste salt on their lips. They bent in the face of it and walked down the hill towards the harbour. Miss Lesley advertised 'beneficial sea air' in her prospectus and she saw to it that her pupils got plenty of it. Katya guessed that she herself would be in her room toasting her feet before a large fire, her eyes closed, her hands folded on her lap.

As they walked within sight of her old home above the harbour, Katya had a sudden vision of her mother standing at the window looking out to sea. Sometimes she had woken in the night hearing her mother going downstairs because she was unable to sleep. The wind had been tearing round the house, the sea roaring beyond the harbour bar and the cries of the seagulls the cries of drowning sailors in the angry sea.

They had passed her old home now. Refusing to give it a backward glance, she called on the crocodile to turn. They were back at three-thirty and trooped into the dining room (still smelling of stew and spotted dick) to

186

partake of a very dull repast of tea and bread with bloater paste.

Distaste for her dull life depressed Katya as she refilled cups with over-brewed tea. For a wild moment she felt the urge to throw down her own cup and run for her life away from this dreadful place that was Hill House School. But run where? Where could one find adventure in Whitby in November – or at any time, come to that? Her sense of humour righted itself and a little quiver of laughter shook her as she visualized herself picking up her skirts and running helter-skelter down the hill with Miss Lesley calling frantically, 'Come back, Katherine, come ba-a-ck!'

'You're smiling, Miss Croxley,' one of the girls said in surprise.

Katya hurriedly straightened her face. Smiling? In Hill House? That would never do!

Back to the last class of the day before high tea at six. At long last the boarders were in bed and she was free. She still had a pile of exercises to go through but her face was cheerful as she hastened upstairs to put a match to the fire and light the lamp. Crouching over the struggling fire that refused to draw, she marked essays recklessly, her pencil flying over the paper. The fire at last began to draw nicely and there was a flurry of raindrops against the window. She shivered as she paused in her work; suddenly, such a sense of desolation assailed her that she felt tears spring to her eyes. What's the matter with me? she asked herself desperately.

10

The Fair Stranger

1

The *SS Mersey Queen*, bound for its home port of
Liverpool, was making its way with the aid of tugs out of
Boston harbour. On this early November morning a mist
still hung over the shoreline although it was just noon as
the ship's sirens heralded her departure for England. The
air was icy cold, for winter had gripped the coast of New
England and there had been a light fall of snow. Rumour
had it that gales were raging in the Atlantic and the
prudent had already gone below to their cabins.

The younger element among the passengers stood in a
solid phalanx at the rail and waved to the rapidly receding
groups of friends and relatives who had come to see
them off. There was an air of gaiety among the waving
passengers, for most of them were going on holiday to
Europe and their excitement spilled over in laughter and
chatter.

Yet one woman stood alone. She was still young,
perhaps just thirty, and yet she stood looking stricken,
her shoulders bowed under the dark brown sable cape
that she held tightly to her neck with one hand gloved in
biscuit kid: the other held the rail in front of her. A dark
brown velvet toque was securely pinned to her thick fair
hair but tendrils had escaped and were being whipped
against her cheeks and across her sad eyes by the wind

that was growing stronger all the time. She was very pale and frightened, her hands showing it in the tenseness of their grip on coat and rail. People standing near cast curious looks in her direction: she looked so forlorn.

Anastasia Barinskaya was going home to St Petersburg and she was leaving behind her the husband she had come to loathe. Her marriage now lay in ruins. During the time Barinsky had been an attaché at the Russian Embassy in Washington they had rented a small but delightful home in a pretty part of Washington. They had made many friends for they were handsome and rich and always ready to be entertained or to throw their doors open to others. Everyone said that no people had a greater sense of enjoyment or more vitality than the Russians.

When the marriage broke up it sent shock waves through the diplomatic circle and Barinsky had resigned from the service. He was, after the divorce, going to marry one of the richest women in the States: Mrs Gertrude Haltmann, the beautiful middle-aged widow of a steel king. She had been determined from the beginning to become the Countess Barinskaya. A Russian title had a certain cachet; besides, Sergei was very good-looking and, moreover, was like putty in her hands.

Knowing full well that he risked the Tsar's displeasure with a divorce, he had decided to settle for good in America. There was, after all, no longer any need to work. The children, he decreed, would stay with him, their legal guardian. 'There are splendid opportunities here and Gertrude will launch them into society when they are older. They are my children by Russian law. You can have no claim to them, Stana. I should go home if I were you.' Then he had summoned his valet to pack for him and had left the same day.

If he had taken the children then and there, Anastasia

189

would have had a battle to obtain custody of them and she shrank from the publicity in the papers. She had learned during her years in Washington that the most delicate matters were often revealed in the newspapers; a barbaric custom, she had thought it. Galvanized by terror at the thought of losing Tanya and Maia, she had acted with uncharacteristic speed and cunning. She had taken her magnificent jewels to a well-known jeweller in Washington (whom she had been used to dealing with from time to time) and offered him her box of fabulous gems. Overnight she had become rich in her own right with thousands of dollars tucked under the lining of her dressing-case. When she got to England she would put most of the money in a bank there: English banks were so safe. She had gone straight down to the shipping office and booked a suite on the *SS Mersey Queen*. With hurried stealth, she and her maid, Corinne, had packed the big trunks and despatched them to the goods depot. When the children were dressed and ready to leave, she had made the sign of the cross over their heads and sent them off with Corinne. Ten minutes later she had slipped out herself and had walked quickly to a cab rank in the next block, leaving lights blazing all over the house and the staff preparing a dinner she would never eat. Her stratagem had worked and no one had attempted to snatch the children as they boarded the night train to Boston. Not that she had been able to breathe freely until the *Mersey Queen* was well out at sea.

Back to Russia! She had to be vigilant until she reached St Petersburg again. Having no fixed home in Petersburg she intended to stay with her sister Laura. She would be safe at Tsarskoe Selo – the Tsar's village, fifteen miles from St Petersburg. Some people called it an artificial little town for only certain privileged people were allowed to live there. The Imperial Family lived for part of the year in the small Alexander Palace set in eight hundred acres of lovely parkland. The Tsarina was said by her enemies (and she had many) to have ruined the royal apartments with modern furniture from Messrs Maples in London. 'That dowdy German woman,' Laura called her scornfully. The little town was surrounded by a dense belt of fir and birch trees that would be covered with a canopy of snow now but in early summer a small forest of lilac would be filling the air with its heavy scent. Every corner of Anastasia Barinskaya's soul was filled with longing for this place that spelled sanctuary to her. Laura's lover, the Grand Duke Philip, had given her the charming house she still occupied near the royal park, although now her dancing career was over she taught at the Imperial Ballet school in Theatre Street. When Anastasia reached England she would telegraph Laura that they were coming. Until then it was better that no one should know.

She turned away from the rail, for they were now out of sight of land, and made her way back to her suite. Corinne was unpacking one of the trunks and lamenting the crushed condition of the clothes they had thrown in so hastily. 'Are the children with you, *excellence*?' she paused to ask.

'Are they not with you?'

Corinne immediately looked distracted. 'With me, *excellence*? But haven't I enough to do? *Mon dieu*, where then can they be, the poor little ones?'

'Don't worry. They will be all right. Tanya is nine and not a baby. She will look after her little sister, I think.'

'It is to be hoped,' Corinne muttered. Her own opinion of the Countess Tanya was not high. A spoilt self-willed girl, that one. Removing her mistress's cloak she said coaxingly: 'Come, *excellence*, you must lie down for a little. You look fatigued.' She bustled about fetching her mistress's negligee and slippers and helping her to step out of her velvet skirt.

Anastasia did as she was bid; she felt too tired and depressed to think for herself now that the first flight from Washington had been achieved. As she lay on her bed, feeling the uncomfortable movement of the boat beneath her, she tried unsuccessfully to still the nervous ache in her body. She turned restlessly on her side and felt a stab of pain under her ribs that made her gasp. She had forgotten it temporarily, this pain that lived in the centre of her body. Sometimes it was a ball of fire making her cry out . . . Carefully, she turned on her back and felt relief. Pray God she reached Petersburg before it altogether devoured her!

'Mamma?' Tanya's anxious young face hovered over her. 'You were groaning. Are you sick?'

'No, dearest, just tired. Where is Maia?'

'She's here. She is such a pest, Mamma!'

'Poor little Maia! You mustn't be unkind, Tanya. She's much younger than you are.'

Maia pushed her way into the stateroom,.past her sister who tried to restrain her but Maia neatly bit her wrist.

'Mamma! Did you see – '

'Hush, children, hush! You're making my head ache. That was naughty, Maia. Beg your sister's pardon.'

'She's worse than a little animal!' Tanya shrilled, holding out her wrist to display teeth marks. 'I shall die of blood-poisoning or something!'

The countess held her head. 'Go and wash, both of you. Luncheon will be in the saloon by now. Be very polite, Tanya, to the steward who is looking after you. Don't treat him like a *moujik* because the English don't understand that.'

'The English don't understand,' Maia repeated, nodding her head. 'And Tanya is rude always,' she confided to her mother.

Anastasia concealed a smile. 'Run, sweetheart, Corinne is awaiting you.' Then she turned to the elder girl. 'Remember, Tanya, she's only four and a half and you must look after her for me until we get home. Everything will be all right when we get home. Old Olga will come back as nurse, I'm sure, and there are always plenty of English governesses to be found.'

Tanya stroked the tails on her ermine muff and avoided meeting her mother's eyes. She was tall for her age with aquiline features and her blue eyes never sparkled with fun. Her hair was always neatly dressed and she wore her ermine cap with chic. There was a decided air of consequence about her that made her seem far older than her years. But that she was still very young became obvious when she suddenly blurted: 'Where is Papa? Why isn't he coming home with us? Why didn't he say goodbye?'

Her mother had been dreading this inevitable question. 'He isn't coming back to Russia. He doesn't want to live with us any longer. Tanya, you are old enough to be told: Papa wishes for a divorce in order to marry Mrs Haltmann.'

Tanya's head jerked back and her nostrils dilated. '*Mrs Haltmann!* I don't like her, Mamma. I think her quite horrid. How can Papa do such a thing?'

'Now you will understand why we had to leave Washington so quickly. I feared he would keep you with him when he married Mrs Haltmann.'

The little girl's face was white with fury. She breathed fast, the ermine tails on her hat and muff jerking perceptibly. 'I hate him for doing this! Yes, I do, Mamma, so don't try and stop me saying it! I'll never live with him – I would run away if he made me – ' She had slipped from the French they spoke at home into Russian. Words poured out of her in a cataract of sound as she castigated her father.

What a good hater she is, her mother thought uneasily, and growing so like Sergei's sister Nada!

Suddenly, the girl's tongue tripped and she stuttered to a stop as she burst into floods of tears and threw herself against her mother. 'Oh, Mamma, why couldn't you have stopped him!'

'There, cry if you must, but don't let your little sister see. She wouldn't understand. Don't worry: I shall never let either of you go although in law you do indeed belong to your Father and I have no rights over you – '

'Mamma!' Tanya was aghast. 'The law must be mad!'

'Hush, Tanya, don't say that! It is our beloved Tsar who makes our laws and therefore they must be for the best. You see, mothers aren't able to provide for their children. Everything they possess becomes the husband's on marriage – children also when they arrive. It is a wise law really, child, because it means a father must provide for those weaker than himself.'

'*I* don't think it's wise!' Tanya scrubbed at her eyes and gave an enormous sniff. 'But how did you get the money to take us home? How shall we live when we get there?'

Her mother pointed to her crocodile-covered dressing-case that still waited to be unpacked. 'Under the lining are thousands of dollars. We are quite safe! I have sold most of my jewels.'

'Not the Barinsky emeralds? Not Grandmamma's pearls? The diamonds? Mamma, how could you?' Tanya leapt off the bed. 'They were to be mine some day! Papa said so! Those jewels are not really yours – the shop must be made to return them!' She stamped her foot. 'Mamma, I insist!'

Poor Anastasia was speechless and stared at her daughter almost in terror. How like – how terribly like! –

194

her old enemy and sister-in-law the child looked now with that expression on her face! The Princess Nada Gurievna was forty-five and Tanya not yet ten but the face was the same: haughty, cold and forbidding. Nada Gurievna had, Anastasia was certain, helped to break up her marriage. Hadn't she always referred to her as a nobody who had captured Sergei by underhand means? A girl who had used sexual attraction to make Sergei forget that he was marrying out of the nobility? No, Nada Gurievna had never approved of the marriage from the first, and now here was Tanya, Anastasia's own daughter, speaking to her in much the same voice. She sat up very straight and said firmly (although her heart was beating fast): 'Don't speak to me like that! You are a silly child and know nothing about it. Most of those jewels were given to me by my Father. They were mine and I have now disposed of them.' She rang the bell that connected her with Corinne and when the maid came she said: 'Countess Tanya is ready for luncheon. Please summon our steward, Corinne.'

'Oh, *excellence*, he has been already – a nice man he is, too. The food is being kept warm. I shall bring you in a tray and you must sleep.'

Anastasia sighed with relief when the door closed behind them. What a difficult girl Tanya was becoming! She put a hand to her side as the pain – jagged and sharp – ripped through her. There was something wrong just *there*: putting a hand on the spot under her right rib she pressed tentatively. Yes, it hurt. When she got home she would ask Doctor Tchelitchev to examine her. A sigh escaped her for it seemed as if everything unpleasant was descending all at once on her shoulders.

When Corinne brought in a wicker tray of food she announced: 'The captain's personal steward has called

195

with a message, *excellence*. Captain Mackay wishes to pay you a call at four o'clock.'

'Is that his name? Very well, you will get me up at three o'clock, Corinne. Take all this away.' She flapped a hand tiredly. 'I'm not hungry.'

'Now, *excellence*, I beg you be sensible!'

'Leave me, please. I am too tired to argue and, truly, I am not hungry. I will wear a grey gown with my pearls,' she added, pretending not to see Corinne's buttoned-up lips and angry eyes.

If only everyone would leave me alone! she cried inside herself.

2

At Liverpool, ten days later, a horse-drawn ambulance waited on the docks to take a seriously ill passenger to hospital. People crowded the rails to watch as the pretty fair-haired first-class passenger was carried off on a stretcher. Following the procession came her personal maid clad in black clutching her dressing-case, and two little girls, red-eyed and looking scared. The thickset man who hustled the children into his waiting cab was said to be the Russian consul at Liverpool.

'Where are we going?' Tanya whispered to Corinne.

'To a very nice hotel where you'll be well looked after,' the consul assured her. He had a prominent gold tooth that flashed in the light; Maia couldn't take her eyes off it.

'*Monsieur*.' Corinne leaned forward eagerly. 'I have remembered something. Her excellency has a sister in England! Yes, in the north, I believe. A Mrs Croxley.

Her husband is a captain on a boat from Hull.' She pronounced it Ull and the man looked at a loss.

'Hull,' Tanya said, turning from the window. 'He is a chief captain with the Howarth and Hawksley Line.' Her impeccable English and air of command made the consul look at her respectfully: the little countess certainly had her head screwed on. 'Her name is Marie Croxley and she has a daughter, my cousin Katya. We have never met her, though, and I do not know her address.'

The man was scribbling in a leather notebook which he then replaced in an inside pocket. Again the gold tooth flashed as he smiled. 'Splendid. You have given me just the information I need. We shall soon find this aunt of yours I've very little doubt. Ah, here we are at your hotel. I'm sure you're hungry so we'll eat luncheon directly we've seen your suite.'

3

'There's been a telegraph from the Russian consul in Liverpool,' Sir Abel Howarth said. He rumpled his sparse hair. 'Apparently an aunt of that girl we educated – what's-her-name Croxley – yes, yes, Katya Croxley – has been taken ill crossing from America to England. She's got to be operated on – let me see – '

'Can I see the telegraph, Pater?' Robert held out a hand that was surprisingly steady considering how his heart had leaped at the name Katya Croxley: she had been out of his life for a year now but she was certainly not forgotten. He read the long message swiftly. 'It seems they don't know that Captain and Mrs Croxley are dead. That's strange. I'm pretty certain Katya wrote to tell her grandfather but she got no reply, I know.' He looked directly at his father. 'Shall I handle this? I know where to get hold of Katya: she's teaching in Whitby.' He turned to the door, hesitated then said over his shoulder: 'Don't worry, Pater, she wouldn't have me when I asked her last year.'

Sir Abel looked at the closed door, outrage on his face. The minx! Wouldn't have his son, wouldn't she? A pauper, a girl without a penny to her name, an orphan educated by his own company and she wouldn't have his son, his Robert, the next baronet and head of Howarth and Hawksley. 'Mad,' Abel Howarth said out loud. 'But then she's Russian. I'd like to meet her to give her a piece of me mind.'

4

On Tuesday morning, Katya woke up feeling as if something was about to happen. How ridiculous, she chided herself as she splashed in tepid water. What could be about to happen in a life that had become as uneventful as hers? It was probably the weather: the fog had gone and it was a dry crisp morning at last. There was even a pale sun coming up over the sea. She must get a breath of sea air before she went on duty at breakfast. She pulled on a knitted cap and was just tucking strands of hair into it when Maggie knocked on the door.

'Oh, miss, you're wanted urgent by Miss Lesley.'

Now what had she done? Throwing the cap on the bed, she ran downstairs to tap on the study door.

Miss Lesley was talking into the telephone on the wall – 'the instrument' as she always called it, regarding it with extreme apprehension and only to be used in emergencies. 'Quite so, Mr Howarth. I do understand

and would be delighted to help if I could. But how am I to manage? Yes? I mean until the end of term. That's a month away. Miss Croxley has charge of my top class – oh, I see. Well, I should certainly consider that generous – more than generous, Mr Howarth. Under the circumstances, what can I say? I will let you know as soon as I can. Miss Croxley is here now – no, I think not. Better I explain it to her. Goodbye, Mr Howarth.' She hung up the receiver and turned impressively. 'Well, Katherine, you are a lucky young girl!'

Katya who had heard the name of Howarth mentioned felt colour staining her cheeks. Robert. Now what was he proposing to get her involved in? She would refuse, of course, knowing full well that it was simply a ruse for them to meet again. It was a terrible temptation they must resist: she missed his friendship sorely but he must forget her and find a suitable wife. It was high time he married. She opened her mouth to make a flustered excuse but Miss Lesley wasn't listening to her.

'Your aunt, Countess Barinskaya, has been taken ill in Liverpool. Apparently they had to rush her to hospital to have her gall bladder removed – dear me, most unpleasant. Mr Howarth was asked to find you. She needs you, Katherine, to take charge of your cousins. Of course I said I couldn't spare you but Mr Howarth insists on paying for a replacement for the rest of term. Well, how could I refuse? So go and pack at once. You are to catch the earliest train – '

'To Liverpool?'

'No, no, child, don't be stupid. To Hull. To the Howarths' *own house*,' Miss Lesley said impressively. 'The little countesses will probably be taken there to meet you and you will escort them to St Petersburg.'

Katya sat down suddenly, an unheard-of thing to do in Miss Lesley's presence, but that lady was happily rolling countesses round her tongue: the Countess Tanya and the Countess Maia Barinskaya. She paused to look at her plainly dressed teacher sitting staring at her. Who would have thought the little fool had all these aristocratic relations in her background? She had never breathed a word about them. Why, if Miss Lesley could squeeze in some airy reference to them next time she met a parent just think of the impact on them! Their Sylvia Mary, their Freda actually being taught by the niece of a Russian countess!

'I don't understand,' Katya said obstinately. 'I haven't heard anything of my mother's family for years. Why do they suddenly need me?'

'I've told you. Really, Katherine, I wish you'd listen.' Miss Lesley's large bust heaved as she took a deep breath and began to explain. At last Katya was in possession of the bare facts and realizing that only when she saw Robert would she get the full story, she went upstairs to pack her clothes while Miss Lesley looked up trains to Hull and ordered a cab.

Standing at the window of her room for a moment she suddenly began to feel excitement. St Petersburg! The name was like a clash of bells. At last she would see her mother's adored home, meet the sisters whom she had talked about so often and so longingly, get out of Whitby at last! She laughed aloud. How very extraordinary life was, she told herself dazedly.

Robert met her at Hull. She saw his ruddy face and stocky figure waiting as the train drew in to the station and it gave her a tremendous sense of comfort and homecoming that surprised her. He came forward and kissed her on the lips and then held her from him to examine her.

'Katya.'

'Robert.'

'You're thinner.' Oh, my love, his heart cried out, how I long for you! How I long to keep you for ever! Katya, I love you. Aloud he said prosaically: 'I've got a motor waiting.'

It was the family automobile – a tall and shining Rolls Royce – with a chauffeur. They tucked her up with fur rugs and then Robert climbed in beside her.

As they drove along he told her about Anastasia Barinskaya and the children marooned in Liverpool. 'I'm going across tomorrow to collect the little girls and I want you to come with me. Will you, Katya? You see, the mater thinks our reputations will be ruined for ever if we go unescorted by a third party. For two pins she'll insist on coming with us! Well, Katya, do you mind coming with me?'

'Of course not! It's right that I should. She is my aunt after all, even if I've never met her. When is she being operated on? Is it a dangerous operation?'

'Any operation is, isn't it? She was undergoing emergency surgery last night. She'll feel better when you take charge of your little cousins. You see, she's worried her husband will follow and kidnap them.' He launched into all that he had learned· over the telephone from the consul.

'Poor thing,' Katya said. 'She married very young. I remember Mamushka telling me. What a tragedy for her.' She shivered as she thought of gay, pretty Tante Anastasia (as Marie always referred to her when speaking to her daughter) unhappy and in pain in a foreign land.

Presently the motor's acetylene lights were lighting up a fine pair of gates and they were bowling down a wide drive.

'Home,' Robert said with satisfaction and his eyes rested wistfully on her in the dark interior of the motor. He could just see her luminous eyes as she turned her face towards him. How wonderful it would have been if he had been bringing her here as his bride-to-be! He fumbled for her gloved hand and squeezed it. Very gently – and not so suddenly as to offend him – she removed it. He turned his face away and said too heartily: 'Here it is!'

She gasped as she looked out, her words an echo of Lady Howarth's on first beholding Wentworth Park. 'Why, it's a palace!'

'It does strike one as rather large at first but the mater's made it cosy in her style, you'll see.'

He helped her out as the chauffeur opened the door. Turning, she saw a small man with a kind little face like a gnome's standing under the huge porch.

What he had expected to see Abel Howarth couldn't have explained but as the slight blue-eyed girl came up the steps towards him he felt his heart give a gasp of relief. Harry Croxley's girl was *all right*. 'Miss Croxley, I knew your father well. A fine man and one of my best captains. I'm delighted to welcome his daughter to my house.' There was no mistaking the genuine warmth in his voice and Robert looked at him gratefully. As they went in, Abel said in his son's ear: 'Well, m'boy, I see you've inherited your father's eye for a pretty girl.' All his prejudice against 'the Russian' had vanished in a blink of an eye. He could understand now why Robert had hung around her all last year, and she'd refused him, the saucy puss! He'd have to see about that.

From the moment she met Robert's mother, Katya felt at home. There was no need to feel shy and over-awed at the size of Wentworth Park and the multitude of servants everywhere. Lady Howarth was a homely little woman who would never be spoiled by her wealth and position. Her voice was no different to the housemaid's who came to unpack for her, while her hostess sat in a chair and examined everything with great frankness. 'My dear, those drawers will never be warm enough for Russia! We shall have to get flannel ones and petticoats to match. You'll freeze to death in those lawn ones. Have you a fur coat and hat? Then as soon as you return with the little girls we shall go shopping for all your things. No need to look worried, my dear, Sir Abel will pay. I'll get him to write me a large cheque and we'll go shopping the day after your return. It'll be difficult to squeeze everything in to be ready by the end of the week when you sail – oh, haven't they told you? You're to sail for Hamburg in your father's old boat the *Sylvie-Rose*.'

Left to herself, her head whirling from all the information she was receiving, Katya changed hurriedly into her best dress, a plain but well-cut merino with a white lawn collar and a great deal of braiding round the hem of the skirt. It wasn't an evening dress but it was all she had and she was old enough now not to be embarrassed because she had nothing better. Nevertheless, she was relieved to find that Lady Howarth was equally plainly dressed while the two men simply wore velvet smoking

203

jackets: that this was due to Robert's instructions she never knew.

Dinner was a well-cooked satisfying meal and she soon found herself chattering easily to her host and hostess. Robert was very quiet, his whole attention taken up with watching the girl he loved.

For her part, Katya hadn't changed. Robert remained the brother she had never had since Matthew died when she was ten.

11
Journey to the Unknown

1

Anastasia had only been aware of pain as she came in and out of her drugged sleep. Now she was awake again and out of the mist swam a face. 'Marie!' Her cracked dry lips tried to form the name and a nurse bent over her and moistened them with wet lint. 'Marie . . .'

'No, I'm Marie's daughter. Your niece, Katya.' Katya looked with pity at the pale drawn face lying on the pillow. The pretty flaxen hair was dark with sweat, the lips drawn back over beautiful teeth. When well, no doubt her Tante Stana would be very good-looking, the girl thought, stroking Anastasia's hand. 'Can you hear me, Tante Stana? Good. I'm going to take the children back to St Petersburg for you. That's what you wanted, isn't it?'

'Yes. Sergei must not – ' Anastasia closed her eyes.

Katya pressed her aunt's hand. 'I'll be back later,' she whispered and stole from the room. Robert sat in the corridor outside, waiting for her. 'I think she'll be able to talk tomorrow,' Katya said. 'Let's go to the children.'

He took her arm as they left the private wing of the hospital. 'I'm not staying in the same hotel, Katya. The mater impressed on me that I mustn't. So I'll take you there and leave you to make friends with them. We must leave by train tomorrow, so have them ready by eleven-thirty for us to call at the hospital first.'

She nodded, grateful for his support. Meeting these relations for the first time was proving something of a strain. Although their colouring was not the same, there was a likeness between Anastasia's face on the pillow and that of her dying mother. Tears had stung her eyes as she leaned over this unknown aunt and it was obvious that she had seen in Katya's face a trace of her sister. *Marie*, she had said twice.

Robert had booked a room for her in the quiet hotel where the Countess Barinskaya had taken a suite for herself and her children. Leaving her overnight bag to be taken up to her room she allowed herself to be escorted to the suite on the first floor.

'Remember, eleven-thirty tomorrow morning,' Robert said. 'Remember, you know my hotel. If you meet with any difficulty at all ask the clerk downstairs to telephone and I'll be over at once.' He rapped on the door and it was opened by a sour-looking woman in black, her iron-grey hair scraped back from a prematurely-aged face.

'Mademoiselle Croxley? Please enter, I am Corinne, the countess's maid. My English not good.'

'Then we shall speak French,' Katya said briskly. She cast a longing glance at Robert's retreating figure, wishing he could have stayed to help her over this difficult first meeting.

Two children were standing in the sitting room: with linked hands they stared at Katya. The younger, a fat little thing with round pink cheeks, curtsied prettily, but the elder girl made no move. With cool pale blue eyes she examined her unknown cousin.

Katya looked admiringly at this slim tall child who looked older than her nine and a half years: how pretty and distinguished she looked! Tanya wore a dark red skirt and white silk blouse with a broad black belt of shining leather encircling her tiny waist. Her fair hair was shining and well-brushed, held in place at the back by a black moiré bow. Beside her, the younger child looked an untidy bundle of petticoats and fat legs in black stockings. There was ink on her fingers and a spot of it on the smocked *delaine* dress. She looked as if she had dressed herself that morning for her stockings were wrinkling round her ankles and some of the buttons of her dress were wrongly fastened: Corinne did not consider it part of her duties to act as nursemaid to the Countess Maia.

The hostility in the elder girl's face did not lessen as Katya held out her hands and said simply: 'I'm your English cousin Katya Croxley.'

'How are we to be sure that you're not a stranger?' Tanya demanded.

Katya shrugged. 'Why should I be?'

'My father could have sent you to take us back to Washington.'

'I don't know your father. Please take my word for it.' Katya spoke persuasively because Robert had explained fully why her aunt wanted the children to proceed to Russia as soon as possible. If Barinsky learned that his wife was lying ill in Liverpool and the children only in the charge of the French maid he would be over by the next boat. 'Please don't be scared of me. I really am your cousin. My mother was the eldest of the three sisters: Marie, Laura and Anastasia. She married an Englishman. They're both dead now but – see – here is her likeness.' She opened the locket that had been Marie's. The little painting inside was a copy of the head that had been in the old timber merchant's picture of his three daughters: he had had each girl painted separately on ivory and each wore it in a gold locket round their necks.

Tanya's face changed. 'Why, that is like Mamma's!'

'And Tante Laura has one too, hasn't she? So you see

207

I'm your cousin Katya. Have you really never heard of me?' She felt a stab of pain as both girls shook their heads: how very thoroughly they had put the errant Marie out of their lives! 'Well, I've known about all of you. I know that you, Tanya, were born in Tokyo and Maia in Paris. Am I right?'

Maia nodded vigorously and taking Katya's hand led her to a sofa. 'I want to see Mamma,' she said with quivering lips. 'Tanya says she's p'obably dying.'

'Oh, I didn't!' Tanya denied swiftly but Katya guessed that she was lying and that she rather enjoyed frightening the younger sister.

'Of course she's not dying. I've just seen her and I'll take you to see her tomorrow before we leave – '

'Leave? Where are you taking us?' Tanya's voice was suspicious again.

'Home to St Petersburg. You'd like to go home to Tante Laura's, wouldn't you?'

'To Tsarskoe Selo?'

'Yes, to Tsarskoe Selo. Tante Laura has been telegraphed and will expect us.'

Corinne came in from an adjoining room. 'Is the waiter to bring up the children's supper, *mademoiselle*?'

'No!' Tanya said. 'Maia of course must have her food here and go to bed. Corinne, please see to it. Cousin Katya, I would prefer to dine downstairs tonight. I'm five years older than my sister. I can sit up much later.'

Katya hesitated. Then, remembering it was a very quiet expensive hotel, decided that they could safely dine together downstairs. Besides it was a chance to get to know Tanya who seemed to be a haughty, prickly girl. 'Very well. We'll go down at seven.'

'May I speak to you alone, *mademoiselle*?' Corinne asked.

Aware of Tanya's suspicious eyes following them,

Katya went into the adjoining room, a bedroom, and closed the door.

'First, how is her excellency?'

'In much pain. But Mr Howarth who accompanied me from Hull today saw the surgeon and tells me that with careful nursing my aunt will be perfectly well again. She had a stone in a certain part of the liver, you understand, and they have removed it. She must stay some weeks in hospital and wishes you to remain here until she is allowed out. After a short convalescence, she will be ready to travel.'

Corinne nodded. Opening a crocodile case she removed a handful of green bills. 'These are dollars, *mademoiselle*. Tomorrow I would like you to change them into English pounds for me. £200 I am to hand to you. It is more than enough to see you all home and to provide for your immediate needs. Laura Nicolaievna will see to everything else. You understand?'

'Certainly. Please keep the money for the moment. Tomorrow we will go to a bank near at hand and exchange it. At seven I shall take my elder cousin downstairs to dine. Please look after my little cousin until my return.'

'It is not my place,' Corinne began obstinately.

Very decisively Katya interrupted her. 'We each have to do what we are not used to in order to help the countess. I'm sure you'll not object.'

'Very well,' Corinne agreed sulkily. 'But I have no wish to be a children's nurse and my mistress understands that.'

Stiff-necked creature! thought Katya, smiling with false gratitude at the whey-faced Frenchwoman. How can Tante Stana care for such a creature round her?

Next morning she was up early and was soon in the Barinsky suite supervising a swift packing of the children's clothes. Then she took Corinne round to a bank to change the dollars into English sovereigns. She had already sized up the characters of each one of them and realized it was only Maia she would have no trouble with. Corinne, thank heaven, would be left behind in Liverpool but Tanya and she would have to learn to get on together during the next few weeks. Tanya, she had found, was far more difficult to deal with than all the Hill House girls rolled into one. Weak English governesses had had charge of her all her life and, a naturally headstrong character, she now seemed quite out of hand and far too old for her years. She had calmly acted the part of hostess in the dining room last night, ordering the most expensive dishes, and rejecting them as uneatable when they were brought. From now on, Katya vowed silently, I intend being in charge. It will be our first battle.

2

Anastasia was propped up this morning and the ghastly drawn look and dark rings under the eyes had faded. She had a tiny tube inserted in one nostril but was able to talk. With her lovely hair spread over the pillow and her delicate hands now wearing their magnificent rings again she looked a very different person already. Everything about her was expensive and beautiful, from her pale pink marabou jacket to the small golden clock on the table; it was formed like a birdcage and a tiny gold bird ticked the minutes away. Crystal vases held hot-house flowers on this dark November morning: roses, lilies, even mimosa, and their delicate scent filled the air.

Katya approached her aunt shyly.

'Yes, I was right. You are the living image of Marie as

I remember her! Come, kiss me, Katya. I'm so glad we meet at last!'

'So am I, Aunt Stana, and I'm especially glad you are so much better.'

'Do I look better? I feel . . . uncomfortable.' Stana smiled back. 'Now sit where I can see you, please. The children?'

'They're outside, longing to see you. I've come only for a few minutes to tell you the plans we've made.' Rapidly but gently so as not to tire her, Katya explained that they were leaving for Hull that afternoon with Robert Howarth and would go by sea to Hamburg on Saturday and on by train to Russia.

'My sister, Laura Nicolaievna, has been telegraphed? She will see to everything. I pray you reach there safely.' She paused and wiped her lips with a handkerchief. 'I must explain: I have left my husband Sergei for good. He wishes for divorce but although I am willing for that I am not willing he should keep the children.'

'Indeed, no!' Katya sat up straight and an indignant flush swept her face. 'It is iniquitous that women have so little legal power! To be a wife is to lose control of everything in England.'

'It is so in Russia: worse, we have no control over our lives even if we have no husbands! So I must emphasize, Katya, that the children are in danger of being abducted by him. You see, our embassy in London knows I'm here now. They sent these.' She indicated the flowers. 'I must get the children away before Sergei arrives to claim them!' Tears had sprung to her eyes. The door opened and the nurse came in, looking sharply at her patient.

'Please give me a few more minutes, nurse,' Stana pleaded.

Katya got up. 'Don't worry. I understand. We're leaving now. I'll send the children to see you.' She bent and

211

brushed her lips against Stana's forehead. 'I cannot call you *aunt*: you're too young!'

A mischievous look lit up the tired face. 'Thank goodness for that! I don't relish being aunt to a grown-up young woman! Goodbye and God go with you all.' She made the sign of the cross over one who was about to travel.

'You can go in now,' Katya told the children. They passed her in a rush. To Corinne she said: We must leave in five minutes. Has Mr Howarth arrived?'

'I'm here,' said a voice behind her and there he was smiling reassuringly.

She was amazingly glad to see his stocky figure standing there. They clasped hands.

'All well?'

'Yes, everything. I will fetch my cousins.'

Maia began to howl as Katya lifted her down from the bed. 'Mamma! Don't die!' she sobbed. 'Tanya says you might die and we'll have to live with Mrs Haltmann – '

'Tanya.' Her mother closed her eyes wearily. 'Try not to frighten your little sister, I beg. Goodbye, my darlings. Be good girls and kiss Tante Laura for me. I shall be with you for Christmas.'

Both girls sobbed as they were led away by their cousin and Robert Howarth. Katya felt sorry for them; after all it was hard to be put in the charge of complete strangers and to leave one's mother in hospital. Nevertheless she was surprised at this more childish side of Tanya manifesting itself without restraint: she had thought the girl too proud to show emotion. She watched her in the cab as they drove to the station and quickly spotted that when Maia began to leave off sobbing, Tanya howled the louder until the little girl began to weep again. Why, the little wretch is doing it on purpose! she thought indignantly. It's just to upset us. And her right hand itched

212

with a desire to spank the girl until she cried in earnest. It was not a good omen for the beginning of their relationship.

To while away the journey they played silly games, most of them devised by a desperate Robert who had never had anything to do with children before. At Manchester four little luncheon baskets awaited them and the children dived in with pleasure, even Tanya showing a normal childish greed as if she had forgotten her role of troublemaker.

Katya guessed that of the four only she had not been used to travelling first-class until her journey to Liverpool. The comfort, the attention of the conductor and the peacefulness of a compartment to themselves were an unexpected pleasure that she hoped (with the puritan side of her nature) she wouldn't get too used to. All too soon she would be plunged back into the world of school-bells, bad food and tepid water for washing. Who was the idiot who had said sententiously that this regime was good for the soul? she asked herself indignantly. She already felt a *nicer* person on smoked salmon sandwiches, fruit and chilled white wine than she ever had on porridge and pea soup! Robert's firm manner of handling railway staff, the luggage and even the Barinsky girls secretly impressed her: it was delightful to be travelling with a man who took all the burden off her shoulders.

At Hull, the Howarth carriage and pair awaited them together with a dogcart for the luggage. Soon they were driving through the brightly lit streets of Hull out on to the Beverley road. The children were tired and inclined to be quarrelsome with each other but when they at last drove down the drive of Wentworth Park, Tanya viewed the huge house (every window seemed to be showing a light) with impressed approval. The huge Palladian porch had recently been fitted with electric lights and under these stood the proud owner himself, curious to see what the little Russian countesses looked like.

'It's bigger than Tante Nada's!' Tanya exclaimed.

'Who's that man?' Maia asked cautiously.

Sir Abel came down the steps and greeted them heartily. 'And how's your mother, my little girl?' he asked Maia as he helped her down.

She curtsied. 'Mamma isn't going to die, Katya says.'

'Die? Of course she's not going to die! The idea.' He peered at the tall figure of Tanya. 'Is this one of 'em?' he whispered to Katya. 'She's going to prove a handful for you, m'dear,' he predicted as he led the way indoors.

Lady Howarth clucked round the children like a motherly hen, anxious there should be no tears or tantrums. She accompanied them to the adjoining rooms prepared for them and then drew Katya aside. 'The elder one's very stiff for her age, isn't she? My dear, she stands on more ceremony than royalty! I'm only trying to be friendly and she simply stares at me in the haughtiest fashion. Am I doing anything wrong?'

'Of course not!' Katya said warmly. 'It's best to take no notice of her. She seems a difficult girl and I'm afraid, as Sir Abel has already told me, I shall have my work cut out to get her home without crossing swords.'

'If anyone can do it, you can.' Lady Howarth patted her arm for she considered this former company orphan as her very own protégée. She'd do champion for our Robert, she told herself happily.

The children were put to bed and trays of supper were brought to them by a friendly housemaid who was only too delighted to act as audience with a gaping mouth, while Tanya told her about their life in Washington. 'You'll never have seen the President, will you?'

'Of course, often,' Tanya said scornfully but with scant truth.

It was a fine dry morning when Lady Howarth and Katya drove into Hull next day, armed with a shopping list for warm clothes. As so often on the east coast in winter, the sky was a bright blue with white streamers of cloud blowing in from the sea. The air was filled with a raucous crowd of seagulls rising and falling on the roofs. Katya's spirits rose and her apprehension about the journey into the unknown, beginning tonight, began to evaporate. After all, hadn't she been longing for something unusual to splinter the smooth surface of her dull life?

Lady Howarth was in her element swooping into shops where she was evidently well known. 'Good morning, Miss Hodgson, is Miss Tynmont in? Tell her I want her, m'dear.'

This was the furriers where no furs were on view until Miss Tynmont, the head saleswoman, hurried in to unlock cupboards. 'How's the moleskin wearing, m'lady? We're well on with your spring set of sables – beautiful, they are. For the young lady? Full length, no doubt.' She dropped a coat over Katya's shoulders, whipped it off again and replaced it with another, talking, talking all the time. 'And a hat to match, of course. To St Petersburg? Well, I never!'

As they saw the first parcels into the carriage Katya murmured: 'It's costing a great deal, I fear. I feel sure that last dress – the evening one – was not needed. Dear Lady Howarth, shall we take it back?'

Lady Howarth chuckled. 'My dear, what an unusual girl you are! And you know nothing about men: the more you spend, the better pleased they'll be because they can call you extravagant! I'm not seeing you go to St Peters-burg looking like an orphan – '

'But that's what I am, have you forgotten? A company orphan,' Katya said firmly.

Lady Howarth stood stockstill and looked at the girl. 'That's what you were, m'dear. Now you're a young lady going to visit her smart relations and you're not going to disgrace us by going there in that fur tippet.'

Katya smiled. 'It was Miss Lesley's. She thought I could get a lot more wear out of it when she gave it me.'

'It's dead, m'dear. I advise you to bury it,' said Lady Howarth tersely, leading the way into a large emporium to buy woollen combinations and petticoats by the half-dozen. Katya guessed that she wouldn't stop until both seats of the carriage were overflowing. Not that she wasn't delighted with her new clothes – what girl wouldn't be? It worried her though that she was still being subsi-dized by her benefactors. She saw her hard-won indepen-dence dwindling away under Lady Howarth's direction.

When everything had been packed into a trunk of Lady Howarth's and they had eaten a large tea, the time came for them to set out with Robert for the docks. The *Sylvie-Rose* was due to sail for Hamburg at six o'clock. They parted from Sir Abel and Lady Howarth with regret: even Tanya had begun to enjoy herself for Sir Abel had played billiards with her all the morning while Maia played with her dolls.

'Goodbye!' Katya leaned out of the carriage and waved to her host and hostess who stood on the steps until they turned a corner of the drive. 'How kind they've been!' she said impulsively to Robert. 'I hate to think how much your mother's spent on me this morning!'

He smiled down at her flushed, excited face. He felt sad and apprehensive, seeing the girl he loved leaving

216

him for three months. She fitted in so well with them all. His ambitious father wanted to see him marry into one of the great Yorkshire families who were not averse to commerce in the family lineage if it meant they could keep their great houses. But his mother had always been against such a marriage and he had seen how she had taken to Katya. They had returned this morning like a pair of conspirators – he had wanted to hug them both. Now, under the folds of her skirt, he squeezed Katya's fingers. 'Don't forget me,' he said in a low voice. 'Remember that the *Sylvie-Rose* calls at Hamburg every other Thursday and if ever you want to get away you've only to contact our German agent. I've written all the addresses down. I shall write to you. Please write to me, Katya.'

She smiled up at him. 'All right, Robert.' She was going to say more but Tanya on the seat opposite suddenly turned her worldly-wise eyes on them and they fell silent.

The *Sylvie-Rose* was a sturdy little vessel flying the company's flag, with a Norwegian captain on board. Robert had explained that as heavy snow had fallen early in Eastern Europe, St Petersburg was closed as a port until April. The party would disembark at Hamburg and Captain Halvorsen would personally see them on to the express from Berlin. They would have to change only once and that would be on the Russian frontier. 'The Russian gauge is wider than the European,' Robert explained. 'Don't ask me why! Probably to keep out invading armies. Shows how much the Tsars trust their German neighbours, doesn't it? Promise me one thing, Katya: be very careful in Russia. It's a queer place and they employ secret police. Don't be too trustful. At first sight, St Petersburg will look like any great city in Europe. It isn't. Russia is sitting on a powder keg so never get involved in anything political.'

'Oh, no, of course not,' Katya assured him but she was

only half-listening. Her apprehensive eyes were on the little vessel: surely it was very small?

It was a cold night with a stiff breeze and although Katya was a sailor's daughter, she knew she was a poor sailor. Her stomach dropped at the thought of facing the German Ocean tonight.

Captain Halvorsen, who had been supervising the loading of crates into the hold, came forward to greet his passengers at the top of the gangway. 'So many beautiful ladies!' he said with satisfaction as he shook their hands. He was a broad-shouldered, red-haired man with bright blue eyes. His whiskers and beard were brindled with grey and he had pushed his cap to the back of his head. He grinned broadly, displaying splendid teeth like large white stones. He swung Maia in the air and looked as if he might do the same to Tanya so she scowled and retreated behind Katya. She was very much on her dignity since leaving her mother, Katya noticed. When she saw the cabin she was to share with Maia she said disdainfully: 'Tell the captain this won't do at all. It's nothing but a cupboard! I require a better one.'

'Sorry,' Katya said dryly. 'You'll have to stay behind if you can't sleep in this one. There are no others. I have an even smaller one which I'm sure you wouldn't like. Captain Halvorsen doesn't usually carry passengers and as we're not paying for our passage we mustn't grumble. We are his guests. So please make the best of it, my dear, and keep your little sister happy.' After four days' acquaintance, she had come to know Tanya more than the girl realized. She needed firm treatment otherwise she became a bully, getting her own way to the discomfort of others. For one so young she was decidedly swollen-headed and arrogant.

The girl looked at her, a dangerous light in her eyes,

218

but she said no more. No doubt she was storing up resentment against the treatment she was receiving.

Maia had no complaint about the quarters allotted her and she begged for the upper berth, 'so that I can use this darling little ladder. And I shall be able to see out of this porthole – oh, Tanya, look!'

'Stop being a baby and help me unpack,' her sister snapped. 'It's absurd we have to look after ourselves. Mamma could easily have spared Corinne – after all, she won't need her in hospital. We are expected to travel like *moujiks*.'

No, Tanya was scarcely an endearing child, Katya thought, as she went back on deck to say farewell to Robert Howarth. There was no sign of him however and, following her instinct, she searched for the captain's cabin. Loud laughter issued from it and she was met by the smell of whisky and billows of cigar smoke as she opened the door. Both men had their feet on the table and the whisky bottle was being pushed to and fro while they sampled the cigars Robert had brought the captain. They looked blankly at Katya for a moment as if they had completely forgotten her existence, then Captain Halvorsen brought his feet down with a crash.

'Miss Croxley, have you settled in? We shall sail in a few minutes. Have you come across my sister? Her cabin is next to yours.'

'No, I didn't know she was aboard.'

'Indeed, yes. She is a shy mouse, poor Astrid, but she is to act as chaperon, you understand.' Captain Halvorsen looked her full in the eye. His own, she noticed, was full of a roguish light.

'Beware, Katya,' Robert Howarth's voice was dry. 'My friend Nils is something of a lady's man – or so he tells me!' The eyelid furthest away from the sailor drooped

219

in Katya's direction. *Harmless and kind*, telegraphed Robert's eye.

'Come,' said Halvorsen, taking out his watch and squinting at it. 'Two minutes to seven. Robert, we must put you ashore. I'll just go up to see to things,' and he left them alone.

'Well, Katya? Not scared?'

Katya firmed her lips. 'No,' she lied bravely.

He took her hands: they were icy cold. 'You're a brave little thing,' he said. 'Katya, don't forget me.'

She smiled. 'How could I? You and your mother have been so kind.'

He looked exasperated. 'All right, I'll say no more until you come home. Take care of yourself, company orphan.' He bent and planted a kiss on her warm curving mouth. Then he had gone.

She went up on deck to lean over the rail and flutter her handkerchief as they left the lights of the docks and headed down the black waters of the Humber.

She turned to go down and found a woman standing behind her. She looked sufficiently like Halvorsen for Katya to guess she was Astrid, his sister, but she was as he had said 'a shy mouse' of a woman with grey-blonde hair, a pale skin and the same splendid teeth as her brother's. She wore a grey frieze cloth coat and skirt and had a hideous hat pinned on her head. She was nervously twisting her hands together, obviously forcing herself to speak. 'Miss Croxley? I am Astrid Halvorsen. My brother – er – '

Katya staggered a little as she walked towards her. 'Oh, dear, I haven't got my sea-legs yet!' she laughed. 'I'm not a good sailor, I'm afraid. Is it going to be rough?'

'The German Ocean is always so – ' Miss Halvorsen made an expressive gesture with her hand. Katya's stomach lurched.

A strong wind suddenly caught them, knocking Katya's breath away and causing her to lean against a door. Miss Halvorsen smiled reassuringly at her. 'Come down to your cabin. You will feel the motion less down there. But we are not yet out at sea,' she added with another smile.

'I suppose not,' Katya conceded in a hollow voice. She clung to the handrail as they made their way down. Opening the door of the children's cabin, she said with false gaiety: 'Well, children, we are on our way now – ' Her voice stopped, cut off by the leap of fright her heart had suddenly given. For the cabin was empty. No children, no luggage. No coat flung down nor Maia's book of fairy tales lying on the upper bunk.

'Maia! Tanya!' She whirled round, nearly knocking her companion over. 'They're not here! They've gone!' She pushed open the door of her own cabin and nearly fell inside. 'Tanya! Maia! Where are you?' But only her own luggage was here. 'Oh, help me!' she cried in panic, clutching Astrid Halvorsen. 'Someone's taken them – taken them while we were talking – their father – or someone sent by him! And I promised my aunt I would take care of them – I promised!' Anastasia's warning echoed in her head. 'The children are in danger of being abducted.' This was the reason they were making the first part of their journey in an unknown little boat like the *Sylvie-Rose*. 'What shall I do? I've failed!' Katya burst into tears.

'Come, let us go at once to my brother,' Astrid Halvorsen urged. 'Nils will know what to do, you will see.'

'Yes – your brother – ' Katya gasped and ran ahead, bursting into Halvorsen's cabin without ceremony, crying out that the children had vanished. As she was incoherent from agitation and tears, the astonished Halvorsen turned to his sister and demanded to be enlightened. He took the opportunity of putting a comforting arm round his

221

weeping passenger while he interrogated Astrid. Then he touched a bell and put Katya in a chair where she mopped her eyes with the large clean handkerchief he provided. When his steward appeared he asked him to fetch Mr Edwards. 'My mate was in charge of sailing arrangements. He will know if anyone left the boat. Depend upon it, they are playing a game on you.'

But Katya shook her head: Tanya could hardly be described as bubbling over with fun.

The mate, Edwards, was a black-jowled man with the grim expression of one who permanently expects a disaster. 'There's been no one on or off this vessel, sir, except Mr Robert. I had a man posted at the head of the gangway as usual. I didn't want to risk a stowaway like the lad we picked up at Hamburg in the summer.'

'Have the place searched,' Halvorsen said firmly, following the mate out of the cabin.

Katya sniffed and mopped her eyes as she accepted the cup of coffee Astrid Halvorsen had brewed. She was aware that over and above her anxiety for the children was a furious disappointment. It was selfish to be thinking of herself no doubt – but not to see Russia after all! That would be awful.

The cabin door opened and Halvorsen bent his head to enter. He was smiling broadly.

'Dry your eyes, Miss Katya! We have found the young ladies.' The twinkle in his eyes belied his dry tone as he added: 'They didn't approve of the accommodation offered them, it seems. My mate has just found them tucked up in his berth! I've never seen a man so astonished. Perhaps you'll come and persuade them to return to their own quarters? I don't want to lose my mate and at the moment he looks fit to swim back to Hull!'

Katya had flushed scarlet. 'Oh, thank you,' she managed to stammer. She felt deeply mortified. What a fool she had been! She had lost her head at the very first hurdle . . .

'You must be very angry with them,' Miss Halvorsen urged indignantly. 'Show them that they cannot behave so.'

'I will try,' Katya promised. 'Only it's difficult to be cross with them. Poor children, their home is broken, their mother ill and they are being taken home by a stranger.'

Halvorsen patted her shoulder. 'Just so. Let us all forget this silly incident and get them back in their own cabin. The little Countess Tanya has just ordered Mr Edwards out of his own quarters. *He* is the one we must soothe, Miss Katya!' He burst into a guffaw of laughter in which she felt bound to join even as she wiped the last traces of tears away. 'Thank you. You've both been very kind,' she said shyly.

4

They reached Hamburg on time despite the rough seas. Katya, a poor sailor, had spent much of the time in her bunk with the storm rail caging her in. She had hazy memories of the children staring through the rail at her but, mercifully, Astrid had taken charge of them and kept them occupied.

On the last day, in comparative calm, she dressed and ventured shakily on deck. Oh, how good the sea breeze smelled after being below for so long! She took great draughts of it and felt better immediately.

Halvorsen, all concern, was at her side at once offering his arm for a short walk round the deck. 'Remember, Miss Katya, if you should need me, I shall be in Hamburg every other week. You have only to telegraph me care of the harbourmaster and I will wait for you.' His blue eyes were sober for once and he pressed her arm to his side. She felt very small and protected as she walked in his lee.

'Let me tell you one thing, Captain. *Never* will I venture on that horrible German Ocean again! I'd rather die.'

He sighed. 'If only you hadn't fallen victim to it what friends we should have become!'

12
City of Golden Spires

1

Next day he took them to Berlin and saw them on to
their train for the Russian frontier. They had sleeping
berths booked for it was, Captain Halvorsen reminded
them, a thousand miles to their destination. The last
Katya saw of him was his huge figure towering above
everyone and his red hair gleaming under the station
lights as he stood and waved his cap after them.

'Remember!' he shouted, and Katya waved and
laughed back at him.

'He is in love with you, *n'est pas*?'

Startled, Katya drew in her head and straightened her
sable cap. Tanya, a knowing look on her face, was
watching her from a corner seat.

'Nonsense. What gave you that idea?'

'The way he looked at you – like a sheep!' the girl said
savagely and mimicked a foolish expression. 'I daresay he
has a wife already, you know.'

Katya flushed and then, laughing, took off her heavy
fur coat. 'It's extremely hot in here – how shall we be
able to bear it? Why, Maia, poor little girl, you look
unhappy! Darling, we're on the way home – to your
home.'

The child raised heavy eyes. 'My head hurts,' she
complained.

225

'It's because you're hungry. Perhaps you need something to eat.' Katya took her hand and led the way to the dining car.

But Maia didn't want to eat. Persuaded to try a little clear soup she took a spoonful, put it down and leaned against her chair. 'I feel funny,' she protested.

Katya bit her lip. Here was a complication. 'Very well, I'll take you back to our compartment and tuck you up for a rest. I daresay you're tired, darling. You carry on, Tanya, and I'll rejoin you shortly.'

Before tucking Maia up with the travelling rug, she took a thermometer out of her dressing case, smiling to herself as she did so for Lady Howarth had insisted she take one to 'that Russia'. It was going to be useful after all, it seemed. She saw that Maia's temperature was just a hundred degrees. Shaking it down, she said cheerfully. 'You've got a little chill, I'm afraid. Go to sleep if you can and I'll come back after lunch and read to you.'

The child nodded heavily. Her small face was flushed but she could still ask sleepily: 'Will you read me *Alice*? I've got it in my bag.'

'*Alice* it shall be.' She kissed her. 'Have a small snooze first.'

'Snooze,' Maia said drowsily. 'That's a sleepy word.'

As Katya made her way back to the dining car she acknowledged that she was worried. They had a long journey ahead of them and she no longer had Robert Howarth to support her. For a moment she longed for him: he would have known what to do. How ridiculous of her! She must stand on her own feet from now on. She was in charge of two children on a German express train crossing East Prussia. She could have stayed dully in Whitby for the rest of her life, teaching at Hill House and going to the Choral Society every Tuesday. Instead she had been offered a chance of adventure. True, responsibility for others went with it but she would cope. Lurching from side to side, she smiled with excitement as she thought of the unknown future.

Her smile faded when she reached the dining car and was confronted by the sight of Tanya carrying on an animated conversation with a handsome youth who was now in Katya's seat. The ermine tails on Tanya's fur hat tossed merrily as she threw herself into what appeared to be an arch remark delivered with a sideways look that was a copy of an adult's. The youth leaned even closer.

'Excuse me, but this is my seat.' Katya's tone was repressive.

Startled, the boy looked up, then jumped to his feet, mumbling apologies in French.

'Please return to your seat or I shall complain to the steward,' Katya said coldly.

Stuttering apologies, the youth fled.

Katya looked across at her charge. 'I don't know yet what is *comme il faut* in St Petersburg, Tanya, but in England a child of your age wouldn't dream of talking to strangers. Your mother would be shocked, I'm afraid.'

Colour ran into the child's face. She kept her eyes down, her expression stubborn.

'Never do it again,' Katya said, summoning the steward. 'I will have the veal now, please.' What a handful the girl was, she thought regretfully. The last thing she wanted was to antagonize her but the situation would become impossible if Tanya were allowed to behave as she liked.

'I'm going back to our compartment.'

Katya leaned across the table. Inside, she felt desperate but she assumed an assurance she didn't feel. 'You will do nothing of the sort. Maia is sleeping and I don't want her disturbed. When I finish this we will both have a

227

pudding and some coffee, I think. Then we shall go back together.' She held her breath for she could see a swelling defiance on the girl's face. Then Tanya subsided, shrugging silently. She remained unresponsive as Katya strove to talk to her and it was with relief on both sides that they returned to their compartment.

Maia was awake and demanding to be read to, so Tanya sat slumped in her seat, staring bleakly out of the window. Katya wondered what her thoughts were. She couldn't help feeling sorry for someone who so obviously had a difficult character. Life was not going to be easy for the Countess Tanya Barinskaya and yet a lot of it would be her own fault, Katya thought sadly.

The daylight waned by three o'clock and the steward drew the curtains when he brought them tea. Maia refused to eat anything but she drank some tea. Her nose had begun to run.

'She'll give us her foul disease now,' Tanya observed darkly.

Katya had ordered an early supper to be brought to them and immediately afterwards their beds were made up. She undressed Maia and sponged down her hot little body. The heat in the train was overpowering and she was not surprised that the child felt it. 'Hurry up and undress, Tanya,' she said over her shoulder.

Tanya reared her head. 'With you here? I insist on being private.'

Katya burst out laughing. 'Don't be an idiot! Undress under your wrapper if you like.' With feigned indifference, she unbuttoned her blouse and stepped out of her skirt.

Tanya remained sitting on her bed, mutiny on her face.

What an extraordinary proud and unbending people these Russian aristocrats must be, Katya told herself as she slipped a nightdress over her head and began to brush

228

her hair. An English child of the same class would merely have laughed and regarded the whole business as an adventure, a sort of camping experience that could be an amusing tale to be told when they returned home. But most English children would not be so travelled nor so sophisticated as this little Russian, Katya thought with a puzzled sigh as she got into her bunk and pulled the curtain. 'Goodnight,' she called.

At last Tanya moved. Katya smiled and turned over. She didn't see the light go out. She was fast asleep in five minutes.

The train tore through the night, rocking them from side to side, its mournful whistle sounding like a lost soul as it crossed the plains of East Prussia.

Maia waking with a cry of 'Mamma!' roused Katya at dawn.

'What is it?' she whispered, scrambling out and putting her arm round the little girl.

Maia's eyes were enormous. 'I dreamed about Mamma. She was dead.'

'Just a dream, darling. Mamma will be following us home soon, you'll see.'

'But not Papa,' Maia whispered. Tearless, she clung suddenly to Katya. 'I'm frightened,' she said hoarsely.

'Hsh. Don't wake Tanya. I'll give you a soothing powder.' She switched the light on over the washbasin and mixed aspirin powder in water. Then she turned the rather hard pillow and settled the child again. 'I think you're hungry. It's a long time since you ate. What about some hot milk and a roll? I'll ring for the steward.'

Tanya didn't stir, not even when the steward arrived with Maia's early breakfast. Her arms flung above her head, her hair wound Undine-fashion across her face, she slept deeply, her clothes neatly folded on the shelf by her bed, an icon peeping from under her pillow.

Katya took Maia's temperature again and saw with relief that it was slightly down. Before getting back into bed, she drew the red curtains and looked out. Her eyes widened. It was not pitch dark outside as she had expected. A milky radiance filled the sky and she could see that they were crossing a snow-covered plain that was broken here and there by a patch of forest and a wide river running like a black thread over the whiteness. She stared out, awed by the vastness and strangeness of the scene. But she was still glad she had come.

When she woke, it was eight o'clock and both children were awake. The steward brought coffee and Katya drank it thankfully for she was parched. The compartment was still a furnace although neither child seemed to notice.

In the dining car, Katya ate the enormous German breakfast, with her eyes on the scene that was flashing past the windows. It was snowing hard and the sky was a leaden canopy over the snow-covered plain. It was an awesome sight: the plain stretching away into dark infinity with nothing to break the smooth snow except stretches of black forest.

Turning from the window she became aware that someone across the aisle and three places away was watching her. A man of about her own age had a pair of bright blue eyes fixed on her with open admiration. Amusement lurked in their depths; he had been watching for some time her barely-repressed excitement and awe at the scene outside the train.

She turned away hastily, colour mounting in her face, and looked steadfastly out of the window again. But the gooseflesh standing out on her neck told her he was still watching her – she could *feel* his eyes on her. She stole another glance – yes! those eyes (and how blue they were) were still fixed squarely on her. He was the best-looking man she had ever seen: twinkling friendly eyes in a tanned face, the face of a man who spent much of his time out of doors. Crisp fair hair covered a well-shaped head and he possessed a humorous mouth that looked as if it were going to smile openly at any moment. She turned quickly away but there was, she knew, an answering smile in her own eyes.

There were many army officers on the train, both German and Russian, but this man was dressed carelessly in a green tweed Norfolk jacket rather like an Englishman. His left hand resting on the table displayed a gold signet ring on its little finger. She wondered if he was English; he hadn't the stiff look of a German nor the haughty expression of most of the other first-class passengers. She strained her ears to hear in which language he spoke to the steward. But even if she could hear, it would tell her nothing for she remembered that all the train's officials were German and seemed to speak nothing else.

She tried not to look again but when he got up to leave her eyes followed him: he was very tall and had to bend his head . . . He had gone and had left her tingling with excitement. A stranger in a train, that's all he was, and yet she had felt the pull of attraction. He had noticed her, too. So that's what physical attraction was! She had never felt anything remotely like it for Robert or Ernest Hanson. But the pull had been strong for this stranger.

2

She spent most of the morning in their compartment staring out of the window at the extraordinary landscape. She couldn't read in case she missed something. The children played ludo together happily for Tanya had stepped down from her pedestal and was glad enough to

231

play with her little sister. Katya joined them in a game of cards and then read to them. When they went along to the dining car for luncheon, she was annoyed to find her heart beating quickly. But he wasn't there. Either he had already eaten and gone or he wasn't eating lunch. She didn't feel much like it herself after the huge breakfast she had consumed but it broke up the day for the children.

They were peevish in the afternoon and she made Maia rest. Tanya went out to stand in the corridor and presently wandered out of view. When she didn't come back, Katya got up and went to look for her, leaving Maia asleep in a corner of the seat.

There was no sign of the girl in the corridor. Katya hurried along to the washroom but it was empty. The girl was a little nuisance, she fumed as she turned to go the other way. There was no sign of her at the other end, either. Maia, she saw, was still sound asleep. She would have to search the next carriage for the errant Tanya. I shall keep her close to my side after this, she told herself, she's not to be – 'Oh!' she gasped as she turned a corner and ran into someone. A man. The stranger.

'My apologies, *mademoiselle.*' He spoke in French and steadied her by holding her elbows. Their faces were very close for a few seconds, so close that she could see a fine white scar running from his right ear to his cheekbone.

He met her eyes, found recognition in them and smiled. 'I apologize again and do hope I haven't hurt you.'

'Oh, no,' she gasped in English, adding hurriedly in French, 'It was my fault, I think, *monsieur.*'

He released her, bowed and passed on his way.

She stayed where she was, trying to regain her breath. It was so strange that she should run into him like this. She put her head round the corner to see where he was going. *Perhaps his cabin is near ours . . .*

232

He was walking rapidly and confidently, quite unaffec-
ted by the train's swaying motion, when suddenly he
stopped. He had paused before the open door of their
cabin: she had left it ajar when she ran out to look for
Tanya. The movement of the train had pushed it open
further. And he had gone inside! Maia was there, fast
asleep in a corner – too late, a horrible thought struck
her. What if he was a friend of Count Barinsky's who had
been following them, seeking this very opportunity to
abscond with one of the children? In a very few minutes
they would be coming into the first of the border towns,
still in Germany but only just . . . And their passports –
she had left them openly on the table for the customs
men who would come aboard.

What a little fool she had been, allowing a handsome
face to make her forget her vigilance over the children!
Gathering up her skirts she started to hurry back to their
sleeping cabin only to see him emerge, close the door
and continue his saunter along the corridor until he
had disappeared into the next carriage. He hadn't even
glanced back in her direction.

Bursting into their cabin she looked wildly about. But
Maia was still asleep and the passports lay on the table.

The fingers of fear that had been holding her heart
relaxed their grip and she sank onto a seat feeling
decidedly shaky about the knees. Now she was feeling
thoroughly ashamed of herself: she was behaving like an
idiot.

A minute or two later, Tanya sauntered in, avoiding
Katya's eyes.

'Where have you been? Don't you realize how anxious
you've made me?' Katya demanded.

Tanya's eyes held triumph. 'I've been for a stroll right
through the train. It was amusing.'

Very shortly after this they heard cries of 'Passports!'

233

in the corridor as the train began to slow down. There was a rush to pack and to put on heavy boots and fur coats again as after a brief pause at Eydkhunen they jolted on a couple of miles to Virballen and the frontier of the Russian Empire. It was very dark as the conductor helped his passengers down from their sleeping compartments. Katya's heart beat quickly with excitement: she was on Russian soil!

And how different it was already from the German frontier town which had been so correct and orderly, built of red brick and with its crowd of uniformed officials, red-faced and paunchy, all saluting each other.

Porters wearing baggy trousers tucked into high leather boots and with fur hats and untidy beards collected their luggage and disappeared behind clouds of engine smoke. They were herded through an iron gate into the customs hall where a dozen officials fussed over their luggage. At one end of the white-washed hall stood a life-sized picture of the crucified Christ and the Russian travellers, including Tanya and Maia, crossed themselves before the icon and purchased candles to burn before it. Presumably because they were thankful to be home again, Katya thought, as she watched her solemn-faced charges going through the small ceremony. She kept one eye on them and another on their luggage as they were jostled from one end of the hall to the other.

'Tanya! Tanya! Please find out about our next train. They don't understand English or French.'

'It won't be for ages,' Tanya reported after a conversation with an official. 'We must take our hand luggage and have dinner.'

Clutching Maia's hand, Katya followed Tanya into a brilliantly-lighted room – almost another hall. Although one end of it seemed to be a waiting room, the other half was a restaurant filled with tables covered with snowy cloths, which were already rapidly filling up. A distinct and different smell assailed Katya's nostrils; a smell combining wood smoke, leather, sheepskin and cabbage together with a strange smell she was later to learn was the sunflower oil used in all Russian cooking.

They were served excellent *hors d'oeuvres* (which the children called *zakouski*), comprising hot and cold dishes of tiny pickled cucumbers, pieces of dried fish, tiny sausages, mushrooms in cream – indeed almost a meal in itself and very different from the heavy German food on the train. This was followed by cabbage soup, fish wrapped in pastry and then *pannkoogid* which turned out to be light little pancakes served with bowls of berry jam.

The meal took an hour but it was an hour after that before the St Petersburg train, with its fixed snowplough in front, steamed noisily into the station.

There was a rush by the second- and third-class passengers but, safe in the knowledge they had seats booked, Katya had time to look round her. The peasants seemed so good-humoured as they clambered into the wooden seats that looked like racks, but she noticed they were shabbily dressed especially about the feet. Most had simply wrapped cloth round their thin boots to keep the cold out. The women with shawls round their heads carried not only sleeping babies but bundles, too. Katya liked their wide-cheekboned faces and the strong way they walked and stood, their open glances and the gentle way they treated the children.

By direct contrast, the first-class passengers being fussed over by railway officials looked richly apparelled and sleek; the women stood with tiny dogs in their arms while their maids held their jewel cases and canvas-covered crocodile dressing-cases. The men wore long coats of fine cloth with astrakhan collars and hats, or thick elk-skin coats with fur both inside and out. There

235

were a good many officers in coats down to their ankles, and large fur caps. Katya wondered where they were returning from over the border. Russia, since the summer, had been at war with Japan so probably they had been on missions to Germany who supported their aims in the war. Remembering that England was hated for taking the Japanese side, she resolved not to speak English to the children on the journey. It was a strange feeling to feel so far from home and so alien.

They set off at last. It was snowing hard now but inside the coach it was suffocatingly hot. The other seats were taken up by a lady and gentleman and a pair of lap-dogs that amused the children for an hour or so. Katya was thankful that she had not seen again the tall man who had so mysteriously visited their compartment. A great weight was rolling off her shoulders with every mile for soon she would have delivered the children safely to their aunt, Laura Nicolaievna Urosova. By ten-thirty they were passing through Gatchina and the children told her they were nearly home. With a great deal of noise the train ran into the Nicholas Station: they had arrived.

3

As Prince Alexander Rakov strode towards his waiting sleigh accompanied by his footman with the luggage, he glanced quickly behind him and saw the girl he had bumped into on the train shepherding the two children to what he recognized as the Barinsky town carriage. He smiled to himself; it was as he had thought and there would be plenty of time to get to know her. He would call on the Barinskys and renew acquaintance with Anastasia.

He found that he was immensely glad to be home when

236

at last they stopped before the Rakov palace on the Catherine Canal. Lights blazed from all floors and two footmen came running out to help him alight and to bow him into his home. A third man waited to divest him of his heavy grey coat and fox hat and inside in the great hall, Constantine Maxse, his major-domo, waited to greet him with ceremony. To each servant, Alex offered a word of greeting, for he was not the man to ignore his servants as if they were pieces of furniture. Most of them had been there since he was a child. Warmth and blazing lights and the heavy scent of hot-house flowers as well as the servants' smiling faces spelled home for him and he looked round in great contentment.

'Ah, it's good to be home!'

'Your excellency has been much missed,' Constantine murmured, lips smiling under his heavy beard.

'Has the princess gone to bed?'

'Your excellency must have forgotten. Her excellency is in waiting on Her Imperial Majesty until next week.'

'Oh, yes, of course.' The periods of his mother's attendances at Court were always a mystery to him. He crossed the hall to the library, his favourite room, and there of course was Henri waiting up for him and fussing over a silver bowl of soup on a tray that had just been brought in for the traveller.

'Henri! Did I not leave strict instructions that you were not to wait up for me?' Affectionately, he clapped his father's old servant on the back: valet, counsellor, surrogate father – what name could be given this indispensable member of the household?

'Your excellency knows I never sleep until my master is home,' Henri said reproachfully. 'Did all go well? You will be tired, I fear.'

'A little.' Alex had flung himself down on the green leather Chesterfield and was yawning. 'All went well after

237

a few tricky hours this side of the border on the way to Germany.'

'God be praised.' Henri served the soup with trembling hands but skilfully spilled none. 'Thank God, the princess suspects nothing! Indeed, this time she was a little cross with you for being so long away and missing Princess Marina's ball.'

'Oh, lord, I clean forgot.' He snapped off another yawn and broke toast into the soup. 'There was no one I knew on the train going out or coming home – at least I noticed no one following me!'

'One must hope there was indeed no one, your excellency. I think you should not go again for several months.'

'Unless I have to.' Alex finished the soup and put the bowl down. 'If the need arose I couldn't refuse.'

'I've said all along that others should do their share,' Henri said crossly.

'Well, we shall see. Now to bed – no, I insist. I'm perfectly capable of seeing myself to bed, you know!' Alex heaved a sigh of relief when the old man obeyed without his usual protests. He wished to heaven he had never told Henri of his work: the man bore the burden so badly. The log fire crackled and sent up a shower of sparks that fused before his eyes: yes, he was tired and there was no point in denying it. He lay back, meaning to go over in his mind the successful conclusion of the last ten days' work: the conference in Paris, finding good lodgings and even work for the refugees, the journey to Germany and France with three nervous companions. But it was useless because his mind would return to the girl on the train. He looked up at a Romney painting that hung on the wall above his desk. It had been brought into the family by his English great-grandmother who had come out as a young girl to St Petersburg and had been captivated by handsome Prince Igor Rakov and so had stayed for good. The portrait was of a young woman holding a bunch of cherries in her delicate hands. A pair of large blue eyes dominated her heart-shaped face and a faint flush ran along the cheekbones as if she had just blushed. A very English face he had always thought and now it reminded him strongly of the girl. He had been confident that the girl was English even before he had glanced at her passport – so carelessly left on the table in her sleeping berth! – and the door half-open, too. Katherine Croxley. That had been the name. Twenty-two years of age and born in some unheard-of town in Yorkshire. Was she governess to Sergei Barinsky's children?

He grinned and stretched: just thinking of Katherine Croxley had made him forget the heavy burden he carried. He *must* see her again.

4

'Will it be possible to get a cab to take us to the Baltic Station?' Katya asked Tanya. She knew that this was the station for the Tsar's village of Tsarskoe Selo, fifteen miles from Petersburg.

The girl shot her a look of contempt. 'Mamma would have a fit if we travelled in a flea-ridden *isvostchik*. We've never been in one in our lives! Didn't she explain that Corinne telegraphed our house steward? Matthew, our coachman, will be meeting us.'

And there indeed he was: an enormous figure as he sat on the box of a smart green carriage, wearing a padded coat and a tall tricorne hat with earflaps. All Katya could see was a large red nose and a beard as he greeted the children; a footman supervised the luggage. As they set off, Katya wiped steam from the window and peered out eagerly. It was disappointing to arrive so late at night that very little could be seen except tall buildings and ill-lit streets. But presently all this changed as they neared the centre of the city: lights were brighter and men with long-handled shovels could be glimpsed clearing fresh snow from the pavements and streets, scattering yellow sand by the barrelful. Trams with shrill bells ringing rocked across their path and everywhere people (a surprising number still were about) hurried along, muffled in thick clothes of sheepskin and fur.

Tanya, who had adopted the role of guide, was so busy pointing out places of interest that she paid no attention to the route they were taking, and Maia (leaning heavily against Katya) was almost asleep. Suddenly they stopped before a huge, brilliantly-lit building and Katya said: 'Are we there?'

They looked out but instead of the Baltic Station they were outside a large mansion, its double doors thrown wide open. Katya saw a fine chandelier ablaze with light and a woman in an evening gown with a fur cloak thrown over her shoulders coming down the broad marble steps. Her head was bare and in her iron-grey hair glinted diamond ornaments. Her breath hovered over her in a small cloud and it was difficult to distinguish her features but she held her head poised at an arrogant angle.

'We're home!' Maia shouted joyfully, struggling with the carriage door. But Tanya shot out a hand, detaining her: her small face was pinched and white.

'No, Maia – wait! This is not Tante Laura's – '

'No, silly, it's *home*!'

Katya drew her back from the door. Her heart was thudding with alarm. Home? But that meant the home of Count Barinsky who was not to have custody of his children. On no account were they to go to the Barinsky home on the Fontanka Canal. 'Why hasn't he taken us to the Baltic Station?' she said angrily. 'Ask him, Tanya!'

Leaning out on the opposite side, Tanya flung a few harsh words in Russian up to the box. By this time, the footman was throwing their trunks down into the snow while the tall figure of the unknown woman gave crisp directions.

'Matthew has tricked us!' Tanya cried, bringing her head back inside the carriage. 'He has had orders from *her* – my aunt Nada! She's Father's sister. Quick, Cousin Katya, let's run for it!'

Princess Gurievna had approached the open window of the coach. 'Get out, girls,' she said in French. 'I have been waiting for you.'

Katya felt Maia's hand creeping into hers: the child's face was bewildered, her lower lip trembling as she sensed the tense atmosphere. Tanya had no doubts. Grabbing her little sister roughly she shouted: 'Katya – quickly – this way!'

The princess's face was suddenly dark with anger. 'Give me those children immediately – immediately.' Katya glimpsed a high-bridged nose and a thin mouth as she held on firmly to the door. 'Do you understand me, young woman? You are their governess, I presume? Then do not dare to disobey me or you will pay for it.'

The arrogant tone sent the angry blood flying into Katya's face. With both hands she held onto the door as she addressed the princess through the open window. 'No, I'm not their governess, I am their cousin. I am in charge of these children and my orders come from my aunt, Countess Barinskaya. We are on our way to Tsarskoe Selo and nothing is going to prevent us –'

'You go no further than here. The coachman has his orders.'

Tanya whispered hoarsely in her ear. 'I'm getting Maia

out on this side. Never mind the luggage. We can get an *isvostchik* on Nevsky Prospekt – oh, come quickly!'

Out of the corner of her eye, Katya watched the children descending onto the snowy street through the door behind her while she parried the princess's questions. Then, grasping her dressing-case, she turned swiftly and leapt down into the snow after them. All together they hurried with beating hearts down the street towards the bright lights of St Petersburg's main street. 'There's an *isvostchik*!' Tanya gasped, waving her hand wildly. A shabby cab with straw on the floor drew up and they piled in. 'The Baltic Station and *hurry*,' Tanya directed in Russian.

They all subsided on the seat, too spent to talk. Then Tanya gave a crack of laughter. 'Tante Nada's face – how I would love to see it now!'

Katya, her breast heaving, looked at her elder cousin: that there was no love lost between Princess Gurievna and Countess Tanya Barinskaya was plain to see. And yet how alike were their looks! Their relationship was self-evident for Tanya's haughty manner on occasion was a pale copy of her aunt's. 'I'm surprised your aunt didn't send one of the servants to catch us,' she said, remembering the burly footmen standing behind the princess.

Tanya turned towards her, her face rigid with horror. 'Even she wouldn't do such a thing!' she proclaimed. 'Why, no servant would ever be allowed to lay a finger on us! We needn't have run so hard. There was nothing Tante Nada could have done to us.'

'Dear me, I wish you'd told me that earlier,' Katya retorted, nettled by Tanya's lofty tone. Would this awful journey never end? She felt mentally and physically exhausted.

Tanya, on the other hand, appeared to be exhilarated

by this latest incident. A flush had transformed her pale cheeks and an exultant smile lit her face. 'How Tante Laura will laugh!' she crowed. 'She and Tante Nada hate each other like poison, you know. Tante Nada is a jealous old cat and has been very unkind to Mamma. Now I've paid her out!' She rocked with gleeful laughter.

The train journey of fifteen miles took only a short time in a pleasant little train that was clean and shining. There was nothing suggestive of a branch line about it but as Tanya explained, the Imperial Family's special train used the line a lot now that they lived most of the year at the Alexander Palace. 'Besides, only privileged people live out here. Tante Laura is a friend of the Imperial Family's, you know.' Her eyes slid sideways to her companion. 'The Grand Duke Philip is Tante Laura's *cher-ami*, you see,' she added with an air.

Katya sighed. Tanya had been far too much with adults – she knew too much, she told herself silently, and also too little. It was a difficult combination.

'Look! There's Peter with Tante Laura's sledge!' Tanya cried as they walked out of the station. She darted forward, calling out questions to the man who sat on the box of an enormous sledge with a small hood. 'He says he's been meeting trains all the evening!' she called. 'Oh, do hurry, Maia!'

Maia stumped along silently, her fur bonnet to one side, her copy of *Alice in Wonderland* held tightly under one arm while with the other hand she clutched Katya's hand. 'Are we nearly there?' she asked pathetically as a fur rug was tucked round them and they set off.

'You baby! You must remember Tsarskoe Selo! Look, Katya, isn't it a pretty place?'

Katya's own eyes were bleary (for it was well past midnight) as she peered out at the broad avenue leading from the station with four rows of trees on either side and glimpses of fine mansions set behind high walls. There was a suggestion of the Bois de Boulogne about the place that she found comforting in so much that seemed alien to her. This wide boulevard ran straight all the way to fine iron gates in the distance which Tanya said led to the park surrounding the Alexander Palace. The carriage did not reach the end but turned sharply down a side road and stopped outside a tall house covered in almond-green stucco. It stood in its own grounds with railings instead of a wall and lights lit it from roof to cellar. They swept in through the gates and drew up at the portico. An old man in a colourful high-necked shirt and baggy trousers came through the inner glass doors and made the sign of the cross as he saw the travellers getting down, calling out something that Katya guessed must be a blessing for their safe arrival.

Katya lifted Maia down, feeling a great surge of relief. Their journey was over and she had brought the girls to their new home and safety.

13
The Tsar's Village

1

A wave of various smells was Katya's first experience of a
Russian upper-class home. For a moment she felt nausea
as a combination of fierce heat and strong drains met her
like a blow in the face and she blinked in the light of the
hall. Later she was to learn that St Petersburg and its
surroundings were built on an enormous quagmire and
the subsoil was saturated with sewage because the town
only stood ten feet above the water level. The double
windows in the houses successfully sealed in the sewer-
gas that was to give her a slight headache every day of
her stay and sometimes a sore throat.

'Your little excellencies!' A broad-faced woman in a
grey cotton gown with a kerchief round her head came
hurrying across the hall. 'Laura Nicolaievna had given
you up!' she told Tanya, clapping her hands. 'Ai! Ai! She
will be pleased!'

Katya listened to the hubbub as if from afar. She
suddenly felt so exhausted she was faint. What energy
they all had, she thought dully, listening to the clamour
of Russian between servant and children. Even Maia was
skipping up and down with a renewal of energy as she
poured out what must be an account of their journey.

Suddenly, a door was flung open across the hall and a
woman emerged holding out her arms to the children.
'*Chéries!*' she cried.

Katya stared at the vision of her aunt, Laura Nicolaievna Urosova, once *première danseuse* of the Imperial Ballet, as she stood in the doorway in this striking pose of welcome. Her white arms shone against the ruby red of her gown and she sparkled with diamonds. Her scent – musky and mysterious – came in waves as she moved towards them, kissing the children first and then enfolding Katya in her perfumed embrace. 'I am delighted to meet you, my sister's child! But how tired you look!' Her English was excellent like Anastasia's.

Katya greeted her shyly. Over her shoulder she could see into the room Laura Nicolaievna had just left. It had red damask walls with crystal lights blooming at intervals round them. A round table held a branch of candles and on its white cloth stood glasses of wine and a great dish of fruit. Sitting leaning back in a chair, twirling a glass in his fingers, was an officer in a white serge uniform, its tight collar unbuttoned, gold epaulets gleaming. He had a heavy face and a thickening neck and paunch but his air of knowing himself to be different came across clearly to Katya. This must be the Grand Duke Philip, she thought.

'You have been too kind bringing these precious children home,' Laura Nicolaievna told her. 'And my poor sister! Soon you must tell me all about it. But first you must all have a good meal – hurry, Olga!' She drew Katya into the room and the Grand Duke got lazily to his feet and bowed over her hand as Laura said: 'This is Marie's daughter. She is called Katya. Katya, this is the Grand Duke Philip.'

'Enchanted, *mademoiselle*.' The eyes raised to her face were grey and very cynical. She remembered to call him 'Your Highness': a grand duke, after all, was royal and this one was cousin to the Tsar.

'Now you eat!' Laura said. Raising her voice, she shouted without ceremony. 'Olga! Olga! Bring food –

much food, at once. The poor little ones,' she added, lowering her voice to its more usual ringing octaves, 'they look famished. Pour them wine, Philip.'

Katya would get used eventually to this calling from room to room and up and down stairs, from mistress to maid. Laura never rang a bell but shouted for what she wanted – even at one o'clock in the morning. How hot it was in here! Katya passed a hand over her forehead, feeling dizzy. 'If you don't mind, I would prefer to go to bed at once,' she said with an effort. 'I am not at all hungry, Tante Laura. We had a very good dinner at Virballen at eight – '

'At *eight*? But that is hours ago. The little ones must be fed – '

'Please.' Katya shook her head firmly. 'I would prefer to go to bed.'

Laura looked as disappointed as a child. The servants were bringing in trays of *zakouski*, a cauldron of soup, more wine. The Grand Duke said softly: 'The English are not a hardy race like the Russians. Come, Laura, do not press your niece further.' There was a veiled contempt in his voice that Katya could not mistake. A flush rose in the tired pallor of her face as she remembered that Robert Howarth had warned her of the unpopularity of Great Britain because they took the side of the Japanese in the senseless war Russia was engaged in. Should she remind him that half her blood was Russian?

Giving in reluctantly, Laura led the way. 'Then you shall go to bed, my dear child,' she said kindly. 'Tomorrow we shall talk.'

Katya put a detaining hand on her arm when they reached the upper floor. Here at last was a chance to tell her of their frightening encounter with Princess Gurievna. Laura stopped dead in the middle of the landing as she spoke. 'What? The old toad!' she exploded indignantly.

247

'I'll have something to say to her when I next see her! So she has all the luggage, then?'

'I'm afraid so. I have my dressing-case but the children have nothing.'

'No matter. Olga will see to it that they have everything.' Before handing her guest to the waiting servant, she took her hand and patted it. 'You look pale and not strong, child. Your stay in Russia will do you good, I know! And how like dearest Marie you are!'

The servant had opened the door of a bedroom. It was a huge chamber and as hot as the rest of the house. In the middle of one wall was a four-poster bed hung with muslin and lace. On the bare honey-coloured floorboards – polished like mirrors – were Persian rugs of every colour. There was a vast dressing-table with three mirrors, a long cheval-glass on a stand, chairs, small tables and behind a chintz-covered screen was a marble washstand. The tiled stove occupied one whole corner. There were two windows, both with double panes and sealed. Heavy damask curtains of deep blue covered them and two armchairs were covered in the same material. It was all in charming taste and more palatial than Katya had guessed it would be but all she could think of was how tired she was and how thirsty. She had been warned not to drink the water so she gestured to the young girl who was waiting to attend her (at one-thirty in the morning! she thought with amazement). Smilingly, the girl pointed to a silver tray containing bottles of icy-cold mineral water then went to fetch hot water for washing and a pile of soft towels. She took away all Katya's travel-stained clothes while she washed herself from head to toe, then came back and helped her into the high bed. And what a wonderful bed it was: soft but not too soft; firm in all the right places and with sheets of silk that received her tired form like a caress. With a groan of exhausted contentment, she buried her head in the pillow and fell into a dreamless sleep.

2

She woke up with a start of fear.

Someone was in the room . . .

Raising herself on one elbow, she stared into the dark, her heart pounding. Then she saw a light: the door was half-open and a dim gleam of light flickered on the ceiling. Stealthy footsteps pattered across the carpet.

'Who is it? Who is there?'

She could dimly see a figure outlined against the light: a small bearded man in the usual Russian dress of shirt, baggy trousers, and leather boots. She was opening her mouth to scream when the door was pushed open and the wall lights were switched on. The young girl who had attended her the night before came in carrying a tray on which was a samovar, a small china teapot and cup and saucer. She said something to the man who grunted and went on attending to the tiled stove. The girl drew the curtains back and revealed what looked like twilight. Then she advanced to the bed and said, smiling and pointing to herself: 'Anna.' Then she pointed to the old man. 'Ivan.'

Ivan, Katya realized, was the old man who had opened the door to them on their arrival. He grinned toothlessly at her, saying something in Russian as he collected his basket of wood and padded away.

Katya sat up. How very nearly she had lost her head again! she told herself crossly. There was a lot she would have to get used to in Russia: old men padding through her room and meals at unearthly hours, among other things.

'Tea, miss?' Anna had evidently been coached because she grinned delightedly as she uttered her first words of English.

Katya smiled back, nodding vigorously, and watched as the girl made tea from the samovar. This was a much more elaborate affair than the one on the train, she noticed, being of shining silver. The water boiled briskly over its charcoal fire and the china teapot was warmed on its holder. Boiling water was poured on the leaves and a very strong brew issued from the spout. This Anna diluted with more water in the cup. With silver tongs she added a slice of lemon and handed it with a smile to Katya. It was delicious, Katya found: hot and refreshing and no longer too strong. She reached sleepily for her watch: two o'clock. It must have stopped. But it was ticking steadily. Puzzled, she looked outside: how could it be two o'clock and so dark? Was it early morning? Snow was falling steadily outside. She held the watch out to Anna who nodded happily and held up two fingers. Then she mimicked a long sleep, closing her eyes and resting her head on her clasped hands.

'Good heavens, I must have slept twelve hours!'

'You did!' said a familiar husky voice and Laura Nicolaievna came like a rush of fresh air into the room. 'The children, too! My God, how you all sleeped – slept. You see how my English needs the brush-up? You, Katya, shall do it for me!' She was dressed for the street in a dark brown cloth skirt and jacket trimmed with golden sable. On her head was perched a sable toque and wound round her arm was a long sable scarf. 'It is gone two o'clock in the afternoon – yes, truly! Anna shall bring you luncheon on a tray and then you shall get up. Those poor children are exhausted!' She perched on the bed and stared at her niece. 'How strangely like Marie you are!'

'Anastasia said so, too – oh, I am to call her Anastasia and not Tante: she is too young to have a niece my age and so are you, Laura Nicolaievna. Need I call you Tante?'

Laura threw her head back and laughed heartily. 'You saucy puss! How right you are! Marie, after all, was – er – a great deal older than her sisters.' She winked mischievously. 'But tell me what happened to my poor beloved sister? Why didn't you let us know?'

'I wrote to my grandfather.'

'When was this?'

'December 1899 – just five years ago.'

'Now I understand.' Laura Nicolaievna got up and took a turn about the room. 'You see, Katya, your grandfather had died six months earlier. His executors – two old friends of his – would have destroyed the letter because neither of them possessed a word of English! Yes, they would have destroyed it rather than admit they couldn't understand. That is Russia for you, my dear. We are not an organized people. I daresay you feel more English than Russian?'

'Yes, I do,' Katya admitted. 'I speak French well because Mamma and I always spoke it at home when Papa was away. My Russian isn't fluent but perhaps it will improve now I am here.'

'Like my English, yes? But first tell me about poor Marie's death. I know nothing. Then I must have a first-hand account of Stana's condition.'

'I'll give you that first,' Katya said.

They talked for twenty minutes and there was a shadow on Laura's pale face at the end. 'My poor Marie! How I wish I had known . . . We corresponded only at Christmas and she always seemed so happy and well I rejoiced for

251

her.' She rose and stood with a hand on the back of a chair. 'There is money waiting for you. Did you know?'

Katya flushed. 'No, I didn't. I never gave it a thought.'

Laura smiled. 'I'm sure you didn't. My father left Marie's share of his fortune in trust for her descendants – that means you. He swore he wouldn't leave a kopeck to her and he kept his word. I shall have to inform our lawyer that we have found you again. You are quite a rich woman, my dear.'

Katya said nothing: how strange they were, these Russian relations! If fate hadn't made Anastasia seek her help in England, would they have bothered to find her, Marie's child?

Sensing something hostile in her feelings, Laura looked quickly away, laughing her deep laugh. 'I'm late! I must fly. Now, rest, Katya. Last night you looked years older than your age – such dark rings under the eyes. Now I see you are a very pretty girl – such skin!' she added enviously. Her own face was heavily made up and underneath were many fine lines: years of living in a centrally heated house set at eighty degrees had taken their toll of Laura Nicolaievna's skin. So had the heavy stage make-up she had been using all her life. A sigh shook her. 'Alas, I was young once!'

'You are very beautiful,' Katya told her shyly.

Laura's face lit up. 'You think? As long as my dear Philip continues to think so . . . You know about him? While the children are here with me, he has returned to his house in Petersburg. We thought it better.'

'That was thoughtful,' Katya murmured. She knew a sense of relief. She hadn't liked the look of Philip and it was a relief to know she wouldn't have to meet him daily.

'I must fly!' Laura repeated. 'I teach at the Imperial Ballet School, you see. One day I will take you there. This evening there is a rehearsal for the end of term display and I must be there.' She raised a gloved hand. '*À bientôt!*'

3

As the light faded, Katya fell asleep again. Outside a bitter wind blew snow against the double windows but she heard nothing. When she woke at last she stretched like a cat, feeling completely recovered and very, very hungry. Within an hour she was up and dressed, having had a long hot soak in the deep bath across the landing with Anna to hold her towels, fetch her robe and slippers and finally to brush out her hair.

I shall be ruined for Hill House after this, she told herself gloomily but an irrepressible smile answered her from her reflected face: who could fail to enjoy such luxury?

The children were standing at the *zakouski* table in a room (almost a passage) between the dining room and what she later came to know as the *petit salon*. Upstairs was a vast drawing room filled with French furniture and rich hangings but this was used only on special occasions and its long mirrors were shrouded in muslin.

'Come and eat, Katya!' Tanya's face showed a natural childish greed as her fingers hovered over dishes. 'Aunt Laura told us not to wait for her when she telephoned from St Petersburg. She's going to be late, Olga says. Take this plate and fill it with a bit of everything. It's the best way.'

Katya stared at the feast that was the *zakouski* in a private house. Ten dishes holding ten different things and all beautifully garnished were set out to tempt the appetite, the whole presenting more of a still-life painting than a meal: pink smoked salmon in wafer slices, speckled sausage cut into cubes, crisp green pickles, curls of red pepper. Some foods were set in aspic, some cut in star shapes, the whole a mouthwatering prelude to dinner. In the middle was a cut-glass barrel of Beluga caviar. There were bottles of different types of vodka and plenty of mineral water standing in ice.

Katya helped herself thirstily to the latter while she debated between herrings in sour cream or pâté on hot toast. The children had taken their own advice and put several things on to their plates. 'You see, we're simply starving,' Tanya explained, reaching for the caviar. 'Do you know, Maia slept so long I thought she must be dead so I shook her – '

'And I slapped her face,' nodded Maia tranquilly.

'Isn't it very hot in here?' Katya asked desperately. Her face was burning, her body on fire. The children seemed not to notice and assured her the house was always hot. Tomorrow, I shall discard these terrible flannel petticoats, she vowed silently. It is perpetual summer indoors although it's below zero outside.

When Laura Nicolaievna arrived at last, they were about to eat dinner and she hurried to join them, still wearing her street outfit. Hot soup with croûtons was followed by smoked fish soufflé and then roast pheasant. Two women waited on them under the supervision of the grey-bearded butler, Pyotr. Laura didn't ignore her servants but tossed remarks at them in Russian to which they smilingly responded.

It was her first meal in a Russian home and one Katya never forgot for everything was light and delicious like the French wine accompanying the meal. The children drank wine mixed with mineral water and ate enormously. When the Rassisky cheese was handed round, Katya felt she had had enough but there was an apple-and-almond pudding to follow.

Looking at her with a smile, Laura said: 'Do you approve of my chef? He is French and one of the best in St Petersburg. He was given me by the Grand Duke who looks after me so well,' she added without a hint of coquetry. She waved a hand at the great vases of yellow roses everywhere. 'From Philip's estate in Georgia. You see how big Russia is? It stretches from these icy regions to the warm south – I wonder sometimes why Peter the Great didn't build his city somewhere in Georgia! But he wanted it to be as like a fine European city as possible – like Paris or Venice, you know.' She threw her napkin down and turned suddenly to the children who had fallen into a surfeited silence. 'I will tell you what I have been doing. I have been engaging a governess for you, girls – ah! ah!' She held up a hand as they responded shrilly. 'Let me finish. I know you would prefer not to have a governess but, my dears, I could not bear to see you idle every day and you would soon tire of it yourselves. Mamma especially wants you to go on with your lessons so tomorrow Miss Ellis comes. And I warn you to behave prettily. Miss Ellis has been with the Grand Duchess Basil teaching her daughter. She will expect much from you two, and so no American manners, please.' She led the way out of the dining room. 'Let us go to the music room and Tanya shall play for us. She plays well for her age.'

The girl did play well, having a natural talent and the best masters. Laura made no pretence to listen. Turning to Katya she said in a low voice: 'I called on Nada Gurievna this afternoon – of course she pretended not to be at home. She would not meet me, I think, because she knows I have Philip's ear and therefore the Tsar's. So then I drove to the Barinsky house and demanded that all the luggage be sent on here immediately – I cowed their house steward! It will be here tomorrow I think and then you must get Anna to press all your clothes, Katya. Soon I shall take you about and show you St Petersburg.'

'You are very kind,' Katya said. 'I don't want to be a nuisance for I know you are a busy person. Please, Laura Nicoláievna, do not change your mode of life because I am here for a short time.'

Laura laughed. 'You mean the Grand Duke's visits, I presume! My dear, it is not because of you but because of the children that I have told Philip he must not come. He understands and he agrees with me. The innocence of children must be preserved.'

'I believe Tanya is very grown-up for her age,' Katya said.

Laura shrugged. 'She is like me. She will marry and take her first lover at twenty.'

'They are not the same?'

'Dear me, no! That is why I have never married. Philip has never married, either. The Tsar would never allow him to marry me. I am a commoner, you see.'

'But Queen Victoria's daughter, Princess Louise, married a commoner!'

'Ah, England. That is different. We are much stricter in our code. So I am Philip's mistress and he is my lover and so it must remain and all Petersburg knows it and waits with held breath for the liaison to break up.' She smiled slowly and a little sadly. 'It never will. We are getting old and settled. But how I should have loved to have had his child – now, Tanya, you have played that badly!' she chided in a different tone and Katya knew it was the end of an intimate conversation.

'Here is Olga come to take you to bed. Children! Children! No fuss, please. Yes, you may kiss me. No, I have no news of Mamma yet. We shall hear soon no doubt.' Turning to Katya, Laura said with relief: 'Thank heaven they have gone without fuss! I felt they must object, it is so early.'

Early! Katya glanced involuntarily at the French clock: ten-thirty. In England the children would have been asleep for hours. She was heavy-eyed herself having drunk two glasses of wine and eaten a large meal. But it was obvious that Laura herself had no thought of bed and indeed it was long after midnight when they parted. Now Katya felt she knew her aunt much better and no longer envied her her lifestyle. There was a lot that Laura Nicolaievna had missed in life although she herself seemed scarcely aware of it.

14

The Fellow Travellers

1

Years of early rising had made it difficult for Katya to stay late in bed. She was awake and impatiently waiting for her breakfast long before Anna brought it. Then she bathed and dressed quickly and went downstairs. It was nine o'clock but the sleepy servants were still half-heartedly cleaning the salon so she couldn't sit there. There were many more *moujiks* about than she had realized the house possessed. Where did they hide in the day, these simple peasants in baggy trousers and soft high boots who were sweeping and cleaning the house? They looked disapprovingly at the English girl who had wandered into their midst so she retreated hurriedly and finding herself back in the echoing hall bolted down a passage with a door at the end of it. Surely there must be somewhere in this vast house where she could write letters or read in peace until the children appeared? So far there was no sign of them. Outside it was still dark and the flickering street lamps burned. She paused to stare out of a side window. Dim figures were clearing away a fresh fall of snow and a horse and sleigh passed noiselessly. She shivered suddenly: it was all so strange, as eerie as a dream . . .

She opened the door cautiously and peeped round it: she was in a sort of gallery with a balustrade through which brilliant light shone. She peeped over. There was Laura Nicolaievna, in tights and a practice tutu, her hair tied back with a band, working at the barre that ran along one wall. She was grunting with effort and sweating freely. Stopping suddenly, she wiped her face on a towel and going across to a phonograph put a cylinder in it. Tinny strains of a fragment from something vaguely familiar came to Katya's ears. She watched, spellbound, as the sweating, grunting figure who had been pushing herself relentlessly through her exercises, changed into a leaf floating gently on the wind, whirling, turning and ending in a constant spinning motion that she would learn later were called multiple *fouettés*.

Unable to stop herself, Katya clapped vigorously as the music stopped. The ballerina looked up with a quick frown but this changed when she saw who was clapping. With a smile she curtsied. 'So! You have discovered me, have you? You love ballet?'

'I've never seen any in my life – and that was wonderful!'

'We shall have to cure your ignorance, Katya! You must come to the Maryinsky to see Kschessinska and our young Pavlova. It shall be arranged.' She wiped her face and then wrapping herself in a big shawl came up the stairs to the gallery.

'I would love to see them, of course. But what about yourself? Shall I see you dance?'

'I? It's a little late to see me, I fear! My best was over long ago. I was seventeen when I graduated from the ballet school and I retired on my pension seventeen years later – yes, I am thirty-seven! Some get re-engaged but although I had been a *première danseuse* I chose to leave and to teach at the Imperial Ballet School.' She turned to switch off the lights. 'His Imperial Majesty pays all

259

expenses for our ballet school and theatre: I am his pensioner now. Is it so in England?'

Katya shook her head. 'Oh no. I think our ballet is run by theatre companies.'

Laura shrugged contemptuously. 'Like a circus, eh? Now I am going into St Petersburg to teach so I hope you can amuse yourself today. I shall be home for dinner. The new governess should arrive at any time. I suggest that you and the children drive out to the park in the sleigh – I will give orders. There is an ice hill for tobogganing.'

'Couldn't we walk there? The gates are only down the road.'

Laura laughed. 'Yes, but there are eighteen miles of park, *chérie*! Yes, the Catherine and Alexander Palaces are both there but you won't be allowed near them. However, you can have the rest of it to run in or to drive and I suggest you do both. We have another park at Pavlovsk – and more palaces! You shall see all in time.'

'Please don't worry about me, Laura Nicolaievna. Everything is so different – so new to me. How could I be bored?'

2

Peter took them out with the troika and sleigh an hour later. Katya had never seen a troika before and was fascinated to see the bulky coachman standing up and controlling not only the fast horse between the shafts but the two galloping horses on single traces on either side. She was warmly tucked under a wolf-skin rug, a child each side of her, and they swept through the park gates and over the snow at great speed. In the spring the place would be beautiful for a jungle of lilac had been planted by former empresses: now one only noticed the dark pines weighed down with layers of frozen snow. The whole area lay within this belt of trees, all heavily guarded and patrolled, making it nearly impossible for anyone unauthorized to enter the Tsar's village. Katya glimpsed two splendid palaces: lights from the smaller blue one glittered under the dark sky. This was where the Tsar and Tsarina now lived most of the year. They were said to dislike the grim Winter Palace at St Petersburg and only went there for Court ceremonies. They tore past, Peter's hoarse exhortations to the horses ringing out on the clear icy air.

The children huddled close to her, each holding a diminutive muff to her face while Katya cowered into the collar of her fur coat and felt tears pouring from her eyes. The sudden change from the over-heated air of the house to the ice outside was a shock to the tender membranes of her nose and eyes. She was glad when they drew up at last by a large ice hill that was still in the process of being made by workmen who were throwing water over it. Each bucketful was pulled up ponderously from a hole in the ice and carried up an iron ladder to be emptied over the artificial hill: about fifteen *moujiks* were working here overseen by a loud-voiced foreman who shouted continually. Soon there would be a perfect surface for the tobogganing to begin.

'Come, let us get out and walk now,' Katya suggested. Her feet were frozen and she needed to run about to restore the circulation to her limbs.

The children shrank back. 'Oh, no! It's too cold!' they protested.

Katya had to agree that the prospect wasn't enticing: the sky was blue-grey and a sombre light fell on the snow. The total absence of sunlight was not conducive to romping. 'Then tell Peter to take us home again. At least we've had some air,' she added thankfully. Shut up in a very hot house had made her feel languid.

Now she felt exhilarated, her cheeks glowing, the headache chased away and it was with some reluctance that she walked back into the house. Ivan, the old man who guarded the hall, came to meet them to help them up the icy steps. He said something to Tanya and her face darkened.

'Bother! A visitor! Tante Laura's out. Well, I'm going upstairs. It's probably our horrible new governess – you go, Katya, *please*. You'll know what to say to her.'

Pyotr, the butler, was in the hall muttering hoarsely to himself. He threw gloomy words at Tanya and looked at Katya pleadingly.

Tanya's alarm became obvious. 'It's Tante Nada!' She grasped Katya's arm. 'I won't – I won't see her – '

'You don't have to.' Katya felt completely in charge of the situation. 'Take Maia upstairs.' She followed Pyotr into a tiny room off the hall where visitors waited to hear whether Laura Nicolaievna was at home to them. It had a high ceiling painted with birds and flowers, two sofas tightly buttoned into green silk, and striped red and white curtains at the single tall window. There was a plain cane chair on either side and on one of these, bolt upright, sat Princess Gurievna. She was dressed in heavy furs and under a fur hat her narrow face was almost obscured.

'Good afternoon.' Katya held out a hand. 'I'm afraid Laura Nicolaievna is not at home. We met briefly two days ago, as I'm sure you remember. I am Katherine Croxley.' *Met* was hardly the word, Katya thought, remembering that short explosive encounter.

Princess Gurievna stared through her veil, her eyes as cold as pebbles. There was no trace of any emotion on her face and she might have been deaf for the amount of reaction she showed.

Katya felt her quick temper rising. She knew the princess was neither deaf nor blind. She sat down hard on one of the sofas and stared at the unrelenting face. The rudeness of this Russian aristocrat! she thought indignantly. The princess, blandly indifferent to her presence, smoothed the fur of her muff and re-crossed her feet.

Katya's fighting spirit rose and cast discretion to the wind. She wasn't going to be cowed by any Russian princess – why, they were two-a-penny in this country! The other night this woman had almost succeeded in snatching the children by a trick – well, she needn't try again! Mentally, Katya rolled up her sleeves and considered her next move. 'Have you come to return our luggage, Princess? The luggage you took from us on our arrival in St Petersburg?'

Silence. The princess stared at a spot on the wall behind Katya's head.

'Oh, I forgot. Of course you don't understand English,' Katya said wickedly. 'I will repeat myself in French.' And she proceeded to do so very, very slowly.

Suddenly, like a tiger poked with a stick, the princess sprang to life. Her eyes blazed. 'You impudent baggage! I speak English perfectly – *perfectly*! How dare you address yourself to me? You – a mere employee of this house – '

'How could you be so mistaken? As I told you when we first met, I am the English niece of Laura Nicolaievna and have accompanied the children from England on her behalf. As a guest in this house and although a good deal younger than you, madame, I feel I am entitled to an apology,' Katya added with a flash of inspiration. The princess, she guessed, would understand hauteur and outrage. 'And please return my luggage at once. If you have not done so by tomorrow I shall be forced to seek advice from my embassy.'

A dark flush suffused the thin face under the veil. The princess opened her mouth to speak then closed it again.

Katya got up and walked to the door. 'Allow me to show you out, Princess. I will tell Laura Nicolaievna that you called.'

Summoning Pyotr, she handed the agitated guest to him and left her with a small inclination of the head. But as she mounted the stairs she found herself trembling from reaction. She realized suddenly that the princess would never forgive her for winning this second round in their battle over the children.

3

But Laura, returning in time for dinner, roared with delighted laughter. 'Oh, my God, how I wish I had been here! No one can ever have spoken to poor Nada Gurievna like that! I feel quite sorry for her. Katya, I salute you! Why are you not laughing, too?'

'Because I know I've made an awful enemy of her. She will never forget it.'

'We hope not!' Laura cried, clapping her hands gleefully. 'Do not worry: she will respect you now – is it not so always with a bully? And how much better to be Nada Gurievna's enemy than her friend! I am not going to change for dinner because Miss Ellis has just come and is not yet unpacked. She will be down at eight-thirty. Dear me, how I dislike these early dinners – I only do it because of the mites.'

Katya suppressed a smile: she had not had time to get

used to the late hours kept in Russia with luncheon at two o'clock and dinner at nine – and now Laura was calling this early! The meals were so vast that she could only eat a little of each course but the gap from lunch to dinner was hard to bear. She would have to get used to it in the few weeks she expected to be in Russia.

Miss Ellis was a self-possessed little woman well past middle-age. She had iron-grey hair and wore a well-cut outfit in maroon broadcloth trimmed with velvet. Her few pieces of jewellery were good and consisted of gold earrings and a watch pinned to a fob, and a magnificent pearl brooch holding the collar of her bodice. As Katya, was to learn, these were all the gifts of a grateful grand duchess. Katya had no need to wonder where Laura Nicolaievna had found this very superior governess; Miss Ellis had for the last twelve years been in charge of the Grand Duke Philip's niece. She had lived in Russia since 1870, she told them over the *zakouski* table. 'The Grand Duchess Basil begged me to stay on with them even though dearest Paula comes out this year but I said no – quite firmly of course, because the dear lady would not take *no* for an answer at first.' She helped herself to caviar and eyed the children, her pince-nez glinting. 'Dear me, what lucky little people to be allowed to stay up for dinner!'

'I'm nine and a half. I'm not a baby,' Tanya snapped.

Miss Ellis nodded to herself. 'A child of nine – I thought so. After tonight, Laura Nicolaievna, I would be grateful if you could arrange for us to eat upstairs at about six-thirty? The Grand Duchess and I are firm believers in the English schoolroom time-table until children are eighteen.'

'Six-thirty?' Laura was aghast, avoiding Tanya's outraged eyes as best she could.

'Well, seven o'clock if you like. Not a minute later.

Nothing rich in the way of food: a nice English stew perhaps and rice pudding?'

'We – we haven't a schoolroom,' Laura faltered, all her natural self-confidence evaporating under the governess's eyes.

'Then we shall have to create one, shan't we? Believe me, it is essential for the children to live separate lives from the rest of the household and to keep to a strict routine. It is all for the best,' Miss Ellis assured them, dipping her fingers into a bowl of rosewater and wiping them on a linen napkin. She leaned forward and murmured: 'Much more suitable in every way, Laura Nicolaievna, believe me.'

Laura agreed weakly. Shades of Miss Hardwick, her own governess, were rising from the past and she would have agreed to anything Miss Ellis suggested. But Tanya's face was a study in fury and frustration.

4

So next evening Laura and Katya dined alone.

'I wonder if the English way really is best?' Laura remarked, pulling a face. 'I endured it for years but Tanya has been much in America and has had more freedom. It will be hard for her and I feel cruel but I must obey Miss Ellis,' she ended virtuously. 'Our Imperial Family are being brought up the English way, you know. They sleep on hard camp beds and have few luxuries. Olga, the eldest, is only nine so perhaps it does not matter yet but where is the point of being royal if it means you are brought up like the daughters of an English clergyman?'

'Do you see much of the Tsar and Tsarina?'

Laura shrugged. '*She* hardly comes out. I am told by one who is close to them that she suffers from a form of suppressed hysteria. No, she does not cry and weep, she just cannot bear to be among people for long. She always looks about to faint. The Tsar is aware of it and most concerned for her. He adores her, you know.'

'How terrible to feel like that if you are an empress!'

'Indeed, yes. There has never been a breath of scandal round the Tsar since his marriage, although when he was young, Kschessinska, our *première danseuse*, was his mistress. A little different from your king, I think? He is a naughty boy, poor Teddy!'

'Maybe, but the British love a sporting king so he is popular. I would like to see your emperor because he is so like our Prince of Wales.'

'They are first cousins, as you know. Well, you shall, Katya. Some Sunday I will take you to the ballet; the Emperor comes often on a Sunday night. He used to do when he was Tsarevitch, you see.'

They had hardly seated themselves in the *petit salon* to take coffee when the door opened and Pyotr announced in his hoarse voice: 'His excellency Prince Alexander Petrovitch Rakov.'

The man who walked into the room was not an officer. He wore evening dress and was well over average height with very fair hair, and bright blue eyes. Katya was near enough to see the thin white scar standing out on his tanned skin and running from his right cheekbone to his ear. She felt the blood leave her heart. It was the man on the train, the man who had entered their compartment to look at their passports . . .

'Alex!' Laura advanced with outstretched hands. 'But this is delightful. No one told me you had returned, my friend. Where was it this time? Paris, eh? She must be very beautiful to keep you so constant! Weeks you've been gone, missing all that's been happening in Petersburg.'

The prince bent his bright head and kissed her hand: he was obviously very used to being teased by the ballerina. 'You are mistaken, Laura Nicolaievna; I've been gone only ten days. I'm sorry that it has seemed longer to my friends!'

'And Feo? He is well? Safe?'

'So far. God grant he remains so. This is a stupid war,' he added in a lower tone, 'only it isn't popular to say so.'

She nodded. 'I am quite of your opinion. We shall win, of course, but to embark on this adventure in the Far East – well, it's madness!' She shrugged contemptuously. 'The Tsar has surrounded himself with bad advisers, I fear. They say *she* is behind much that goes on. Your mother sees her, I know – '

'My mother never speaks about such matters.' His voice, polite and even, was decisive.

Laura took the hint and changed the subject, remembering suddenly that she hadn't introduced the visitor to her niece. She drew Katya to her side with a jewelled hand. 'My dear, I want you to meet an old friend of mine and of Stana's – ' and she flashed him a knowing smile. 'Prince Alexander Petrovitch Rakov. Alex, this is my English niece, Miss Katya Croxley.'

He bowed, his smiling eyes looking into hers with interest. 'I believe I saw you on the Berlin express a few days ago? With the Barinsky children?'

'Yes, I remember. I was bringing them back from England. My aunt was taken to hospital, you see – '

'Anastasia is ill?' There was deep concern in his voice. 'I believed her to be in America!'

'So she was,' Laura told him, lolling back on the sofa. 'However, since Sergei Barinsky has proved to be a very bad husband, my poor sister has left him. For good, I hope.'

'I am very sorry to hear this.' Alex Rakov took the opportunity to sit down next to Katya. 'But not really surprised and nor should you be, Laura Nicolaievna,' he added, causing her to look disconcerted for a moment. 'We all knew what he was like.' Turning to Katya, he said pleasantly, 'You are here on a visit, Miss Croxley?'

'A short visit, yes. I have never been to my mother's home before but she always talked a great deal about Petersburg.'

Enlightenment crossed his face. 'But, of course, you must be Marie's daughter! I never met her but I have heard about her from Stana. A runaway match by all accounts. Have you brothers and sisters?'

She shook her head. Their eyes met and found difficulty in looking away while their voices went on politely talking. I've never felt like this before, Katya was telling herself in near-panic. What is it? He attracted me in the train and now I see him so close – I mustn't! I'm going home in three or four weeks and it would be madness to fall in love with someone out here – a prince, too. I shall probably never see him again. He's married – he's bound to be. Stop it, you little fool! Aloud she talked shyly about England, the journey, her aunt's health and he listened attentively, his eyes never leaving her face.

'We must have some brandy,' Laura decreed. 'Pyotr! Pyotr! The brandy and glasses at once!'

Katya refused the brandy: two glasses of wine at dinner were more than she was used to.

As he sipped his brandy, Rakov told them that he had been to the Alexander Palace to dine with his mother who was in-waiting on the Empress.

'And did you hear how the Heir is doing? My God,

269

how thankful we were to hear those three hundred salvos in August!'

Alex Rakov's face became suddenly expressionless. 'No, she did not tell me. But he is a handsome boy, the little Tsarevitch, by all accounts, and a blessing to Russia, of course.'

'And when may we expect you to be getting married and having an heir, my young friend? Is it not time? It's five years since your father died. If you're not careful, young Feo will beat you to it on his return from the Far East! From all accounts, he has a reputation as a ladies' man. And you, Alex, are wasting your time with your mysterious Parisian! Come, come, it will not do!'

Alex laughed and shrugged. 'I shall marry some day but not yet.'

'Well, you'll certainly have to forgo your freedom before long! It's your duty.' Laura drained her glass and rose. 'Come, it is time I took Katya to her bed. See how her poor eyelids droop! Besides, tomorrow is my day at the Ballet School and I must rise at a horribly early hour.'

'You are coming in to Petersburg tomorrow? Then will you bring your niece to luncheon, Laura Nicolaievna? I have my cousin Marina staying. One-thirty, then? I shall look forward to it.' Alex Rakov's voice was eager.

As he bent over her hand and brushed it with his lips, Katya felt a distinct *frisson* down her spine: she was very attracted to this man. There was no denying it. She suspected he was interested in her, too. Had he entered their compartment on the train to find out who she was? Or (and a cold feeling suddenly sickened her) had he looked in to see if Anastasia herself was travelling with the children? There was no mistaking the warmth of his interest in her pretty aunt who was probably not much older than he.

After he had gone, Laura twirled her brandy glass

thoughtfully. 'How careful he was in what he said! Especially about this stupid war in the Far East. I could not draw him at all. Did you notice?' She looked sideways at her guest. 'Of course, one must always be careful what one says, Katya. In this country the *Okhrana* are everywhere.'

'The *Okhrana*?'

'The Tsar's secret police. Surely you have the same in England? Your king has his secret police?'

'Good heavens, no!' Katya laughed at the idea of King Edward employing secret police. 'Our king is a constitutional monarch, Laura Nicolaievna. He has no real power, whereas the Tsar is an autocrat, as I understand it, and rules without a parliament?'

'That is so. But how strange to have a king who is powerless!'

'We have Parliament, you see.' Katya felt it was a little late in the evening to start discussing the merits or otherwise of parliamentary government. She remembered that Robert, too, had warned her to be circumspect in Russia. 'Perhaps I should go to bed if we are starting early for Petersburg,' she suggested.

'Did you see him on the train?'

'Prince Alexander? I believe I did,' Katya said carelessly as she mounted the staircase.

But Laura was not deceived. 'I wonder where he had been? He is a mystery, that one! A good many people suspect him of working for the *Okhrana*. Secretly, of course.'

Katya shrugged with a great display of indifference.

'And Alex is attracted to you and you know it, you sly puss!' Laura added. 'When you weren't looking, how his eyes followed you – ah! How pretty a blush! I wish I too could still blush like that!' She patted Katya's shoulder. 'I mustn't tease you, my child. Now to bed. There are black rings under your eyes.'

271

15

The Stranger Prince

1

The nurseries in the Alexander Palace were above the apartments of the Tsar and Tsarina and the little feet of their four daughters running across the floors was the happy sound they were used to waking up to. The new baby, a fat and handsome boy, seldom cried and the empress spent much of her day near the child, neglecting her duties in the city and by her husband's side. She didn't like the society of Petersburg: to her rather staid German mind the nobility were a useless lot, bent only on having a good time and creating daily scandals by their reckless living. Alexandra's whole inclination was to turn more and more inwards towards her husband and children, closing the doors against the clamorous world. When she wasn't with her children, she was tucked up on the daybed in her lilac-coloured boudoir writing voluminous letters to all her relations and her English governess whom, as a motherless little girl, she had adored.

This morning she hurriedly swallowed the early cup of herb and lemon tea brought to her in bed and then bathed and dressed hurriedly. It was thus every morning now: her joy at having given Russia an Heir at last woke her early, sent her eagerly to the nursery to sweep aside the nurses and lift the darling little form from its lace-hung crib to strain it to her bosom: her own darling little son Alexis who would one day rule Russia! It was doubly important now that Nicky should preserve the form of Autocracy with which he governed. All this stupid talk of a *Duma*, a sort of parliament, to take over the government of the country was infamous and must be stamped out. They owed it to their little one who had been sent by God at long last to fulfil her dream of giving Russia its next emperor. That feeble Michael, who was weak and immoral and Nicky's only remaining brother since George had died from hard living and tuberculosis, would never succeed to the throne now!

As she entered the nursery, a smile of loving anticipation on her face, she was aware of something alien in the air; something wrong creating sober faces and frightened eyes.

'What is it?' the Tsarina demanded in her usual imperious manner when speaking to servants. She glanced quickly into the cot: thank God, Alexis looked as chubby as usual. But why was he crying, drawing up his legs in pain?

For answer the head nurse came towards her holding the baby's napkin. 'The Tsarevitch is bleeding from the navel and we are unable to stop it, Your Imperial Majesty.'

She snatched at the square of terry towelling and stared at the bright red stain. 'Nonsense! One of you has been careless and pricked him with the safety pin. Who has done this? I will not have such carelessness!'

They remained silent and she heard her own blustering tone die away. Terror dried her throat. Oh, God, no, not this! Not this! *Haemophilia*. That was the ugly word by which the bleeding disease was named. It was carried through Queen Victoria's female descendants to their male descendants. Not all. Only some unlucky boy child in each generation appeared to have the disease. It heralded terrible pain, sometimes early death like her Uncle Leopold, Queen Victoria's youngest son, who had died in 1884. He had only been thirty-one. The Tsarina, always at her best when her children were ill, found herself suddenly helpless. Despite applying every remedy, the bleeding would not stop and the baby refused to be comforted.

At last, her face white, she threw down the napkin and hurried out of the night nursery, her one desire to get to Nicky and be reassured that it was not so, that their darling baby boy, so long awaited, didn't have this horrible disease. He couldn't have it! He mustn't have it! The future of Russia depended on him not having it!

It was from this day that people close to her noticed the change in Alexandra Fedorovna. She became obsessed with the preservation of her one treasure on earth, her son and Russia's next emperor, the Tsarevitch Alexis. Everything else – husband and daughters, duty to the state – came a long way second to what was now her prime object in life: Alexis.

2

Katya had slept dreamlessly. She woke late and sat up rubbing her eyes. The curtains had been drawn back so Anna must have been in. She could see the snow falling relentlessly against the dark sky and judged it to be about nine-thirty. Lights among the trees in the park across the road came from the palace; she wondered idly what life could be like behind those windows. The stove was drawing well and the room was very warm for which she was thankful. Memories of early risings in the freezing dawns at Hill House came back to her and she wriggled her toes luxuriously: it was going to be hard to return there even for a short time. She must get a new teaching post by the end of next term.

There was a flimsy green envelope on the tea tray with her name on. It carried no stamp but Cyrillic characters were printed along the top. It dawned on her that it must be a telegraph of some sort. Tearing it open she saw at once that it was from Robert Howarth.

Countess making excellent progress. After convalescence will be travelling home in three weeks. Have you forgotten me?
                                                            Robert.

She got out of bed, shrugged into a robe and hurried across the landing to knock on her aunt's door. 'May I come in, Laura Nicolaievna? It's I, Katya, and I have news of Stana.'

Laura's maid, an utterly silent girl called Marfa, emerged from the bathroom among a cloud of scented steam and stared stolidly at her. 'Laura Nicolaievna? Can I see her?' Katya said in halting Russian.

The woman shrugged and disappeared once more through the curtain of steam. Katya looked round her aunt's bedroom: what disorder and how typical of its owner! It was a large room with a high beautifully-draped four-poster bed standing in an alcove. This was now a rumpled mess with a telephone, a tray of breakfast, a large diary and pencil, a beaver hat and two open hat boxes cast on its surface like so much wreckage thrown up on a beach after a storm.

'Is that you, Tanya?'

'No, it's Katya! Can I see you for a moment, Laura?'

Laura's voice was raised in strident Russian: she was demanding a towel. Going in, Katya found her aunt rising out of the steam, flushed coral all over and reminding her irresistibly of Venus rising from the waves.

'Oh, it is you! I thought this fool said it was Tanya,' Laura said, allowing herself to be wrapped in an immense bathtowel and helped out of the mahogany-sided bath.

'I've heard from Mr Robert Howarth – a telegraph of all things! He says Stana is making good progress. The children will be pleased.' She offered the flimsy form and with a damp hand Laura held it and frowned myopically at it. Then she looked slyly at her niece. 'Ho-ho! So Mr Robert Howarth wonders if you have forgotten him! Well, Katya, have you?'

'Oh, Laura, take no notice of that! It's just his way. We've known each other five years at least. There's nothing in it.'

'Then that's a pity. It is time you found a good husband, child, and who better than this rich man who owns all those boats?'

'He doesn't. It's his father, Sir Abel – '

'So a title – although a little one – as well. Better and better.' Dried, Laura stepped into slippers and a bathrobe. Tying it tightly round her slim body she went through to the bedroom and sat down at her dressing-table. Marfa took up a brush and proceeded to brush the thick black hair. 'Katya, I've been thinking: when we lunch with Alex today the Grand Duke will be there. I do not think we should mention England or the fact that half of you is English. He does not like England at the moment – no one does, my dear!'

A memory of those pale bulging eyes looking at her coldly on the evening of her arrival came back to Katya. She felt herself going pink with indignation. 'What do you mean, Laura? *No one likes England* sounds very sweeping to me.'

'England is not sympathetic to our cause in this war. She openly takes the side of Japan and has even had the audacity to warn us of the consequences!' Laura gave a little snort of derision. 'Do I speak true?'

Katya nodded unhappily. Then she said defensively, 'But then, you see, Russia isn't popular in my country after the incident in the North Sea last month.'

'To what are you referring?'

Laura's contemptuous tone suddenly irritated Katya. Really, these Russians took some living with! 'Why, your naval fleet shelled a lot of our fishing boats and left the men to drown!'

'Good God, what a fuss over a few peasants! Our good Admiral Rozhdestvensky was bound to be careful and warn off any boat that approached. He was in charge of our huge fleet we are sending to Japanese waters to finish off the war.'

'They were *fishing boats*, Laura Nicolaievna! Unarmed and on the Dogger Bank!' Then she choked back the rest of her anger for Laura's eyes were reflected in the mirror and their expression was hard. She must not have a row with her aunt, Katya reminded herself, smoothing out the crushed telegram and putting it in the pocket of her peignoir.

'Now that is a typically English statement: one must be fair and kind to the peasants. Bah! It is rubbish and very hypocritical, too,' Laura persisted.

Katya had learned self-control in a hard school. She bit back an angry retort and contented herself with a half-smile.

Laura saw the expression and immediately vented her irritation on her maid. 'Don't pull my hair, you fool!'

Beating a hasty retreat, Katya went back thoughtfully to her own room. There was a deep gulf in thought and way of life between her and her Russian relations, she told herself. A depression that was also homesickness

277

seized her. At that moment she would have given anything to see Robert Howarth's open face and hear his blunt voice saying exactly what he thought about these Russians. But not about Stana: she had seen that he was charmed with the Countess Barinskaya. But how strange that Laura took the Howarths' kindness so much for granted! Not once had she expressed gratitude for their help.

I don't like her, she thought bleakly. Worse, I can't bear her! She's a selfish, self-indulgent cruel monster! To hear her talk to that poor Marfa – oh, well, I'm only here for a short time and I'll just endure it.

3

Yet when Laura walked into the morning room an hour later to take her into Petersburg for lunch at the Rakov Palace, she radiated a charm that Katya found hard to resist. 'Ah, you're ready. Good girl! That colour suits you admirably, Katya. Good morning, children. You do lessons this morning, I think? Miss Ellis, please pay attention to their English accents. They have both picked up a vulgar whine that must come from their sojourn in the United States. It must be corrected quickly.' She rustled out into the hall and Katya followed her wondering why she hadn't told Tanya and Maia the good news about their mother. She's going to ignore Robert's telegram, she thought indignantly as they got into the red sledge that was to carry them to the station. Really, the woman's impossible!

She settled into the sledge expecting to be driven off but not a bit of it. Laura was helped out again: she had decided to wear her beaver hat and coat instead of the sables.

Katya waited shivering in the icy air while cries of 'Marfa! Marfa! Run quickly to my room – ' echoed from the house. Ten minutes later, Laura emerged holding a flowered hatbox. 'I must take my sable cap back to Monsieur Paul,' she explained. 'I've only worn it twice and it really doesn't suit me. Now let me see: where is my bag? Oh, it's here. Pyotr, come here!'

The butler, looking thunderous, emerged into the icy air and stood while Laura gave him several last-minute instructions before allowing the sledge to move off at last.

We shall have missed the train, Katya thought to herself.

But Laura Nicolaievna was not in the least perturbed. True, they found the train in the station emitting great clouds of steam but she unhurriedly gave her coachman instructions about meeting them on their return while a porter carried the hatbox and a fur rug to an empty compartment. Only when she was seated did an underling (obeying a gesture of the station master's) raise his green flag.

At the Baltic Station the Tsarskoe Selo train had its own platform: on days when it was used by the Tsar himself a purple carpet would be put down, Laura told her as they strolled across to where a royal blue sledge awaited them. This belonged to the Grand Duke Philip and his arms were emblazoned on the doors. A footman in royal blue and gold livery helped them into its padded interior and then jumped up on the running board behind.

So this is what being a grand duke's mistress means! Katya thought, suppressing a gurgle of amusement: *better by far than being his wife*. For Laura was still very much her own woman although she was under Philip's

279

protection. There's a lot to be said for it, Katya told herself with a secret chuckle as they swept down Nevsky Prospekt, the *droshky*'s iron runners gliding smoothly over the hard-packed snow.

She looked eagerly from side to side. So far she had only seen the city by night. Seen by day, under shafts of thin sunlight that touched the golden domes of buildings with a queer unearthly light, she realized that it was beautiful. Domes and tulip-shaped towers sparkled like something out of a fairy tale, and what queer colours the houses were painted! And how wide the streets were! No wonder it was said that Peter the Great had tried to build a new Paris on the banks of the Neva: there was something Parisian about this very smart street lined on either side by expensive shops. She gasped with delight at the sight of these shops, their windows stuffed with luxuries, their interiors blazing light. That was Elisev's where the best cream pies and sweets were to be found, Laura told her. The English shop; the Ural Stone Shop and the Peasant Shop flashed past and then suddenly there was Fabergé with its granite pillars and its grilled windows aflame with precious jewels.

Katya longed to explore but this morning Laura had no time to spare. 'I must just leave this hat at Monsieur Paul's and then we must go straight to the Ballet School.'

But even from the *droshky* there was much to be seen. A troop of Cossacks passed going on guard duty with their perfectly-matched horses; policemen in long black overcoats with orange facings and astrakhan hats seemed to be everywhere. To Katya's eyes, used to the familiar rotund figure of the British bobby, they looked more like soldiers than police and she felt nothing would induce her to approach one to ask the way. There were beautiful women muffled in grey fox or brown sable; little girls with governesses; old gentlemen weighed down by elk-skin coats – and dozens of peasants in rags trying to keep warm round the bonfires that burned in an attempt to melt the collected heaps of snow. The acrid smoke from these fires made her hide her face in her muff, but Laura seemed so used to it she made no such gesture.

The peasants were engaged in sweeping the snow off the pavements and they had continually to retreat to the well-filled gutters to allow the nobility to walk past unimpeded. There were ragged beggars in London, sweeping the crossings, and sad sights like legless men begging for pennies, but here in Petersburg the poor seemed to be multiplied by hundreds. And the well-dressed appeared not to see them, walking through them as if they didn't exist, Katya noticed. Even small children were earning a few kopecks carrying baskets from the shops to the waiting *droshkys*.

The Grand Duke's *droshky* turned in a half-circle off Nevsky Prospekt and now they were in Theatre Street, a wide short cul-de-sac that was hushed after the rush and babble of Nevsky Prospekt. Here was the Imperial Ballet School, its roof adorned by three bronze horses. Next to it was the yellow and white front of the Imperial Theatre where Laura Nicolaievna had been principal dancer. 'This, Katya,' said Laura Nicolaievna, 'is my real home.'

'Is it a boarding school?' Katya asked as children were filing down the stairs clad in what seemed a very plain grey uniform.

'Yes, you can call it that. They learn general subjects although they are here to become ballet dancers.'

Katya watched the streams of children. 'You have a lot of pupils here. And both boys and girls! How strange – a boarding school for both sexes?'

Laura laughed as she began to mount the stairs. 'Why

281

not? Our girls live here on the first floor and are very closely guarded, I assure you! The boys are upstairs.'

'When are they fully fledged as dancers, Laura Nicolaievna?'

'When they are seventeen or so. Then they must sign a contract to dance for the Imperial Ballet for the next twenty years or so. After that, they may retire with a pension.' She opened a door and beckoned Katya after her. 'Here is my office where I interview the parents and children. I have to explain to them what the life of a dancer involves. They have to say goodbye to their children and give them up to us. It is a hard decision to make. It isn't an easy life. One has to be dedicated to it.' She closed the door and they walked down a corridor. 'Let me show you our little theatre where each year the Imperial Family come to watch a performance by the pupils.'

It was a perfect miniature theatre in blue and gold, the royal box swagged in rich dark blue and gold tassels.

The sound of a piano came from behind a closed door beyond the theatre. 'Come. You shall watch the rehearsal for our Christmas ballet while I go and discuss some arrangements with Leon Ivanov. You'll find it interesting, I think. I will come back for you shortly.'

They had entered a vast room made light with many windows. Here boys and girls of all ages were working in two separate groups.

'They are working on *Casse Noisette*. You know it? By Tchaikovsky? Kschessinska has danced it in London but perhaps you did not see her – it was some little time ago. This movement is the dance of the Sugar Plum Fairy. Charming, isn't it?' She went across to the teacher, a thickset woman with colourless hair who was wrapped in many layers of wool for the room was unheated. She had a rasping voice with which to rap out orders, rather like a

282

sergeant-major on a barrack square, Katya thought. An old man, bent and bearded, played the piano with a crisp touch and fingers that seemed to be years younger than his body.

'So I will leave you,' Laura said and shut the door.

Katya, aware that she was the cynosure of many eyes, sat self-consciously on a hard chair. The air smelled stuffily of sweating bodies and chalk but she soon forgot these discomforts watching the young dancers. She could follow the instructions because they were in French.

'*Élévation*!' screamed the instructress and a girl leaped with seeming effortlessness into the air. They stopped and an *entrachat* was discussed, the woman insisting on an *entrachat-trois* from a reluctant boy. Now the pupils had no eyes for their silent visitor; all their attention was on the shapeless woolly figure screaming at them, demanding the utmost from them. Sweat flowed freely off their bodies. '*Jêté*!' They leaped into the air. Then back to the *divertissement* from *Casse Noisette*.

Across the room, Katya could glimpse another class in progress; this one of older pupils. A man like a gorilla in black tights and a singlet was hurling himself about and coaxing the dancers to reach new heights of effort. It was clear that their concentration was such that the screams of the instructress in the other class didn't penetrate their consciousness. There was no music at this end of the room, only supple young bodies performing small miracles in the shape of a *fouetté* or an *arabesque*.

Much too soon, Katya felt Laura's touch on her arm and she followed her reluctantly downstairs to the waiting *droshky*. She drew a long breath as she sat down, saying impulsively: 'That was the most enthralling half-hour I've ever spent! Oh, if I were years younger and had an aptitude I think I would have chosen to be a dancer! How happy it must make you to dance, Laura Nicolaievna!'

Laura's face seemed to soften from inside. 'It does – it does! But now there is sadness, too. I am growing old and the time is coming when I shall dance no more.' Melancholy flooded her green eyes. 'Even *l'amour* doesn't take its place, Katya.' Then she smiled brilliantly. 'Enough! It is good I can amuse and please you so easily, my dear – ah, we are here.'

The house they had arrived at was in a street full of beautiful buildings off Nevsky Prospekt. It was called Catherine Canal and the house before which they had stopped was a palace of yellow ochre with four rows of tall windows, and had huge double doors painted in dark red. Inside the imposing entrance stood a rigid row of servants in dark red livery with powdered hair waiting to receive them. Katya swallowed in surprise. To think of that shabbily-dressed prince owning this! She felt very shy of him all of a sudden.

They were shown into a small reception room where servants took their coats, and then they were led through a vast hall with a floor of huge almond-green and white tiles, pale green and blue columns holding up the ceiling and a green marble staircase that split into two. There were flowers everywhere and their scent floated on the air, mingling with Laura's strong *Chypre* that floated behind her wherever she went, and the usual drainy smell found even in the great houses of St Petersburg.

Alex Rakov came eagerly towards them and bent to kiss their hands. Again Katya felt that *frisson* down her spine, especially when his eyes looked deeply, if briefly, into hers . . . She knew now without a doubt that he was as attracted to her as she was to him. Already an invisible string seemed to be pulling them towards each other and already she was beginning to feel as helpless as a puppet manipulated by unseen hands.

Having greeted them he took Katya by the elbow and

steered her towards a small group of guests standing round the *zakouski* table. 'Miss Croxley, allow me to make some introductions.'

There was the Grand Duke Philip, his bull neck bulging over his white and gold collar and his round poached-egg eyes goggling sentimentally at his mistress, Katya noted with amusement. How could beautiful Laura bear him?

He was the only other man present, the other guests being an old woman called Countess Betsy Tarpol, very yellow of skin and covered with a careless assortment of gorgeous jewels, and Princess Marina Sergeyevna Drusova who was Alex Rakov's cousin. She was tall and beautiful and reminded Katya of a young lioness with her tawny colouring and broad-cheeked face. Her fascinating eyes were a golden hazel and her voice was a purr. A young lioness indeed and afraid of nothing as she teased the Grand Duke and brought a dark flush of annoyance to his pallid face.

Katya was thankful it was a small party for she felt shy and uncertain at this first venture into Petersburg society. Everyone spoke English in deference to her but her heart sank dismally when she found herself sitting on the Grand Duke's left hand, Rakov having the old countess on his right and his cousin on his left: Laura sat at her lover's right side and they were soon deep in conversation.

Presently, the Grand Duke turned to her and prepared to make stiff conversation consisting mainly of disparaging remarks about Britain. It was soon evident that (as Laura had warned) like many high-born Russians at the moment he was feeling bitter towards England. She soon lost her shyness in indignation at his deliberately pointed remarks but she attempted to parry them with light-hearted retorts of her own.

'England, that *great* democracy,' he said constantly with malicious emphasis. 'Our poor uncle is virtually a

285

prisoner in his own country! Unable to rule like an emperor should, dominated by a lot of shopkeepers! Tragic, *n'est pas*? And there are fools here who would wish the same for us!'

Katya's murmured protests were brushed aside and Countess Betsy, who had been talking non-stop, paused abruptly and said in her deaf old lady's voice: 'What? What was that he was saying?'

Laura repeated it loudly for her benefit and Katya's head drooped over her plate. She felt foolish and alien which was what Philip intended. He regarded her presence in his house at Tsarskoe Selo as the main cause for his own banishment from Laura's bed: sexual frustration and a genuine dislike of England were making him behave boorishly to the young English girl who was making no attempt to defend herself or her country – bah! They were a poor lot! Why, young Marina over there would have sparked up at him and thrown his insults back in his face . . .

Katya took a sip of wine to cool her agitation and her eyes met Rakov's: dark with concern, they suddenly smiled encouragingly at her and he gave her a little nod like a message. Then he said coolly but firmly: 'Miss Croxley is my guest, Your Highness.'

It was enough: Grand Duke Philip took the point. He laughed maliciously but he must have realized he had angered his host for he began to make himself very charming, across Katya, to Countess Tarpol.

Marina Sergeyevna took out a little ivory tablet on which she scribbled with a silver pencil and then gave it to a footman to carry round to Katya: *He's the greatest beast in Petersburg. Take no notice, I beg!* She accompanied this missive with an encouraging and friendly smile.

At this warm-hearted treatment, Katya's courage

flooded back. She guessed that Alex Rakov had invited his cousin because they were of an age. Afterwards, they drank their coffee in a huge drawing room overlooking a snow-covered terrace above a courtyard and they found plenty to talk about.

Alex soon made his way to her side and gradually led her round the room, ostensibly to view the fine collection of paintings, mostly French, adorning the walls. 'This is a delightful Fragonard, don't you think? This Watteau is one of my favourites.' Lowering his voice he said: 'I must apologize for the Grand Duke. I would not have him hurt your feelings for the world. He has always been a tactless fellow and cultivates this brutal manner but I felt I had to invite him for Laura Nicolaievna's sake. They love each other, you know, and have been faithful for years. It's very touching St Petersburg thinks!'

'Please don't worry. After all, you and your cousin Marina have been kindness itself to me.' Their eyes met. The light that had leaped up in his startled her. For a moment they stared into the depths of each other's eyes but all he said was: 'Let me show you this little sketch. It's my favourite.'

They moved on, their shoulders touching. A dizzy sort of happiness possessed her and she hardly heard what he was saying. 'This room was furnished in the French style by my grandmother who was an unashamed Francophile. She and my grandfather were happiest in Paris, and I still retain my *appartement* in their old home in the Bois de Boulogne. The rest is let.'

'Were you returning from Paris when I saw you on the express?'

A broad smile lit up his face. 'So! You did notice me, *mademoiselle*? I'm flattered!'

'How could I not? You stared so hard – it was very rude, your excellency,' she added demurely.

287

He laughed softly. 'I did something much worse than staring! I saw little Maia in your sleeping compartment and went in and read your passport!'

'I saw you,' she informed him calmly. 'I thought you were a friend of Count Barinsky's who had come to abduct the children.'

'A friend of Barinsky's – good heavens!'

'Then of my aunt's? You recognized the children.'

'That is acute of you. Yes, Anastasia and I are friends – good friends. I saw quite a lot of her in Paris from time to time. Tanya recognized me and stared right through me! I think she doesn't approve of me,' he added ruefully.

'Perhaps she has reason not to?'

He shook his head, laughing. 'Oh, no, *mademoiselle*, nothing like that, although I have always found your Tante Stana a very alluring person. There is something of her in you: your nose, the set of your eyes and – yes – when you laugh I see Stana.'

'That is because I'm very like my mother, her elder sister, whom you won't have known.'

'No, I didn't, although Stana has told me her romantic story.'

'Romantic? I wonder. Sometimes,' she said softly, 'her longing for Russia made her ill. She died much too young and my father was drowned the same week when his ship was in a collision on the German Ocean.'

'The same week? My God, what you must have suffered,' he said gently.

She looked up and found his eyes fastened on her face with the tenderest expression. She tried to look away and couldn't. I – ' she said, 'I – ' Then she saw that the old Countess Betsy was being helped to her feet; her little tapestry bag, and her gloves handed to her, her silk shawl being draped about her person.

Laura beckoned her niece. 'Come, Katya.'

'I must go. Thank you very much, Prince, for a most enjoyable luncheon party.'

'I am delighted you could come, *mademoiselle*.' He pressed her hand. 'Until we meet again.'

On their way home Laura said: 'I have asked the family solicitor to let you have some of the money Papa left in trust for you. You need a lot more clothes – good clothes. I can't stand these ready-made outfits you're wearing.'

'They're the first good clothes I've ever possessed and come from the best shops in Hull,' Katya pointed out. 'Sir Abel Howarth paid for everything – even my fur coat – so if I'm to have any money I must send it to him.'

Laura smiled. 'The solicitor shall send him a cheque with your thanks. My dear girl, you are quite rich! Papa was not a poor man and he settled money on you three grandchildren.'

'Then perhaps I shall have sufficient capital to start a school of my own?' Katya said eagerly.

'*A school of your own?* Are you mad? D'you want to be a governess all your life? Of course not! You will marry and marry well when it's known that you have money. Yes, I shall drop hints in the right quarters – '

'Please *don't*, Laura Nicolaievna. I don't want any man to offer me marriage because I have money! Besides, I'm going home after Christmas and that's only three weeks away.'

'Is there someone in England? Aha, of course! Mr Robert Howarth!'

Katya flushed. 'I don't intend marrying Robert and he knows that. There is – no one.' Under the rug she crossed her fingers.

'Then don't set your heart on Alex Rakov, *chérie*.'

She was startled and blushed fiercely.

'He is very attractive and many have been in love with him including my own little sister! But he is known to have a mistress in Paris like his father before him. Then there are his politics.'

'His politics?'

'Yes, he is either a police spy or a revolutionary. He has been seen often at socialist gatherings – a princely socialist, ridiculous, eh? Most people think he is there to give names to the *Okhrana*.'

'But that's awful!'

'Yes, isn't it?' Laura said easily and, having done her worst, turned her mind to other things.

16
Gipsy Music

1

Three days later, Laura Nicolaievna rustled into the *petit salon* where they were gathering before lunch and brandished two letters above her head. 'Good news, children! Your mother will be with us for Christmas!'

Tanya sprang to her feet. Her face went pale with emotion. 'Then she's not going to die? She really is better? Tante Laura, promise me it's true? Mamma won't die after all?' She burst into tears.

Miss Ellis put an arm round the child and led her to a small sofa by the window. 'Dear child, is that what you've been thinking? That your mother was dying and we were keeping it from you?'

Tanya choked and nodded. 'I thought – ' she said incoherently and wept on Miss Ellis's shoulder.

'Well, as you see, it's splendid news. Now dry your eyes. Laura Nicolaievna, I suggest we give her a little wine – just for once.'

Maia scrambled up beside them. 'I'd like wine, Miss Ellis, if you please. Will Papa be coming, too?'

'Papa's never coming back!' Tanya cried in a fierce, hoarse voice.

Whereupon Maia opened her mouth, screwed up her eyes and bawled: 'I want Papa to come back! I do – I do! I love Papa! I do – I do!'

'I don't! I never want to see him again!'

'Tanya, stop it!' Laura said sternly. 'You must not speak of your father like that. He still loves you and some day will want you to go to Washington to visit him – '

'I shall never go! Never – never – never!'

Laura shrugged. 'Dry your eyes, Maia. Just think! Mamma is well again and will be travelling home to Petersburg. I had heard she was getting better but never did I dream of such progress – '

'You knew? Then why didn't you say that you had heard?' Tanya asked fiercely. 'Why did you hide it from us, Tante Laura? Mamma is *our* mamma and you should never have kept any news of her from us.' She scrubbed at her eyes childishly but the look she directed at her aunt was perfectly adult, combining indignation with real anxiety. 'You should have told us – you should have!'

Laura shrugged. 'I wanted to be sure,' she said defensively. 'I wanted to hear from Mamma herself. The telegraph received wasn't from Mamma. Now, here is a letter in Mamma's writing – very weak as you see – but it is from her and there is no mistake this time.' She proffered the other letter to Katya. 'It's from Alex Rakov to me. Read it. He wants us to dine at the Bear Restaurant tonight and go to the gipsies afterwards. I must telephone him at once. It will be a novel experience for you, Katya, for I know you have nothing like our gipsies in England. They live on the Islands and they play our Russian music like angels – and dance like angels, too!' She leaned across and said for Katya's ear alone. 'But beware, my child! Gipsy music is the most romantic in the world and it is plain to see Alex has designs on you – oh! oh! no use denying it! It was written on both your faces the other day. Even Betsy Tarpol noticed and she is almost blind!'

2

Katya wondered what would be a suitable dress for dining in a restaurant. Appealing to Laura that evening, she displayed her wardrobe. 'I like the red taffeta myself. I wore it the other evening, you may remember.'

'It's too plain,' Laura decreed. 'Very nice for dining *chez nous* but – ' She lifted down an elaborate dress in sea-green satin with shell-pink velvet ruching round the low neck and skirt. It had been one of Lady Howarth's extravagant choices and suitable for a grand ball: where, Katya had demanded at the time, would she wear it in Russia? And now here was Laura Nicolaievna nodding approval and saying it was 'quite a nice little dress' and would do very well for a visit to the Bear Restaurant!

'Have you jewels?'

'Just this brooch of my mother's.'

Laura smiled. That pathetic little brooch of Marie's her niece wore every day and seemed so attached to! It would be lost among the magnificent jewels worn by the other women. 'I shall lend you an aquamarine set of mine – no, it's not valuable so do not be silly, I pray. It was given me when I was young and it will be suitable, I think. But we must get you some clothes and quickly.'

Katya accepted the offer of the aquamarine with good grace. She only hoped the jewels were not a gift from the Grand Duke: they would feel like a snake round her neck if they were. She docilely accepted them and the fact that an elaborate dress was suitable for the evening's entertainment.

Dressed in the sea-green satin dress, she thought she

293

really looked quite nice. The colour did things for her skin and her hair.

As she reached the hall, Tanya came out of a room and stared at her. Up and down went her sharp eyes from the aquamarine necklace to the pink flounce on the hem of Katya's dress.

'Will I do?' Katya asked with a smile.

Tanya shrugged. 'I suppose it's all right. It's very much what a governess would wear on her evening out, isn't it?'

'Tanya.' Miss Ellis had joined them silently. 'Go upstairs to your room at once. I shall come up presently.' As the girl sulkily marched up the stairs, the old governess laid a kind hand on Katya's arm. 'I assure you, my dear, *I* never wore anything so fine on *my* evenings out! Really, what an unpleasant child she is. The news about her mother has quite unsettled her. I shall set her a piece of English prose to copy out: that should take her mind off such things for a time.'

Katya kissed her affectionately. 'Like you, I'm a governess really and this does seem to me very grand for dining in a restaurant!'

'Just wait until you see the others! St Petersburg ladies know no limit!'

3

Katya saw how true this was when they entered the restaurant. Under discreet lighting, the women preened themselves, spreading their rustling skirts like birds of paradise. Some were quite outshone by the glittering uniforms worn by their escorts. Heat and the smell of rich food and Egyptian cigarettes rushed to her nostrils as

294

she took her host's hand and curtsied to the Grand Duke who inclined his head and looked through her. Alex Rakov however had pressed her hand and looked eagerly into her eyes causing colour to flood her face: she had the strange feeling of being hunted by this man and she felt panic because she knew it would be impossible to resist him. So, hastily withdrawing her hand, she turned to greet his cousin Marina and her friend Mademoiselle Staropova who was dark, plump and pretty, a complete contrast to the statuesque Marina. Lieutenant Maisky and Captain Sverbeyer made up the party who occupied a table in the centre of the room and were waited on by the head waiter and three underlings whom he communicated with by a crack of his fingers.

Katya hardly knew what she ate only that it was delicious. She was aware only of the proximity of Rakov: from time to time his arm brushed hers. He was the only man in the party not in uniform, yet he lost nothing by being dressed in a white waistcoat and tails.

As the meal progressed and the conversation became interspersed with laughter, or voices dropped intimately to be heard only by one's dinner partner, Katya became aware that she was being singled out by her host, that it was to her he was paying special attention. Skilfully, he drew her out about her life and her attitudes. At first she was reserved for English ideas now seemed out of fashion in this Russian city. Her liberal ideas were listened to respectfully, however. He asked her several questions about England, about politics and the position of women there. Afterwards she had time to be surprised that while the conversation of the others was frivolous and teasing and gossipy, she and Alex Rakov were earnestly pursuing the subject of unions and labour in England – conducted in the low tones of a pair of lovers!

Laura was the first to notice. She gave her shout of

laughter. 'Just look at those two! Tell us, pray, what is the fascinating subject you discuss with your heads so close together?'

Alex raised his glass to her. 'Ah, frivolous one! Katya was giving me the latest figures for infant mortality in England – a little above your head, Laura Nicolaievna!'

Of course no one believed him, Katya noticed with amusement. Everyone laughed and looked at them teasingly. *Infant mortality in England* indeed!

His eyes met hers. 'Tell the truth and no one believes you! You heard that I called you Katya without your permission. A thousand pardons but I intend calling you Katya from now on! My name is Alex.' Under the stiff damask cloth his hand reached out to hold hers. Her eyes had already been caught by his and held against her will. Her breath came quickly and shallowly; she was amazed by the feeling that swept her. His face suddenly swam before her eyes: when it steadied she saw it at close quarters for the first time. There was a brown mole under his left eye and another near the eyebrow; there were creases on either side of his mouth and there was the fine white scar running like a thread from temple to cheekbone.

'How did you get that?'

He put a hand to it, a reminiscent smile on his face. 'A legacy of my mis-spent youth! I was a hothead at twenty-one, I am afraid.'

Then Lieutenant Maisky on her other side claimed her attention and she turned away but she was acutely aware of his sleeve with its inch of starched cuff so close to her arm.

It was past midnight when they set off in troikas for Novaia Derevnia, the gipsy quarter on the Islands as the archipelago formed by the canals was called. To Katya there was magic in this midnight journey under an indigo sky where stars flashed like scattered diamonds. The driver was called a *yamshchik*, a large figure in his padded coat and fur hat, who stood up controlling the horses with great skill. They dashed at speed across the sleigh road over the frozen Neva that was marked by lamps on this bitterly cold and dark night. Soon they had left the suburbs behind and were racing through the snow between the black shapes of forest trees.

Katya shared a troika with Alex. Close together under the wolf rug provided, their bodies touching, she longed for the journey to go on for ever, with Alex beside her and the icy wind clawing at her face for her scarf was soon torn off. Seeing this, he laughed as he put an arm round her and shielded her from the worst blasts of air that threatened to take her breath away.

Her eyes closed she was aware only of speed, of being pressed close to the side of this stranger prince to whom she was already deeply attracted. Dangerously so, she feebly reminded herself. It would be madness to lose her heart to a man who could only be treating it as a lighthearted game. Besides, she was going home after Christmas and would never see him again . . .

There were lights ahead and they were slowing down before entering a clearing and drawing up in front of a long, low wooden building. Dogs bounded out, barking in the darkness, someone was thumping on the door and as it opened and light flooded out on to the snow, Alex threw the rug back, picked Katya up and carried her into the building. She blinked as she stared round the big room she found herself in. It was lit by dozens of tall candles stuck in bottles and was overpoweringly hot and smoke-filled. Coming from the fresh icy air, the atmosphere struck like a physical blow. There was already a crowd of people sitting round the room at small tables on which were gold-necked champagne bottles or samo-vars of tea. At one end of this barn-like room was a gipsy troupe of about twenty men and women dressed in colourful clothes. Ribbons fluttered from their balalaikas as they sang in curious metallic voices a haunting folk tune that the audience echoed under their breath, swaying as if mesmerized.

Soon the rhythm changed and a girl ran on to the floor. Her full skirt of blue and scarlet and green flew out round her hips as she began to dance, affording a glimpse of sturdy legs clad in scarlet leather boots. She danced like a whirlwind, the music going faster and faster, and then she was joined by two swarthy young men wearing embroidered blouses who danced round her until all that could be seen was a mad swirl of colour. As the music stopped, the whole room leapt to its feet calling for *more! more!* But the gipsy dancers ran off to be replaced by a sad-looking man on a stool who began to pluck his balalaika strings to another haunting tune.

Silence fell and melancholy filled the listening faces as the gipsy choir began to sing softly from the shadows. Marina, Katya saw, had tears in her eyes as she laid her head on Lieutenant Maisky's shoulder. With a little throb, the music touched a chord in Katya's being too, and she knew without doubt that she was in love with Alex Rakov and that sadness lay in this very fact for within a very short time she would have gone home. Half turning to look at him, she found his eyes still fixed on her. Word-lessly their hands met again and held, forming an acutely sensitive lifeline between them. Tears stood in her eyes and she blinked them away. She had promised herself that she would be sensible and cautious during this Russian visit and now here she was, her fingers interlaced with Rakov's (a man whom she neither understood nor knew anything about), her heart moved by the treacherous music, her whole body aching for his touch.

Then the music stopped. Marina raised her head from Lieutenant Maisky's shoulder. 'Oh . . . I was in a dreamland – a wonderful feeling! Please, some more champagne for I am about to cry!'

The haunting sadness of the moment was dispersed with a laugh. Alex poured champagne and signalled for more for both tables.

Katya sipped hers in a dream. She felt bewitched by this extraordinary place. Inside the circle of light cast by the candles on their table, she glimpsed Marina's white arm against the red velvet of her dress and the pale fur she had thrown back over her chair; Lieutenant Maisky's uniformed sleeve of royal blue and gold; Alex's black sleeve with a white cuff resting carelessly on the table, her own breast rising and falling, a slice of her own pale dress sweeping under the white cloth: the whole circle round the table seemed to possess a new dimension. She stirred and turned to look round. 'Where are Laura Nicolaievna and the Grand Duke? Didn't they come with us?' For the other table held only Mademoiselle Staropova, Captain Sverbeyer and two strangers.

'No; they went home. For this one evening they wanted to be together,' Alex said.

She nodded. Although she herself couldn't bear the Grand Duke, if Laura felt about him as she now felt about Alex then, yes, she could understand their wish to be alone. She knew that Philip had been banished from the Tsarskoe Selo house while Laura had charge of her nieces, and that this was the penalty they would always pay because they were not allowed to marry and the morals of young girls must be protected – how cruel it all was! she thought despairingly, seeing society as a huge amorphous growth pushing people who loved each other

299

apart. It wasn't enough to love and to be loved in return. One had to conform to the rules and love only within one's own sphere.

The night went too fast. 'It's four o'clock,' Alex said and signalled to a gipsy waiter. He took out his wallet and threw a great deal of money on the table which the gipsy scooped up, grinning from ear to ear.

Like a child, she wanted to cry: 'Not yet! Just one more hour! Don't let the magic stop!' But Alex was wrapping her in her fur-lined cloak and leading her to the door. It was snowing hard outside as he lifted her up and carried her through the snow to the troikas that were arriving for their clients.

As they raced back towards Petersburg, the fresh snow spraying out from under the horses' hooves, they could see an eerie light over the city, the effect of the street lamps on the low snow clouds that had gathered during the night. The fir trees were black conical shapes against this radiance, then tall apartment blocks came in view and soon they were across the Neva again and drawing up outside the Rakov Palace on the Catherine Canal.

'You and Marina will stay here for the rest of the night,' he told her, helping her out. Lights blazed out at them as the old bearded porter who always spent the night in a hooded leather chair in the outer hall, came hobbling down the steps calling out hoarse greetings in Russian to his excellency and his excellency's guests.

Marina was going through a long, passionate farewell with her lieutenant, and her cousin waited with patient good nature for a while. 'Come, Marina,' he said at last, 'you are keeping us waiting.'

Marina bestowed one last kiss then ran lightly up the freshly-brushed steps, her white fox cloak blowing out behind her. She stood waving as Maisky drove off until Alex reached back and pulled her inside. 'Come, we will have a glass of tea before we retire.' He led the way into a room that was evidently a study: books in leather bindings lined the walls and a green leather Chesterfield and armchairs were grouped at one end of the room, a vast mahogany desk and tall cupboards filling the opposite end. Heavy green curtains shrouded the windows and all the lamps were alight. An elderly man in dark clothes was attending to a samovar on a side table and there was a delicious smell of hot aniseed bread warming on the top of the tiled stove.

'*Henri, qu'est que c'est que ça*? Did I not give you firm instructions you were to go to bed and not wait up for us?' Alex threw his heavy coat over the Chesterfield and looked quizzically at his valet.

'Yes, your excellency, you did – as you always do,' Henri replied, gently smiling. 'But I would not have slept – I cannot while my master is out. It was just so in your father's time.'

'You are incorrigible! Now to bed!'

Henri bowed and shut the door behind him.

'Poor Henri! What a life you lead him!' Marina said teasingly. 'He is worse than my old nanny, that one. Oh, but how tired I am! Alex, shall I marry Andrei Maisky? He is not from a noble family, I grant you, but he's rich. I think I would like to be rich and not have to ask Papasha for every kopeck – '

'*Kopecks?* You?' Alex threw his head back and laughed. 'You wouldn't recognize a kopeck if I showed you one, my dear cousin. Now to bed. You and Andrei are not yet twenty years old. You must not think of marriage for many years yet.'

Marina pouted but kissed her cousin in a forgiving manner, making the sign of the cross over both of them before following the woman whom Rakov had summoned to take her to her room.

301

Katya finished her tea and began to rise from her chair but Alex put out a hand to check her. 'Stay while I finish mine,' he said persuasively.

A foolish panic gripped her. For the first time she was alone with him. 'I ought – ' she began.

'Please, Katya.' Putting his glass down he slipped on to his knees and encircled her with both arms round her waist. 'Katya, look at me. Ah!' There was exultation in that low sound. 'My feelings are reflected in your eyes! Katya – Katya – ' He tightened his grip until she was unable to move. She was being crushed against him. To be near, to be held like this by the man she had begun to love! Joy shot up in her like a rocket.

Suddenly he released her to unclasp the heavy necklace from round her neck. 'Such white skin . . . you need pearls not these baubles, my love.' He bent his head and kissed her neck, her throat and the valley between her breasts. She lay in his arms, her own locked round his neck. 'Katya . . .' he murmured between Russian endearments.

She never knew how long they remained like this but quite suddenly he stopped kissing her. Tenderly, he brushed her tumbled hair back from her face. 'Dearest, you must go to bed. It's almost morning. Later we will talk. You are my responsibility while you are in my house and this I must remember. Come,' and he lifted her to her feet.

She hadn't uttered a word for several minutes. Now through dry, burning lips she pleaded: 'Let me stay!'

'No.' He was completely in control again. 'It is time you rested.' He turned to swing the porcelain handle of a bell on the wall and within seconds, the woman servant who had shown Marina to her room came in and curtsied. Like a sleepwalker, Katya followed the woman out of the room and up to a vast bedroom that had been prepared for her. It was brilliantly lit by crystal candelabra placed round the walls and was stiflingly hot. Another woman bustled about preparing a bath which she had placed on a goat-skin rug before the wood stove. A pretty *toile de Jouy* screen coped with any draught there might be and a scarlet satin *robe de chambre* had been placed nearby for her use. By the French clock on the bedside table she saw that it was six o'clock.

She had allowed them to unhook her dress before she remembered that Laura's necklace had been left downstairs. She looked desperately at the women, trying to explain her loss first in French and then in English. But they only looked puzzled, shaking their heads vigorously.

She would have to go down herself. She saw their amazement as she stepped back into her dress and bade them hook it up again. She hadn't replaced her shoes as she let herself out of the room and flitted silently down the cold green marble staircase to the great hall with its almond-green and white tiled floor. There were no servants about although the lights still blazed. She found the door of the study and wondered if Alex had gone to bed by now. Turning the handle she stood on the threshold and said: 'I've left Laura's necklace down here somewhere – ' Then she stopped as if someone had gagged her.

He was still in the room but no longer alone. He stood almost on the same spot where they had kissed not fifteen minutes ago. There was a man with him; a short stocky figure with an untidy beard and wearing good clothes that looked as if he had slept in them. On his left sleeve there was an L-shaped tear hanging loose. There was something so wild and strange about this figure that she drew back quickly, heard herself say explosively, 'Oh!'

They both turned sharply. The stranger's attitude was suddenly defensive and menacing, a man at bay. No one

303

spoke for a few moments then she blurted, 'I'm sorry. I forgot my necklace. Oh, here it is. I'm sorry,' she repeated and slammed the door behind her.

The house, brilliantly lighted and silent, seemed to watch her as she sped upstairs clutching her skirt with one hand, Laura's necklace in the other. The women received her smilingly, stood over her while she bathed, then they closed up the stove and withdrew, leaving only lamps burning by the bed. For some time she sat up staring ahead and seeing the strange man with Alex. He was a fugitive of some sort; of that she was certain. But what was Alex mixed up in? He had seemed at first just a frivolous fellow, good-looking and attractive, with a taste for pretty women. Against her will she had been attracted to him – *no! be truthful*, she told herself sternly, *you have fallen in love with him. And you know nothing about him*!

She slid down in the bed with a puzzled sigh. She thought she wouldn't sleep but when she looked again at the clock it was midday and grey light was edging the curtains and pouring a milky radiance into the room. The women were back, stealthily making up the stove and passing to and fro. When she sat up, they drew the curtains and grinned at her. She shuddered, seeing the snow swirling in funnels outside and sliding down the outer glass. Breakfast was not long in coming. A table was rolled up to the bed. On it were a selection of breads, platters of smoked ham, fish and sausage, white unsalted butter and a smoking samovar.

Her pillows were plumped up and a tray with legs placed on her lap. Under the pretty plate decorated with cherries a note protruded. It was very brief and impersonal.

Urgent business calls me away. I have left instructions for you to be taken to the train at any hour you desire. A thousand apologies for deserting you.

A. Rakov.

'I have no appetite – why do they have to bring me all this food?' Marina complained, coming barefooted through the connecting door to her room. Her limp pale hair was loose on her shoulders and her flesh glowed ruddily through the silk net robe she wore. A huge yawn disfigured her face as she slumped onto Katya's feet. 'Tante Natalia's house is a shrine to food. Who eats it but the servants? What effort for nothing!'

'Alex has been called away suddenly.' Katya showed her the note.

After reading it, Marina looked sideways at her companion. 'Oh,' was all she said. Absently, she broke a croissant in half and dipped a part of it in Katya's tea leaving buttery flakes on its surface. She nibbled in silence for a moment or two. 'My cousin is a strange man,' she said thoughtfully. 'No one, I think, knows the real Alex except Henri. They are very close. One can't get close to Alex himself; there's a barrier.' Again she looked obliquely at Katya. 'You care for him. No, don't deny it, for it shows. And he is very much attracted to you. But if you love him, Katya, then my advice is *don't*. He will bring you unhappiness and he should not be close to anyone. Think of him as someone with a contagious disease and keep him at a distance in case you catch it. It could be fatal to you.'

Katya stared at her. 'What can you mean? Do you have to talk in riddles?'

Marina's faint smile held sadness. 'I hardly know what I mean myself except that we Russians have long shadows at our feet and these shadows are getting shorter. That is my instinct. We have an uncertain future and Alex could be dangerous to know.'

Fishing croissant flakes out of her tea Katya said with a catch in her voice, 'You mean it's something political he's

305

mixed up in. Something that could be dangerous. Oh, Marina, I hope you're wrong!'

Marina slid off the bed. 'I hope so, too. Don't speak of it to anyone. Even Tante Natalia knows nothing. Just think: she is serving the Empress! and that is why no one suspects Alex yet. But his luck won't hold for ever.'

17

The House on Mohovaya

1

'Dear Katya, (wrote Robert Howarth) There! Don't you think I'm very good? I wanted to begin Dearest Most Adorable Katya but I know you would strongly disapprove so instead I write a weak Dear Katya. Then again I wrote you *such* a letter; I wish you could have seen it, Dear Katya, because this pen of mine wrote things that my tongue is always afraid to speak. I can hear you muttering crossly "The man is quite mad" and indeed you may be right. I certainly feel decidedly odd and I'm off my food (always a bad sign with me). My mother talks of giving me Parrish's Food daily. Do you know this patent medicine: It darkened my young life when I was ten years old. My father has detected several mistakes in my work at the shipping office and wonders if I shall ever shape up to his ideal of me (I shan't, of course). You see I know what's wrong with me: my head is filled with only one person. I know I promised a year ago never to mention it again but I do love you, Katya. Seeing you again has made me realize how much. Please write to me soon.'

Katya had laughed at the beginning of this letter but now she folded it quickly and thrust it into her pocket. Her face saddened as she thought of this nice man suffering on her account. To love without hope of return

– yes, it would be anguish. How she wished she could return his feelings! Life would be so simple then – but she couldn't. He didn't stir her in the least. She thought of him as Dear Robert and then forgot him. She wandered to the window and looked out on the snow-covered landscape. If only Robert sent a frisson of excitement up her spine like – like – She turned quickly away from the window and threw herself into a chair. No good could come of having such feelings for Alex Rakov: Marina was right about that. She must guard against showing her feelings. After all, hadn't Marina guessed very easily that she was in love with Alex? Katya groaned; she was never good at dissembling. Laura was already teasing her about it; she had guessed, too.

She sat down at the walnut writing table in her room to write a swift reply to Robert's letter. Suddenly, there was a hurried knock at the door and Tanya came in, her eyes bright with excitement. 'Oh, Katya, isn't it lovely? I've had a letter from Mr Howarth telling me all about Mamma – of course it's for Maia too, but he addresses it to me. He says she is *much* better. Oh! won't it be lovely when she comes home?' She came and stood beside Katya, her face that of a pleased child again.

'Yes, Tanya darling, it will be lovely. I told you she was in safe hands, didn't I? Now it's a question of getting her strength back for the long journey. Are you going to write to your mother today? I should if I were you. She will be longing to hear from you both.'

Tanya nodded. 'Yes, I will and I'll make Maia write too, the lazy thing.' With a whirl of petticoats she was gone.

Katya was smiling as she took up her pen again and continued with her letter: 'Tanya has been in with your letter clasped to her bosom. She is quite a different child now she has heard that her mother is convalescent. How wise of you to write directly to her, Robert! She is furious with her aunt for withholding your telegram from her but I have told you all about that.' She stopped and tapped the pen against her teeth. Then resolutely she went on: 'I have met Prince Alexander Rakov and Laura has taken me to his house for luncheon. Another time we all went to see the gipsies.' She paused for thought and then wrote frankly: 'I must tell you I like him a great deal.'

As she signed the letter, folded and sealed it she thought of Robert as he read those last lines. But she wouldn't alter them even though he might not write again. He must know – it was only fair – that she cared for someone else, however hopeless it might be.

2

Now that the children knew their mother was coming home they became more difficult to manage, especially Tanya. 'If Mamma were here,' she said stormily, 'she would give me permission to go with you to that bazaar –'

'Don't be a silly child!' Her aunt had reached the limit of her patience. She was arranging a fetching hat on her head before her dressing-mirror and Tanya was leaning over her chair talking to her image. She raised her eyes and frowned: child or not, Tanya was beginning to mature too fast. It made her miserably discontented being classed with her little sister, and therefore she was unbearable in the house. 'Pass me the pin with the diamond head, please. You cannot have forgotten that I've already told you this Christmas Bazaar is organized by the Grand Duchess Vladimir to launch the new social season. Young girls about to make their debut will be there with their mammas. Your day will come, darling, when you are sixteen or seventeen and then you will be grown-up and able to wear some of the Barinsky jewels – '

'I shan't. Mamma has sold them.'

Laura Nicolaievna nearly stabbed the diamond pin into her scalp. '*Sold* them? My God, is she mad? They are not hers to sell!'

'That's what I told her.' Tanya nodded with a degree of smugness in her tone that would normally have irritated her aunt.

'Sold them!' she repeated uneasily. 'Barinsky will be furious. It was a stupid thing to do! How could Anastasia be such a fool?'

'Well, we had to get home,' Tanya pointed out, 'otherwise Papa would have kept Maia and me with him. Imagine if I had had to live with Mrs Gertrude Haltmann!'

Laura looked sharply at her niece: she knew more than was good for her, she told herself angrily. Really, Barinsky ought to have had more sense! Of course, an alliance with the rich American would solve all his financial troubles and no doubt these were pressing, but didn't he realize that if he were divorced he could not continue in the diplomatic service? He had burned his boats with a vengeance and would probably never see his children again. Of course, if she had been short of money it would seem Anastasia had done the only thing possible – but why was she short of money? Their father had left her a great deal . . . unless of course Sergei had got his claws on it! Oh, what a fool Stana was!

Looking up, she saw Tanya's anxious eyes fixed on her face. Forcing a smile she said: 'I'm sure Mamma did the wisest thing under the circumstances. Now run and tell Katya we're going. I don't want to be late.'

310

The bazaar was held in the Hall of the Nobles in the Winter Palace and as usual it had drawn high society to it like pins to a magnet. Everyone who was anyone had to be seen here at the beginning of the social season. So some dragged themselves from sick beds to don a smart new outfit and to stroll about under the autocratic gaze of the Grand Duchess Vladimir who had become the leader of St Petersburg society instead of the very retiring Tsarina who obviously loathed social life. Since the birth of the Heir last August, even less had been seen of Alexandra Fedorovna and it was whispered in horror that she was rumoured to be *breast-feeding* the baby herself! A thing no one but a peasant woman would do.

The Grand Duchess Vladimir, whose husband was an uncle of the Tsar, was eminently suited to the task she had taken on herself. She was a stout and regal woman with a proud face and a stiffly-corseted body. Her aquiline nose was always at a certain angle; never did she look down. On her greying hair today she wore a hat that outdid in decoration every hat present. A bird, fruit and flowers flourished among the silk and velvet and Katya for one couldn't take her eyes off it. What it must weigh! she thought. And how expensive it must have been! For, hideous as it was, it had been beautifully constructed and even boasted a hovering butterfly. With her satellites, the Grand Duchess was going from stall to stall encouraging people to buy; the bazaar was in aid of the Empress's charities and would be open for four days.

The noise reminded Katya of a crowd of greedy starlings feeding on the bird table at home.

'Ah, here is Philip!' Laura observed as the Grand Duke broke away from a group of officers to kiss her hand. He bowed stiffly in Katya's direction. Here I go playing gooseberry once again, she thought ruefully; no wonder he detests me! She had plenty to look at and would have wandered off on her own if Laura's gloved hand hadn't plucked at her.

'Wait, Katya. You must not walk alone – but here is Prince Nikita. Tanya's cousin, you know. Quite providential! Nikita, please escort Miss Croxley while I have a word with the Grand Duke,' she added after introducing them.

'Charmed, Miss Croxley.' But Nikita Guriev's face looked anything but charmed. It was puffy and there was something about his pink-diffused eyes that filled her with foreboding. As she was led away by this son of the dreaded Princess Gurievna, she smelt brandy on his breath and realized that he had been drinking heavily. His deceptively cherubic look of innocence made his near-drunkenness even more nauseating, she thought. But then all these Russians were deceitful, she told herself angrily as she remembered Alex Rakov. Six days had passed since they had visited the gipsies and she had surrendered to his kisses – so easily, she reminded herself bitterly. Not one word had he sent her since that austere little note on her breakfast tray. If she ever saw him again she would simply bow stiffly and pass on her way.

So she was feeling decidedly prickly when Nikita attempted to draw her arm through his and hold her close to his side. He was being a great deal too familiar, she thought furiously and attempted to pull herself free. For answer, he threw an arm round her shoulder and, breathing fumes of brandy all over her, actually attempted to kiss her.

'Why so cold, Miss Croxley? Come, let us be friends –

312

f-friends of the bosom!' He gave a giggle that ended in a loud hiccup and several heads turned. 'Do not be cold with me,' he cried and lurched against a stall loaded with highly-priced objects.

Vainly, Katya tried to withdraw her arm but he held it tightly against his side. 'Your excellency, please release me!'

People were turning, surprise on their faces. Katya's own face burned with rage and shame: how dare he make a fool of her in front of them all? And where was Laura to rescue her?

He was making his way towards a certain stall and Katya saw the foxy face of Princess Gurievna framed in the greenery of hot-house plants and creepers that she was selling. 'Look at my mother!' he entreated as he pulled her along. 'What does she remind you of, Katya? A little woodland animal coming out of its hide!' He roared with malicious laughter.

Nada Gurievna's thin pointed face turned suddenly in their direction. Her expression hardened and she began to make a pretence of being very busy. But Nikita wasn't fooled: he knew she had spotted him and, still roaring with laughter, he drove a way through the crowd calling out: 'Well, Mamma, does this satisfy you? I have a lady friend at last! Bow to my honoured mother, Katya! Make her eat her words! You see? I *am* like other men! I have a woman!'

Tears of rage spilled out of Katya's eyes as everyone in the vicinity stared at her. Her hat had been knocked sideways, and she was furiously aware that she must look as drunk as her companion. 'Let me go!' she entreated. 'Your excellency, please let me go!'

Suddenly, someone stepped in their path. 'Your excellency, may I have a word with you?'

It was Alex Rakov: his face grim, he was holding anger

313

in check with the greatest difficulty. Gazing at him, Katya could hardly believe her eyes. She had never guessed that she would be so relieved to see him. Restraining herself with difficulty from throwing herself in his arms and pleading with him to be rescued, she gave one more wrench of her numb arm and succeeded in freeing herself. Breathing fast, she hastily wiped the tears off her face and straightened her little hat.

Nikita seemed to recollect himself suddenly. He bowed stiffly. 'You wish to speak to me?'

They both turned away and Katya saw Alex speaking tersely: beneath its tan, his face was white, its expression grim. She turned away herself, pretending to inspect a stall but she was so deeply upset by the scene Nikita Guriev had created that she saw nothing. Now, thank goodness, people were moving on at last. Feeling as if she were about to faint, Katya looked wildly for a chair. A hand came under one elbow. 'I am here,' said a voice and she felt untold relief. 'You're not going to faint, are you?' There was a teasing note in Alex's voice that restored her.

'No, of course not!'

'Good. I have an infallible remedy for fainting females.'

Curiosity caused her to look up at him. His expression was now quite different: the anger and hostility displayed to Nikita Guriev had gone and good-humoured pleasure shone from his face. 'What is it?'

'It never fails. I throw them over one shoulder and carry them off to tea. Come: let us go and have some. It will restore you. But first let us go and meet the Empress who is on the point of arriving. Her appearance will stun these good ladies who have been laying bets that she would not lend her presence to the bazaar. My mother will be with her and I would like you to be presented.'

Katya stopped dead. '*Me*? Presented to the Empress? Oh, no!'

Inexorably, he led her on, smiling down at her. 'Why not? She won't eat you! She is a much maligned woman, poor Alexandra Fedorovna. Desperately shy, she gives the appearance of great *hauteur* but is a very ordinary woman, really. And she will be delighted to meet someone from England, her second home.'

Katya's stomach was lurching nervously. The last thing she had expected was to be presented to the Tsarina. To Alex, she realized, it was not in the least nerve-racking for his mother was at Court and so he must often meet the Imperial Family. She glanced swiftly at the man walking beside her: hadn't she been determined to cut him when next she met him? Instead, gladness and relief were warming her and she felt decidedly buoyant. 'Is – is my hat straight?' she asked in a whisper.

'You look beautiful,' he told her softly.

A small group of people had come into the huge hall and Grand Duchess Vladimir was hurrying across to greet her Empress and niece by marriage.

Katya, who now had a good view, whispered: 'Why does she look so unwelcoming – even angry?'

'The Grand Duchess? Poor dear, she's having rather a lot to swallow at the moment. One of her spoilt sons – Cyril – intends marrying the divorced Grand Duchess of Hesse. And who is she other than the sister-in-law of our Tsarina? It would hardly do if after the marriage the former wife of the Grand Duke of Hesse settled in Petersburg! I fear the Cyrils will be banished. Nicholas is said to be very angry on the Tsarina's behalf. Besides, first cousins are not allowed to marry in Russia – now's our chance!' He gripped her arm and propelled her forward, giving a quick little bow of the head as the

315

Tsarina recognized him and turned with relief from the forbidding Grand Duchess Vladimir.

'Why, Alex, I didn't expect to see you here! You haven't been back to finish that game of chess with Olga and she won't let anyone touch the board until you do!' The cold expression with which Alexandra Fedorovna had entered the hall quite vanished in a delightful smile as she recognized a friendly face. 'I believe you allowed her to beat you!'

'Indeed, Your Majesty, the Grand Duchess may only be nine years old but already she plays like a veteran!'

Katya eagerly devoured the picture presented by the Tsarina as she talked to Alex Rakov. Unlike the other ladies present she was not dressed in the height of fashion nor was she rouged and powdered. For a young woman she appeared rather matronly and wore a large and dowdy hat on her red-gold hair. Chatting away easily now, she seemed to forget the hostile faces looking on: colour came and went on her face, and her grey eyes, so cold earlier, positively danced with fun. No wonder she was called 'Sunny' inside her family, Katya thought, swallowing nervously as Alex turned to her, saying, 'Your Majesty, may I present a friend from England, Miss Katherine Croxley?'

Katya felt her hand taken as she curtsied.

'From England!' There was a wealth of yearning in the voice. 'My second home, I always say. My happiest memories are being with the Queen at Windsor – how much I miss her letters! Tell me, Miss Croxley, what part of England do you come from and what brings you to Russia?'

Katya found herself chatting easily, remembering to throw in an occasional *Your Majesty*. When the Tsarina moved on, she was left flushed and elated. How natural and friendly Alexandra Fedorovna had been! She had almost forgotten she was the Empress as she had talked to her about England.

'Mamma, may I introduce Miss Katherine Croxley?' Alex drew his mother to one side as she stood in the wake of her royal mistress.

'How do you do, Miss Croxley? I hear you are staying at Tsarskoe Selo with friends? You like St Petersburg?' The princess was so like her niece Marina that Katya had recognized her as Alex's mother at once. She possessed the same tawny colouring and hazel eyes but the hair had patches of grey in it and was untidily arranged under an unfashionable hat. Indeed the Tsarina's entourage was notable for their dowdy appearance amongst the gorgeously attired ladies of St Petersburg.

As Katya finished exchanging pleasantries with Princess Rakova, she was swept away by the press of people wanting to see with their own eyes the seldom seen Empress of Russia.

Alex rescued her and hurried her off to a corner of the hall where tea was being served.

'To think I've met the Empress – or the Tsarina as most people call her!' Katya murmured, allowing herself to be steered towards a table.

'Nicholas prefers the old Russian title, you see. The Petersburg people insist on Emperor and Empress, though!' He shrugged. 'Not that it matters. I think the Tsar tries to encourage old nationalist feelings – he has a great fondness for all the old institutions and not much enthusiasm for anything new. I think he hopes to keep Russia on a different time-scale to the rest of the world!' There was a curious bitterness in his voice that made her glance at him. 'She's far nicer than people give her credit for, I think,' he went on. 'You see, she's desperately shy and crowds unnerve her. She'll leave quickly if they don't give her breathing space, you'll see.'

317

Tea was brought to them in a small china pot, English-fashion, and Katya poured it out. She felt utterly happy again. It no longer mattered that she had been advised not to trust him: he was here with her, if only for ten minutes. To be near him, she realized, filled her with well-being and made her light as a feather with happiness.

'I wanted my mother to meet you,' he said, smiling into her eyes.

'How like your cousin Marina she is!'

'And in character, too. Yet her father is black-haired and quite humourless and he is Mamma's brother! Odd, isn't it?' He put a slice of lemon in his tea and was silent suddenly. When he spoke again it was in a hurried subdued voice: 'The other night – I ought not to have behaved as I did. I must apologize.'

She put her cup down with a bump and stared at him, all the light dying in her eyes.

He looked back at her unhappily. What huge expressive eyes she had! he thought. They were dark blue with little flecks in them – like a butterfly's wing. Her skin was pale – so pale that fine blue veins round the eyes and temple were discernible. She looked fragile, a creature of heart and feeling and he was having to deal her a horrible blow. It was for her good in the end. He hoped she would understand that. The remembrance of her warm responsive body in his arms weakened his resolve for a moment but he hardened his heart: he would never forgive himself if he embroiled her in danger. 'You must forget the things I said.'

She found from the recesses of her soul the courage to smile. 'There's no more to be said, then.'

He could see how her hand shook as she drank her tea and for a moment he weakened. Then he steeled himself: to involve her would be cruel for there was no knowing

318

what the future held. She must go back to England, to safety.

They sat in miserable silence. Then she said with an effort: 'I-I expect to be going home after Christmas. Tante Stana should be coming back to Russia any day now so there will be nothing to keep me here. Besides, I teach at a school and the new term will be beginning.' She gave a wry smile to herself at the thought of Hill House after all this.

'You are leaving Russia?' His head jerked up.

'Yes, for good.' It was a bitter thought to her that he wouldn't care as she would care that they might never meet again. She felt tears sting her eyes.

'Katya.' His hand, warm and strong, covered hers. 'Let us live in the present – enjoy what today holds for us. Believe me, it will cause less pain in the future: there can be no future for us.'

His quietly spoken words stabbed like a knife. Controlling her voice with an effort she whispered: 'I understand.' There were too many stumbling blocks to make a future possible: perhaps he was committed to another woman, someone suitable to fill the role of his wife. Despite her Russian blood she was an English girl without background, a person from a totally different world. Oh, yes, she understood everything now. She had been a fool. But she felt rebellious all the same. Nothing he said or did would make her change her feelings. She loved him as she had never loved any man before and with this love burned a stubborn sense of hope in the future – that future he said could not exist for them.

As Alex went into his dressing-room to change for dinner that night, he found Henri waiting with a look of badly-controlled fear on his face.

'Your excellency, there has been a telephone call.' He stopped speaking to dart across the room and close the door into the bedroom.

'There's no one there, you old idiot!' Alex railed him. 'Now what's the secret?' He looked more closely at his valet and his tone changed. 'News?'

'Not of that sort, excellency. The message came from General Davidov.' He paused. 'From the house on Mohovaya.'

Alex raised his brows. Everyone knew what 'the house on Mohovaya' meant. An unobtrusive white house that had once belonged to the Prince of Oldenburg, it now housed the *Okhrana*, the Tsar's secret police. 'What did he say?' Alex's tone was calm.

'He wishes to see you tonight after dinner.'

They looked at each other. Two tears had emerged from the corners of Henri's eyes, making little pinpoints of light. Making no attempt to brush them away the man said in a low voice: 'I beg your excellency to give up . . . your work. Before it's too late – before it breaks the princess's heart – and mine.'

Alex patted the thin shoulder under the well-brushed black cloth coat. 'Who took the message?'

'One of the footmen who came to ask me if you were at home. When I heard who it was I went immediately to the telephone myself and spoke to Captain Bokorny, the general's *aide*.' Henri eased Alex's jacket off his shoulders. 'At one time, excellency, General Davidov was a frequent caller at this house so it would be as well to treat the call as one from a friend of the family – '

Alex turned. 'At this house?'

'He was just Lieutenant Davidov then and nothing to do with the *Okhrana*.'

'He was a friend of my father's?'

Henri hesitated. 'Yes, excellency, of both your parents.'

Alex shrugged and pulled his shirt off. From its folds he said in a muffled voice: 'Perhaps he wants to renew an old friendship!'

'Your excellency will be careful?'

Alex emerged from his shirt. 'Don't worry, old friend, I shall play a cat-and-mouse game with the fellow. Now is my bath ready?' Outwardly calm, his brain was seething with questions. Why was he being asked to call at the house on Mohovaya? And by General Davidov of all people who had been a friend of his parents.

At dinner, he made no mention of Davidov to his mother. They were dining alone tonight, an unusual occurrence, and while they had coffee afterwards in the small yellow drawing room, he mentioned casually that he had to go out.

'Will you be long, dearest?' His mother signalled to a footman to remove the tray. 'I rather wanted to talk about Tatarskino affairs since we are alone and I'm going back into waiting at the end of the week. Gedconovsky called with the rents this morning and we had a long talk. He doesn't approve of all you are doing on the estate, I'm afraid, and says that unless you raise the rents this year our income will be affected.'

'Mamma, I can't discuss it now. Perhaps tomorrow? Why Gedconovsky should discuss our money affairs with you I cannot imagine. I am the head of the family now. Rest assured, I shan't ask you to make money sacrifices for my experiments at Tatarskino.' He bent and kissed her. Out in the hall he shrugged into the heavy fur coat held by a footman and went out to his green sledge that had just been brought round from the stables. Dismissing his groom, he drove off alone.

5

General Davidov, a prey to nervous indigestion that would probably keep him awake all night, was prowling round his office. This morning, he had had to witness a triple hanging at the Fortress of St Peter and St Paul. He loathed hangings, but a firing squad that was quick and painless was reserved for 'honourable' executions. These three were traitors to the Tsar and had been found guilty of a plot to kill him. Ever since the assassination of the present Tsar's grandfather, Alexander II, on the Catherine Canal twenty-three years ago, the Imperial Family had been nervous about their personal safety. Now with the growth of revolutionary feeling in Russia, the secret police had to be more on the alert than ever.

The worst of it was one of the criminals had been a young woman. Davidov shuddered. She had taken longer to die than the others for some fool had not taken into account that her body was many pounds lighter than those of the two men. A pretty girl with yellow curly hair . . . twisting and twitching on the end of the rope. The memory of this slow death would be with him for days and if he had had anything to do with it, he would have had the fellow responsible flogged for his incompetence.

There had been a chance of getting her off the death sentence and sending her to Siberia, but the Tsarina had been against it. She had pointed out that the girl was an enemy of the Tsar's who had plotted to kill him; she must be put to death with the others. So, in Davidov's presence, the Tsar had uneasily signed Vera Vianenka's death sentence: she had been nineteen years old.

Davidov poured another stomach powder into a glass and added water. He was just about to swallow it when Captain Bokorny announced: 'His excellency Prince Rakov.'

Draining the glass, Davidov went forward to shake hands. My God, he's a handsome fellow, he thought. Was I ever as good-looking as this? Yet he is like me – he is!

Alex, finding his hand held overlong and the one piercing eye summing him up, could barely conceal his surprise. He had not expected such a warm greeting from one of the police at the house on Mohovaya! So this was to be a friendly occasion, was it? He refused a glass of vodka and sat down in the chair offered him. Now he could see the other more clearly he was struck by something: tall, fair hair turning grey, the fellow reminded him tantalizingly of someone . . .

Davidov, seated behind his desk, appeared to be studying a list: it looked like a list of names.

It was a list of names: the names were of suspected liberals who were helping political prisoners to escape over the borders to Finland and Sweden, Germany and Switzerland. There were several secret routes and safe houses waiting to give them beds and food and money. Among the names was that of Prince Alexander Petrovitch Rakov.

Davidov looked up and stared at the young man: was he really mixed up with these wrong-headed fools and did Natalia know?

'You asked me to call on you on urgent business,' Alex reminded him.

323

Davidov grunted. 'I believe your views are of the so-called liberal persuasion?'

Alex smiled. 'Hardly *so-called*, General! They *are* liberal views and I'm not ashamed of them. I believe that wc should have a *Duma* and should share in the government of the country, that all this censorship only makes the people feel more frustrated – '

'Enough. You hold views that would displease His Imperial Majesty if he knew of them. This is an Autocracy, your excellency, and you from one of our princely families should be grateful for it.'

'I would prefer a democracy,' Alex retorted. In his imagination he could see Henri wringing his hands at these words but he had decided it would be more incriminating to deny being a liberal at all than to confess it. The secret police knew of his views without doubt but they were only guessing when it came to his implication with the secret escapes. 'I must point out, General Davidov, that I'm by no means a revolutionary in thought and outlook. I simply want to see Russia modernized and brought into the twentieth century like the western democracies.'

'You talk nonsense. The peasants are not ready. Why, they are completely uneducated!'

'Exactly. That is what I complain about. On my estate at Tatarskino we are beginning to educate the young people – '

'Good God!' Davidov sat up, flushing angrily. 'It is people like you who are traitors to their class! Why don't you leave well alone? The peasants are happy enough.'

Alex smiled and was silent.

'I knew your parents.'

'So I understand.'

'Your father should not have allowed you to go to Law School after the army. The Law School is a breeding ground for discontented revolutionaries and I believe you yourself became infected there.'

'One commits many follies at twenty! I did go to dull meetings in cold cellars; they had little or no effect on my thinking. I repeat, I'm not a revolutionary and never have been.'

'You go a great deal to Paris?'

Here it comes. 'Oh, not a great deal. We have an apartment in the Bois and I like the occasional trip there to enjoy the – er – sights of the place. No doubt you did so too, General, at one time?'

Davidov looked at him sharply. Could it be that the young fellow knew that it was in Paris – 'You go out of season, Prince. You've just been there to attend a conference – a conference composed of revolutionary forces plotting against Russia.'

Alex laughed easily. 'What nonsense! It was a conference of a lot of hot-air balloons! That's how the French papers reported the so-called revolutionary speeches. I certainly didn't go to Paris to attend this affair – in fact, I never went near it and you can't tell me I did. I went for – other purposes.' He looked slyly at the general. 'To see a pretty lady in fact.' *To take her husband disguised as my valet to her before you got your hands on him.*

'You are telling me it was an affair of the heart that took you there in November?'

'Certainly.'

'And in September?'

'That, too.'

'And in May, June and August?'

Good heavens, they had been busy at the house on Mohovaya! 'I'm afraid so. She's married, you see, and there are complications. Why else was I there?'

'You know why I'm asking you these questions. There have been far too many escapes by those enemies of the

325

Tsar whom we have wished to interview. What I want to know is this: who gives you advance information, Prince? Someone working here?'

'Look, you're talking nonsense. You can't seriously believe I'm mixed up in all this?' He threw back his head and laughed.

'We suspect you belong to a group of people with dangerously liberal views who are going to a great deal of trouble on behalf of traitors to the Tsar. And you, Prince, are one of them.'

'A traitor, General Davidov?' Alex retorted softly. He sat up very straight and stared at the eye opposite: why did a black eyepatch look so particularly sinister? 'No one has ever called me a traitor,' and he rose from his seat to tower over the other.

There was silence. Davidov's hands were tied in a way the younger man didn't suspect. *This is my son, my own flesh and blood. I can't see my son thrown into Peter and Paul to rot.* Remembering the twitching bodies on the end of the rope that morning, Davidov shuddered inwardly. He remembered almost too clearly the night this boy had been conceived: passion had carried them both further than they intended, to the point of urgency whence there could be no return. He had begged Natalia to elope with him but she was committed to marrying Peter Rakov by then. It was impossible to back out; her family depended on it. Soon after, their relationship broke up for good. No, he couldn't destroy his own son.

Rising, he held out a hand. 'Then remember my words of warning, Prince. This is what this interview is meant to be: a friendly warning not to become implicated in a dangerous activity on behalf of a lot of worthless traitors.'

Driving home in his sledge, Alex's brain was working feverishly: there were people to be warned; Henri's contact at the house on Mohovaya would have to cease his activities for a bit. *A friendly warning*, indeed! But why had he done it? The old fox knew more than he let on, Alex told himself. I suppose I should be grateful to him – Davidov of all people!

18

Across the Neva

1

The spirit of discord was broad in the house next morning – or so Laura said. It had begun with a letter from her brother-in-law in Washington. He informed her that 'since Anastasia has chosen to run back to Russia taking with her my children without my permission, our marriage must be considered over'. In fact, he added, he would now take steps to have it annulled.

Laura gave a scream of rage. In the eyes of the world he would make Anastasia seem to be the culprit! There was no mention of his involvement with Gertrude Haltmann. How could he *annul* a marriage that had produced two children? Did he intend making bastards of them? She groaned aloud, feeling a headache beginning behind her eyes. She would have to consult Philip without delay. He would have to approach the Tsar and counter-measures would have to be taken. Barinsky was even threatening a court action for the return of the family jewels! He obviously intended blackening Anastasia's character in one swift move after another.

It said much for Laura's family feeling that she didn't brush her sister's troubles away as of no concern of hers. Bent on action she called loudly for Marfa to bring her tights and practice tutu.

She danced fiercely that morning, forcing her body to

attempt feats it hadn't attempted for years and she was aching when she returned to her room for a bath. But her headache had gone and her mind felt clear again.

It didn't help things to find Miss Ellis standing waiting for her. 'It's Tanya, Laura Nicolaievna. I have been up several times in the night and I really don't feel like facing the journey in to Petersburg, yet she ought to see a doctor at once. It's a splinter under the nail – painful but hardly serious. Will you take her in, Laura Nicolaievna?'

'But I have my class and other business to see to! *You* are her governess – '

'I am far too tired after the night I've had. I'm no longer young, as you must realize. Indeed this gives me the opportunity to hand you a month's notice. The children are too much for me, I'm afraid. As duenna to older girls I would have been happy: forgive me, Laura Nicolaievna, but I fear that for my health's sake I must make another move.'

Laura groaned loudly as the door shut behind the governess. The woman had lied about her age – that was now evident. She must be seventy at least. Oh, well, Anastasia could see about a replacement when she came. She took up the telephone and dialled the number of Doctor Mikhail Tchelitchev in St Petersburg.

2

Applied to by her aunt, Katya readily agreed to take Tanya to the doctor.

The child was downstairs nursing her sore finger and crying into her coffee. She raised a face of terror. 'Will he have to cut if off?' she quavered, and hot tears spilled from her eyes. 'I wish Mamma was here!'

Laura hugged her. 'Now don't be silly. You're much too big to cry over a little thing like a sore finger. Eat up, *chèrie*. We have a train to catch.'

Tanya sniffed miserably throughout the journey but still had enough spirit left to object to going off with Katya in an *isvostchik* when they reached St Petersburg. 'Why can't you take me in the Grand Duke's *droshky*? Mamma will be horrified when she hears. She's never allowed us to travel in one. There'll be fleas – '

Laura was fast losing patience. 'Do your best,' she told Katya significantly before being driven away.

Dr Tchelitchev lived across the Neva. Apart from giving the directions, Tanya took no further interest as they drove over Palace Bridge to Vassili Island and a tall apartment block where Dr Tchelitchev lived on the third floor.

Katya wondered why the rich Barinsky family patronized a doctor in this unfashionable quarter and Tanya gave her the answer as they toiled up the stone staircase.

'Dr Tchelitchev was the son of our factor at Nosar,' she informed Katya. 'Old Tchelitchev is dead now. Papa says Dr Mikhail is a very good doctor because my grandfather paid for him to go to the best place to be trained.'

'Is Nosar your country estate?'

'Yes. It's a dull hole. We hardly ever went and I've forgotten it.'

They stopped outside one of the identical green doors: this one had *42* painted on it in white and Tanya pressed the bell.

The door flew open immediately and a tall girl with fair hair worn in a plait round her head stood smiling at them. 'Countess Tanya! How you've changed – how you've grown!' she said in Russian, then looked interrogatively at Katya. 'Your governess, I believe?'

'No, she couldn't come. This is my English cousin. She doesn't speak Russian so shall we speak French?' Turning to Katya, Tanya explained in her best grown-up manner: 'I have said you do not speak Russian so we shall speak French. Anna Andreyevna, the doctor's sister, does not speak English, I'm afraid.'

'I am Katherine Croxley.' Katya held out her hand and smiled.

'Anna Andreyevna Tchelitchevna.' The girl bobbed her head and displayed splendid white teeth in the friendliest of smiles. She had a wonderful skin of clearest peach and dark blue eyes but she wasn't pretty. Everything about her was too large: her large nose and her big frame could have belonged to a boy. There radiated from her a warmth and interest that was most attractive. With Anna Andreyevna you would always believe you counted.

'My brother awaits his patient. Come, Countess.'

Tanya went pale. She threw Katya a look of desperate appeal like a puppy who is about to be whipped.

'Perhaps I ought to have gone with her?' Katya said when Anna returned.

'No, no. My brother is splendid with children. Besides, we must all learn to face pain, *mademoiselle*.'

This was a new point of view to Katya who believed in avoiding pain wherever possible. She took a fresh look at the tall girl who sat on the edge of the table swinging her legs. Her clothes were well worn but clean and mended: a brown tweed skirt and brown knitted cardigan over a starched blouse all showed signs of renewal in one form or another. A disfiguring pair of badly-made boots peeped out from under the skirt. They were a peasant's boots and not made of shining kid like Katya's and Tanya's. Her hands were red, the nails cut short and her only ornament was a heavy gold brooch at her throat.

'From England!' she said, looking searchingly at her

guest. 'All my life I have longed to go to England. Some day, my brother has promised me, we shall go. But first we must save enough money and that is not easy! Indeed, I think we shall both be old when the time comes!'

'Couldn't you get a job teaching French or Russian? Give lessons here in your flat?'

Anna's eyes lit up. 'That is a splendid idea! Oh, if only I could go to England – I mean Great Britain, of course! – and live there a little just to see how your great democracy works. It is what so many of us long to see here in our beloved Russia but we are not supposed to say it out loud.'

'The *Okhrana*?' Katya said with a wry smile.

Anna nodded vigorously. 'Mikhail feels as I do, of course, but he would lose his more lucrative patients if his views were known. The Barinskys have been very kind and many of their friends are now Mikhail's patients. Slowly – very slowly – my brother is building up his practice. He has also an appointment at the hospital,' she added proudly. 'We shall not always be poor but when one is young one is impatient, I think.' She leaned forward. 'Are you rich, *mademoiselle*?'

Katya laughed. 'No, indeed! I am a school teacher, teaching modern languages and English literature at a girls' school. Not a very good school,' she had to admit, 'but I hope to find a better post before long.'

'You go home soon?'

'After Christmas.'

A ludicrous look of dismay crossed Anna's face. 'So soon! Then we must waste no time. Please come to supper with us so that we can talk about England, *mademoiselle*.'

'Why, I'd like that very much.'

'Tomorrow, perhaps?'

332

'Not tomorrow as I believe Laura Nicolaievna has invited friends in.'

'She is Urosova, the dancer, yes? The mistress of Grand Duke Philip?' Anna's expressive face had hardened alarmingly. 'He is a bad man, that one. And you live in his house?'

'Well – yes – but he doesn't live there himself, you know. I certainly don't like him and I imagine he could be cruel – '

The door behind them opened suddenly and a much relieved-looking Tanya emerged nursing a bandaged finger. 'It was *agony*,' she informed them, 'but Dr Mikhail says I've been very brave.'

A thickset man with brown hair worn *en brosse* had followed her out and was polishing his pince-nez. He replaced them on his nose and regarded Katya with interest. 'You are Mademoiselle Croxley? Please tell the countess's nurse that she must bathe her finger twice a day in the antiseptic mixture I have made up.'

'My brother, Dr Mikhail Andreyevich Tchelitchev,' Anna introduced him with a note of pride. Turning to her brother she added excitedly: 'Mademoiselle Croxley comes to supper with us one night soon, Mikhail! So that we can talk of England. Please, the night after next?'

Katya nodded. 'Thank you. I'm sure that is all right but I will telephone you on my return to Tsarskoe Selo.'

'That will be pleasant,' Mikhail said. 'I must go to the hospital as I am late – yes, yes, Anna, I will have something to eat there. *Au revoir, mademoiselle*, Countess Tanya.'

'He works too hard,' his sister sighed as the door shut behind the doctor. 'He is only twenty-five but already he looks forty. Now will you have a glass of wine before you go?'

'No, thank you.' Tanya's tone had become repressive

and she was evidently trying to convey some message to Katya. 'I think we should go now.'

Katya bit her lip. She would like to stay and talk to this new friend but it was impossible to ignore Tanya's very pointed signals. The girl stood with her coat buttoned, one hand on the door, the injured one tucked inside her chinchilla muff, departure in every line of her body. Katya had to follow her, albeit reluctantly. She paid the bill as Laura had instructed her, and obtained Anna's receipt.

As Anna handed it to her, she said wistfully: 'Perhaps you will not come to supper on Friday?'

'Of course I shall! I am looking forward to it. Goodbye, Anna Andreyevna, I have much enjoyed meeting you.'

'And I, *mademoiselle*! Goodbye, Countess Tanya, take care of that hand. When does your dear mamma arrive home? Please remember me to her. She was so kind when my beloved father died and I have never forgotten. Till Friday, *mademoiselle*!' On the point of closing the door, she called: 'You like *kolbasa varionaia*?'

'What is that?' Katya whispered.

'Cold beef sausage – horrid!' Tanya's face expressed distaste.

'Yes!' Katya called back from the head of the staircase. 'Of course I like *kolbasa varionaia*!'

'You won't, you know,' Tanya said confidently. 'And I don't think Tante Laura will be at all pleased.'

'Why on earth not?' Katya paused on the next landing.

'The Tchelitchevs are little people – *petite bourgeoisie*. Not the sort we know socially. Papa says they are usually revolutionaries and make nuisances of themselves.'

Katya glanced at the girl's haughty little face. Laura was right: Tanya was becoming the image of her aunt, Princess Gurievna. 'Perhaps they are not the sort *you* know, your excellency,' Katya retorted mockingly, 'but

334

they are my sort of people and I'm going to like them very much, I think.'

Tanya changed the subject because she was not at all sure that Katya was not making fun of her. 'My hand's hurting abominably,' she said pettishly. 'Do hurry up and find us a cab.'

3

When Katya returned to the Tchelitchevs' for supper on Friday it was evident that Anna Andreyevna had made a great effort with her preparations. The main room (a bleak, half-empty room it had seemed two days earlier) had been freshly cleaned and smelled even more strongly of carbolic soap. The few ugly pieces of deal furniture had been polished and rearranged so that the table (now covered with a starched white cloth, much darned), with three chairs round it, could be placed near the stove and the lamps. The *zakouski* had been arranged on a large tray with some pieces of fish, pickled cucumbers and *pashtet* (a liver pâté). There was a new bottle of vodka to be drunk with this before they all sat down at the table to partake of sorrel soup, *kolbasa varionaia* and cheeses. A bottle of red wine had been warming by the stove and was poured out by the doctor.

'Russian wine,' he said with satisfaction. 'Yes, red wine from the Caucasus. We never drink French or German wines in this house. Russia is a wonderful country, *mademoiselle*, producing everything her people need. But Petersburg – bah! It's a foreign town filled with imitation Russians – people who prefer all things French, including the French way of life. I would prefer to speak in Russian

335

to you but that is not possible. Can you not help Anna with her English? Then she could teach me.'

'I should be delighted,' Katya replied, 'but you must remember that I shall be returning to England in a week or two, as soon as the Countess Barinskaya arrives. But Anna must come to England when you can spare her and stay with me there. That will be the best way for her to learn.'

Anna's face lit up with longing. Then, glancing at her brother, she smiled and shook her head. 'How can I leave Mikhail to manage on his own? I shall come when he marries – yes, Mikhail, you must marry one of your pretty nurses then I can leave you and go to England!'

Mikhail's answering smile was wry. 'Marry? I? Impossible on my income.' He handed Katya some hot bread and she glimpsed the bitterness lying deep in his eyes. That they were struggling professional people had been obvious to her from the first but she hadn't guessed how poor they were until now, sitting at their table and hearing the weariness in her host's voice. Her eyes took in the furnishings of the room: there were several icons collected on a corner chest and badly-printed pictures depicting heroic Russian incidents in the past hung on the walls, relics no doubt of their dead parents. There were several shelves of books, piles of periodicals and even a new-looking phonograph on a table by itself. It was not unlike the home of a young and struggling English doctor, she thought, and Mikhail should not be so bitter for he surely had every chance of rising in the world and joining more prosperous colleagues before long. It was only later that she realized he had pledged himself to work for the poorest in St Petersburg, the so-called 'Black People'. His connection with the Barinsky family meant a little icing on a very small cake but that was all.

Halfway through the meal, there was a knock on the

door and another pair of young Russians came in. The man was a lecturer at the university, his wife worked at the Alexandrovsky Hospital as a nurse. The charcoal under the samovar was lit, hot bread and cucumber brought and the visitors pressed to partake although they protested they had just eaten. Talk flowed easily as they sat on and on with their elbows propped on the table, little bursts of laughter punctuating the conversation. Katya suddenly realized how much she had missed this sort of evening at Laura Nicolaievna's: these *were* her sort of people.

They were all eager to learn of conditions in England: indeed, they seemed to see it through a rosy haze as a sort of Utopia. Surprised though she was to find that they were not in any way Anglophobes, she had to warn them of the many things (like terrible poverty) that were still wrong with her country.

'But you are *free* people.' The young lecturer's voice yearned over the world *libre*. 'We could endure much if we were free to decide our own fates.'

'There is great unrest in Russia,' Mikhail agreed. 'We are fighting for our freedom with our lives.' Land, he went on, was in such short supply that the peasants couldn't live on what they raised themselves. The nobles on the other hand (and here his voice deepened with bitterness) had vast estates and sold the grain for profit while those who helped to produce it went hungry! He knew what he was talking about, he reminded them hotly, for hadn't he and his sister been brought up on just such an estate of which his own father was factor?

'And the population grows yearly yet the land is still tilled by hand – there have been no technical advancements which would produce grain for everyone,' the lecturer added. 'The land is so rich! It could provide well for all of us! It is time for change – we need to look

337

towards America where things are managed the modern way. We are living in the far distant past – ruled by one man!'

'You are a socialist, then?' Katya asked and almost immediately realized she had said the wrong thing for the young man flushed and the others dropped their eyes.

'We prefer to call ourselves liberals,' Mikhail corrected her.

'You see, we are not anti-monarchist,' Anna interceded quickly. 'Please don't think that! But the Emperor should not rule as an autocrat. That is wrong. We need a *Duma*.'

'Please repeat none of this in the Grand Duke's household,' Mikhail requested her earnestly. 'I could lose my job at the hospital – never work again!'

Anna murmured assent, her eyes uneasily on their new friend. Katya sensed a new reserve in the group round the table, as if they had just become aware they had a stranger in their midst. The lecturer's wife clasped and unclasped her reddened hands and in the lamplight Mikhail's eyes seemed to withdraw behind his pince-nez.

'Don't be uneasy. I won't repeat anything mentioned here. I'm no spy,' she said shortly and Anna, sensing they had hurt their guest, leaned across and clasped her hand.

'Of course you won't! Mikhail is a fool to suggest it,' she said warmly and Katya sensed she had kicked her brother under the table. But the spell had been broken and the lecturer and his wife rose to leave. It was late and Irina was on early shift at the hospital.

As it was past ten o'clock, Katya decided it was time for her to go, too. Mikhail announced he would accompany her to the station. He put on a long elk-skin coat with fur both inside and out that had belonged to his father, jammed on a shaggy fur hat and told Anna that she was not to wait up.

338

Anna, who was annoyed with him, told him that she had no intention of doing so and he could come home at dawn if he had a mind to do so. Katya she kissed warmly. 'Please, please, come again!'

Her brother led the way out of the apartment into the icy night.

'Shall we find an *isvostchik*?' Katya suggested for a light snow was stinging their eyes.

'An *isvostchik*?' He laughed grimly. '*Mademoiselle*, we never hire a sledge while we have two legs to walk on! Your time in the Grand Duke's home has softened you.'

'Of course it hasn't!' Katya was becoming irritated by this bossy, cocksure young man. 'But it *is* snowing and the Baltic Station is a long way away – '

'Not if we go my way. Come.' He offered her an arm. 'We are young and strong. It's good to feel we have strength and to use it this way. The walk will be good for us both. Anna keeps the rooms too warm.'

Katya, who had been driven everywhere since her arrival in Russia, soon realized that she was sadly out of practice and that Mikhail's remark was probably all too true. She had grown soft living among people like Laura Nicolaievna who adored comfort and had plenty of money. She also missed the polished, gentle manners of a man like Alex Rakov. Mikhail Tchelitchev was not polished: he was bitter and rough-tongued and hard-working and although she couldn't warm to him, she admired him.

Soon she began to enjoy the walk along the frozen quays where the buildings rose as tall as cliffs on their right as they hurried along. There was something lowering and evil in the look of the vast palaces where lights shone out onto the snow from every floor. Snow was falling thicker and faster now, mantling the dirty snow packed on the roads with a briefly clean covering that shimmered in the lamplight.

Mikhail ploughed on through it, talking without pause. Indeed, Katya suspected he had suggested the walk to the station as an excuse to continue his lecture on the state of Russia and what should be done about it. He mentioned several times a priest called Gapon for whom he had a grudging admiration. Father Gapon worked in a terrible district on the swampy outskirts of the city, called ironically the Haven. Here were the hovels and hide-outs of the very poor and the criminals. Here disease and death stalked, and here it was that Dr Tchelitchev found most of his work. 'Some day I'll show you my district,' he told her, 'and you shall meet Father Gapon – he is a Christ to those poor people. You will understand better then the problem of my country.'

'We have such districts, I believe,' Katya interposed but Tchelitchev was deaf to her interruptions and intent only on lecturing her. 'There is not enough food in the country districts – not enough in a country the size of ours! Ridiculous, isn't it? So the peasants flock to our cities to find work. There is none so they soon have to steal or starve. Yes, I must show you the Haven. It is unlike anything on earth. A hell of dirt, disease, dying children and human misery – '

Katya's head was beginning to ache. Mikhail Tchelitchev was proving a very exhausting companion and she was thankful to reach the station at last.

'My sister and I have enjoyed meeting you, *mademoiselle*. You will come again? Anna is alone so much and tonight I can see she has been happy.'

'I now look on you both as my friends,' Katya told him as they shook hands. 'Oh, the train is moving! Please get down!'

He was quite unhurried: perhaps he understood Russian trains better than she did. 'You have everything for your comfort? Then goodnight, Mademoiselle Croxley.' He jumped down and slammed the door. She watched his bulky figure walking away across the dimly-lit station. He was going into the refreshment room, she saw, perhaps for vodka, more likely for tea which the Russians seemed to consume in even greater quantities than the English. And of course he would fall into more talk with strangers and wouldn't see his bed for hours.

4

'Katya, I shall take you to see our lawyer this afternoon,' Laura announced a couple of mornings later. 'He is anxious to settle Papa's Will and this money has been making interest for five years.'

Katya rose and faced her aunt. 'I would prefer not to receive it – oh, please understand, Laura! Grandpapa wouldn't leave it to my mother; how can I take it?' She had thought about this a great deal and although the possibility that it would buy her a school of her own had delighted her at first, she now saw that it wouldn't do at all.

Laura paused and turned round. 'You would *prefer not to receive it*! What madness is this? I for one will not allow it. Papa earned this money – every kopeck – by the sweat of his brow and being clever in business. I will not have you repudiate it. It is an insult to him!'

'It is an insult to my mother, you mean! *She* should have had it, not I.'

'You are very young in some ways, Katya. Don't you really understand? Papa adored Marie: she was his favourite daughter and she ran away from him and married against his will. Both Papa and Marie were stubborn people: she never begged pardon of him and he swore he wouldn't leave her a penny. They died without reconciliation and it's very sad. The money is for you, Marie's daughter. It is a great deal and makes you a rich girl. No way can you refuse it as Monsieur Koffsky will tell you this afternoon.'

Monsieur Koffsky was even more horrified than Laura when it was mentioned that Monsieur Urosov's grand-daughter did not wish to inherit the money he had left her. Muttering 'Nonsense! nonsense!' under his Vandyke beard he put a pen in her hands.

Meekly Katya signed. Laura had been so kind to her and obviously regarded it as an insult to her father if she were to reject it. Nothing must spoil the last few weeks in Russia.

'Tell me, *monsieur*, what does this money mean in English terms?' Laura pressed.

Monsieur Koffsky summoned a clerk who went away for a few minutes. He brought the answer on a piece of paper.

'Forty-eight thousand pounds,' Katya said with a gasp. She went white, Never had she dreamed it could be such a sum. Why, two thousand pounds would have been a fortune! Feeling sick, she looked from Laura to the lawyer. 'I can't – ' she said faintly but Laura cut off her sentence.

'It's essential that you receive the very best advice on your return to England,' she said crisply. 'You will ask the bank to give my niece every facility, Monsieur Koffsky? Thank you. Now we must go. There is a great deal to do.'

She was now in her element. Stifling Katya's protests she led the way out of the lawyer's office and into the

Grand Duke's *droshky*. 'We will call at Madame Brissac's first. She is the court dressmaker and quite the best in Petersburg. I cannot wait to see the end of these Hull garments. You need a small but carefully chosen wardrobe to carry you on to spring. We will look in at Monsieur Paul's for hats when we have swatches of material to show him. When you return home you must order your clothes in Paris twice a year – '

'Laura, Paris clothes would just look silly in Whitby.'

'Of course they would. But you surely aren't expecting to go on living there? My dear child, you can settle anywhere now. You will have to get yourself a dull good woman to live with you and then you can travel and enjoy life.'

Katya was silent as they travelled from noisy Znamenia Square down Nevsky Prospekt to Madame Brissac. Laura's blueprint of life for her was not in the least to her taste. It bore out her forebodings that the money might prove to be the worst thing that could happen to her.

5

Christmas was fast approaching and with it the expected return of Anastasia Barinskaya. Although there was no definite news of her arrival yet, the children asked daily with increasing eagerness and impatience: 'Will Mamma arrive today, do you think?'

Katya went with them and Miss Ellis on a shopping expedition to Nevsky Prospekt where the most fascinating shops were to be found. Bright lights and a smell of spice hovered on the air; there was little daylight now but it didn't seem to matter.

As she shopped and drank hot chocolate at Elisevs,

343

Katya was all the time conscious of a feeling of pain which she tried to pretend wasn't there. Everything she now did was done with a sense of imminent departure and she hadn't seen Alex Rakov since the day of the Christmas Bazaar, nor was she likely to since he had told her so honestly that there could be no future for them. She wished she could forget him but those words echoed round her mind as she chatted with the children, helping them choose presents for the family and gaily concealing her own purchases from them. They had sampled two American Christmases and were quite determined to have a splendid one now that Mamma was coming home.

Yes, he had been honest with her, she admitted as she helped Tanya select a gold chain for her little sister. He had been right, of course. Their ways lay in different directions and she must be courageous and forget him for it was now unlikely that they would ever meet again. She couldn't regret what had happened for it had taught her what was meant by love. The response of her body to his, yes: but more than that, she loved his mind and its strength and gentleness. Her feelings for him were despite what the world thought of him: a man who probably kept a mistress in Paris; who went from relationship to relationship quite selfishly; a man who was either a police spy betraying those who trusted him or a bitter revolutionary. Whatever the world said, the man she knew was none of these things. He couldn't be. Of that she was almost certain.

19
The Dividing Line

1

'Dearest Katya (you see how I am progressing?), Of course you are only trying to break my heart *and* succeeding, need I tell you? So you like Prince Alexander Rakov very much, do you? Katya, Katya, beware of having *your* heart broken, too. Russian princes are notoriously volatile. How can you be sure he's an honest man? My little company orphan, I feel very responsible for you since it was my idea that you should go to St Petersburg in the first place. I am thinking of running over on the next boat to see you – '

There were three pages from Robert this time and he ended:

'More in sorrow than in anger, your worried friend, Robert.'

Katya cast the letter from her. What a fool she had been to tell him about Alex! *Running over to see her*, indeed! A week's journey just to satisfy his jealous heart that she was simply teasing him. Good heavens! the man really was in love with her and she had treated it lightly! Of course she liked him very much and she felt his solid reliability behind her like a well-built wall. But she was in love with a Russian and nothing – *nothing* could change that fact. She didn't expect to get any happiness from it: they were worlds apart as he had made so plain and so delicately to her at the bazaar. But she was drawn to him with every fibre of her being: it was both an agony and a pleasure.

Wilfully, she decided not to reply to Robert's letter.

2

The weather began to close in. Clouds of snow blew like duststorms along the frozen Neva. Workmen toiled night and day collecting the fresh drifts of snow to melt in the huge bonfires they built on every street corner. What they burned to keep these fires going no one seemed to know but an acrid, rubbery smell made people choke as they passed. Trams clanged and swayed through the city packed with people buying food for the feast next week.

The children begged to be taken to the Pavlovsk Park on the outskirts of Tsarskoe Selo where they might join other young people tobogganing down the ice hills in the three short hours of daylight that was their allotment now. Laura Nicolaievna suddenly decided to accompany them and Katya, and they all crammed into her fur-lined sledge for the short drive.

The park was full of people enjoying themselves. Laughter rang out like the sound of bells in the icy air. Down the nearest ice hill, a crowd of off-duty guards officers in their long grey greatcoats and fur hats were racing each other and hurling snowballs.

Katya watched in amusement: it was difficult to picture their British counterparts behaving in a park like a troupe of riotous children!

Laura knew them and hailed them delightedly.

'Boris! Nikita!'

They swarmed round her, laughing and talking, their faces stung by the cold, their breath in clouds round their heads. 'Laura Nicolaievna, introduce us! Introduce us at once!' they clamoured.

'I don't believe I know this lady,' and a laughing lieutenant bowed to little Maia causing her to hide her face in her muff.

Captain Boris Skernevitsky bowed to Katya and offered her a seat on his toboggan. Nikita's bow in her direction was stiff and he devoted himself to Laura, while Tanya (very adult all of a sudden) was borne away by a handsome boy lieutenant.

There followed half an hour of high fun, such as Katya had never experienced before. How these Russians enjoyed even the simplest pleasures of life! she thought enviously as she climbed the steps for another toboggan run. The ice hills were a wonderful idea. Man-made, they were now as hard as iron and the toboggans shot down them like bullets, leaving one's stomach behind.

Pavlovsk was a very pretty park. In it was a big yellow palace where the Grand Duke Constantine (son of the Grand Duke Vladimir who was commander-in-chief of the military at St Petersburg) lived. The private grounds of this palace were patrolled by soldiers who had worn a grey path across the clean snow. There were carved bridges, Chinese pagodas and wooded dells – all now outlined in crisp white snow. It was a delightful playground for the noble families living in Tsarskoe Selo and Katya soon felt as carefree as the others.

Soon, lamplight starred under the trees and human voices tinkled like glass in the frosty air. Daylight was over at two in the afternoon.

An old man who was clearing a path paused in his work to watch them, simple pleasure on his bearded face as he leaned on his long-handled shovel for a well-earned rest.

Katya had noticed him earlier. She was just finishing a

run down the ice hill when she heard him protesting vigorously and she saw Prince Nikita, childish malice on his face, running up and down kicking the cleared snow back on to the paths and laughing hysterically as he did so. The work of a morning was soon demolished beneath his boots and the neat paths were piled high with snow again.

'Look at Nikita!' cried someone. 'What a child he is!' and they all roared with laughter.

To and fro, to and fro ran Nikita, hiccuping weakly with breathless laughter. The old *moujik*'s protests seemed only to egg him on and he pushed the shabby figure aside as he turned to destroy another path. The peasant, his feet bound with rags against the cold, was clumsy and stumbled, falling and picking himself up, talking volubly all the time as he begged his excellency not to ruin his work.

Katya glanced about her: only she seemed to feel shame and anger that Prince Nikita was depriving the old *moujik* of a day's wage. When the overseer came, the old chap wouldn't get a kopeck for work not done.

Suddenly, finding his protests unheeded, the peasant shot out a horny hand in its ragged mitt and plucked Nikita's uniform sleeve as he rushed past kicking up the snow and shouting at the top of his voice. Arrested in his flight, Nikita turned his head and saw whose hand held his arm. With a blow he felled the man.

'How dare you touch my Tsar's uniform?' he hissed, his face transfigured from childish delight to a mask of fury. 'You have defiled it, you cur!' Seizing the old man's shovel he knocked him senseless as he attempted to rise from his knees.

One of the other officers called to a foot patrol outside the yellow palace. 'Remove the dog! Throw him into jail!'

A couple of soldiers hurried up and seizing the limp body by its legs dragged it away. A ragged fur hat and blood marked the spot where he had fallen.

Katya, transfixed with terror and amazement, seemed rooted to the ground. Her hands to her face, she stared from the blood on the ground to Nikita who was being patted on the back by his brother officers. No one seemed to think he had behaved appallingly. Indeed, Laura was at that moment praising his action in defending the Tsar's uniform in such a manner. 'Their impudence goes beyond anything!' she declared. 'If we weren't constantly on the watch, the Black People would be at our throats like wolves!'

They're mad, Katya thought, trembling with shock. *Mad as hatters and not one of them realizes it!* She felt physically sick as she stood on the fringe of the group of excited officers who, with Laura and Tanya, made up the crowd round Nikita. She realized now that she was centuries away from these people in thought and spirit. They were still in the middle ages – this was 1904! How could she pretend to understand them? Perhaps, she thought, Alex too would have approved of Nikita's action in half-killing a peasant for touching his uniform sleeve. The fact was, she didn't know what Alex's reaction would have been. She didn't really know him at all. He was a Russian and therefore an enigma to her.

A touch on her skirt recalled her from her depressing thoughts. Maia had buried her head against her and was shaking and sobbing. 'Katya! Katya! Let's go home! Is that old man dead? I want Mamma – ' and she opened her mouth and roared with fright. Katya led her away a little distance and knelt in the snow to comfort her. 'Ssh, darling. Yes, we're going – look, there's Peter with the sledge. Shall we get in under the warm rug and wait for Tante Laura?' Tenderly, she mopped the small face and

349

straightened the fur bonnet, thinking sadly that in a few years Maia wouldn't cry at the sight of a peasant being killed before her eyes: she would have imbibed the creed of the nobles and such a sight would no longer upset her. She glanced over her shoulder and saw that the others were preparing to go home, laughing and bantering as if nothing had happened. Tonight, the old peasant's family would wait in vain for his return.

Anger made her voice shake when they were all seated again in the sledge and the fur rug was fastened across them. 'That was a terrible thing to do.'

Laura glanced across. There was contempt in her voice. 'Do not presume to condemn what you cannot possibly understand. You know nothing of a Russian officer's code of honour. Nikita acted with commendable loyalty to his Tsar.' She patted Maia's head for tears were still rolling down the child's cheeks. 'Come, Maia, wipe your eyes. That was a nasty old man and Cousin Nikita did what was right. The Black People must learn to keep their places,' she added and her face tightened ominously, 'or we shall have to show them how to do so.'

3

Next day, Katya went into Petersburg with a present for Anna Andreyevna of an English grammar, a small dictionary and a book of fairy tales in English for her to translate. She had found everything at the English Shop on Nevsky Prospekt and Anna was so excited that she begged for her first English lesson there and then. Mikhail was at the hospital and the girls were free to chat. A deep flush swept Anna's face when Katya told her of the ugly incident at the Pavlovsk Park.

350

'We are hundreds of years behind the times,' she said in a low voice, closing the books and piling them one above the other on the red-chenille-covered table. 'How will we ever catch up? You see, *they* want it to remain the same – and with all that power who can blame them? Do you wonder that we are followers of Father Gapon? He is not a revolutionary as some people make out. He simply wants democratic government here in Russia, a vote for everyone over a certain age. And why not? We are told we're not ready for it – we never shall be if *they* have their way!' Her eyes alight, Anna was embarked on her favourite theme. Father Gapon had said that the first step must be a *Duma*, a parliament to which deputies could be elected. 'But I fear it will be a long time before anything like that happens,' she ended with a long sigh. 'Nicholas wishes to remain an autocrat, to rule absolutely – ' She broke off, listening. 'Is that someone at the door? Please excuse me; it may be a patient.'

Katya waited, her eyes thoughtful: so the brother and sister did not think alike. Mikhail made no bones about wanting a violent end to the Tsar's rule: Anna on the other hand was a monarchist wistfully hoping to see the old order changing democratically. Did Anna fully understand how her brother felt?

Anna came back leading a young man in a rough sheepskin coat. With his shaggy hair and beard he looked like a peasant but he soon dispelled that idea when he spoke in French to her. Anna's innocent face was wreathed in blushing smiles as she introduced him as 'Dmitry Igorovich Anadory who was brought up with us on the Barinsky estate.'

The man looked with interest at the English girl as they shook hands but he said little to her, addressing his remarks to Anna: now and again he stole a glance at

351

Anna's guest but always his eyes moved hastily away again.

Anna had rung a bell with all the air of a society hostess and presently Lisaveta, the little servant, came padding along the hall bearing the samovar. She proceeded to light this and at the same time exchanged jokes in Russian with Dmitry Igorovich with whom she appeared to be on the best of terms. As they drank their glasses of tea, Anna and Dmitry exchanged small items of news and then – inevitably with these young Russians – they drifted to politics and the future of their country.

'The Autocrat will have to go,' Dmitry declared, thumping the table. Then he stopped; his eyes slewed round to Katya. 'Can I rely on your discretion, *mademoiselle*? You would not have me in the Peter and Paul Fortress?'

'Of course you can trust Katya!' Anna said angrily. 'I told you she's my *friend*! But it is *I* to whom you ought to be afraid to address such remarks! Such talk is seditious and I will not allow it. Both Mikhail and I are monarchists as you very well know – '

'Oh, come now, Anna Andreyevna! You know as well as I do that Mikhail is as revolutionary as I am!'

The pretty pink colour drained from Anna's face. 'In God's name, what do you mean, Dmitry Igorovich?'

There was silence in the room.

Then Dmitry moved uneasily on his chair. 'I don't mean anything,' he said crossly. 'How quickly you take me up, Anna Andreyevna! I just thought – '

'Mikhail is as loyal to the Tsar as I am. Like me, he is a follower of Father Gapon and you know *he* is no revolutionary! He abhors the Bolsheviks and Mensheviks – '

'We all know Gapon is a lap-dog of the *Okhrana*,' Dmitry muttered under his breath. 'He's in their pocket and that's why he's allowed to be the mouthpiece of the workers.'

Anna was seriously disturbed, Katya could see; tears rose in her eyes. 'You must not say such things. You know they're not true!' The glass of tea trembled in her hand. Katya glanced angrily at the cocksure young man who seemed determined to undermine Anna's faith in the young priest.

He caught her hard look and scratched his head uncomfortably. 'Well, well, don't fuss yourself, Anna Andreyevna. We shall change the subject.' Turning again to Katya he said affably: 'And how do you like Petersburg, *mademoiselle*?'

'It is a beautiful city. I shall be sorry to leave it so soon.'

'Katya is staying with Urosova,' Anna began. 'She goes home when Countess Barinskaya returns – '

Dmitry Igorovich whirled round. 'With Urosova? In the Grand Duke's ménage? My God, Anna, where are your wits? Why did you let me speak as I did with one of *them* among us?'

Both girls stared at him. A feeble protest began to issue from Anna's lips but Katya's voice cut her off. 'Perhaps in future it would be wiser to keep your revolutionary ideas to yourself, Dmitry Igorovich, instead of annoying Anna with them. But don't worry,' she added contemptuously. 'I shan't repeat them to the Grand Duke! You are safe this time.'

It was the young man's turn to look awkward now. He scrambled to his feet, bowed to Katya and said in a dignified voice: 'It is time I went, Anna Andreyevna. Please give my felicitations to your brother.'

When Anna returned from seeing him out, she was indulgently smiling. 'The silly boy! He got a good fright and it will do him good. He works in one of the ministries

353

and will be frightened of losing his job. But I wish he wouldn't come and talk to Mikhail in this way. It's beginning to influence him. Talk, talk, talk. That's all they ever do, these so-called revolutionaries.'

'Not always, Anna. Didn't one of them kill the Minister of the Interior last summer?'

Anna sighed and sat down. 'You're right. Now and again, a hot-head throws a bomb and conditions are tightened for everyone. Plehve was a hated man – so cruel – he deserved it. But it hasn't furthered the cause of freedom in Russia. And Dmitry is always telling Mikhail that blood must be shed! I'm so afraid for Mikhail: he will lose his job if he is unwise – if people think he has revolutionary ideas. The Barinskys have brought us many patients. He would lose all of them and we should have to start again.'

Katya got up and reached for her coat. 'Don't worry, Anna, I imagine Dmitry Igorovich is all talk. At home, many young men are the same and no one takes much notice of them.'

Anna smiled sadly. 'But this is not England, Katya. Here it is dangerous to talk so. People vanish who do so.'

As she buttoned her coat Katya said thoughtfully: 'If I were a Russian citizen, I daresay I would talk in this manner. Remember what I saw yesterday?' She clenched her hands. 'Change is badly needed here; even I, a foreigner, see that.'

Anna nodded as she followed her out. 'It is what Father Gapon is working for but *with* the Tsar – always *with* the Tsar! We feel he does not get told about the plight of the people. If he knew, he would help us – I'm sure of it!'

Katya looked doubtful. This seemed a very naïve point of view to her. They promised to meet again and Katya ran down the three flights of stairs to the street.

A figure who had been walking up and down outside threw away his cigarette and detained her with a hand on her arm.

'*Mademoiselle.*'

Stifling a scream, Katya turned. Although still only the afternoon, it might have been midnight outside. Under the light of an overhead lamp she saw Dmitry Igorovich's worried face. 'I startled you?'

'Of course you did,' she said crossly.

'A thousand pardons. But I had to speak to you.'

She peered at him suspiciously. 'What about?'

'About what I said in there. You will not repeat it to Urosova? I could get into trouble.'

'Laura Nicolaievna and I rarely talk politics. I will not repeat it. But I do beg you not to worry Anna about her brother. I feel sure you must be wrong about Mikhail.'

He was silent for a moment. Then he said in a low voice: 'No, I am not wrong, *mademoiselle*. Mikhail meets with the Bolsheviks. But do not repeat this.' Still in the same cautious voice he added: 'The time for revolution is nearly ripe. The war is a fiasco. A man has just told me that Port Arthur has fallen. I bid you goodnight, *mademoiselle.*'

When Katya returned to Tsarskoe Selo, Laura left her in no doubt of the truth of this news. Her nostrils pinched, her eyes like slits, she said between her teeth: 'You have heard? We have suffered a miserable defeat! Our great Russian empire to suffer so at the hands of the Nippons!' She leapt off her chair and paced to and fro. 'My God, what cowardice to *surrender*!'

'Does it mean the war is over?'

'Never!' Laura's bosom heaved with outrage. 'The whole world will be pleased – oh, England has been a false friend to us and we shan't forget!' She collapsed again on her chair and mopped her eyes.

Katya stood awkwardly not knowing what to say. She remembered how everyone in Britain had mourned during Black Week in the war with the Boers. There had been such despair. She wanted to say something comforting but could find no words. At home, she knew, Nicholas had been condemned for going so foolishly into this war with Japan after grabbing territory Russia had no right to, and sending out a huge army and now the entire navy, too! Heaven alone knew when the Russian navy would enter Japanese waters – it was having to go round by South Africa as passage through the Suez Canal had been refused and that was another reason for hating England, she thought glumly.

Laura blew her nose and sat up. 'We shan't give in,' she announced as if she was the commander-in-chief himself. 'We shall send out more men – we have thousands more men we can equip and train! Many more than the Japanese! We shall win, you'll see, even if it takes years!' She glanced at the clock. 'You know that I go out tonight? Yes, it is our performance at the Ballet School before the Imperial Family. I have to be at the rehearsal so will change and dine there. Marfa! Marfa! Have you my things? Then help me on with my coat. If only it wasn't tonight of all nights! I feel sick with nerves. Is Peter here with the sledge? Then I will say goodnight, Katya. The children expect you for supper with them tonight.' In the flurry she always created round her, Laura swept to the door and Katya watched her drive off. She turned away with a sigh as Pyotr closed the heavy double doors. This Russian defeat wouldn't make her more popular among her Russian friends, she thought glumly. She wondered how Miss Ellis was feeling.

'My dear, I've weathered far worse than this during my time in this country,' the governess told her as they sat down to their meal in the children's room (an English stew floating with grease, Katya saw ruefully). Afterwards she played Snakes and Ladders with Maia while Tanya sat curled up in a chair disconsolately turning over a fashion paper and yawning. How strongly one got the impression that Tanya was counting the hours to maturity, Katya thought with amusement. It was only nine o'clock when she said goodnight and went to her own room to read. It was such a pleasant room to be in for an hour's leisure, she thought as she looked round, and she seldom got the opportunity. She sat down on a low chair by the stove and opened *Middlemarch* that she had brought with her but barely started. Next month she would be back in her room at Hill House: she shuddered with distaste at the memory of its ugliness. Laura was right; she must leave Whitby and start afresh somewhere else.

Luxury has ruined me, she told herself with a rueful smile. She got up and began to unhook her bodice for although it was early, she would be far more comfortable in her robe. She undressed completely and got ready for bed. If she became sleepy over her book, she could climb straight into bed.

But she didn't read. Busy thoughts crowded her head as she stared at the glowing wood through the little window in the stove. She had thought she would be glad to return home when the time came. Well, the time had come now and she was dreading it. It was nearly Christmas and Anastasia had not yet arrived so it looked as if she, Katya, was saved from spending Christmas at Hill House with the Miss Lesleys.

The truth was she didn't want to leave Russia: Russia held Alex and she couldn't bring herself to believe that she would never see him again. She loved him and this love burned and ached in her day and night despite the fact that he had told her there was no future for them. To be told this was one thing: to believe it meant destroying

357

something precious – something like hope and faith together with love. He had been honest and strong and had deliberately kept away from her since the day of the Christmas Bazaar; but didn't they say love flourished on neglect? Hers was stronger than ever now. She longed for his touch and the sound of his voice, the look of sudden tenderness in his eyes. Had she no self-respect? Wasn't there this other woman in his life, the woman he kept in Paris? Surely it was madness to go on loving him? She wished she could forget his tender words as he held her, forget the feel of his body pressed close to hers, the rough feel of his face as he kissed her.

Longing swept her and she put her hands to her face and held them there like a shield, for the memory of those few minutes was making her burn with desire. 'Alex,' she whispered, trying to conjure up his presence. 'Alex . . . Alex . . .'

A sound made her jump. The hands dropped from her face and she half turned. Was there someone outside her door? Someone who was opening it very softly without knocking.

'Who is it? Who is there?' She held her lamp high so that it cast its light full on the gently opening door.

Suddenly, the door crashed open and she was startled and amazed to see the Grand Duke Philip framed there. His stiff white and gold tunic was unbuttoned, his hair was rumpled, his heavy jowls flushed. On his face was a strange look of malicious glee.

'Well, English girl, shall we drink to Russia's defeat?' he slurred, unsteadily placing a bottle and two glasses on a small table.

He's drunk, she thought. Knowing that it took a man of his habits a good many bottles to get drunk, he must have been drinking for hours – probably at the barracks.

Standing up, she strove to appear calm and matter of

358

fact despite her trembling legs. It was silly to be afraid of a drunken man, she told herself firmly: someone with fuddled wits would surely be easy enough to deal with. 'No, thank you, your highness, I am about to go to bed as you can see. I don't believe I heard you knock? Will you leave at once, please?' She glanced towards the bell but he was too quick for her. Drunk or not, he moved with the silent precision of a panther and grasped her hand as she was about to swing the handle on the wall. Giving her a little shake he pushed her, causing her to stumble against a stool and almost lose her balance.

'You're going to drink to it whether you want to or not,' he told her in a hard voice. Slopping the wine into both glasses, he held one out. 'Here, take it. Join me in wishing perdition to our brave army in the East!' The bitterness in his voice caused her to shrink back as he thrust his face close to hers.

'I – I don't want it.'

'Take it! By God, d'you want me to force it down your pretty little throat? Come on, after me: perdition to the brave Russian army in the East.' He tossed his drink down and threw the glass to crash in smithereens against the stove. 'They've brought us to our knees – the laughing stock of the world – ' he muttered hoarsely, half to himself, his hands opening and closing.

She sipped her wine, measuring her distance from the door. If she rolled over the bed, she might beat him to it. She glanced at him and saw that he was watching her with a strange look in his eyes. She stood defenceless in the lamplight, her dark hair loose and cascading round her shoulders, her robe delineating every line of her shapely body. He chuckled suddenly and sprang at her, knocking her sideways onto the bed and spilling the red wine over the silk cover. 'Get out!' she screamed, trying to push him away but he was much stronger with a heavy, bulky body that threatened to crush all the breath out of her as he rolled on to her. His hands were everywhere, pulling at her lawn nightdress and thin woollen robe while she fought and bit and found the breath somewhere to scream and scream. Would no one hear? The walls of the house were very thick, she remembered, and only Laura slept on this landing and Laura was out until the early hours as he well knew.

'Stop it, you little fool!' His hand hit her sharply on a corner of her mouth and she felt the taste of blood as it ran down her throat. Her violent struggles seemed only to increase his desire for her and he chuckled hoarsely again as he held her down and began inexorably to tear her nightdress off. The blood had mounted to his heavy-jowled face and his eyes glittered greedily as he succeeded in revealing more and more of her naked body.

Her strength was nothing against his and she was crying weakly now.

'We Russians may lose a war but we always conquer our women,' he said in her ear as he pressed her naked-ness against the gold buttons and gold lace of his uniform. She shrieked once more with pain and fright as he held her pinioned and with his free hand fumbled with his own clothes.

'Katya?' The door had opened behind them and a small figure blinked in the light as Maia in her nightdress looked for her cousin. 'I can hear Mamma's voice calling! Katya! It's Mamma! I'm sure it is – ' She rubbed her sleepy eyes, trying to focus them on the dim figures in the room.

With an oath the man released his victim and pushing past the half-asleep child left the room.

Katya lay bruised and breathless on the blue silk bed-cover, hoarse sobs shaking her. Remembering the child,

360

she made an effort and sat up, wrapping herself in the cover and trying to smile reassuringly.

'Oh, Katya, you're bleeding!' Maia exclaimed. 'Who was that horrid man? Did he hurt you?'

So she hadn't recognized the Grand Duke, Katya realized thankfully. It was not surprising: Philip's face had been transformed from the one she was used to seeing. 'No, darling, he hasn't hurt me. Just help me bathe my face – I think I've cut it somehow.' Her teeth were chattering with shock; cold nausea rose in her throat. Oh, God, I'm going to be sick! she thought and leaned against the bedpost. Wide awake now, Maia had fetched a sponge dipped in water and carefully and gently was wiping blood from her face.

'You mustn't cry. I won't let him hurt you, Katya.'

'Thank you. You're a kind little girl – '

'Mai-a!' Through the open door came a familiar voice. 'Tanya! Maia! It is I – Mamma! Where are you, darlings?'

'There! It *is* Mamma! I *did* hear her – ' Barefooted, Maia sped joyously out of the room and Katya heard her rushing down the stairs. 'Mamma! Mamma, you're home!'

Squeals and the sound of laughter echoed up the stairs. Anastasia Barinskaya had succeeded in surprising her family by arriving on the last train from Petersburg.

Tanya and Miss Ellis were roused and one by one came downstairs to greet Anastasia as she stood in the hall with Maia in her arms. She was flushed with excitement, wisps of fair hair falling from under her toque. Dressed in a becoming prune shade, her furs cast on a nearby chair, she looked very different from the pale invalid in the Liverpool hospital, Katya thought as she came slowly down the stairs, attempting to smile with her very sore mouth. Miss Ellis, a wonderful sight in a pink boudoir cap and a man's Jaeger dressing gown, was introducing herself with dignity. Anastasia looked up and saw a pale girl with a cloud of dark hair down her back standing on the bottom step. Why, she's lovely – I hadn't realized, she thought, coming impulsively forward and taking Katya's icy hands in hers.

Katya's eyes had been looking fearfully round the hall. Had he gone? Was he still here? But the only other people were Corinne and Pyotr supervising the disposal of the luggage.

'Katya, my dear! I have so many messages for you from Mr Howarth!' Anastasia leaned forward and kissed her. 'My child, you're trembling. What is it?'

The others were staring now.

'I b-blundered in the dark and hit my – my face on the doorpost. It's nothing.'

'A bad man hurt her,' Maia told them, nodding her head.

They all laughed and Katya tried to smile but her mouth had swollen alarmingly and it was difficult.

'Come back upstairs, my dear,' Miss Ellis commanded briskly, 'and I will bathe it with arnica. Will you excuse us, Countess?'

'Of course. I am to have a meal Olga tells me so I will keep the children with me. We have so much to talk about and then my sister will be home in an hour or two – oh, it is so good to be back in Russia!' Anastasia cried, clasping her children to her.

'Those children won't go to bed tonight,' Miss Ellis murmured with a shrug as she led Katya upstairs. 'Wonderful people, these Russians, with a great deal of misdirected energy. One would think that poor woman hadn't a care in the world.' She placed Katya under a strong lamp and said in quite a different tone: 'Now, the truth, please. Who did that?'

Katya's tears began to spill over again. She attempted to speak but her voice was too choked and for a minute or two she could only cry unrestrainedly. A mannish linen handkerchief was thrust into her hand but Miss Ellis left her alone while she fetched arnica and gauze from her own room. Her sharp eyes saw the torn white lawn nightgown on the floor, the state of the bed and a smashed glass near the stove but she still said nothing as she bathed the girl's sore face.

'The Grand Duke,' Katya said, her voice shaking.

It wasn't long before the old governess had the full story and her wrinkled face set in lines of grim anger. She put the cork back in the arnica bottle. 'My dear child, what an escape! I haven't liked the *feel* of this household since I arrived. One can always sense when things are wrong. On no account must Laura Nicolaievna be told of this. Why? Well, what good would it do? She is the only refuge Countess Barinskaya has and this is the Grand Duke's house – or one of them anyway. Now of all times, her liaison with Philip mustn't end. He has the ear of the Tsar and is a powerful man. Through his aid I know that Laura Nicolaievna hopes her sister will be vindicated and her fortunes rescued. You understand?'

Katya was mopping her eyes and nodded reluctantly. But how cynical the old were! 'You're right, of course. I shall leave today – ' She glanced at the clock with a ghost of a smile. 'It is today, isn't it? Perhaps on an evening train to give me time to pack.'

'But you can't rush away like that! It would look so strange, leaving without warning.'

'I don't mean to leave for England yet. I shall say I've been asked to spend Christmas with the Tchelitchevs at Petersburg. We've become very friendly, you know, and I'm sure they would have me if I telephoned them. Oh, Miss Ellis, I daren't stay another day in this house in case of meeting that horrible man again!' She shuddered with horror.

363

Miss Ellis saw the point at once and they agreed on the story that was to be told Laura: the Tchelitchevs had asked Katya to spend the last week of her Russian visit with them, for now that Anastasia had returned Katya would be returning to England in the New Year.

Laura had been overjoyed to find Anastasia had arrived when she at last returned home on the Imperial Family's special train, an honour that had flushed her cheeks and put a sparkle in her eyes. The evening had been a tremendous success in every way and for part of the performance she had been asked to the royal box and congratulated on the high standard attained by the Ballet School children. Then to come in and find her sister and the children feasting by the fire, everyone ready to talk for hours, had put a seal on the evening's activities. She didn't come down until midday and found Katya, her valises packed, waiting to say goodbye.

Laura accepted her explanation for her departure with secret relief for now she could discuss Anastasia's affairs without her niece's continuing presence. 'But you will come back for a week or so before you leave? I shall keep your room just as it is, Katya!' The melting green eyes rested on her guest's bruised and swollen mouth but her lips said nothing about it. She was no fool. Pyotr had told her his highness had been to the house last evening – an evening when he perfectly well knew she was at the graduation performance – yet no one else had mentioned him. What had happened she could only guess at, but that something had caused this sudden flight she was convinced.

And Katya, looking into her aunt's eyes, knew that she hadn't been hoodwinked. 'You've been so kind to me. Are you sure you don't mind me rushing off like this?'

'No, I quite understand. The Tchelitchevs are your own age after all. But you'll have to return: there is much

364

to talk over and you will have to collect the rest of the clothes Madame Brissac is making for you. I'm *so* glad you've got the royal blue street outfit, it's perfect under your fur coat.' Chatting easily, they went downstairs together.

'All my Christmas gifts are hidden in the cupboard in my room.'

'And here is yours, my dear. The children too have gifts for you.'

Katya's eyes filled with tears. These were her mother's sisters and it was here, among her own at last, that she should be spending Christmas. 'I wish – ' she said and choked.

Laura hugged her and Anastasia came out with the children to kiss her goodbye. They seemed genuinely sorry to see her go, she thought forlornly as she got into the sledge to be driven to the station. A thin sunlight had broken through the clouds and lit up the fairytale town: now it looked like a stage set with puppets moving about. It's unreal, she thought, a place hidden from the harsh realities, the glaring imperfections of the twentieth century.

Giving it one last look, she knew that some day it wouldn't exist; reality would have swept it away like a flood tide.

20

A Russian Christmas

1

Anna met her at the door of the flat, her arms full of big square pillows for Katya's bed. 'Come in! Come in! I am very busy as you see. Yes, you shall help me but first Lisaveta must bring in the samovar. You are cold after your journey.'

It was three o'clock and dark outside so they drew the curtains and sat with the samovar between them under the flickering gas jet hanging from the centre of the ceiling. Its crude light carved out harsh shadows on their young faces.

'Your brother?'

'He is at the hospital as usual after midday. He is delighted you are to stay with us. I think he admires you, Katya! You make intelligent comments that he finds helpful. And you promised to teach me to speak English so we are both happy!' she ended gleefully, reaching for the tea box.

Katya smiled. She realized that her new friend was a very lonely young woman, shut up as she was in this third-floor flat with only Lisaveta for company. Mikhail was out a great deal and when he was at home he would be in his surgery most of the time, reading medical journals and making up medicines. Sometimes, he did late visiting, Anna had told her.

There was one subject that must be spoken of and cleared up at once: money. 'While I'm here as your friend and guest,' Katya said, picking her words with care, 'I would like to share the household expenses. Even one person makes a big difference, Anna, so do not protest – no, *please* – I shall go back to England at once if you are unreasonable!'

They both laughed and Anna accepted gratefully. No one knew better than she that her shabby brown purse contained few roubles to see her through each week.

The two girls made up Katya's bed in a narrow slice of a room off the main living room. The few pieces that furnished it were of no value and the curtains and bed covering had been washed countless times but Katya's heart was lighter than it had been for several weeks. There was a warmth and friendship here that had been lacking at Tsarskoe Selo. These were, after all, her sort of people.

She unpacked very little and the rest of her luggage was stowed away in a box room that contained an odd assortment of household things including an old sewing-machine of Swiss make. 'My mother's,' Anna explained. 'I am always intending to use it but I'm a very poor sewer, I'm afraid.'

'Well, I'm a good one,' Katya announced. 'So we shall buy materials and I'll make you a dress for the New Year.'

Joy flashed across Anna's face. She clasped her hands. 'Truly? A dress perhaps in dark red with ruffles round the neck? And here a bow – and sleeves – so – oh, Katya, how clever you must be!'

'Remember I can't do the things you do. I can't cook or order a household or see to medical instruments – '

'May I join this admiration society?' Mikhail's voice came from the hall where he was shrugging out of his coat. His face ruddy with cold, he shook Katya warmly by the hand. 'Welcome to our home – why, what have you done to your face?' He took her swollen face and turned it to the light. 'What is this cut on your mouth?'

'I too wondered but I didn't like to ask,' Anna murmured. 'You have had an accident, Katya?'

Katya shook her head. 'It is why I am here so precipitately. You have become my refuge, dear friends.' She tried to smile. Instead, under their puzzled gaze, tears welled in her eyes and she ducked her head.

The brother and sister glanced at one another.

'Come, let us sit comfortably, and Katya will tell us what has happened – that is if you would wish to, Katya?' Anna added delicately.

It didn't take long to tell the sordid little story. 'I think he only did it because his pride had been wounded by the war news. He feels very bitter towards my country – he feels we ought to have come out on Russia's side like Germany,' Katya ended. 'So he took his revenge on me.'

Mikhail said something in Russian under his breath. 'That place! You ought never to have gone there! Those people have too much of everything – they are spoilt, like children with many, many toys. They are satiated by the good things of life, things people like us only dream about. We have to strive for everything – they haven't to strive at all. It is all there, waiting for them, from the time they are born. It is time we were rid of them – they are a cancerous growth on society. It is time for revolution and change, for blood to be shed – '

'Mikhail, I have never heard you speak so!' Anna whispered. Her face was suddenly pinched.

Her brother shrugged. 'No? That doesn't mean I haven't thought like that for a long time. I'm getting surer every day that they must all be swept away – yes, even the Tsar, Anna!'

'Oh, Mikhail!' She jumped up and opened the door an inch, then closed it again. 'Lisaveta,' she explained. 'I wouldn't like her to hear. Mikhail, I beg of you, be careful what you say!'

'Don't look so frightened, Anushka!' He patted her arm affectionately. 'What a milk-and-water fighter you are, my dear sister! You are getting more like Father Gapon in outlook every day. You want everything that I do but you don't want trouble, you don't want to fight for it.'

'But you admire Father Gapon! Mikhail, what do you mean?'

He shrugged. Perhaps he was already regretting his hasty words, Katya thought. 'I'm depressed sometimes,' he tried to explain. 'Things get worse not better. Sometimes I wonder why we all carry on. We are like ants on an anthill. Getting nowhere. Doing the same thing every day.'

But he cheered up when the evening meal was spread on the table, Katya noticed. There was a bottle of vodka and he drank two glasses of it. Anna had bought a small barrel of Beluga caviar of which he was very fond; before long, he was talking enthusiastically about his work to a new attentive audience while Anna unobtrusively served the meal and looked at him proudly now and again.

But when she was in bed that night, Katya reflected on the evening and came to the conclusion that Mikhail, while not ready to admit it to Anna, had indeed become a Bolshevik. That was the strangeness about Mikhail Tchelitchev that she had puzzled over. The night he had walked with her to the station he had been testing her opinions, trying to find out how much their views clashed or coincided. I must be careful not to get involved in politics, she thought remembering Robert's advice. But it would be difficult because these middle-class young Russians thought of nothing else.

2

She woke next morning to the appetizing smell of coffee being ground and smiled to herself, guessing that this was a treat in her honour. Outside her door, the little servant with the rosy freckled face who represented the total working force of the household was scrubbing the linoleum and singing a Russian folk song under her breath. There were quick footsteps; Anna's voice was calling out; the shrilling of the telephone.

She lay quietly for a few moments, allowing thoughts of Alex to steal back into her mind. It was twelve days since the Christmas Bazaar, twelve days since she had seen him. Now she had left Tsarskoe Selo, would he seek her out? Would he want to?

'I won't think about it!' she said aloud and jumped out of bed onto the thin little mat that was the only thing between her and the icy linoleum. She opened the curtain and saw that it was pitch dark outside with snow whirling ceaselessly across the yellow lamplight. This was the northern mid-winter, the bleakest part of the year, and Christmas Day was tomorrow.

With this in mind they decided to go shopping for food but first there was morning surgery and already a few patients waited on the bench in the hall. While Anna busied herself with them, Katya wrote a hurried letter to Robert Howarth telling him of her change of address. Then it was time to sally forth armed with bags to buy food for the feast.

How different the shops were to those across the river!

Here was a small bakery with a queue waiting to buy from twenty sorts of bread. Anna bought *churek* with sesame seeds, *balabusky* which were sour dough rolls, and *khalach*, golden braided twists of dough warm from the oven. There were black breads, sweet white breads and a beautiful cheese loaf that was a speciality of this baker who came from Georgia, Anna told her.

In the dark grocery shop along the street with its huge green scales on the mahogany counter, they were hard at work weighing out raisins and dates for eager buyers. A boy was cutting from an enormous slab of white unsalted butter and another was filling customers' bottles with golden sunflower oil.

Anna talked in her rapid Russian to the other housewives standing about the shop. They all seemed to know the doctor's sister and by the way their eyes turned to herself, Katya guessed that Anna was explaining her to these acquaintances.

At the butcher's, white veal from Archangel (very expensive) was purchased for Christmas Day and at the pastry cook's across the road, Katya insisted on buying a tower of flaky pastry stuffed with cream, fruit and nuts to finish the meal with.

The morning sped and the afternoon was spent in helping Lisaveta prepare for next day. At five o'clock, they set out by tram to serve tea at one of the Gapon reading-rooms. This one was on Vassiliefsky-Ostrov on the left bank of the Neva. Anna worked here two evenings a week. 'Our movement is small but it's growing,' she told Katya. 'We now have three reading-rooms as we call the meeting places and the workers call in on the way home from work. We teach many to read and write – it is ignorance we are fighting, you know! Three-quarters of our population are illiterate. It is a terrible thing. That and disease, Mikhail says, are a Russian's two worst

371

enemies – worse than the *Okhrana* even!' In her capacious leather bag she had a bundle of newspapers, Katya had noticed. 'These are copies of *Liberation*. They are printed for us in Germany, you know – oh, yes, it's illegal, of course.'

'Isn't that risky for you?'

'Yes,' Anna agreed. 'But sometimes it is necessary to risk a little to achieve a lot. This paper is uncensored news and passes from hand to hand until it falls apart. No, no, I carry these – Mikhail says you must not be allowed to do this work. *You* must not get into trouble.'

Katya followed Anna into the tea-cum-reading-room feeling a new respect for her. She was ashamed to remember that she had rather smiled at her friend who had such naïve aspirations; now she felt humbled. Anna was risking her liberty by distributing this news-sheet.

In the reading-room Katya noticed young men in black with peaked caps moving about distributing pamphlets. She nudged Anna. 'Who are they?'

Anna looked annoyed. 'Students from the university. They're all revolutionaries or think they are,' she said ironically as she dumped her leather bag and unwound her snow-spattered scarf. 'They have no business here and are misleading these poor people. But what can one do?'

Sitting on a stool hoping she looked unobtrusive, Katya watched Anna handing out *Liberation*. Two other women were making tea and a third was lending out books from a shabby-looking library of a few dozen volumes. She saw Anna clash with one student and an argument breaking out. The secret police must know this is going on, she thought, letting her eyes wander over the crowd as she wondered which of them was a police agent: the Tchelitchevs said they were everywhere. Now that elderly grey-haired workman was probably one in disguise – but his hands were black and blue with toil, the nails bitten down. As he grinned, she saw how bad his teeth were. Then who? She twisted on the stool and the breath left her body. Standing near the door was Alex Rakov.

He wore a heavy beaver coat and hat and was eagerly talking to a young priest in a black cassock who had a thin intelligent face and a black beard. That must be Father Gapon, Katya thought. A way opened before them as they walked towards the samovar, talking earnestly. Anna was now buttering hot bread at the table. She looked up, flashing a smile and speaking both to Alex and the priest. Alex was talking animatedly back to her, easily, laughingly, in the manner of an old friend.

Katya turned away quickly. Her heart was beating nervously. *Anna knew Alex.* He was on good terms with Gapon, and others had called out greetings to him. Could *he* be the police spy who must be here somewhere? Were all her early suspicions of him correct after all? A man who encouraged friendships to learn all he could only to denounce those who trusted him. She suddenly felt sick.

'Katya!' Anna's voice close at hand made her jump. 'Katya, I want you to meet a friend of mine, Alexander Petrovitch Drusov.'

She swung round and met his startled eyes. Colour had drained from under his fair skin leaving it grey. It was evident that he was as amazed as she was. But not by the flicker of an eye did he give her away.

'Mademoiselle Croxley is spending Christmas with us before she returns home to England, Alexander Petrovitch.' Anna beamed on both her friends.

He was carrying three tin mugs of tea on a tray. Bowing, he offered her one. 'You like Russia, *mademoiselle*?' The voice was that of a stranger.

'Very much – *monsieur*: I go home in the New Year with much regret.' Her voice was flat.

373

'Katya is teaching me English,' Anna went on. 'Already I can read it a little but the grammar is difficult. How lucky you are, Alexander Petrovitch, that you can speak English as well as French. Alas, I was not taught – but I mean to learn now and visit my friend in her country!'

They smiled, sipping their tea and hoping she would drift back to the table to continue buttering bread. But Anna was enjoying herself, introducing her English friend to all and sundry. Presently, Father Gapon himself joined them. Unfortunately he could speak neither French nor English and presently he drew Alex away and they walked off, talking earnestly.

'Who is he?' Katya asked casually.

'Alexander Petrovitch? A friend of Mikhail's. They met at one of the study circles. Mikhail never comes now and he was asking after him. Now we must go for there is supper to eat before we go to Midnight Service.'

All the way home in the tram, Katya replied in mono-syllables to Anna's chatter. She was still shaken by her meeting with Alex and the discovery that he went by another name. That he was Prince Alexander Rakov she had no doubt: but Alexander Drusov? Then she remembered that his cousin's name was Marina Drusova. It looked as if Alex was using his mother's family name to cover his identity. Could he really be a police spy? She had been told that every stratum of Russian society had its police spies. She had become almost sure that Alex wasn't one, that he was simply a liberal-minded noble-man. There were, after all, many of these, all rather jeered at by their fellows as odd characters who were harmless fools.

Inside her muff, her hands were clasped nervously. The meeting had roused all her feelings for him once more. She must remember to keep before her eyes that sentence of his that had struck her to the heart: *There can be no future for us*.

Mikhail was already home, they found, and soon they were hungrily eating a festive supper of fish wrapped in puff pastry and *medivnyk* to follow. This last was a delicious spiced honey cake that Lisaveta had made. Then they set out for Midnight Mass at the church round the corner. Even Mikhail who professed agnosticism accompanied them and Katya noticed Anna's ill-concealed surprise when he put his coat on.

The whole neighbourhood seemed to be streaming in the direction of the church and the huge congregation stood for an hour (there were no pews or chairs), each holding a slim, lighted candle: these were the only lights in the church. Round the altar figures in gorgeous robes that caught the soft lights chanted and in the outer ring of half-darkness a choir sang. Moved by the music and the whole scene, remembering all the doubts and despair that beset her, Katya's eyes filled. Slowly, one by one, tears rolled down her cheeks.

From behind the flame of his candle, Mikhail's unfathomable eyes watched and noted, but Anna's eyes were on the altar and full of shining faith. Katya realized that Anna's life was empty and dull with a daily procession of small duties. It was so like her own life at Whitby that she felt an empathy with her friend. Indeed life for both Tchelitchevs was a constant struggle to achieve something in life, to break down barriers that prevented them from reaching fulfilment in their lives. No wonder both fought so hard for freedom for themselves and others. To Anna, her faith in God and the Gapon Movement represented her only hope for the future.

'Why are you weeping?' Mikhail asked Katya in an undertone as they left the church.

She felt irritated with his attempt at intimacy. Her thoughts were hers alone.

'You are homesick?' He had cupped his hand round her elbow.

She jerked her arm away and then felt foolish: he was only trying to guide her down the steps after all. 'A happy Christmas,' she said, smiling at him. To her discomfiture he bent and kissed her awkwardly. He smelled of antiseptic and the long thin cigars he smoked. 'And to you, Katya.'

Quickly she turned away to kiss Anna and to repeat: 'A happy Christmas!' Then she took Anna's arm and walked quickly through the icy darkness to the tall apartment, dimly aware that Mikhail strolled unhurriedly behind them.

3

On Christmas Day the flat was filled with a stream of people drifting in and out. Some brought small presents of caviar or preserved ginger, others were empty-handed and just as welcome. They brought with them their own bottles of vodka or wine and sat about drinking and talking for hours. The university lecturer and his wife were there and recognized Katya with shy smiles. Their names she discovered were Ivan and Irina. Shy and inarticulate though they were, they managed to convey a feeling of friendliness as they asked her (inevitably) about England. What had been achieved by the Women's Movement? Nothing? What a very great pity! What was the average wage of a factory worker? Did children still work in the mines?

Years afterwards Katya remembered that strange

Christmas Day when earnest young people sat about Anna's living room and discussed the future of their country, when a slightly drunk doctor from Mikhail's hospital had drunk 'damnation to the Autocrat!' and had smashed his glass after the toast. The girls had all said 'Ssh!' and looked frightened until the talk had risen like a wave again to drown the doubtful incident.

'Here for at least ten years we have been asking for some form of constitutional government,' Ivan said, leaning earnestly across the table to Katya. 'The Tsar has swept our requests aside as "senseless dreams". Why should it be senseless? Other countries have it!'

'Russia is ripe for change,' Irina nodded. 'The war is going badly and people are getting bitter – '

'Only a swift and bloody revolution will resolve our troubles,' said Mikhail behind them. He put his arms round Ivan and Irina. 'Why is it, my friends, that you do not see this as plainly as I do? Gapon – ' He made a contemptuous sound. 'He will never succeed in bringing about change. He is milk-and-water. We need men prepared to shed their blood for the cause.'

'What a hot-head you are, Mikhail,' Ivan said indulgently. 'But we all know it's just your way. *Mademoiselle* here mustn't take seriously the things you say.'

'Afraid she'll report me, eh?' Mikhail's eyes slid towards Katya and he dropped his voice. 'She looks very innocent, I know, but how do we know she isn't a police spy?' It was a sly joke he had made before and as usual Ivan and Irina looked uneasy, exchanging glances with each other.

'Take care they don't believe you, Mikhail!' Katya said drily. 'Your friends' reaction to your joke shows me plainer than any words could how little freedom of speech you enjoy in your country. At least in my country we are still free to speak our minds, we can talk without fear of being locked up! We can criticize our Prime Minister, curse our MP, and exchange doubts about our King – no one will imprison us!'

Ivan laughed uneasily and presently drew his wife away.

'All talk as usual!' Mikhail said, his eyes following them. He bit off the end of his cigar and lit it. 'The worst trait of my compatriots is that they're windbags! Talk, talk, talk – have you ever heard so much talk? This room is loud with it. But when you ask them to join you in *doing* something, they melt away. They've suddenly remembered they have their university appointment to think of or an old mother to keep. They dare not risk it, they tell you – yes, the same fellow who five minutes earlier had been leading the revolution! Bah! They'll get nowhere fast that way. Believe me, Katya,' and he fixed her with a wholly serious stare, 'revolution is inevitable in this country. It will come in the next year or so. Remember I have said this. All Gapon's bleatings will get us *nowhere*. It is a case for bombs and blood,' he ended as someone came to claim his attention.

Yes, it proved to be a queer sort of Christmas Day.

4

Two days later she found herself accompanying Anna to a study-circle at the Narva Hall, which was in the Narva district where most of the factories and steel plants were to be found. That morning she had bought herself a woollen cap like Anna's. With the brim rolled up several times and a muffler round her neck, she now could identify with the other similarly-dressed women.

The hall was full of workmen, their wives and children

378

and the smell of dirt and sweat and babies' urine was indescribable. So was the noise. But the enthusiasm was unmistakable when Father Gapon came in and addressed them.

He was no orator. Indeed his manner was shy and self-deprecating as he spoke earnestly to the faces turned towards him. The audience hung on his words, grunting approval and clapping. No chairs were provided and groups were bunched together, enthusiasm running like an electric current between them.

'What is he saying?' Katya asked.

'He's telling the workers to set their ambitions higher, to expect more from life, to believe in themselves and to remember how much the Tsar cares for each one of them,' Anna paraphrased for her.

'The Tsar?' Katya raised her brows.

'Oh, yes! Father Gapon is a monarchist, Katya. He believes as most of us do that if the Tsar understood the truth – if things weren't kept from him by those wicked ministers – he would never allow these terrible conditions. But how can he know what long hours the people have to work and how little they are paid?'

Katya said nothing. Anna – Gapon, too! – must be very naïve if they really believed that. But then people usually believed what they wanted to. She was about to reply when she suddenly saw Alex Rakov come into the hall. He stood leaning against the wall on her left, his arms akimbo, his bright blue eyes roving in search of someone. Could he be looking for her? She averted her own eyes quickly, afraid that her gaze would catch his. For suddenly she didn't want to see him – not in these surroundings. She couldn't look at him without seeing the police spy that was behind his face. All these people – Mikhail and Gapon, too – accepted him as a middle-class adherent of the Gapon Movement. What if she were to denounce him? Expose him as a prince of the house of Rakov? Perhaps an interloper with evil intent?

Oh, God, make him go away! she prayed, shutting her eyes tightly. A burst of clapping startled her. Father Gapon, his face alight with enthusiasm, had just made a popular point. Faces around her were beaming with delight, heads were nodding. She turned to ask Anna what it was he had said only to find Anna had moved away and there in her place was Alex.

'Katya, I must speak with you.'

'Please, not here – not now – '

'But I must. In the name of God, what are you doing here, you, a foreigner? Don't you realize how dangerous it is, getting mixed up in politics? It will bring you trouble.' All this was said in a fierce whisper as he grasped her wrist.

She tugged free. 'It's none of your business!' she hissed back. 'Leave me alone! I'm with friends – '

'Who will lead you into trouble if you're not careful. Do you realize that Tchelitchev and his friend Anadorv are both flirting with the Bolsheviks? You don't believe me? Tell me this: do either of them come with you and Anna Andreyevna to these Gaponist meetings? No? It's because they have moved away, become extremists. I beg you, Katya, have a care. Please listen to me.' He gripped her fiercely. 'I love you, you little fool!'

Another burst of applause nearly drowned his words. But she had heard them. She turned and looked at him wonderingly and he, not letting go of her, pulled her out of the crowd and led her through a side door into another small room where two women were preparing samovars of tea. They glanced without interest at the man and girl who stood so quietly talking at one end of the room.

'Alex, say that again.'

'I love you. You knew that, didn't you?'

Her smile seemed to come up slowly from within, lighting up her eyes, her whole face. 'I've wanted to hear you say that! That you love me as I love you – oh, I do, Alex, I do!'

'Oh, Katya . . .' His voice broke. 'I didn't want to say it and I ought not to let you say it, either. I told you there can be no future for us. That remains true. I want you to go back to England and safety. Please, Katya, do as I say! Terrible things might happen here any day and I don't want you to be here when they do. Do you understand, darling?'

'Will you tell me who you are?' She held one of his hands tightly in both of hers and stared into his eyes.

His eyes widened in puzzlement. 'You know who I am!'

'But here they believe you are plain Alexander Petrovitch Drusov and I know you as Prince Rakov. Are you a police spy? Please tell me the truth, Alex.'

'*A police spy?*' He threw back his head in silent laughter. 'Is that what you've been thinking? That I've disguised myself in order to betray my friends?'

She nodded unhappily. 'Yes, I did think that lately.'

'Do you remember how we saw each other on the Berlin express when you were travelling with the children? I fell in love with you then,' he told her softly. 'There, I said to myself, is the sort of girl I've been looking for all my life. I had to find out who you were and shamelessly looked at your passport. I admitted it, didn't I?'

'Who was that man who was with you when – when I stayed at your house? I burst in on you both the night – the night we went to the gipsies,' she added in a low voice.

He, too, remembered that night. He gently kissed one of her hands, retaining it in his own. 'The night we

381

discovered each other, my love. That was George Meyendorv, one of my oldest friends. He and I shared a tutor as boys. He came to me in much distress for he had been forced to go into hiding and was under threat of arrest. He, like me, is a member of the Kadet Party – in other words, liberals. When you saw me on the train I was returning from Paris, having helped three friends to escape across the border and so evade a prison sentence. If this were known in Russia, I and my friends would be in deep trouble and without doubt would be prevented from going on with our work. That is why I call myself Drusov here. That is why we have to work clandestinely – we can do nothing from prison! We are not revolutionaries like the Bolsheviks and Mensheviks who want to kill the Tsar and take the reins of government into their own hands, exchanging one autocracy for another. That night we went to the gipsies, George came to seek my help. The fool had been indiscreet at a dinner party and had recklessly made known his views. It wasn't the first time, either – he comes from a reckless family! He had been reported by one of those present and was about to be arrested. So he sought my help. I had to leave Petersburg that night and take him to my *dacha* on the Gulf of Finland and hide him. From there, he could get to Finland and to Sweden and thence to England. Natalia, his wife, has now joined him there and they are both safe. I was sorry I had to leave you – I would have much preferred to stay!'

The relief made her feel lightheaded. She wanted to shout for joy. The fact that he had been so frank meant that he trusted and loved her.

Perhaps he read all this in her expression for his own became grave again. 'Dearest, it's too soon for joy. I shall be a wanted man myself before long. My luck cannot hold for ever and I have helped too many dissidents to

382

escape. I refuse to drag you down with me when that time comes. Go home, I beg you. We none of us know what the future holds.' The melancholy that was under the surface of every Russian's nature showed suddenly. 'Go home. Please, Katya, listen to me. For your own safety.'

'Not yet,' she said obstinately. 'Alex, let me help! I could act as a courier, too – no one would suspect me, I'm sure. And in my heart and soul I'm sure you are right in what you are doing. Let me be part of it, please. I've learned so much from Anna and Mikhail of the horrors – '

Suddenly they were no longer alone. People were streaming in from the main hall looking eagerly for the tea and bread that had been promised. Anna spotted them and hurried across. 'Wasn't that a splendid speech of Father Gapon's?'

They nodded, pretending they had just preceded her from the hall. Katya was deeply dismayed that their brief time together was over already. There was still much to ask him. People pushed them apart and Anna claimed Katya's help in feeding the mothers and children. As she worked, she was aware of a well of joy pumping fresh hope into her heart. He loved her. They loved each other. Surely nothing mattered except that?

Fifteen minutes later, she escaped to hunt for him. But nowhere was there a sign of him. He had gone.

383

21
Miss Ingram

1

Because she had thought that he had only half-heard her, she didn't expect him to follow up her plea to be allowed to help. So the note that came from him a few days later was totally unexpected. She read it in the privacy of her own room.

Katya dearest, If you really want to help, please go to 81 Znamenia Square at five o'clock tonight. It is an apartment house. Look for the name Alexandrovsky on the board in the entrance. You can take a tram there quite easily and without being noticed. I would like you to accompany a friend to the Nicholas Station to catch the five-twenty-five express to Berlin. If you cannot go, telephone my house and ask to speak to Henri only. With my love and gratitude always, Alex.

Her heart jumped with a fearful excitement. This meant that he trusted her – trusted her enough to let her accompany one of his refugees to the station – her presence would act as a blind, no doubt.

She told Anna that she had a little shopping to do: was there anything she wanted? She thought Anna looked at her strangely; neither of them went shopping late in the afternoon when it was so cold and dark. Nevertheless, Katya took the old canvas holdall they used for collecting the bread and said she would be back at six. Letting herself out into the dark street, she hurried quickly across the bridge from the Islands. An icy fog circled each dim street lamp; people loomed suddenly out of the darkness nearly bumping into her. She was glad when she reached the Alexander Garden for here she would find a tram to take her down Nevsky Prospekt which was at least two miles long. Znamenia Square was at the bottom, only a stone's throw from the Nicholas Station.

She found the apartment house easily: a shabby cliff-high building with a flickering gas jet on each floor. The name *Alexandrovsky* on a yellowing card in the entrance had told her that the flat she was looking for was on the third floor. As she climbed, she wondered suddenly if Alex would be there.

But a stranger opened the door; a tall woman dressed in grey with a large grey fox hat on her head. She said in Russian: 'Yes? Who is it?'

'My name is Katherine Croxley. I am expected.'

The woman repeated the name, then switching to French said: 'Yes. It is I who await you, *mademoiselle*.'

The flat was small and dark and smelled of old clothes and general mustiness. A rough wooden table with the remains of a meal on it and two carved wooden chairs that seemed to have strayed from grander surroundings were the only things in a room that appeared to double as a kitchen of sorts: a small tin oven was balanced precariously over an oil burner and there was an earthenware sink.

The woman vanished, leaving Katya standing uncertainly in the bare room. What a strange-looking woman, Katya thought, remembering the gruff voice and gawky stance of Madame Alexandrovsky – if that is who she was. She turned, uncannily aware of being stared at: the woman was watching her from the door. She was now wearing a shaggy fur coat of old-fashioned cut and had lavishly powdered her face.

'Come, *mademoiselle*, I do not wish to lose my train.'

'No, indeed,' Katya agreed and began to walk through the door which the woman held open. Then she stopped. Her mouth opened and shut again. The hand holding the door was a man's hand: broad and strong with dark hair covering it. Round the wrist was a broad scarlet mark – at least two inches wide: the mark of manacles. Her startled eyes went to those of the disguised man and saw that he was smiling mockingly.

'Alex did not tell you, then?'

She shook her head speechlessly, aware of fear. If this man was in deep trouble, then of course he would have to wear a disguise. An escaped prisoner, perhaps. If he were caught, she would be involved in something far beyond that originally intended: which was to put on the train someone who needed to leave St Petersburg in a hurry.

'There is time to draw back, *mademoiselle*.'

She shook her head, pride coming to her aid. Brushing her hand across dry lips, she said: 'No, I won't draw back.'

'Good.' The man patted her arm. 'Then let me tell you that I am Miss Ingram. I have been governess in the Rakov family for many years and I am going home for good. Home is Aberdeen in Scotland and I speak French as fluently as English – but my Russian has never been very good! Do you notice the Scottish tinge to my voice? No, these are not her clothes! They once adorned the old Princess Rakova – dreadful taste she had.'

'Your voice is very good but – ' She shook her head. 'That terrible powder won't do.' Extracting a handkerchief she reached up and dusted it off the man's cheeks. Then she pulled the fur hat lower over the face and surveyed him critically. 'That's better. Don't take such long strides when you walk and stoop a little: Miss Ingram is old, remember. And whatever you do, don't sit with your legs crossed: it would look very fast and quite out of character.'

'Thank you, that is very helpful. I haven't had much time to practise – I only left Peter and Paul this morning,' he added ironically.

She was horrified and perhaps her face showed it for he closed the door again and came towards her. '*Mademoiselle,* let me go alone. We thought that a young woman seeing off the old governess would attract less attention than if she were to leave by herself. There are bound to be soldiers at the station. We have been warned – '

She was very frightened but determined not to show it. After all, Alex had thought her capable of doing it and she must have faith in his judgement. 'I've told you already that I will not draw back. Have you a pencil?'

'A *pencil?*' He shook his head. 'No, wait – there is a pencil on the windowsill. But we must go if I'm to catch that train.'

'This will not take a minute.' She reached up and began to make faint marks about his eyes and down the sides of his mouth. 'In artificial light these should look quite authentic.' She felt a quiver of laughter for little had she thought when they acted scenes from Shakespeare at the end of term at Hill House that one day her skill in make-up would be put to deadly purpose and perhaps might even save a life.

'Thank you.' He seized her hand and kissed it. 'You are a brave girl, *mademoiselle.* Your fresh pretty face is the best thing I've seen in two years.'

Two years. So that was how long he had been in prison. She hid her pity and helped him turn down the gas jets that they had nearly forgotten to do. The outer door was left unlocked, she noticed. Someone would no doubt be visiting the flat before long to see if the bird had flown safely.

They walked briskly towards the station, Katya insisting that it would look better if she carried Miss Ingram's grip. The ticket to Berlin seemed to have been procured earlier, she saw with relief, but this didn't prevent 'Miss Ingram' making a great fuss about her other travel documents when they got to the station. 'Here's my ticket – and my passport. But where is my visa? Do you know, my dear, Russia is the only country that insists on a visa *and* a passport? Silly, isn't it? You must always remember to carry them about with you, too – ah, here it is, thank goodness. Ask that nice official which is my train – oh, I forgot, you don't speak Russian yet.' Mispronouncing one word in four, Miss Ingram questioned an official covered in gold braid. Nearby stood two soldiers with fixed bayonets guarding an individual in plain clothes who was examining all travel documents. By their bored stance, Katya guessed that they had been at their task for hours. One yawned widely. She realized how right her companion was to establish her character before being submitted to examination. She played up, calling her Miss Ingram at the end of every sentence, standing with ill-concealed irritation while the old woman fussed, and warning her that the train was in and getting up steam.

'Very well, my dear, let me get on. Now remember what I've told you: stand no nonsense from young Natalia. A firm hand, my dear, that's what is needed. I hope you'll be very happy in my old position – twenty-five years I've been with the family. Do you know, I wish I were not going home. I shall miss so much – '

'You'll certainly miss your train,' Katya warned her. 'Dear Miss Ingram, thank you for all your advice. I will certainly write and tell you how I'm getting on.' The plainclothes policeman, she saw, was waiting impatiently for the old governess to produce her documents; behind them a queue of people waited and some were beginning to push past. Miss Ingram placed her own documents triumphantly on the table. 'There! I have found everything I think you will need. Maud Ingram is my name and I'm returning home to Scotland – is that all? Thank you.'

'I am not travelling,' Katya said, quickly producing her own passport.

A cursory glance and she was allowed through. Miss Ingram had found a seat and Katya climbed up to say goodbye. They looked at each other, relieved that the first hurdle was over.

'You were wonderful,' Katya whispered.

Miss Ingram enveloped her in an audacious bear's hug. 'You're a darling,' said a man's voice in her ear, 'and Alex is a lucky fellow.'

'Good luck to you, too,' Katya whispered and jumped down, lightheaded with relief that her part was now over. The train began to move and steam belched in an enormous cloud from the engine, obscuring Miss Ingram's face and taking the fugitive out of her life for ever. She wondered fleetingly who he was and what he had done to condemn him to the fortress without trial.

She turned to walk out of the station and found her path blocked. Two burly men in long overcoats and grey astrakhan hats stood in her way.

'Mademoiselle Croxley?'

The alarm that paled her skin must have been apparent even in the blue light of the station lamps for one of them said, 'Make no fuss, please. Come with us.' His hand on her arm was like steel.

She never knew how her legs supported her as she was

led through the booking hall while people turned to stare at the young woman being taken away by the secret police – for there could be little doubt as to who they were, especially when one stopped to exchange quick words with the policeman who was still checking documents. He sucked in his cheeks, staring at Katya as she stood with her head bowed by the side of the other man.

The waiting *isvostchik* smelled sour and airless. The men pushed her down between them and lit evil-smelling cigarettes. She felt nausea rise in her throat and fought a strong desire to burst into tears. Oh, she was so frightened! She knew now that she was not of the stuff of heroines, that she could not – as so many were doing in Russia – take enormous risks for the sake of others, and the thought shamed her, giving her the stiffening that she needed to say: 'I am a British subject. You have no business to take me away like this. I shall demand to see my ambassador.'

One turned to her. 'Just wait and see, *mademoiselle*.'

The horse was old and slow and they seemed to be going down numerous side streets and crossing canals. She tightened her lips. At any moment they would be crossing the Neva and entering the courtyard of the terrible fortress. I mustn't give way, she told herself. I must be strong. Afterwards she was glad to remember that not once did it occur to her to reproach Alex for getting her into this predicament.

'You are nearly home, *mademoiselle*.'

She turned to stare at the man who had spoken. 'Home?' she echoed.

A lamp swam past. Then they stopped. It was difficult to see where she was for a thick snowstorm was suddenly whirling down but it looked – it really looked as if she were back at the Tchelitchevs' . . .

One of them said in a low voice: 'Alex thought it

imperative we get you away quickly. The secret police were due at the station. Thank God, you made no fuss but came like a good girl!' She was pushed out, the door was slammed and the *isvostchik* ambled off.

Relief flooded her, making her weak so that she nearly fell in the snow. She had been too hot in the cab; now she shivered violently as the tension seeped out of her. Trying to collect her wits, she staggered towards the apartment block, icy snowflakes blinding her. As she entered the dimly-lit hall, a hand came down on her arm and she stifled a shriek.

'Katya – Katya darling!' The whisper was low but she heard it at once and hurled herself into his arms. They pressed close for reassurance and she wept silently against his shoulder.

'I've been through hell – never again will I allow you to risk yourself.' His low voice shook with feeling. 'Oh, Katya, I was mad to use you but Andrew Nilov was my friend and I feared that the police would have me and all his old friends under surveillance. I dared not risk it and I was committed to helping him after he got away this morning.'

'How did he do it?'

'He was being moved to Siberia with a whole lot of other political prisoners. There was an accident on the railway outside the city and he gave them the slip.' He glanced uneasily about in the empty hall. 'But we can't talk here.' He held her close again. 'I shall never be able to thank you enough, my brave girl.'

'I haven't been at all brave,' she confessed. 'I was terrified all the time.'

'But you did it – that was what was so brave.' One last kiss and he pushed her from him. 'Go, darling, or Anna will wonder where you are.'

She stood on the stone staircase and watched his

shadow slip out into the white night. She felt exhausted. Had it only been a couple of hours since she had started out from here? And Alex was doing this all the time. Dimly she began to realize the knife's edge on which he lived.

2

That Saturday, news came that the workers at the Putilov Ironworks were out on strike. Mikhail heard the news at the hospital and brought it home to the girls. It was startling news. During the past year, many more had joined Father Gapon's Assembly of St Petersburg Factory Workers, a mild sort of union smiled on by the authorities because it was considered a safety valve for those who would make trouble. It was these men and their families who filled the reading-rooms and listened spellbound to their leader, the young priest.

But, suddenly, anger had swept like a fire through the Putilov works: it was alleged that four workers had been dismissed because they belonged to the Assembly. Their foreman Tetyarkin denounced them as trouble-makers; they said Tetyarkin spied on them.

Mikhail who had been bandaging heads after an angry clash, added that the men had denounced the works manager as a two-timing blackguard whose promises meant nothing.

'What will happen?' Anna asked, watching him wolf down a meal before returning to the hospital.

Mikhail cut himself a hunk of rye bread. He was grinning. 'There's to be a show of solidarity this time. If they don't reinstate those four fellows, other plants will come out in sympathy. The factory gates all over the

Narva district will be locked, their chimneys will go cold. And serve those fat-jowled owners right! They've been getting rich standing on the backs of starving women and children.' He pushed his chair back. 'Don't be worried if I'm late back. I shall probably stay around to see the fun.'

Anna stood at the window watching him walk rapidly across the road and disappear down a side road. 'Mikhail is a firebrand. He never looks ahead.'

Katya, anxious to turn her thoughts from impending trouble, asked her to try on the dress she was making for her. It was of dark red material scattered with tiny flowers and Anna was delighted with it. Privately, Katya thought the material very poor quality. They spent the rest of the day sewing hard so that by the time the samovar was brought in at five o'clock, the dress was almost finished and both girls had aching eyes and backs. However, Anna was able to wear it under her long fur coat to church next day and her delight was touching as she proudly fingered the cheap-looking dress, now her 'best'.

'You are so clever, Katya! I could only make the ruffles – you have made the whole thing. Such beautiful feather-stitching too.'

It was good she had the new dress to distract her thoughts for Mikhail had not been seen since lunchtime on Saturday. They devoted the afternoon to an English lesson and at five o'clock they heard his key in the lock. He opened the door and called out in a voice hoarse with weariness, but exultant as well: 'The strike is spreading! They'll all be out this week, you mark my words!' Flopping into the old leather chair that had been his father's, he closed his bloodshot eyes.

Anna hovered over him. 'Have you eaten anything? You look terrible!' He hadn't even shaved, they noticed.

'Don't fuss,' he grunted. 'For God's sake hurry that

girl up with the food. I could eat a horse. I'm all-in but it's been worth it! We spent all yesterday and this morning meeting the men and telling them to come out. They'll all be out this week,' he repeated exultantly. 'The Neva Spinning Mill, Franco-German Shipbuilders, the Ekaterinogov Mill – yes, all the big ones as well as the Putilov works. They're refusing to take up their tools again until all demands have been met. It's the only way.'

'They'll be shot – '

'It's the only way, I tell you. It's a risk they must take.'

'But their families? How will they eat? They won't get a kopeck while they're on strike.'

'They'll have to manage somehow,' Mikhail grunted as he set about the tray of food Lisaveta had brought in. When he had finished, he lit one of his thin cigars and began to retail all that had happened. It didn't escape Katya's notice that he was quietly jubilant at the turn events were taking. Remembering Alex's warning about Mikhail, she watched him uneasily. It was the Bolsheviks who were stirring up the workers. He kept repeating that 'bloody revolution was at hand'. He found it difficult to conceal his glee. Soon he went out again to another meeting.

Anna said uneasily: 'He's changed. A year ago he would never have talked like this! It's Dmitry's fault! He has influenced Mikhail, I'm certain of it. It makes me most uneasy, Katya. You see, anything could happen.'

By next day, the strike had spread and even the trams had stopped running. People stood on street corners talking in groups. There was a strange sense of unease in the air as the girls went as usual that evening to the reading-room near the university. Anna had at first insisted that Katya stayed home, but Katya had equally insisted on accompanying her. The thought of Anna walking alone through the dark streets made her shudder:

it was better to be two girls together, especially as Anna had a bagful of *Liberation* to distribute.

The reading-room was full to the door. The smell of bodies and the heat made Katya turn pale as she battled her way in. Rumours were circulating that Father Gapon would be visiting each room in turn to speak to them. He had tried to stop the strike, had failed and had realized he must go with the workers if he were to keep his influence over them. But his plan was to petition the Tsar in person on behalf of the workers and he had drawn up a seven-point plan to present. Surely, once the Tsar understood their grievances, he would put things right?

Excited talk filled the room, babies wailed and a man sitting on his haunches in a corner began to pluck the strings of his balalaika. Soon they were all singing a folk song while the samovars brewed and a team of helpers cut up cheese and bread. Where did the money come from to run these rooms and provide food for hundreds? Katya wondered. She asked Anna who shrugged. 'Behind the scenes, a lot of the nobility are interested. Perhaps they give the money. I don't know. Someone does. There's always food here and it brings the people in.'

Katya nodded thoughtfully as she apportioned cheese to pieces of rye bread. People like Alex, she thought – perhaps Alex himself. There was no lack of money to run these places. Looking up she caught sight of the students wandering round among the workers, talking earnestly and pressing Marxist literature on them. Anna's eyes met hers.

'I don't suppose they can read it. Three-quarters of our people are illiterate.'

'But they can speak,' Katya reminded her, watching the black and green caps bobbing through the crowd. No one took steps to put them out although they were obviously adding fuel to the smouldering fire of resentment that was spreading.

She jumped nervously as a hand came down on her shoulders. It was Alex. He wore the collar of his coat up to muffle his face. Obviously, he didn't want to be seen. 'I must speak with you,' he whispered urgently.

She dropped her knife, looking apologetically at Anna who was staring at them with surprise, and followed him through a rear door. Outside, in the darkness of a narrow passage, he held her close for a moment. 'Katya, dearest girl, I beg you not to come here! There is trouble brewing and you might so easily get mixed up in it and I'm not going to let you get involved after what happened earlier this week.'

'But, Alex, I can't leave Anna to walk alone now the trams have stopped – '

'You must think of your own safety. It has come to my ears that the police are mentioning an English girl who is being seen at what they choose to call revolutionary gatherings. You know how unpopular England is here! I'm worried about you – I worry so much that I cannot do the work I'm called upon to do! They say you are hand in glove with the revolutionaries, people like the exiled Vladimir Ilyich Ulyanov – '

'But it's ridiculous! I don't know any revolutionaries – certainly not this man you name.'

'He is beginning to call himself Lenin which makes it simpler for you. He works from *London*. Now do you understand why they connect you with this man? And they have their eyes on Mikhail Andreyevich and know you are living there. Indeed they class you as his woman! Believe me, darling, that is how the narrow official mind works. You are getting involved. The secret police send their ferrets down burrows and come up with answers to satisfy their suspicions. I believe you to be in danger.'

There was no mistaking the worry in his blue eyes, fixed on her so urgently. As he spoke he kissed her again. 'Please, Katya, go home! They have their finger on *you*, my precious girl. My God, I couldn't bear to see you thrown into the Peter and Paul Fortress! Do you have any idea what it's like to be a political prisoner, a prisoner without trial, in my country? It means a living death.' He shuddered and clung to her. 'For myself, I could endure it – but not for you – not for you – ' he muttered against her hair. 'After the risk we took with you in helping Andrew escape, I've been in hell.'

It was then she realized the depth of his feeling for her and she shivered as she clung to him. She could feel joy that he loved her so much but it made the possibility of being parted for good so much worse.

'Who is behind this story about me?' she asked, looking up at him.

'Grand Duke Philip. You made an enemy there.'

'You don't know why, do you? Then I must tell you.' Rapidly, she disclosed the real reason for her sudden flight from Tsarskoe Selo.

He held her close again. 'I could kill him.' His tone was savagely cold, full of deadly purpose. 'It makes it all the more imperative that you return to England as soon as possible.'

'I have written to Hamburg to ask for the dates that the *Sylvie-Rose* will be sailing. Captain Halvorsen will take me to Hull and that is only fifty miles from my home. I should hear soon.'

'I shall come to England some day,' he promised. 'It may not be for a long time but I *shall* come.'

She thought of all the dangers that beset him in his work. Some day the secret police would discover who it was who helped to save so many dissidents from a dungeon in the dreaded fortress. He made the promise of coming to England 'some day' because he, too, knew his days were numbered.

'Too much is stirring in the cauldron,' he told her. 'It's only when I hold you in my arms that I weaken.' He kissed her quickly and released her. 'Go. Take Anna Andreyevna with you. And be very careful because you are precious to me.'

As she and Anna hurried home through the freezing darkness, Anna said tentatively: 'Do you know Drusov well? Had you known him before?'

Katya was fond of Anna and hated to deceive her but for Alex's sake she must lie. 'Oh, no! But he *will* follow me around asking questions about England! He's worse than you – and half the time I don't know the answers.'

'Forgive me, Katya, but I thought you were flirting – and after only meeting him three times, too.'

'Dear me, that would be dreadful,' Katya agreed with mock solemnity. 'To fall in love after only three meetings? Why, it should take years!'

Anna began to chuckle. 'You tease me. You are thinking of my feelings for Dmitry!'

'Something like that.'

Their combined laughter rang out like bells on the thin air.

22
Blood on the Snow

1

Next day was a day of thin sunshine and Anna suggested that they walk to the Palace Bridge to watch the ceremony of the Blessing of the Waters by the Tsar. Great crowds were surging in that direction and soon they were carried along against their will to crowd the bank of the Neva and the bridge overlooking the site where a wooden pavilion had been built out on the ice. Soon a procession came out of the Winter Palace to stand under the pavilion's canopy: the Imperial Family and the Metropolitan of St Petersburg, an imposing figure in a gold mitre and robes that flashed in the sunlight. By his side, Katya could make out a small fair-bearded man in a soldier's uniform. Was that insignificant little figure the Tsar of All the Russias, the Autocrat himself? He looked amiable and very like his first cousin, the Prince of Wales.

The ceremony ended with the guns of the First Battery of the Mounted Artillery on Vassili Island firing a salute. Suddenly there was a loud explosion and a flash as one of the charges turned out not to have been blank at all. Shrapnel rained down on the officials standing nearby and people shrieked with horror as smoke obscured the scene for a minute or two.

'My God, they've killed the Tsar!'

So great was the pressure of people that Katya could

hardly breathe. She clung desperately to Anna's coat, terrified of being cut off and mown down. Then the smoke cleared and a long sigh of relief ran through the crowd for the Tsar could be seen standing immobile on the ice. On one side, several police lay badly wounded and there was a crashing of glass as windows in the Winter Palace splintered and fell out. Soldiers and police hurriedly cleared the wounded out of sight and the ceremony continued; the Tsar's figure seemed carved of stone. A choir began to sing and the two girls looked at each other with white faces.

'I thought that was it.' Anna's voice was a thread but Katya heard and understood. They began to edge their way out of the crowd, all their interest in the spectacle spoilt. They felt they had so nearly witnessed an assassination.

They found Mikhail in his surgery when they got home and they poured out their story to him.

He finished cleaning a pipette and put it back in the rack. 'Pity they missed,' was all he said.

2

She was writing a letter to Robert in her room next afternoon when a round-eyed Lisaveta knocked on her door and said in the halting English she had been learning from her mistress (who believed in passing on every scrap of knowledge that came her way): 'The Countess Barinskaya to see you, *mademoiselle*. A very grand lady she is – '

'Thank you, Lisaveta. Have you shown her into the room? Yes?'

400

Lisaveta's total English knowledge fled at this sentence. She shook her head and spread her hands.

Katya tidied her hair, feeling a little troubled. She had written to thank Laura Nicolaievna for her hospitality: what now brought her Aunt Stana out to the suburbs? Perhaps it was the doctor she wanted but surgery was over now.

Anastasia's statuesque figure clad in almond-green and furs was outlined against the window in the living room. Seeing Katya in the doorway she came forward holding out her hands.

'Katya, forgive me for not coming before now!' She kissed her affectionately, noting that the girl didn't look well. She was thinner and blue shadows lay under her eyes – and not surprising either, Anastasia told herself, living in a hole like this. Really, these Tchelitchevs didn't know how to *exist*. 'It was neglectful of me but you'll understand when I tell you all that has happened.'

'Let me take your furs, Stana,' Katya said, pulling forward Mikhail's leather chair. 'I'm so glad to see you. Please tell me how everyone is.'

For five minutes or so they talked about the children, then Anastasia paused a moment and said at last, 'Katya, I know now what drove you from my sister's house – no, it was not Miss Ellis who told me, but my little Maia. I found her in tears one night, fearful of going to bed and it all came flooding out. The Grand Duke was muddled up in her mind with the bad demon in one of her fairy tales. He had been cruel to Katya and made her cry. My poor little girl believed that Philip was hiding in the house somewhere – that he would hurt her next – oh, it was too awful!' Anastasia pressed a scented handkerchief against her lips. 'My dear girl, you should have told me – the man's a beast!'

'Miss Ellis and I agreed it would do no good for Laura

401

Nicolaievna to learn how the Grand Duke had behaved, Stana. It might mean an estrangement just when you had joined her.'

'It was kind to think of me but the last thing I would have wanted. Katya, you and Mr Howarth have been the soul of kindness to me: this is no way to repay you both! I haven't told Laura. No doubt she guessed something, however. But I could not stay in his house a second longer than need be. Then I heard from Sergei! You'll never believe this, Katya, but he's coming home! Yes, he's decided not to marry Mrs Haltmann after all.'

Katya stared at her. 'Is this really what you want?'

Anastasia got up and swept to the window. Over her shoulder she said: 'Yes – no – oh, I'm confused. I don't love him, I never have and this gives me a guilty feeling. But he wants us all to live together again. D'you understand?' She turned and looked miserably at her niece. 'I shall have status again: I shan't be a divorced wife! The Grand Duchess Vladimir is such a stickler for these things, you know, and I would be excluded from so much.'

It seemed to Katya a strange reason for taking back Sergei Barinsky as a husband after the way he had treated his wife.

'We're going back tomorrow to our own house and I can start having it done up just as I like, Sergei says.'

With my grandfather's money, Katya thought sardonically. Really, silly trusting women like her aunt made things too easy for cads like Sergei Barinsky. But she smiled and kissed Stana's anxious face. 'The children will be glad – especially Tanya. I think she loves her father because she denies it so hotly.'

'She is like him, you see.' Stana sighed. 'So will you come to us there, my dear, in a few days' time? I can't bear to think of you living in this hole,' she added in a low voice.

'You want me to come and stay?'

'For as long as you like. And I thought of asking Mr Howarth over as well.' She pinched her niece's cheek.

Katya laughed. 'Oh, Stana, how transparent you are! There is nothing between Robert and me – at least not on my side. But it's sweet of you to ask me. Perhaps later. I'd like to stay a little longer here. I find it . . . interesting.'

Anastasia looked alarmed. 'You're not falling in love with Mikhail Tchelitchev?'

'Indeed, I'm not!' Katya retorted. 'What an idea! But Anna and I are great friends now and I'm enjoying myself.'

It was obvious that Anastasia found this difficult to believe. She looked round the shabby room and shook her head.

As Katya showed her out, she pleaded with her again. 'This is an *awful* place, my dear. The doctor and his sister are a kind pair but they have no idea of comfort. You're sure? Then come to us for a time before you leave for England – that you must promise me!'

From the window she watched her aunt entering her own sledge: it was dark red with black horses, the servant riding behind wearing black and red livery. 'Very smart,' she said approvingly, dimly understanding Anastasia's satisfaction at her restored status. 'But I couldn't do it myself – ' She broke off, her eyes widening. Surely that was Alex crossing the street and coming towards their block of flats? Anna had gone out soon after lunch to buy essentials for Mikhail's surgery: for once they would be alone.

She flew out of the door and was waiting on the landing as his head appeared above the stairs. She opened her

403

arms and he stooped, gathering her to him. Wrapped thus and in silence they stood on the landing; then he began to press his lips passionately against hers, as if he drank her in with every breath. 'Katya – Katya – ' he murmured.

'Oh, Alex, at last!'

It was the first time they had been alone since confessing their love for each other and it was a sweet long moment to savour. Then, with arms still round each other, they went into the flat and closed the door.

'Anna's out but Lisaveta shall make us some tea.'

'Katya,' Alex said, staying her. 'I must tell you at once. Gapon has arranged for a huge march on Sunday. The workers are to march to the Winter Palace where he will present his petition to the Tsar. *You must not go.*'

'But, Alex, Anna will go. It will look strange if I refuse.'

'I don't care how it looks. I'm only concerned with your safety. *Stay here*, dearest Katya. I believe this huge gathering is folly and the authorities will react sharply. I was at a luncheon yesterday where Prince Sviatopolk-Mirsky, Minister of the Interior, was present, and from what he said I believe there could be trouble. Try to persuade Anna to stay here in this apartment.'

'But I know she won't do so! The Tsar is to meet the workers – ' She paused. 'He will be there, won't he?'

Alex's laugh was mirthless. 'I know from my mother that he will not be leaving the Alexander Palace. Only fools believe he will come.'

There was silence. Then Katya said sadly: 'Trusting fools like Anna and Father Gapon and a thousand others. Why won't he come? It is to be a peaceful demonstration, a chance to present the workers' petition – '

'He won't come because he never does face up to the reality of a situation. Besides, *she* will persuade him to

404

ignore the petition: *her* mind is only too ready to be made up. She is not a wise woman and he listens to her in all things. Well, if you go, Katya, then I insist on accompanying you.'

'Oh, Alex, will you?' A delighted smile lit up her face and she clapped her hands. 'I shall be perfectly safe with you to take care of me.' The joy of having his company that day outweighed all other considerations and she suddenly saw that Sunday would be a happy outing for them all.

He looked at her with a curious expression. He hated the thought of her naïvety causing her to run into danger. But if she must go, then he would go with her every inch of the way despite what he feared might be the outcome.

3

Mikhail hooted with derisive laughter when he read Gapon's seven-point petition that Anna had brought home from a meeting. He was sitting eating a hearty breakfast and it was Sunday, January 9, the day of the march to Palace Square. 'The priest has got you in his grasp, Anushka! Yet the man's a fool! You have only to read this rubbish to see that – ' and he tossed it contemptuously across the table. 'You have read it, I suppose?'

'Why, yes, that's my copy,' Anna said serenely. Mikhail's railings against Father Gapon no longer roused her anger: he was just being obstinate; the events of this afternoon would make him eat his words.

'The man's a donkey, I tell you. Does he really believe *this* will have any effect on that stupid Nicholas?'

'Mikhail! Don't speak of our Tsar in that disrespectful way – '

'I shall speak as I like. It will make no odds. He is a fool and so is the priest – you're all fools to believe you'll do any good.' He hit the piece of paper with the petition printed smudgily on it. 'You're demanding everything at once, a new Russia overnight. Nicholas won't spare it a glance. He'll be sitting on his bottom – '

'Mikhail!'

' – at the Alexander Palace and won't move out of it all day. And Georgii Gapon intends leading you and all those others to Palace Square on a fool's errand! I tell you it's useless. Only a bloody revolution will achieve anything – any one little concession for the workers – and, mark you, it's coming. Oh, yes, it's coming all right so you needn't waste your time this afternoon.'

Anna put her knife down to stare at him. 'What has happened to change you, Mikhail? Only a month or so ago you were as enthusiastic as I was about the Gapon movement. You've given up coming to the meetings – even Father Gapon himself has noticed it. Why, Mikhail?'

Katya sat silently drinking her coffee while the argument raged. She felt that Mikhail was on the point of telling his sister the truth: that he was a Marxist; that he wanted to sweep away the past and create a new society run by the workers. She could see the words hovering on his lips and she kept very quiet.

'Things have changed now. Our big chance is coming.' His eyes glowed suddenly. 'I have friends who *know*. Yes, I was like a child a few months ago, allowing the priest to hoodwink me as he's hoodwinked you, dear sister – why, he's a milk-and-water revolutionary, that one!'

'You cannot be meaning all you say.' Anna put a hand on his sleeve. 'Say you are joking.'

He shrugged. 'On the contrary, I am deadly serious. This stupid war has taught me a lot – it's opened my eyes. Now that it's going badly for us revolution is in the air: I can smell it. Very soon now it will be the time to strike a blow for freedom – for *our* freedom and a new order in Russia.'

'My God, Mikhail, you *have* become a revolutionary!' There was fear in Anna's voice. 'If you should get mixed up with *them* – if you should get sent to Siberia what will become of me – of us both?'

'Don't be so melodramatic!' Mikhail lumbered to his feet. 'If you'll excuse me I am due at the hospital. But I must warn you both that you are going on a fool's errand.'

After he had left the flat, Katya said persuasively: 'Perhaps he's right. Perhaps we should stay at home, Anna. Father Gapon is assuming too much – that isn't a wise document he has prepared.'

But Anna's gentle mouth had folded obstinately. 'I didn't think *you* would let us down, Katya! Father Gapon is relying on people like us to support him, not only the workers. I shall certainly go. Lisaveta must prepare bread and cheese for us. It's going to be a long day.'

Alex came running up the stairs at midday and Katya opened the door to him. Their eyes and hands clung longingly but they had to break apart when Anna appeared to greet their escort. 'See, I have your lunch in here with mine, Katya.' She held up a coloured kerchief from which issued a strong smell of pickled cucumber.

'Wrap up well,' Alex directed them. 'It's bitterly cold.' He himself was clad in a long elk-skin coat and a cossack hat of grey fur.

Katya noticed that his eyes were full of laughter again as if he had shed all his doubts and was determined to enjoy himself. His high spirits soon set both girls laughing too, and they gaily bantered as they crossed the bridge to Palace Square.

It was indeed bitterly cold, grey and raw with hard snowflakes stinging their faces as they trudged along with bent heads. The weather had worsened during the night and heavy black clouds now pressed low over the tall buildings on the banks of the Neva. Here on the quays the snow was packed hard and the girls stumbled a good deal so Alex reduced the length of his strides and gave each of them an arm to lean on.

As they walked Katya had time to reflect on the character of the man accompanying them. She knew him as a prince with many servants, a huge palace on the Catherine Canal, a brother fighting for the Tsar in the Far East, a mother who was a lady-in-waiting to the Tsarina. To Anna he was plain Drusov, a liberal with idealistic dreams for Russia, a friend of Gapon's. He fitted both roles, Katya thought wonderingly. Two different men yet the same man under the skin.

As other groups joined them, she saw that Alex was quite at ease with these simple people who were rough and good-humoured and sang hymns as they marched along.

'That's a pretty pair keeping you warm, brother!' shouted a red-faced man with a wink. It made Anna blush and Alex laugh and they both refused to translate for Katya which made her cross with them. Anna tended to be shy but Alex it seemed was only too ready to exchange repartee in kind. He encouraged the group round him to continue singing and from the look on his face he appeared to be enjoying himself thoroughly. Only Katya noticed that his eyes were looking alertly about him as if in search of something.

They reached the Narva Hall at last. Crowds were swarming inside and out and there was a holiday air of anticipation and excitement. Gapon read out the seven-point petition once more, first inside the hall and then to those outside. His voice was high with enthusiasm and he stood grinning delightedly as they cheered him uproariously.

Alex translated it point by point for Katya's benefit. It asked for a constitutional assembly, civil rights, political amnesty for prisoners, the separation of church and state, an eight-hour day for the workers, the legalizing of unions, and an end to the war. 'He wants Utopia granted in a morning,' Alex said in a low voice. Then he shrugged. 'And why not? He might as well ask for everything at once because he's going to get nothing.'

They ate their rye bread and cheese, and after prayers were said they set out for the march to the Winter Palace. The crowd was divided into sections, each section taking a different route so as to converge on the square at the same time but from different directions.

In their section a group of young men led the way carrying banners and portraits of the Tsar and Tsarina. Everybody sang. First, 'God Save the Tsar', then hymns and folksongs to keep the blood coursing in their veins as they shuffled along. Only Katya was silent, having no Russian, but all round her bobbed happy faces, friend greeting friend, exchanging jokes and news. The collective excitement seemed to stoke their energy and they were in danger of arriving at their destination too soon until their leaders called on them to slow down.

They were going to see the Tsar! Father Gapon had promised them! The Tsar would understand and grant them what they asked – God Save the Tsar!

Anna was the first to notice groups of soldiers clustered at street corners holding rifles with bayonets fixed. She plucked Alex's sleeve. 'Why are they here? It's not because of us, is it? We shan't create trouble!'

409

Alex didn't reply. The alert look was back in his eyes and he took each girl by the arm.

It had been a long walk to the Narva Hall and now back to Palace Square and Katya at least was weary. Her legs felt weak with fatigue and she was glad of Alex's arm. It was nearly two o'clock: at any moment now they would be pouring into Palace Square and the Tsar would come out and speak to them. Louder rose the voices as all roared out their national anthem. Katya felt excitement rising in her throat; now it felt dry and her breath came quickly. She was going to see the Tsar –

Alex halted abruptly. 'Look.'

Near the Narva Triumphal Arch leading into Palace Square a line of soldiers and police was drawn up barring the way. The crowd halted, a puzzled grunt rising from them. What right had the soldiers to bar their way?

Katya looked at Anna, then they both turned to Alex. He avoided their eyes as he strained to see ahead. But it was only what he had expected: that weak Sviatopolk-Mirsky had been persuaded to use force after all and Grand Duke Vladimir was there in person with his guards.

An officer on horseback called to the crowd to halt. Those in the front rank did so reluctantly, glancing at each other with anger. Why, the soldiers and police were preventing them seeing their Tsar! They were confronting the workers with guns, the fools!

'Come on, brothers!' roared a huge man waving his arm.

From the back, the crowds pushed on, not aware that the front ranks had been stopped. Cheering and singing filled the air as they approached their goal. To the waiting soldiers the sound was ominously like a threat.

'They ought not to push forward like this!' Alex swung round, gesticulating. 'Good people, stay quietly here! You will be crushed if you press ahead – remain here, I

410

beg – ' But his words were swept away by the sound of those eager to see and hear the Tsar. And from the side streets more and more poured into the main confluence like tributaries joining a great river. They were one and all convinced that their Emperor was waiting to greet them on the steps of the Winter Palace.

'Go back! Go back!' Others joined Alex now in frantic shouts.

'What's happening, friend? Can you see the Tsar?' shouted a broad-cheeked man holding one end of a banner proclaiming *Long Live the Tsar*.

A volley of shots shattered the air. The broad-cheeked man's face registered surprise as a red hole spread along his temple. He crashed to the ground, the banner collapsing on his neighbours.

Katya didn't realize her mouth was open, releasing scream after scream of sheer terror as bullets whistled past her face to find their marks in the soft flesh of others. She couldn't move. One hand held Anna in an iron grip as if she would never let go. Alex pulled cruelly on her other arm, shouting her name over and over again: 'Katya! Katya!' But she was frozen to the ground.

Anna too was dazed. Blood from the dying man had splashed over her as he crashed to the ground. She put her hand up, wiped it away and then stared at her white woollen glove. Dazedly she walked on with Katya pulling at her and screaming, 'Anna! Anna! Come back – don't go on – '

She turned to look at Katya, to say something. Instead she pitched forward and slumped to the ground.

'She's been hit – Alex, quick, Anna's hurt!'

They stooped and tried to raise her inert body but a red stream was running from a wound in her neck. She held one hand pressed to it and her white glove became

411

soaked in blood. Her eyes, beseeching and frightened, stared into theirs.

Katya fell on her knees in the snow. 'Anna! Oh, Alex, she's badly hurt!'

Anna's eyes – the wide innocent eyes of the child she was at heart – met Katya's pleadingly. The red stream from her neck wound was widening rapidly now and as she tried to form words with her lips she fell back against a mound of snow.

Alex could see the bright arterial blood and realized the girl was past all help. He knew, too, that Katya would never leave her while she lived, so he stooped and took her inert body in his arms and stumbled on, Katya following and brushing her tears away with one hand. She could hear herself crying loudly as once she had done in childhood when some small cloud had temporarily darkened her sky. Now it was from fear of death that she wept: Anna's, Alex's, and her own.

They somehow made their way down a narrow passage between two tall buildings where the pounding hooves and gunshots resounded against the walls. Alex's breath came in hard rasps as he struggled along with Anna in his arms. Then they were out in the street again, a multitude of people pouring in the same direction, jostling them, pushing them frantically out of the way to escape being ridden down by the soldiers. Anna's cap had fallen off and her yellow hair streamed in the wind slapping against Katya's face as she ran – her breath almost gone – trying to keep up with Alex and his burden. Then she fell to the ground, taking great groaning breaths. She no longer cared. She couldn't go on.

People ran over her, pushing her first to one side and then the other. She had lost sight of Alex. All she wanted was to be left alone, here on the snow, until the pain that racked her stopped hurting.

412

More shots and shrieks rang out. Instinctively she stumbled to her feet and went on running drunkenly, every breath an agony, crying Alex's name.

'Katya!' A hand grasped her skirt and Alex pulled her down into the semi-safety of a doorway. The crowd and the pursuing soldiers swept past and they were left with the dead and dying lying all around them on the blood-stained snow. Anna was propped against the wall, her eyes wide open, shining through the curtain of hair that covered her face. A scarlet stain soaked the whole of her upper body but she no longer held a protective hand against the wound.

'Anna,' Katya whispered. Gently, she pushed the hair aside. 'Can you hear me, Anna?'

The large lustrous eyes looked at her without recognition and Katya suddenly saw that they were glazed with approaching death. Anna's lips moved, then her head fell sideways.

'She's dead,' Alex said gently.

Katya hardly heard him. Dazed with shock she continued to hold Anna's icy hand in hers. She couldn't be – not Anna, so warm and laughing and sweet. But the figure lying on the step seemed not to be Anna's any more: death had transformed her into a huddle of shapeless clothes.

Alex lifted an arm with infinite weariness and drew Katya towards him. Wordlessly, she looked into his face and he nodded. Only then did she see how white he looked beneath his healthy tan, that he held himself stiffly and was obviously in pain.

'I've been hit in the shoulder.'

Suddenly, she became quite calm. Cold fury took over. They had killed Anna; they were not going to claim Alex, too. Unbuttoning his elk-skin coat she thrust a hand in and withdrew it red with blood. She had seen how he

413

had winced when she touched his shoulder and hope strengthened her: the bullet was nowhere near the artery but had ripped through the muscle and he had lost quite a lot of blood. All modesty now fled, she lifted her skirt and stepped out of her lawn petticoat which she rolled up and placed as a pad at his shoulder. 'This will stop the bleeding. Can you walk?'

He nodded. Shots echoed from Palace Square and his expression tightened: the soldiers would be finishing off the wounded. They must get away as fast as possible. He staggered to his feet. 'Come, we must go.'

She looked down at Anna's body, tears blinding her. Goodbye, she said silently, and turned away.

He let out a breath: he had been afraid that she would refuse to leave the dead girl. It was becoming rapidly dark now and this would be an advantage. Without looking back, Katya helped him down the step to the road. Then she stumbled over a small object and looking down saw that it was a child's doll lying on the cobbles. With sick horror she remembered how many of the peasants had brought their children with them 'to see the Tsar', as they had gaily told each other less than twenty minutes earlier. Like a sleepwalker, holding his arm, she hurried along resisting the temptation to look behind for their pursuers. Then they had turned a corner and were in Nevsky Prospekt where the crowds were still being harried by the cavalry as if they were a flock of sheep. The glint of swords cutting through the air with an evil whine made Katya shudder. Cries and oaths and the snorting of the horses filled the street which had been turned into a battlefield with the pursuing army putting the enemy to flight: only the enemy were unarmed.

Here at the intersection with Gogol Street in front of the lovely colonnaded cathedral of Kazan, the crowds were jammed to suffocation point: another crowd was still making its way to Palace Square from a different direction, unaware of what was happening ahead of them. A dawning surprise spread over their faces as they stopped and saw the cavalry galloping towards them. Then, screaming, they too turned and fled back the way they had come.

Dazed from loss of blood and pain Alex staggered drunkenly and nearly fell. Her heart straining in her breast Katya pulled him up, supported and then pushed him further and further from the eye of the storm. It was obvious he couldn't go far in his condition and she was frantic with terror that he would fall down on the snow and not move again.

But there was the cathedral. Surely the soldiers wouldn't follow them there? Church meant sanctuary. Somehow they stumbled up the steps and passed into the dim incense-haunted interior.

A service was in progress and candles flickered from wall sconces. In between were deep wells of shadow. In a corner she noticed a large icon under a canopy with some candles lit round it. She knelt in the shadows as if praying before it and with her fur coat she sheltered his body. He was breathing quickly and shallowly like an animal in pain, his body a dead weight against hers.

She closed her eyes. *Oh, God, Anna is dead! She'll never come to England now. Please help us. Don't let Alex die – please, I beg you, Jesus Christ in Thy name –*

The incoherent words poured silently from between her lips. In the nave the congregation was making its responses. The drone soothed her and she was still, her whole body a wordless prayer for her lover's life.

415

How long they stayed there she never knew. She was aching and stiff with holding him against her under her coat.

Presently a woman came across and lit a candle under the icon. She glanced down at Katya, no doubt taking her for a penitent for after a brief prayer she turned away.

'My love, can you move?' Her warm breath was against his ear.

He stirred, weakness flooding him. But the sight of her white and anxious face roused him. 'I shall be all right. Is it dark yet? Then we can go.'

'Be careful,' she whispered. 'Hold your arm so – that way you won't disturb the blood clot that's formed. It's probably only one bullet and if it can be got out quickly – oh!' she gasped as she suddenly received his full weight.

They stood locked together while he took several breaths. 'It's all right. I'm ready now.'

'I don't know where I should take you.'

'Take me home to the Catherine Canal. It's not far. My mother is at home.'

'Will she – ' She hesitated.

'She's a very understanding woman. Whatever I've done she'll stand by me,' he said with a faint smile.

With one arm across her shoulders, holding the other close to his chest he was helped from the cathedral and down the icy steps to the street. Soldiers were still in evidence everywhere and the hollow thud of horses' hooves, shouts and screams, echoed between the buildings. A large cart trundled up the street and by the lamplight she could discern bodies piled inside. *Anna*. She was too fatigued to cry. Soon she would be able to feel grief again, to feel pain for the violent ending of Anna's life. It would be like blood rushing back into a frozen limb. But not yet. There was too much to do and she could think only of saving Alex's life and her own. Of one thing she was sure; out of the ugliness of today's events would come a new outlook on life.

Slowly and carefully she guided his steps towards the Rakov palace. Every time a troop of soldiers came up the street, they would stop, pretending to watch them like wide-eyed country bumpkins who had never before been to the city. At last, with the utmost relief, she saw the yellow ochre of the Rakov Palace. The blazing windows threw a golden radiance on to the snow and ice outside, and through them she could see the glistening crystal chandeliers in the downstairs rooms.

She rubbed her side where a stitch had formed. Her strength was almost spent; his weight had become almost unbearable and she knew he was very weak too. Propping him against a wall she struggled up the steps and pulled at the bell. The double doors opened immediately and the old grey-bearded hall porter wearing the Rakov livery came out, regarding her dismissively. I suppose I must look like a beggar, she thought. Unable to speak, she pointed to the figure of the prince at the bottom of the steps.

'Timotei, it is I,' Alex said in Russian.

The man's eyes opened wide in horror. Calling out over his shoulder for help he ran down the steps. 'Your excellency! In the name of God!'

Five footmen tumbled down the steps to help lift him from the snow where he had fallen. He must have fainted and he was completely inert as they carried him past

Katya and into the house. The doors closed leaving her leaning against a pillar.

I must get home, she thought dully. She closed her eyes as suddenly the memory of Anna returned: she would have to go back to the flat and tell Mikhail.

She felt dizzy as she struggled down the steps and along the road towards Palace Bridge. Too late she remembered she had left her purse in her room that morning and had no money for an *isvostchik* or a tram. Slowly, wiping the freezing tears from her face as she walked, she crossed to Vassily Island, every step of the way filled with pain, fatigue and heartache. How gaily she and Anna had set out that morning! No thought of this disaster had crossed their minds despite Alex's reluctance to take them. Had he guessed what awaited them?

The memory of that gruesome cart full of bodies trundling down the street filled her with a wave of terror. 'Oh God!' The words were jerked out of her. 'You were so harmless! Such a gentle being!'

A man passing her stopped and stared.

She put a trembling hand to her mouth. She must stop calling out in pain. She looked wild, mad.

She reached the apartment block and pulled herself up the stairs: never had the three flights of bare stone stairs felt more like the side of a mountain. By the time she reached the Tchelitchev door, she was spent and could hardly fit the key in the lock. The flat was cold and dark. The stove must have gone out and Mikhail was probably still at the hospital.

She fumbled her way into her bedroom and found matches to light the gas jet. She took off her coat and let it fall to the ground. Underneath, her knitted jacket and white blouse were stiff and caked with blood. A huge patch of it was on the front of her skirt where Alex had

418

lain in the cathedral. Taking it off, she saw that the blood had soaked through to her drawers and chemise. He must have lost a terrible lot, she thought as she stripped and washed herself down with a sponge wrung out in icy water from her pitcher. Her head ached. 'Anna,' she kept repeating under her breath. 'Oh, Anna!'

She had just finished changing when she heard Mikhail's key in the door. She heard him fumbling with the chain of the gas jet in the hall. 'Anna!' he called. 'Are you in?'

She came out of her room to face him, dread in her face and heart. 'Mikhail.'

He turned round, shading the match with one hand for he had been about to light the second jet. He said something in Russian, startled by her sudden appearance and the strange look on her face. 'Where is Anna?' he demanded. 'Why are you in the dark?'

She swallowed nervously. 'Something very terrible happened this afternoon. I hardly have words to tell you.'

'Anna?'

She nodded, clasping her icy hands in anguish. 'Oh, Mikhail, she was shot through the neck in Palace Square by the Tsar's soldiers. Just after two o'clock this afternoon.'

He gave a terrible cry of grief and anger. 'By God, they shall pay!' He put his hands to his head. 'Did she die? Tell me! Are you sure of it?'

'Yes, she died. There was no pain.' She paused and took a breath. 'Then Alex Rakov was shot – '

'Who?'

She raised her eyes. 'Prince Alexander Rakov whom you knew as Drusov.'

'So we had one of *them* in our midst – a spy – '

'No, no! You're wrong. He's a liberal, a member of

419

the Kadet Party, certainly not a police spy. I knew him before coming here – '

'So you too deceived us!' He turned his twisted face, awful in the half-light, towards her. 'So we were harbouring two snakes in our bosom! Anna was too simple a person – '

'You're wrong, I tell you! It was nothing like that! I knew Alex was no spy but simply didn't wish people to know his true identity, and he had his reasons for it too. I love him and I know him.'

He flung off the hand she had put on his arm. Then he went into his bedroom and shut the door.

She sat down on a chair, shivering with shock, hunger and fatigue. From the clock on the wall, she could see that it was past eight o'clock. Movements went on behind the door. In the light under it she could see his shadow moving to and fro. What was he doing? She began to weep, pressing her hands against her face.

Suddenly the door was flung open and he confronted her dressed for the street and carrying an old-fashioned valise.

'I'm going.'

'Where are you going?'

'To throw in my lot with the Bolsheviks.' He went into his surgery and picked up his medical bag. Turning to her he said almost casually: 'The rent's paid until the end of the month. You can stay here until then unless you care to come with me.'

'I? Come with you?' She shrank back.

He looked at her searchingly and shrugged. 'It's too late to ask you, isn't it? You're in love with that fellow, Drusov or whatever he calls himself. His lot are doomed. Much better you come with me, Katya.' He put down his bags and seized her hands, saying urgently, 'Yes, much

420

better you come with me! The revolution is about to break! The *boyars* are doomed, I tell you!'

She pulled her hands away. 'No, I can't come with you. I'm going home.'

'Back to England? Good. That will be best.' He bent and kissed her roughly, then opened the front door. From his pocket he took a piece of white paper and a drawing pin with which he fixed it to the door. 'This is to say the practice is closed. Goodbye, Katya, I don't suppose we shall meet again.' He picked up his bags and closed the door.

23
Sanctuary

1

For a moment she stared blankly at the closed door. She could hear his feet clattering down the stairs. He had gone. Anna was dead. She was alone.

She went into her room and fell on to the bed. Wrapping herself in the heavy duvet but not bothering to undress again, she fell into a deep exhausted sleep filled with terrifying images from which she couldn't escape. When she woke again it was morning and Lisaveta was standing looking down at her.

'Where is Anna Andreyevna? The doctor?' she asked in the halting English she had been learning from her mistress.

Katya struggled up. Her hair had tumbled halfway down her back and her eyes were heavy. 'What?' For a moment she could remember nothing, then it came flooding back and she lay feeling sick with grief and horror.

Lisaveta shook her impatiently. '*Mademoiselle*, wake up!'

Katya opened her eyes and stared up at her. Tears rolled down her cheeks. Haltingly and slowly, using a mixture of French and English, she told her. When at last she understood, Lisaveta jerked back, naked hatred transforming her good-humoured face. A torrent of Russian words poured out of her and she shook both her fists. Then she burst into tears, rocking herself to and fro. When she had recovered, she began to talk again in Russian. Seeing Katya's blank incomprehension, she rushed out of the room. When she returned she had drawn a crude picture of men digging a huge grave. She nodded. 'Today. Preobrazhensky. I take you.'

It transpired she knew a great deal about the massacre for many of her neighbours had been involved, some killed. Being a practical girl, she wiped her tears away and briskly set about preparing breakfast for Katya. It was an hour and a half later that they reached the Preobrazhensky cemetery only to find that the huge mass grave had been closed already and soldiers surrounded it with fixed bayonets. Despite this, relatives of the dead were attempting to uncover the bodies but were being driven off only to return again and again. It was obvious that the soldiers had orders not to shoot and that the authorities had been in a great hurry to conceal the number of the dead by burying them in the night.

The two girls stood in the biting wind, helpless, not knowing what to do. Then Katya said in slow, careful English to Lisaveta: 'Go to the officer – that one over there. *Ask*.'

But the only answer the officer gave the girl was a rough shove, shouting at her as he did so. He was young and obviously apprehensive of the crowds of relatives coming to seek their dead. Desolately they turned for home, taking an *isvostchik* back to the flat.

'Mademoiselle Croxley?' Two men who had been standing in the shadows by the Tchelitchev door suddenly stepped forward. Lisaveta screamed and clutched Katya's arm.

'Yes? What do you want?'

They were big, burly men. One had a thick grey moustache, the other was clean-shaven. Something about

423

their bearing warned her they were policemen although they were in plain clothes.

'We are from the security branch, *mademoiselle*. Can we come inside?'

She felt her stomach drop. 'No. It's not my house. I have no authority to ask you in.'

'Open the door,' one of them said, pushing Lisaveta forward. Obediently she inserted the key and let them in: she was too trained to the voice of authority to refuse and she looked apologetically at Katya as she stood back.

The men walked straight into the living room and looked around. Then they turned to Katya, their faces grim. 'Now, *mademoiselle*, no fuss, please.' The clean-shaven man spoke excellent English. 'We want the truth. Where is the traitor, Prince Alexander Petrovitch Rakov?'

She pretended amazement. 'How on earth should I know?'

'Don't play games with us.' The man's voice was silky as he leaned forward and whispered: '*You* pretended he was Drusov.'

'Yes, I know Alexander Drusov. He's not Prince Rakov.' She managed a laugh. 'Drusov is a friend I met through Dr Tchelitchev. I saw him last – let me see – '

'Yesterday.'

Thank God, Lisaveta had not been at the flat yesterday! They would get nothing out of her. 'Not yesterday, *m'sieur*. Last week. At the reading-room on Vassiliefsky-Ostrov.'

They exchanged exasperated looks. 'Come, *mademoiselle*, the truth, please. You and Anna Andreyevna Tchelitcheva went to the socialist demonstration at the Winter Palace yesterday – '

'Not socialist, *m'sieur*. A workers' demonstration

424

arranged by Father Gapon who I believe is a friend of the police?'

'Father Gapon is a traitor. We are searching for him, too.' Suddenly the younger man shot out a hand and gripped her arm. Bringing his face menacingly close to hers, he hissed: 'The truth, *mademoiselle*, or it will be the worst for you.'

Somehow she kept her voice steady, her eyes contemptuously returning his stare. 'Release me at once, please. I am a British subject on a visit to Russia. I know nothing of your politics. Leave this flat at once or I shall take a complaint to my embassy.'

He realized his effort to intimidate her had failed and he drew back, giving his colleague a chance to try other tactics.

'You will be sorry your friend has been killed, *mademoiselle*.'

'Yes, I'm deeply grieved. Anna Andreyevna was simply an innocent bystander. We were amazed at the action of the soldiers who were ordered to fire on us. A good many innocent people have perished, *monsieur*. It was a bad day for St Petersburg.'

They had not expected to be attacked in this way and were nonplussed. Certainly this young woman did not seem frightened. 'So you cannot tell us where Prince Rakov is now?'

'At home on the Catherine Canal, I suppose.'

'So you know him!'

'Certainly, I have met him. He is not Drusov. Everyone knows the Rakov Palace: it's one of the biggest houses in the city. The Princess Rakova is at Court, I believe? A friend of the Tsarina's. Why should you suppose that Prince Rakov – of all people – is a traitor?'

The man shrugged and motioning to his colleague

walked to the door. With a terse 'We shall be back, *mademoiselle*,' he left the flat.

She stood in the living room with bitterness in her heart. Mikhail had done this. He knew she loved Alex so he had tried to destroy him. In a way, it was a revenge on those who had killed his sister. He must have telephoned the police this morning. She remembered that not once had they enquired for the doctor, the tenant of this flat, nor had they commented on the card on the door informing his patients the practice was closed. One thing only lifted her spirits: she no longer had any doubts as to where Alex stood. He was what he said he was: a liberal secretly working against an intolerable regime, for a democratic Russia. And what a dream it was! she thought sadly.

Since they must have called at the Rakov Palace before coming here, it meant that Alex had been well-hidden somewhere. She must get used to the idea that she would never see him again.

She could hear Lisaveta in the kitchen, making the tea and crying noisily. Suddenly making a decision, she went across the hall to Anna's room. It was so like the girl herself in its utter simplicity, she thought, sick at heart. One of the first things she saw was the red dress they had only finished a week ago: Anna's best dress.

She sank onto a chair and let the tears flow. Oh, this cruel and hateful country! To kill Anna who would not have hurt a fly! She let herself cry unrestrainedly. Mopping her tears away five minutes later her brain felt clear again: there were things to be done. Mikhail had gone off without a thought for the personal possessions in the flat that he had left to strangers. She swept Anna's few things into a straw valise and went through to Lisaveta.

'These are Anna Andreyevna's things.' She opened the

straw valise. 'You look after them until the doctor returns. Understand?'

Wiping her eyes, Lisaveta nodded.

'Go home now, Lisaveta.' She took out her purse and counted out some roubles into the girl's hand. Patting her shoulder she repeated: 'Go home. Goodbye.'

Lisaveta, crying bitterly, went. Under her arm she carried Anna's few personal possessions. As her footsteps died away, Katya shut the door and leaned against it. She must leave a note for Mikhail, in case he returned, telling him what she had done. In the living room were icons, photographs in cork frames, books. She found a cardboard box and filled it, writing Mikhail's name on the lid. Whoever came to live here would know that those things were his: perhaps the janitor could be persuaded to care for them.

She was deadly tired. The samovar had been lit for hours so she made herself a glass of tea, tried to eat a piece of bread and a slice of cheese and found she couldn't; her stomach revolted against it suddenly and she was sick. Throwing off all her clothes she got into bed and fell deeply asleep.

2

She slept until noon next day, waking to a thin sunlight that would be fading in an hour or two. She washed and dressed hurriedly, again tried to eat and managed a little piece of dried fish and bread, then put on her outdoor clothes and went out. The trams were running again but each had an armed guard on its platform; there were soldiers everywhere as she rode over the frozen Neva and went to the bank where she kept her money. Twice she was stopped and her papers were inspected by the police. St Petersburg had lost its easy-going air; it was evident that revolution was expected and being sternly frustrated by the authorities.

At the bank she found she had a surprising amount of money left in her account. Her grandfather's legacy would be sent to her bank in Whitby but this was more than enough for her needs. She withdrew it all and then took an *isvostchik* to the Nicholas Station to purchase her ticket to Berlin.

'When do you travel, *mademoiselle*?'

'Tomorrow or the next day.'

'I will mark it valid for a week.' The clerk stamped it and handed it through the grille.

She put it carefully in her purse: this small pasteboard ticket represented the end of her Russian experience. Tomorrow or the next day she would be crossing the border to East Prussia. She would never see Alex again nor know how he fared. She dared not call or telephone: his house was being watched.

On the way home she stopped to buy a little fresh food to carry her over the next day or so: some fresh bread, a pat of white unsalted butter and some cuts of cold sausage. With these she would be able to make English sandwiches to keep herself going.

She let herself into the flat and instantly knew that someone had been there. There was an alien smell in the air; pomade and tobacco, unlike anything Mikhail used.

Her heart hammered with fright. With a dry mouth, she called out: 'Who is it? Who is there?'

There was silence.

Where were the matches? She tried to remember where Mikhail had put them – no, wait, Lisaveta had used them to light the charcoal under the samovar. It was almost dark. The windows were grey slabs of light in the gloom.

Leaving the outer door open she went into the kitchen and fumbled for the matches on the shelf where they were usually kept. They were there and in a trice she had struck one and lit the gas jet. She went into the hall to light up there and saw at once that the front door was now closed. She had left it open – she was sure she had left it open! She went round the flat, lighting all the jets. The air was icy for the stove had been out for hours. Now it was fully lit up, she went from room to room. It didn't take long to find that every drawer and cupboard had been ransacked, and the contents thrown on the floor. In her own room the intruder had searched her portmanteaux so thoroughly that they had even torn open the canvas linings. She sat back on her heels feeling no fear, only anger now. This was of course the work of the *Okhrana* searching for evidence of Alex in her possessions. Letters perhaps that would hang him. She thanked God that she possessed nothing that could harm him. So they had gone away empty-handed: they wouldn't be back. Quite calm again, she repacked her possessions and placed the portmanteaux in the hall. There was a train to Berlin at ten A.M. tomorrow: she would be on it. This latest incident had made up her mind for her.

She cut sandwiches and mastered the intricacies of the samovar to make a refreshing glass of tea, her first drink that day. Her throat and mouth had been parched, she realized. Then she put the chain on the door and prepared to go to bed for she was weak with tiredness and emotion. She fell asleep almost at once, secure in the knowledge that she had made all arrangements for her departure. She had only to get on the train and go.

3

Two hours later, the doorbell pealed.

At first, she was sleeping so deeply she didn't hear it. Then her eyes flew open and her heart began to hammer nervously.

They were back.

Perhaps this time they meant to take her away for good – perhaps to the St Peter and St Paül Fortress from which it was difficult to regain one's freedom. She wouldn't answer it. But the bell went on ringing remorselessly. Throwing on her robe, she crept into the hall and lit the gas jet. The light gave her courage. It also gave the ringer hope of an answer for he stopped ringing the bell.

'Who is it? Who is there? I won't open the door until you identify yourself.'

'It is Henri – valet to his excellency. Is that Mademoiselle Croxley?' The whispering voice was low but quite clear.

She opened the door and, with the chain still on, inspected the man outside. He removed his black astrakhan hat and she saw his face clearly.

'Henri, *mademoiselle*. I was at the house when you were a guest of his excellency after a visit to the gipsies. Her excellency his cousin was also there. You remember?'

'Yes.' Her lips moved stiffly: he had come to tell her Alex was dead. She couldn't move.

The man's eyes stared at her through the crack. 'It is important I talk with you, *mademoiselle*. I have a message – please open the door.'

Shivering, she took the chain off and opened the door.

Henri stepped inside and bowed. '*Mademoiselle*, are you alone?'

'Yes. But this flat was searched while I was out this morning.'

Henri nodded. 'Just so. They found nothing? Then they won't be back. Will you place your trust in me, *mademoiselle*, and come with me?' He fumbled in an inside pocket and produced a slim gold half-hunter watch. Snapping it open, he showed her the crest inside. 'You will have seen this on the prince's person, I believe? As you know he was wounded badly on Sunday and is now in a place of safety. Her excellency, the princess, wishes me to take you to him. I ask you again, *mademoiselle*: will you trust me?'

'Where do you wish me to go with you? To the Rakov palace?'

'He is no longer there.' Henri smiled suddenly and the tiredness and strain lifted from his face. 'We smuggled him out of the palace on Sunday night. He is somewhere safe – it is better I do not tell you more at present. I have a sledge waiting – one that will not be connected with the prince so no one will recognize it, I think. Will you dress quickly and come with me?'

'Very well. But first give me news of the prince. Is he recovering well?'

Henri hesitated. 'He is young and strong. A doctor operated on him on Monday and removed two bullets from the shoulder and lung. He is weak from loss of blood, of course, but her excellency has nursed him with her own hands. Between us we have done it. But she is due to return to her royal mistress and she hoped you would take her place for a while. So dress quickly, *mademoiselle*, and I will take your luggage down.'

The door closed again and she stood staring at it, joyous excitement making her dizzy. She was going to

431

see him after all! She couldn't quite believe it yet. Tucking her hair under her woollen cap, she locked the flat for the last time. Goodbye, Anna, she said silently, before running downstairs to the janitor in his hut. It was empty so she left the key on a shelf.

Outside a strange brown sledge, old-fashioned and badly-sprung by the look of it, waited with two horses between the shafts and the bulky figure of the driver immobile on his seat. She crept under the hood and Henri solicitously fastened the wolf-skin rug round her. Seating himself beside her he provided himself with a separate rug thereby making the distinction between them delicately clear. 'Until we are free of the city there is a little danger, *mademoiselle*, so do not be alarmed if our route is unpredictable,' he warned her.

Presently she saw in what direction they were speeding: they were heading for Novaia Derevnia where the gipsies lived. Soon they were in the forest and there were the lights from the long wooden house they had visited on that memorable night. They drew up in the clearing before the house.

'We leave all your luggage – others will see to it,' Henri murmured. He paid the driver and they turned away. As if there had been someone watching, the door opened and light and the sound of music and laughter flooded out. A gipsy man bowed to them and escorted them inside.

She followed bewilderedly, wondering a little. But Henri had warned her not to be worried so she said nothing as they followed the man down a narrow corridor skirting the main rooms. Their feet echoed noisily on the bare boards but no one noticed and presently they came to another door and another rush of icy air. With a sign, the man bade them follow him across an open yard to the dark trees beyond. She smelt the horses before she saw them or heard them whinny. A troika was concealed in the trees with three horses harnessed to it. The driver was already standing with the reins and whip in his hands, and when she got in she felt her portmanteaux at her feet. Henri climbed in beside her and they were away, picking their route through the trees and going faster and faster. She had lost all sense of direction but instinct told her she was being taken to Alex's *dacha* on the Gulf of Finland, that these same precautions at dead of night had been undertaken many times before for other fugitives. She too had become a fugitive; so now had he. How strange and topsy-turvy life had suddenly become.

It was long past midnight when she felt the horses slowing down. Lights glowed among the trees and she saw them as a symbol of hope. She knew that scattered round the Gulf of Finland were *dachas* used only in summer, and she supposed that that was where she was now. But it wasn't a small wooden villa they had stopped at; looking round her, she saw that it was a small farm by itself. Dogs on chains barked and she heard the lowing of cows in their byre, smelt them, too. Men's heads bobbed about in the light and she was helped out. Henri's voice coming through the blackness guided her to a door.

'Is it a farm?' she asked, puzzled.

'It is, *mademoiselle*. The Rakov summer house is several versts away. We never use it for *our work*,' Henri said with a pride that made her smile.

Light and warmth flooded out once more and she stood blinking dazedly at the tall slim woman with greying hair under a dowdy hat who stood facing her. It was Princess Rakova, she realized with some alarm.

'Poor child! You look quite bewildered and I'm not surprised!' The princess kissed her with affection. 'I knew you would come although Henri, the old silly, insisted on taking Alex's watch with him: he felt sure you would jib

433

at accompanying him on this strange errand.' Her voice was low and musical, speaking English with barely a trace of accent. 'Thank you, my dear, for saving his life. If you hadn't been so persistent in bringing him home he would have either bled to death or been captured. We owe you so much. You were quite splendid.' She indicated a deep chair in front of the huge log fire.

Opening her heavy fur coat, Katya sat down and held out her hands to the blaze, feeling shyness numbing her.

'How is Alex?' Her voice was low and tinged with dread.

'Very ill, I'm afraid.'

Katya felt an iciness round her heart but she could not speak. Her strained eyes fastened on the face opposite.

'He has had two bullets removed. One wound is healing well – the other – ' She shook her head. 'It is the lung. The good little doctor from the village has done his best and is draining the wound. But I fear he needs hospital treatment and we cannot give it him. We must just nurse him and hope against hope – ' She broke off and leaning across put her hand over Katya's. 'I must not scare you. There is a chance: he is young and strong and will fight with all his might. I have sent for you because I have to be back at the Alexander Palace tomorrow and I must pretend – ' Her voice broke. 'I must pretend that nothing has happened. No one must ever guess at Alex's part in the demonstration. Not only would he be imprisoned – he would die for certain for they would not lift a finger to save him. He is far too much an embarrassment to our ruling class.' She lifted her eyes. 'You understand?'

Katya nodded. 'You are leaving him in my charge while you go into waiting on the Empress. Thank you for trusting me. Will Henri stay too – in case – '

The princess tightened her lips at the 'in case'. 'Henri will look after my son – he is as good as any nurse and has been devoted to him all his life. But there must be two people with him for he must not be left alone at all. He must remain in one position if the hole in his back is to drain.' She was fastening her furs as she added almost casually: 'I know you must care for him or you would not have risked so much to bring him back the other night. You do care for him?'

'Very much.' Katya's voice was a thread.

'Then I trust his life to you, *mademoiselle*.'

His life. For a moment it seemed too much of a burden. Katya swallowed panic and managed a smile. 'I'll look after him, never fear, Princess.'

The princess nodded and made the sign of the cross over Katya's head. Then, walking swiftly and lightly, she left the room. The troika had had fresh horses put in and was drawn up at the door. Katya lifted a corner of the curtain and saw lanterns lighting the tall figure in grey furs stepping into the troika. Then they had gone.

4

A sound behind her made her turn round quickly. A woman in a brown skirt and a blouse with a kerchief round her head had entered the room. She said something in Russian and beckoned. Katya followed her to a door in the wall that, on being opened, revealed narrow stairs going upwards. Again the servant beckoned, leading the way up to an uncarpeted landing. Knocking gently on a door she pushed Katya in and closed it behind her.

Henri was sitting near a narrow iron bedstead. He put his finger to his lips as she tip-toed towards the bed where Alex lay tossing in a feverish sleep. A small head pillow and a rolled blanket were propped against his body to keep him in one position and Henri was struggling now to prevent him lying on his back.

'He is very feverish, you see.' He wiped his master's face with a lawn cloth rung out in toilet water.

'How changed he looks!' Katya hardly recognized the man on the bed. His face was gaunt, the eyes half-open and unseeing, the lips drawn back in a grimace of pain. He looked much older.

'He is under a powerful drug,' old Henri explained. 'The pain would be too much otherwise. When it wears off we give him warm milk or some broth. *Mademoiselle*, does it frighten you?'

'Yes, it does but that does not mean I'm unable to help. I just fear so much for him. Henri, will he die?'

'He is in God's hands and we are doing everything possible,' the old man said gently. 'He is a strong young man. All his life it has been the same when he was ill: he has fought to overcome it. Perhaps he will do it again. He is in God's hands,' he repeated as if it were a prayer.

I wish I were religious, Katya thought. She knelt by the bed stroking one of his hot, dry hands. Poison from the wound had raced through Alex's body, transforming him into this stranger she barely recognized. But his hands were the same: well-shaped with short nails. She noticed that he had no growth of beard so Henri must be shaving him daily. His hair, too, had been recently brushed and smelled faintly of verbena tonic water. Even as she was making note of this, Henri approached.

'Go and eat, *mademoiselle*. It is time for the prince to be washed and changed for the night. I will stay until you are ready to return then I, too, will eat. The night we will divide between us.'

Katya went down to the room with the open fire where food had been set out on the table. She was fatigued to the point of nausea and when the woman brought in a bowl of greasy soup with dumplings she felt disinclined to touch it. Everything was of the plainest: just the soup, bread, cheese and some sliced cold sausage with a jar of pickled cucumbers set baldly on the table. She toyed with it and was thankful when the samovar was brought in and she could drink the fresh fragrant tea.

She left her place at the table to crouch by the fire, staring into the heart of the glowing logs. For some reason, she found herself longing for Robert Howarth's presence: he would know what to do for the best, she felt sure. Outside the house, the wind had whipped up and was howling like a wolf through all the cracks of the poorly-built house. If Alex dies, she thought bleakly, part of me will die with him.

5

All that night, and all the next day, Alex tossed and muttered on his bed. There was an iron stove in his room keeping it warm and on this Katya kept an enamel cup of broth with a little brandy in it. He would take a spoonful in his half-drugged state, his head heavy against her arm as she gently raised him. Once he opened his eyes and looked at her. It seemed that he recognized her, that he tried to speak her name. The tube running out of his back sickened her and she had to grit her teeth to put a new one in while Henri held his writhing body. Tears would pour down her face as she inflicted this agony on him and once when she went out to empty the bowl she was sick in the snow. She saw no sign of the fever abating, although the doctor who arrived in his sledge on the second night said she mustn't worry as it was too soon. She found the nursing the hardest thing she had done in

437

her life, though instinct told her that Princess Rakova had a much harder role to play, being at Court with her royal mistress and not allowing her anxiety to show. For all his mother knew, Katya thought as she stretched her aching back, Alex might by now be dead. Yet it was too dangerous to send her a message that might relieve her anxiety.

Every day she took a short walk round and round the little wooden house, well-wrapped in a cloak of Alex's she had found. She discovered that the family who lived there occupied the back of the house and lived almost on top of their few cows, goats and chickens, all of them keeping warm together. It was impossible to communicate with them because of the language barrier and the woman was dour and unsmiling. Katya didn't like or trust her and yet, she argued, she must be trustworthy or Alex would not have been able to go on using this house as a centre for his activities for so long. Presumably she was well-paid and prepared to take risks and one day she did something that reassured Katya that she was to be trusted.

She was trudging through the snow round the perimeter fence one morning when the woman, a black shawl over her head and two large dogs running ahead of her, came out of the house and ran, stumbling and almost falling, across the snow to her. Her face agitated, she pointed towards the dark line of trees beyond the boundary and urged the dogs through the wire. Katya, her arm in the woman's iron grip, looked in fear towards the trees. The two dogs, baying and snarling, were leaving a dark trail across the snow as they plunged through it towards some quarry. Straining her eyes, Katya saw a figure standing there his arms raised holding something. A gun? She gesticulated to the woman who shook her head and raised her hands to her eyes and held them there. *Binoculars.*

Katya's heart bumped with fright: somebody was standing in the shadow of the trees watching them.

The figure had disappeared now and so had the dogs whose savage barking could still be plainly heard on the clear thin air. She stood with the woman watching and waiting until presently the dogs emerged and trotted back to the house. They had lost their quarry. Without another word, the woman went back into the house and Katya followed her. She decided to say nothing to Henri: the old man was beginning to show signs of strain and Katya hoped and prayed that he would last out until the princess returned. She would persuade him to go back to Petersburg for a good rest; she herself intended staying until Alex was better.

The next day, the stormy skies cleared for an hour or so and the light of a sun that was very low on the horizon suddenly lit up the snow and instantly raised Katya's spirits. She went briskly indoors after her walk and found Henri at the foot of the staircase. His head trembled with excitement.

'*Mademoiselle*, come!' He beckoned and she ran after him up the stairs. As she entered the bedroom, Alex's head turned on the pillow and recognition shone from his eyes.

'Katya! My God, can it be you? Oh, Katya darling!' He held out his good arm and drew her down, repeating her name under his breath as he rubbed his face against hers. 'How did you get here?' he asked faintly at last: he still had great difficulty in breathing, she saw.

'Thank God, you're better.' Words she had never dreamed of being able to utter were torn from her. 'You're going to recover – oh, Alex, I can't believe it! Ssh, don't talk yet, not yet, not yet,' she urged softly, holding his face to hers. Silently, they lay close together,

Katya so full of thankfulness that she could only smile at Henri who watched them with great benevolence.

'I will make some tea,' he whispered. 'In his state it might revive him. You, too, *mademoiselle*.'

When they were alone Alex said against her face, 'You came in and out of my jumbled dreams, Katya. I woke up wanting you here and you *were* here.' He laughed and coughed. 'It was like a miracle!'

'Ssh, don't talk, don't say anything, my love. I'll tell you what's been happening.' In a low voice she told him how his mother had brought him out here, compelling Henri to reveal this safe hiding place. 'If you had gone to your summer villa on the coast, they would have found you by now.' She remembered the figure standing by the trees and decided to say nothing about it yet. 'I'm afraid Mikhail must have denounced you to the authorities. I blurted it out like a fool that Drusov and Rakov were the same. He became very bitter when he learned that Anna was dead. Can you remember that day?'

'Yes, I remember it as if it were yesterday. How long ago was it? Two weeks?'

'Two weeks and two days. The doctor who is attending you tells me there have been strikes and riots in Petersburg ever since.'

'The fools didn't foresee that,' he muttered. 'What did they expect? They're only putting off the evil day when the Tsar's autocratic rule will be broken for good. One can only pray that it won't be left so late that the Marxists take over.' He closed his eyes, and withdrawing her arm she put his head back on the pillow. When Henri came with the tea, she put her finger to her lips and they both withdrew.

'Henri, he's going to be all right!'

'God be praised!' There were tears in the valet's eyes

440

as they drank to Alex's returning health in tea with lemon.

When next he woke, his voice was stronger. Katya brought the lamp close at his request and he scrutinized her face. 'You're much thinner. Katasha, where would I have been without you? You saved me by hiding me in the cathedral. I remember that woman who came and stared at me – I thought we were finished then. I owe you so much.'

'Your mother did most – and the dangerous part, too. Bringing you here to this place was a stroke of genius. She took a terrible risk for you might have died on the journey.'

'Mamma always was a wonderful woman. I grew up knowing it. But *you*, Katasha! I didn't realize you had so much strength of will, little one. I have to confess that I regarded you as young and pliable but the way you carted me home on that awful day is a memory I'll always treasure.' He turned his head to lay his lips on her wrist. 'Henri tells me that only this morning you snatched the last egg on the farm to be made into my supper tonight. He talks of Mademoiselle Katya with a sort of glee – never was there such a woman! He has also just informed me that I am to marry you. He was shaving me at the time so I had to agree. I always obey Henri, you know. He is a sort of father to me.'

She met his eyes shyly but could not speak.

'Don't say anything; I know.' He kissed her fingers. 'We can make no plans until we get to Sweden – oh, yes, that's the plan! This was the way of escape for all the people I hid in this house. As it's winter, we must wait until the ice breaks up at the end of March before we can take the boat. Going across land to the north would be like going to the North Pole – impossible.' He held her hand tightly. 'You will come with me, stay with me always, Katasha?'

She nodded, unable to speak, her love for him choking her.

'We can be married in Sweden, and then travel to Paris to the family apartment – that famous apartment where you thought I kept my lights o' love! We shall have to stay there for some time – perhaps for years until the political situation here changes. It's bound to change!' he added strongly and then fell silent, his eyes suddenly haunted. What was he asking of this girl? What sacrifices would she be forced to make? *Forgive me*, he said silently. *By marrying you and asking you to share my life I may be compelling you to partake in a tragedy.*

Her eyes continued to look trustfully into his as she whispered: 'It will be our happy ending! I know now that I can only be happy with you, Alex.'

6

The following night, the princess was expected and Henri spent the day tidying the rooms and wringing his hands because there was so little food in the house. True, she had promised to bring plenty of provisions with her. Meantime, Henri doled out the invalid's meat extract with miserly fingers. The doctor came as soon as it was light and pronounced Alex as 'much better'. As he left he put a couple of recent newspapers beside the bed. 'I daresay you would like to know what's going on in Petersburg,' he said drily.

Alex pored over both papers and told Katya of the strikes and demonstrations tearing the city apart. 'If only the Tsar would agree to a *Duma*!' he said again and again. 'There'll be civil war if this goes on.' He didn't tell her that they were hunting for Gapon and had rounded up many of his supporters who were now in prison; that stern measures were eroding the citizens' last small freedoms: the Tsar had become a frightened man.

The day wore on slowly and, as darkness fell, Alex began to worry about his mother. To pacify him, Katya went to the window several times but every time could only report that there was no sign of life in the drift of snow outside. Henri unsuccessfully hid his anxiety by fussing about the room and getting on Alex's nerves.

It was about nine o'clock that Katya heard the jingle of harness outside. The farmer, who had been carefully piling fresh logs by the side of the fire, heard it too and turned to grin at her, saying in Russian, 'She is here!' He brushed the brick hearth, got off his knees and hurried to the back of the house to inform his wife.

'Henri, the princess is here!' Katya called softly up the stairs in case Alex had fallen into a doze. Then she went and flung open the door.

But it was not the princess's troika that had drawn up outside. Two men in long grey coats and fur hats were advancing towards her in the light from the open door. They were civilians and there was something about them that reminded her so forcibly of the men who had confronted her at the Tchelitchev apartment that she prepared to slam the door in their faces as she cried frantically: 'Henri! Come quickly – oh!' She was too late: they had thrown themselves against the door and knocked her down.

The old valet was hurrying down the stairs. 'What is it, *mademoiselle*? I thought you called – ' He stopped, the colour draining from his face.

One of the men produced a revolver and gestured with it as he spoke in Russian.

443

'Neither of us speaks Russian,' Katya said in French. Now that the fears at the back of her mind were standing before her with hard, brutal faces, she had become icily calm. 'Please state your business,' she added, primly folding her hands in front of her. 'This is a private house and you have disturbed us enough.'

'You have here Prince Alexander Petrovitch Rakov?'

'No. We have a Monsieur Drusov who is very ill and must not be disturbed.'

Without a word, the other man strode to the stairs. At the foot he said harshly: 'Do not move.'

Katya, her face rigid, refraining to glance in Henri's direction, sat down and looked straight ahead. Presently she heard the man's footsteps returning on the wooden stairs and he stooped as he entered the room to smile coldly and sarcastically at her.

'As I thought, it is Alexander Rakov lying up there. I know him well for we were at university together.' He turned to Henri and looked contemptuously at the moisture of fear on the old man's face. 'You are his servant? Then prepare him at once for the journey back to Petersburg – '

'No! He cannot go!' Katya stepped forward to confront the men. 'I am his nurse and I know he isn't fit to travel.'

'That is certainly a nasty wound,' agreed the man who had been Alex's friend. He smiled amiably. 'I daresay it will kill him before he gets his just retribution but he should have thought of that before he committed treason – eh, *mademoiselle*? He will travel tonight as I say – no, stay here, please. His servant will see to him.'

'I insist on going to him – ' Katya had taken a leap towards the stairs. Like a panther, the man sprang after her, grasped her arm and twisted it behind her, forcing a scream of pain from her.

The man smiled, as if he enjoyed hearing this. 'Did you not understand me, *mademoiselle*? I said *stay here.*'

She pulled herself free and sat down again, sick with pain and trembling with apprehension. What were they going to do to him? Glancing at the cold implacable faces before her she realized it was useless to appeal to them.

Presently, Alex, leaning heavily on Henri, came stumbling down the stairs. He was barely able to walk and his face was ashen. She jumped up and ran across to him, clinging to him in wordless agony for a few moments. 'Where are they taking you? she whispered at last.

'To the Peter and Paul Fortress, I suppose.' He leaned against her, trying to smile reassuringly, the wound in his back an agony. He harboured his strength before making the effort to speak to her for there was something he needed urgently to say. 'Sweetheart, go home – go back to England. Everything is finished here. Promise me that you'll go back to your friends? Promise? Please, Katasha, I beg of you *go.*'

'Don't worry about me.' She spoke hurriedly, one eye on the two men. 'I shall stay here and talk to the princess – between us we shall move heaven and earth – '

'She will not be coming. Kersinsky there informs me she has been banished to our country estate – the Tsar's orders. *They* are very angry with us!' He tried to smile, but there was a terrible sadness in his eyes. 'So you see, our little effort to change to a democracy has been abortive. God knows what awaits our beloved Mother Russia in the future.' He stopped: he had been about to say that he would not be a part of that future but the fear in her face was like a hand across his mouth. 'Let me look at you, Katasha. This must be goodbye.' He held her close. 'I would be happier if I knew you were safe. They won't detain you, I think. Go home to your friends, my dearest girl. Make a life for yourself – forget me – '

'No, never!' she cried, clinging desperately to him. Hands like steel were tearing them apart. 'Alex, I love you – love you – '

They were dragging him between them through the door, down the wooden steps and across the snow to the waiting troika. Another troika had appeared now, was wheeling in a half-circle. They threw Alex into the first sledge and Katya heard him cry out in agony as they showed scant mercy for his wound. 'Alex! I love you!' she cried cupping her hands. She thought he replied but she couldn't be sure as the troika jingled away into the encircling darkness.

The second man, a sharp weasel-faced individual, now approached and pushed her back up the steps, slamming the door behind him. 'Hurry, *mademoiselle*. Pack your things, I'm taking you back to Petersburg. With luck we'll catch the midnight express for Berlin – oh, yes, *mademoiselle*, we're sending you packing back to your precious motherland! We don't want the likes of you in our country,' he added with a sneer. He threw himself into a chair and took out of an inner pocket a gold cigarette case from which he selected a black Turkish cigarette. As he lit it his small eyes glanced at the silent girl who was leaning against a wall. 'Quite a little baggage,' he murmured, blowing scented smoke in her direction. 'Nikita Guriev has told me all about you – a typical English adventuress was how he described you. The sooner we're rid of you, the better. *Move*, will you?'

With feet like lead she climbed the stairs once more. Her world was in ruins and she felt old and finished. They had taken Alex away to that dreaded fortress across the Neva. There, in a dark unheated cell he would languish without medical attention and possibly die. No one would dare enquire after him or visit him. It would be the living death thousands of others had experienced before him. Countless others had escaped this fate thanks to him. But for him the luck had run out and he was trapped.

Hot tears blinded her, began to run down her pinched cheeks. Standing there she thought: I wish I could die and be out of all this pain.

24
A Farewell to Love?

1

Thirty-six hours later, she crawled out of the train utterly exhausted and hungry. She had been thrust in the lowest class of seat available, her valise and ticket flung at her. At the frontier, she had been able to buy some food but it had been the middle of the night when the train stopped again and Katya had been in an uneasy sleep, propped between the window and an ample peasant woman. It was certainly a very different journey from the one that brought her to Russia. She remembered with a jolt of pain how she and Alex had looked at each other that first time in the dining car. They had recognized themselves as the lovers they were to become. It was cruel of fate to have parted them in their first weeks of happiness; perhaps they would never find each other again – no, she mustn't allow herself to indulge in self-pity, she told herself sternly. Yet from behind her closed eyes, hot tears were forced out to fall slowly down her pale cheeks. Her travelling companions, realizing the foreign girl was in some sort of trouble, showed their sympathy by averting their eyes.

Now here she was in Berlin, standing dazedly among the hurrying crowd and trying to make her mind work. She didn't even know what day of the week it was. First, she must go on to Hamburg and find out when the *Sylvie-*

Rose was due. Wearily lifting her battered valise she struggled with it to the ticket office.

At Hamburg she took a motor cab to the docks and the offices of Howarth and Hawksley. To her relief she learned that the boat was due the following evening, a Wednesday. It would sail, the clerk told her, at midday on Thursday. She scribbled a note and asked for it to be delivered to Captain Halvorsen as soon as the boat berthed. Her one anxiety now was that he would not have room for her, especially as the clerk had told her that there were several passengers booked for the journey to Hull.

Then she had herself driven to a boarding house in a quiet street well away from the docks and the noisy centre of the city. She had no German marks on her but the proprietor told her he would be delighted to accept English gold.

She bathed and went to bed but couldn't sleep. All she could think of was Alex and what he might be suffering in his fortress cell.

2

On Friday evening, the *Sylvie-Rose* was approaching Hull having made good time in a calm German Ocean. The icy winds and snow of Russia were now only a memory for here a gentle February wind, carrying a hint of rain, caressed Katya's face as she stood at the rail as they came up the Humber. She was very glad to be home again after three months: already it seemed like a bad dream she had left behind her. She knew she wasn't the same person who had sailed away filled with a blithe excitement on that November morning: how naïve that girl seemed to her now! She felt years older and immeasurably weary as she gripped the rail and tried to push the memory of Alex out of her thoughts. It will do no good to be bitter, she repeated over and over to herself.

Behind her a noisy group of Yorkshire wool men who had been selling their wares in Germany kept up a continual buffoonery, one eye on the pretty lady passenger who had kept herself so aloof on the journey home. She hardly heard them as she glanced up at the bridge: Captain Halvorsen had been kindness itself as if he instinctively sensed the sadness in her. He had telegraphed the Hull office that she was aboard and she had no doubt that Robert would meet her. She dreaded that meeting because she dreaded having to talk about what had happened. If she didn't talk about it she might be able to endure it, she told herself shakily.

Suddenly she saw him on the quayside, a thickset figure in an ulster and cap, his shoulders hunched, a pipe between his teeth. She raised a hand and his eager eyes found her: as soon as the gangway was secured he was up it in long strides.

They met in the lee of a bulkhead. He snatched off his cap and said: 'Katya.' His voice shook with suppressed emotion and his eyes were anxious as they fastened on her pale face with its new sharp outlines. 'My God, what have they been doing to you?' he said explosively, pulling her into his arms and kissing her hungrily.

She submitted to the luxury of being held close and to her horror, tears began to course down her face once more. 'Robert . . . oh, Robert!' was all she could whisper.

He scrutinized her face. 'Something's happened. What is it?'

She shook her head, tears choking her. With an effort she pleaded, 'Please don't let me talk about it yet – not yet. I will tell you later – but not yet, Robert.'

His eyes continued to examine her, seeing the new sharp edges to her face. Under the rolled brim of her woollen cap there was a dark area from which her eyes glittered feverishly. She looked exhausted, as if she hadn't slept for weeks. 'I'm taking you home. Mother insists you must stay with us for a while. She'll be horrified to see how ill you're looking. Katya dear, it's all our fault; we ought never to have let you go out there.'

'Don't say that. It's my fault not yours,' was all she could say but it was obvious he didn't understand.

Lady Howarth was in her element with an invalid on her hands: that was how she classed her young guest. 'You've only to look at the girl – well, I hope it's not consumption. I told your father it was madness to send the girl to that place!' She bustled about seeing Katya into bed, harrying the maids who came in and out with trays of food, hot-water bottles and – finally – a bottle of Sir Abel's finest port. 'Now I insist you take a glass of this. It will put some life into you, poor little thing!' She chafed Katya's hands, her eyes anxious.

In vain, Katya tried to placate her kind hostess. 'I'm just tired. The last weeks were difficult ones. I'll tell you about it soon. I'm . . . just tired,' she said forlornly and the tears began to flow again.

They sent for Doctor Richards, Lady Howarth's pet physician who dropped everything to attend his most important patient only to find it was some waif of a girl needing his attention. He pronounced her 'exhausted and with a weak pulse' and prescribed a sleeping tablet, forty-eight hours in bed and plenty of light food and fluid.

Downstairs, Robert paced restlessly, unable to settle to anything. All his pleasant young life, he had had everything he wanted. Perhaps he was a little spoilt in consequence, as his father was apt to remind him. Now he was beginning to realize that he would never have his dearest

451

wish: Katya's first fresh young love. It didn't need explaining; every instinct told him he was the loser, that in those three months in Russia she had given her love to another man. As he walked to and fro across his study floor he tried to remember what she had written to him. Something about meeting a prince and 'liking him very much'. Maybe, he thought with a spurt of hope, it was just a girl's romantic dream. On reflection, he had to admit that she had not appeared to be romantic in her outlook: life had given her little cause to be that. Whatever her emotion had been, it was something very real and now she was deeply unhappy.

3

Katya stayed a week with the Howarths and Lady Howarth had the satisfaction of seeing her guest fill out and even laugh once or twice. She insisted that she must be back in her place at Hill House by Monday morning and would therefore leave Hull on Saturday. 'I have been away much longer than Miss Lesley bargained for,' she reminded Robert when he tried to dissuade her. They were walking in the rain across the park to a gate that gave on to ploughed land. The furrows glistened like metal rails in the damp and there was a soft feel of spring in the air despite the rain. There was even a hint of birdsong. 'It will be strange going back there after all that's happened.'

There was silence between them. Under a tree, Robert paused to relight his pipe. He glanced across at Katya, his face serious. 'Are you going to tell me, Katya?'

She hesitated, brushing the rain from her lashes. 'I haven't wanted to hurt you,' she said in a low voice.

'I must know!' Robert said angrily, his patience suddenly running out. 'Can't you see what it's doing to me? I love you, you little fool!'

'Oh, Robert, I know – you've been so good to me, far too good. I feel miserable about it. You see, even though I value your friendship so much, I can't love you in return.' She put her hand on his arm, but he turned away and her hand fell to her side. 'I'm truly sorry about it,' she said haltingly to his averted face. 'You see, I love Alex Rakov and he loves me.'

He turned round and stared at her. 'If that's true, why are you so unhappy? Where is your prince that he doesn't marry you?'

The forlorn look was back on her face. 'I don't know. He could be dead. Shall I tell you what happened?'

They sat down on a fallen tree, under the shelter of a belt of firs. Speaking quietly but steadily, she told him all that had happened.

He listened without interruption, the stem of his pipe clenched between his teeth. Absorbed in the telling of her story she didn't notice that the man at her side was suffering pangs of terrible jealousy until, finishing her tale, she turned and looked at him.

'Well, that's it, then,' he said flatly and knocked his unsmoked pipe against the trunk of the tree.

'You mean . . . you think Alex is dead?'

'How can I possibly know that? I meant that I now realize you're never going to care for me after him. He will have ruined your life,' he added bitterly. 'You probably won't see him again but he'll always be *there*, spoiling your future with a forlorn hope. You'll never marry anyone now, Katya. What a waste!' His miserable eyes met hers: hers were full of tears he saw unhappily, but he wanted to hurt her as he'd been hurt. This damned prince had stolen her affections and now she would spend the rest of her life pining for somebody she couldn't have.

'People have escaped from the Fortress; he helped them.'

'Yes, but he's inside himself, now.'

She turned away, a dry sob making a lump in her throat as she remembered Alex's agonized cry of pain as they threw him into the sledge on that terrible night. For a long time they sat in silence. Then she said, her voice steady now, 'If my grandfather's money ever does arrive in England as Laura arranged then I shall leave Whitby and go to London.'

'London? For God's sake, why? You don't know London,' he said roughly.

'Not yet but I shall do. I shall buy a house there and keep it open for Russian refugees.'

He was horrified. 'Katya! You're mad! The most awful Bolsheviks will turn up and you'll be embroiled in politics before you can say Jack Robinson!'

'Not if I organize things carefully. I shall get in touch with someone I helped in Russia.'

'How? It's impossible!'

'How? I shall put an advertisement in *The Times* asking Miss Ingram to get in touch with me.'

'Who is Miss Ingram? Someone's governess?'

'You could say that,' Katya murmured. Suddenly her whole face changed, lit up with sudden joy and relief: somehow, somewhere she would go on helping Alex in his work. If he were dead, then it would be her memorial to him. Getting up, she brushed bark off her raincoat. 'Now I know what to do! It will occupy the rest of my life!' she announced confidently and began to walk back to the house.

He went on sitting on the tree trunk, as profoundly unhappy as he had ever been.

'Come on!' She turned and beckoned.

Slowly, he got up and went to join her.

4

On Saturday she left Hull. Robert put her on the train and this time didn't attempt to kiss her.

'You know where I am, Katya. If ever you should need me, let me know and I'll come.'

It was, she realized, a generous gesture. While there was hope for Alex, he would not bother her. As she waved to his receding figure standing so solidly on the platform, she felt genuine regret that she couldn't love him. Married to Robert Howarth she would be safe and loved all her life – but it was no use thinking of what might have been. Alex Rakov had all her love. If he had died, she wouldn't cease to love him; there would just be a wound inside her that would never heal.

Whitby was wrapped in the same rain as Hull had been. It looked exactly as it always did, she thought, as she stood outside the station while her valise was put in a fly. Everything and everybody was the same: only she had changed.

She rang the bell of Hill House and Maggie opened it, smiling with pleasure to see her back. 'Well, miss, what a time it's been! I said to Cook: we'll never see our young lady back at this rate, you mark my words! Miss Lesley's out but you've got your old room same as usual.' She took up the battered valise and led the way upstairs.

Katya lingered in the hall. She could feel her heart sinking at the familiar smell of her old life: cabbage water, carbolic, furniture polish and Miss Lesley's lavender water mingled on the air. Tomorrow she would be on duty, rousing the girls and keeping order. They would ask her about Russia and she would have to talk brightly to them, giving them the benefit of her travels. She closed her eyes, feeling the old restless rebellion gripping her again. *Alex*, she thought, *Alex, Alex, Alex*. His name would always be her talisman. Just repeating it gave her a renewal of courage.

That night she told Miss Lesley that she would like to leave at the end of the term.

Miss Lesley sat bolt upright. 'Katherine! How can you be so thoughtless?' she said indignantly. 'There's only six weeks of this term left. No, no, you must give me longer notice than that. How could I possibly find anyone in such a short time?'

Katya could feel the shackles being locked again. She had guessed Miss Lesley would make things difficult and was determined not to be deterred. 'I will pay you a term's salary, Miss Lesley. Will that do?'

Miss Lesley's eyes became knowing slits. 'Where would you get the money? Are you intending to marry Mr Howarth?'

'No.'

'Then tell me how you intend to pay me *twenty-five pounds*, my dear!'

'Was it as little as that? I'd forgotten.'

'And your keep, don't forget!'

Thinking of the stiff, cold porridge and the greasy stews, Katya was unable to conceal a shudder. 'My Russian grandfather has left me a great deal of money. It should come through to my bank before long. I intend buying a house in London and going there to live,' she said. 'So I shan't be staying after this term, Miss Lesley.' She went to the door and turned: it gave her pleasure to see that Miss Lesley was both scarlet and speechless. 'Goodnight,' she said sweetly.

In no time at all she had slipped into her role of schoolmarm again. She hated it. The early rising; the tepid
water to wash in; the terrible food. The very smell of
the place had become anathema to her. Outwardly she
behaved with quiet conformity while inside her a jubilant
voice kept telling her that soon she would have finished
with Hill House for good.

She wrote to Anastasia to explain that she had had to
return to England and to ask if she had any news of the
Rakovs. It was the end of March before the expected
letter came from St Petersburg. It was brought to her by
Maggie just as she was about to take a class and she had
to slip it into the pocket of her skirt. She could feel it
crackling against her as she moved to the blackboard and
wrote out some lines from Milton. As soon as the bell
rang, she ran swiftly up to her room, banged the door
behind her and opened Anastasia's letter with shaking
fingers.

Despite every effort I have been unable to find out what you
most desire. If Philip knows – and this I doubt – he will not
enlighten me. Yesterday I drove to the Rakov Palace to find it
shut up and the old porter was unable to help. He said that
everyone was away and only a skeleton staff in residence. I
wish I could have given you better news.

Katya threw the letter from her and wept as if her
heart would break. She had so much hoped for encouraging news; something that would give her the strength
to go on. She paced to and fro feeling an agony of
disappointment. If Stana couldn't help, where was she to

turn for news of the one person she was tied to on this earth? He couldn't just vanish without trace. His mother – but would the letter reach her? She would try. This very night she would compose a letter that would on the surface appear innocuous if opened by the secret police.

Outside a warm spring sun danced across the roofs and seagulls mewed as they tossed hither and thither in the March breeze. She paused to look out of the window at the last shreds of winter being chased away, at the new leaves turning and rustling on the trees below. Spring. What could it mean to her now when in her heart there was perpetual winter?

Meanwhile the legacy had arrived in England and was safely banked. She had had an interview with the manager, Mr Hodgson, and he had advised her how she should dispose of it: a sum set aside for a house; a sum for maximum income; a sum for growth. He rubbed his hands as he explained it all to her: he liked nothing more than a good round sum to dispose of and forty-eight thousand pounds had a nice round sound to it.

Katya cared little for the details of these fiscal arrangements although she had to pretend that she did or Mr Hodgson would have been dreadfully shocked: money, he tried to explain to her, was a sacred trust and she must guard it against beggars and confidence tricksters who would try to get their hands on it. The shock to his system would have been awful if she had told him about the Russian refugees . . . Meanwhile estate agents plied her with descriptions of houses in various parts of London and she, knowing nothing of the different areas, wrote to Robert for advice and help. Reluctantly – but conscientiously – he gave her advice and eventually they decided on a large brick-built house with eight bedrooms in Highgate: she was to go and see it at Easter before making her final decision.

Rounding up the girls for their afternoon walk Katya felt lighter of heart. She had taken the first step away from this depressing establishment, she told herself as she glanced back at it. They wound down the hill, the girls chattering like magpies as they headed towards the beach. Katya was on her own with them today because Mademoiselle was nursing a cold by the schoolroom stove: fires were no longer allowed in bedrooms when March arrived.

When they reached the bay with its expanse of clean, ridged brown sand, Katya let them break ranks and run about. Why not? she asked herself hardily. Miss Lesley's wrath meant nothing to her any more and it did the young creatures good to play in the sharp and salty air. She sat on a breakwater and watched them searching for shells and getting their boots wet.

'Oh, Miss Croxley!' that dull girl, Sylvia Mary Hodges, exclaimed. 'I've never enjoyed a walk more! Look at this razor shell! Oh, do let's do this again tomorrow.'

'Why not? You're only young once, Sylvia Mary.' And as the girl ran off to rejoin her friends, Katya thought bleakly: I was young once myself. Now I feel old. The old never look forward. They live each day as it comes. That way I won't hurt any more. That way this pain will go. Given time.

She got off the breakwater and brushed seaweed off her skirt. She called to the girls and they obediently formed a crocodile again, falling silent as they walked back up the hill hungrily thinking of tea that was still two hours away.

As they turned into the road past the church, they noticed that the station fly had just deposited a fare at the school gate. A man had got out and was paying the driver: he had his back to them. Then he turned and looked with amused interest at the straggling crocodile wending its way up the road towards him.

Katya bringing up the rear was the last to see him. She stopped, one hand creeping to her throat in a gesture of uncertainty. Her breath seemed to be forcing its way through her rib cage. Suddenly she let it go in a long gasp. Her heart was hammering in her ears and she had to cling to the railings. It was – it couldn't be – The tall man wore a shabby tweed jacket, rather crumpled trousers and a soft corduroy cap. As he removed the cap, the spring sun fell mercilessly on a gaunt face with a white scar running like a thread from cheek to temple, on bright unchanged hair and the bluest of eyes.

Katya began to force herself through the ranks of girls. She sensed their curious stares but her own eyes were fixed on the man who stood facing them, his thin face breaking up into a familiar smile. Her woollen cap fell off her head as she ran forward gasping his name. 'Alex! Alex! You've come – you've come – ' Her arms opened and with a long stride the man reached her and gathered her in his arms, crushing her as he murmured her name over and over.

The crocodile was dumbfounded, but being curious by nature it gathered round in a protective circle while the two adults embraced and threw words at each other.

'I thought I'd never see you again!'

'And I. Oh, Katya, I thought I'd never find you!'

'But how did you get out of that place? I thought – '

'Beloved, I've been banished by my Tsar. I'm lucky. So many others have died. But he can never bring himself to spill princely blood – ' He shrugged. 'So I have had to leave Russia and my estates and become a refugee.'

'You're safe – oh, thank God, you're safe!'

They kissed and the crocodile heaved a sigh of pure bliss.

Both of them had forgotten their audience. He said eagerly: 'Sweetheart, we shall make our home in my apartment in the Bois. Will you mind that? Paris for a few years then perhaps I shall be allowed to return home.' He looked up, caught the eager eyes fixed on him and laughed suddenly. 'We are being well-chaperoned, I see. Perhaps, girls, you will allow us to go indoors to complete our wedding plans?' With Katya within the circle of his arm he pushed open the iron gate and led the way to the front door.

Peeping over her lace curtains, Miss Lesley was unable to believe her eyes. A stranger, and foreign at that by the look of him, had taken possession of the Hill House crocodile and with Katherine Croxley *hanging round his neck* was approaching her front door. As she was to tell everyone afterwards: 'I was never so surprised in my life.'